TERROR IN

Erin was unsure of herself now, and she turned to go back downstairs. Yet something was wrong . . . She felt it in the cold tension of her skin and the pull of the hair at the back of her neck.

She realized that she was afraid of the dark up here, of the long hall stretching past old bedrooms and a playroom not used since Great-granddad was a child. She was afraid of something that still lingered in the old house. As if in burying Great-granddad, they had freed something else.

As she started back down the stairs, she saw the figure. Small, still, it stood to her left, beyond the corner of the wall. It had a round face and fair hair, and even in the shadows in which it stood she could see the little red smiling lips and the white teeth.

Why would Kara and Susan bring their beloved doll up here and leave it standing against the wall? Why? And suddenly she knew they hadn't.

She heard the slight creak of movement as the antique doll lifted both of its arms. As Erin watched, stunned with horror, the perpetually smiling doll walked out of the shadows and toward her. . . .

A FEAST OF TRUE CRIME FROM ZEBRA BOOKS

DADDY'S GIRL (2955, $4.95)
by Clifford Irving

On June 19, 1982, James Campbell, successful Houston lawyer, and Virginia, his wife of forty years, were found by their grandson, brutally shot to death in their bed. With only allegations of family greed, sexual abuse, and a missing will, the murder went unsolved for two years. The finger of guilt pointed at daughter Cindy Ray Campbell and her survivalist boyfriend, David West. But the two had an alibi the cops couldn't crack, until a sexy private eye coaxed a confession from West and the story exploded across a stunned nation.

Author Clifford Irving masterfully untangles the web of events that led Cindy Ray, a tortured woman driven by perverse love and bitter hatred to commit the most heinous and unnatural of all acts known to man—the premediated, cold-blooded murder of her own parents!

THE WOODCHIPPER MURDER (3113, $4.95)
by Arthur Herzog

Helle Crafts, attractive Pan Am flight attendant and mother of three, was full of holiday plans: planning her Thanksgiving Day dinner, her Christmas shopping spree, *and* proceeding with her divorce from her womanizing and brutal husband, Eastern Airline pilot Richard Crafts. November 18, 1986 was the last time Helle's friends saw her alive.

When Helle suddenly disappeared, her husband said she was visiting her mother in Denmark. But Helle's lawyer and the detective investigating Craft's extramarital affairs suspected foul play. Their investigation led to the most scandalous murder trial Connecticut had ever witnessed, and the entire country watched breathlessly until Crafts was found guilty of murdering his wife and running her frozen body parts through an industrial-sized woodchipper.

Zebra has updated the hardcover version to include the newest information about the second trial and the dramatic conviction of the Woodchipper Murderer, and the crime which will be remembered for decades to come!

Available wherever paperbacks are sold, or order direct from the Publisher. Send cover price plus 50¢ per copy for mailing and handling to Zebra Books, Dept. 3235, 475 Park Avenue South, New York, N.Y. 10016. Residents of New York, New Jersey and Pennsylvania must include sales tax. DO NOT SEND CASH.

VICTORIA

RUBY JEAN JENSEN

ZEBRA BOOKS
KENSINGTON PUBLISHING CORP.

For Gayle, my daughter, with love.
Take time to relax with Victoria.

ZEBRA BOOKS

are published by

Kensington Publishing Corp.
475 Park Avenue South
New York, NY 10016

First printing: December, 1990

Printed in the United States of America

Prologue

"Can we go outside?" Andy asked the woman who had made their breakfast and lunch, and she said, "Yes, keep your voices down. Your grandfather's in his coffin in the front parlor, and people will be coming for the funeral services. So you young'ns keep quiet."

She was a round woman with round glasses, and her hair was in a curly permanent. When they had first arrived she'd patted Andy's head and told Susan she was a pretty little girl and looked a lot like her cousin, Kara. Then she had hugged them both and kissed their cheeks. After that she had shown them upstairs to their room. And this morning after breakfast she had kind of pushed them out onto the big, screened back porch.

So they had gone into the back yard, which to Andy seemed as huge as a city park, with trees of all kinds and sizes, bushes beginning to bloom, and birds fluttering away as they approached.

In the distance, through trees and shrubs, they could see an iron fence with spikes at the top, and there was the ghostly rise of big old tombstones, and when they went closer they could see the fresh pile of dark earth that had been piled to one side of a new grave. Part of it was now covered with a dark green velvet cloth, and a kind of awning had been put overhead and chairs were placed in a row beneath the awning, also dark green.

"Is that where he's going to be buried?" Susan whispered, and Andy shushed her and pulled her back in another direction.

"Andy," Susan said, after she had followed him through paths, beneath shrubs and around trees, and the cemetery was no longer in sight. "He's not really our grandfather, is he?"

Andy was older than she. Three years older, and he knew a lot of things she didn't. She looked up to him, and followed him, and asked him questions. He had taught her to read long before she went to school. Sometimes he got tired of her, but then she waited around and he got to feeling sorry for trying to leave her behind. She thought he was old and wise, especially now, since his eleventh birthday. They'd had his party just before their mama had gotten word that Granddad Mason was ill.

After a while Andy said, "No, he's Mama's grandfather."

"If he had still been alive when we got here, what would we have called him?"

"Probably Granddad, like Mom did. Or maybe Great-granddad."

"That's hard."

"Well."

Susan was quiet, and Andy understood. Their great-grandfather's death made them both sad. They both had wanted to know him, maybe sit on his lap the way their mom used to. Mama had told them stories about how Granddad had taken her on his knees when she fell out of the sycamore tree. But instead of scolding her for climbing, he'd said she should have climbed the cherry tree instead because it wasn't so far to the first limb or so far to the ground.

Susan followed Andy through a group of shrubs, bending to keep the branches from tearing her hair, though he tried to hold the branches up. Her pale hair was long and curly, with bangs, and it could get tangled. She hated having their mother comb her hair because Mom always found tangles she never found herself.

"What is he to us? Really?" Susan asked.

"Our great-grandfather, of course."

"That's what I thought, but if I was wrong, you'd tease."

"No, I wouldn't. I would just tell you."

"You'd laugh."

"No, I wouldn't."

But Andy felt a little guilty because she was right. He could tease at times, especially when he was kind of bored, like when their mom was late coming home from work and the TV show was a rerun. But he tried to remember that Susan was just a little kid, only eight, and she didn't have anybody but him.

She bumped into Andy when he stopped. They stood staring up at the high roof of the big house. It had angles and pitches and little windows in high peaks.

"What, Andy?" she asked. "What's up there?"

He shrugged, and put his hands into his pockets. "It's just so big, that's all."

"Is it bigger than our house?"

"Yeah, but our house is an apartment house, Susan, and it's got a lot of families living in it."

"I *know* that. But altogether is it bigger?"

"It's different. It's real old. Everything here is antique, Mama said, except for the new wing. And he lived here all alone."

"What about Martha?"

"Well, yeah. But she's mostly his housekeeper."

"Well, but she lives here, doesn't she?"

"Yeah, I guess so. But alone means without family. Kids or something. I think it means not having a wife living with him, or Aunt Laura or Mama. Martha's got her own place downstairs, while Granddad lived up in the tall part of the house alone."

They walked in silence, Susan following the erratic path Andy chose. He thought of Granddad Mason in his coffin in the parlor at the front of the big house, and a cold chill brought goosebumps up his arms and spread ice into the hair at the back of his neck. He had never seen a dead person before. Somehow it was like being in a place where there was no sound, ever. The coffin was so narrow, so close around the silent man who lay there, and the man's face, strange to Andy, looked white and artificial, as if it were made of wax. The quilted satin of his coffin bed and pillow didn't look comfortable either, though he had heard Martha say it did to Mama. It looked smothery.

These were thoughts and feelings he would never tell Susan. It might scare her, and make her think he was scared too.

He had been so glad to be able to leave the room. He wished he didn't have to go back, but he knew they would. "You can go with Martha," Mama had said. "Until one o'clock. Then you have to get dressed for the services."

Chairs had already been arranged in the parlor. In neat rows, like the chairs out under the awning in the small graveyard under the trees.

"Just a few close friends," their aunt Laura said. "That's all he wanted."

Andy stopped again, and Susan almost ran into him. He said nothing when she touched him. Sometimes he got tired of her always bumping into him when he stopped, and he'd yell at her. But today he didn't feel like yelling. Ahead of them he saw a pile of discards. The kind of stuff that back home was put out for the Salvation Army to pick up.

"Hey, look," he said. "Junk. All kinds."

It was near a gate that was closed. Beyond the gate

was a narrow little track of a road coming through the trees and making a circle as it dead-ended by the gate. The place where the trash truck would turn around, Andy figured. It was different here at the edge of town than it was in the city.

"What is it?" Susan asked, always expecting him to be able to answer her.

Andy had begun to climb. A broken chair fell, and he slid with it. Beneath the broken chair were two black plastic bags of bumpy stuff and another broken chair. Andy dug through the pile.

"Old antiques too broken to fix, you think? I bet you I could fix this one up."

He hauled out a small, wood rocking chair that looked as if it had belonged to a child a long time ago. One rocker was missing, and part of the back poked up like broken teeth.

"I could fix this, and then we'd have us a rocking chair."

"One that belonged to us? Not rented like the rest of our furniture?"

"Right."

"Let me find something. I need a chair for myself."

"You can use this one sometimes."

Susan peered down into the pile of things that looked as interesting as treasure. "Andy, was our great-granddad so rich he could afford to throw away things like this? Before he died, was he so rich?"

"I don't know," Andy answered. "But he must have been."

They had hardly even known of him. They had never seen a picture of him. And they hadn't really known there was an Aunt Laura, their mother's sister, or three girl cousins. Coming here had been like finding treasure all in itself, except for their great-grandfather being in his coffin already.

Andy saw, beneath a pile of discarded stuff, the rounded and carved metal top of something that looked like a trunk. The glimpse gave him a strange, odd thrill, as if he had done something forbidden and dangerous. It was almost the way he'd felt when he took Susan across a street alone for the first time.

"Andy . . . look!" Susan had seen it too.

For a moment his shoulder touched hers as they looked down at what they had found.

"A trunk," Andy breathed. "A real old trunk."

"Can I have it, Andy?"

"Golly," he said, pushing junk away from its top. "Why would they throw away a real old antique like that? I bet you it's a mistake. Maybe whoever cleaned out the closet didn't know it was an antique."

He had begun to uncover it and drag it aside.

"Did *all* this stuff come from a closet?" Susan asked in disbelief. "All three of our closets together wouldn't hold this much stuff."

"I don't know. Maybe from an attic. Maybe from that funny old building back in the trees that doesn't have any paint. *A shed,* Martha said it's called."

Later, he promised himself, he would go up high in the house, to the third story, maybe to the attic. But now the trunk was the most fascinating thing he had ever seen. Susan helped Andy pull it away from the pile of discards.

"It's not heavy," he said. "It must be empty."

"Can we open it, Andy?"

Andy tried, but the tonguelike latch remained firmly closed against the side of the metal trunk.

"It's locked."

They sat on their heels looking at it for a while.

Andy got up and began searching through the discards again, and Susan tried to open the trunk. Overhead, a bird squawked and flew away through the trees and Susan ducked, as if it were diving at her. Andy looked up to see black wings. The bird flew away toward the open sky.

"Crow," Andy said.

"What?"

"That was a crow."

"How do you know?"

"Because I know. When I went to camp that time I saw some. Here. Maybe this will open it."

He came back with a flat piece of metal that looked as if it had been the handle of something. He stuck the end under the latch of the trunk.

"Andy," Susan said in a lowered voice, remembering that Martha had told them to keep their voices down. "What are you going to do?"

"I'm going to open the trunk."

"But . . . it's not ours. Don't we have to ask?"

"They're going to throw it away."

"Yeah . . . but . . ."

She sat on her heels and waited, and he began to feel nervous. They were crossing the street again, after having been told and told by their mother not to ever cross it alone. But on the other side was the ice-cream parlor where they could buy a cone with the dollar Andy held in his hand.

Andy saw Susan was holding her breath. The handle under the latch creaked as he pried. The latch began to bend outward, and Andy stood with one knee on the trunk and both hands on the handle. His face twisted and turned red, he grunted, and then something popped and he fell forward onto his face.

"It's open! You did it!"

Andy grinned and got up, brushed his knees and face, the back of his hand swiping moss and specks of black soil from his chin.

Susan pushed the lid of the trunk up, and then stared

and stared.

Andy leaned beside her, staring too, surprise and disappointment dragging his chin down.

Nothing but an old doll. In an old trunk.

Around them was silence, as there had been in the parlor.

There was something very strange about the inside of the trunk.

It looked as if it had been made into a coffin too, with quilted satin lining the top and sides, the color cream, no longer white.

Andy looked at Susan, and saw her staring with eyes wide, sparkling, as they did at Christmas. As if she had never in her life seen anything so beautiful.

A big old doll in a coffin trunk, and Susan looking dumb. *Girls!*

"Andy," she breathed. "Oh, Andy! Isn't she the most beautiful doll you ever saw?"

He looked down. The doll's eyes were closed, long lashes that looked real lying dark on its pink and white cheeks.

Fine golden hair curled on its forehead and on its cheeks, and the tip of one small ear held a gold earring.

Its hands, as perfect as Susan's, only with longer, more adult fingers, lay palms down on the coffin lining.

On the right wrist was a gold bracelet, a name engraved on it in fine penmanship.

Susan started to reach in to pick up the doll, but Andy pushed her back.

He stood frowning down into the trunk that was a small coffin.

It was almost as if they had dug up a grave.

The doll's eyes were opening, slowly, the long lashes rising.

Chapter One

Coming home was the second hardest thing Fawn had ever done in her life. The hardest had been leaving, eighteen years ago when she was nineteen. But leaving was something she had to do, she'd felt at that time, with her feelings hurt and her pride crushed. To leave everyone who meant anything to her and go toward the unknown.

But there had also been a sense of adventure, of a rainbow to find, and a pot of gold. She'd had no one to worry about then. She was nineteen, and devastated after losing the man she loved to her sister, so she had gone off alone.

There had been a satisfaction in dealing out her revenge too, as if by leaving she had said, See, you can't treat me this way, Jim, Laura.

Only later had she wondered if she ran too soon and for no reason beyond her own fears and imagination. But her pride kept her away. And she kept going.

Coming home was a bittersweet experience. She had missed Granddad, and Laura, too. She had yearned to come home years ago, but had felt such a fool. Laura hadn't married Jim after all. She had married someone else just a year after Fawn left home, and a year later became a mother.

The only communication Fawn had with Granddad was through Christmas letters, and he had asked her to come home in every one she'd received since those excruciating days in her youth. But time had a way of bogging a person down and taking the adventure out of life. There came the reality of making a living alone in a big world, and then protecting the children she eventually had.

She had gone first to Kansas City, not too far from home, and gotten a job as a waitress. Finding out her skills were not worth more had been the first blow. As she'd filled out the form at the employment office that day, so many years ago, she had thought of Granddad who had hoped she would finish college. What had he thought of the note she had left him? "Dear Granddad," she had written, "forgive me, but I have to leave. Give my best to Laura and Jim. I love you." Her note had revealed nothing of her feelings, of why she was leaving, she realized. The reference to Laura and Jim was perfectly natural since Laura was her sister, Jim her boyfriend. The note hadn't gone on to say, I hope they choke on each other, as she clearly remembered thinking.

At the time she had thought it enough to leave a note telling Granddad she loved him. Now, with two children of her own, she realized how heartbreaking that must have been.

Coming home had meant getting to see her aged grandfather again, the old gentleman who had been mother and father as well as grandfather to her and Laura since their parents were killed in an accident. But Granddad was ill, Martha had warned. If she wanted to see him again, she'd have to come quickly.

With her two children, Andy and Susan, she had gone up the walk to the tall, old house the town had always called "The Mansion." But it was Laura who met her at the door, a Laura with sad eyes, a changed, older

Laura. And Fawn knew the moment Laura's cold hands grasped hers that it was too late.

Granddad was dead.

For the first time in eighteen years she had wept hard, that night when she was alone in her old room. Wept so hard her chest ached the next day at the funeral services when she was unable to weep. Harder than she had when her brief marriage broke up. She cried for all the years she had missed being with Laura and Granddad, and Laura's children—and for Jim, whose picture still sat on her dresser, on the nightstand by her bed, on her desk. Handsome Jim, dark hair falling over one side of his forehead, the dimple in his chin a small dark shadow in the high-school graduation photo. Where was he now? What had happened to him during these years? She hadn't asked, hadn't heard his name. He hadn't been at the funeral. She had cried for an unretrievable past.

At the last she knew how much she had wanted to come home, to be with her family again, to sit with her grandfather in quiet companionship and feel the security of his presence.

The figure in the coffin hadn't seemed real. That frail, white-haired old person couldn't be Granddad. The skin on his face as thin as tissue paper and stretching across the bones, sinking between, the chin jutting, the mouth fallen against the teeth. The granddad she remembered was round and plump, with a fringe of dark hair around the bald spot. She could remember him teasing, "You may grow bald, Fawny, but you'll never be gray, not if you take after your old granddad."

He had though, sometime during the years, turned gray.

In the three days since the funeral she had tried to leave again. She had a job in Chicago as a hostess in a restaurant. There was also the apartment which they would lose if they didn't go back and pay the rent.

But every time she'd mentioned leaving the kids complained. "Why can't we stay here, Mama?" Susan had pleaded. Andy had joined her the second time.

And Laura had said, "Don't go, Fawn. You've been away far too long. We want you to stay. We need you."

And today, at the reading of the will, she had learned she could stay if she wanted to. Although everything was left to Laura and to Antique Village, which Granddad had helped found thirty-five years before, Granddad's big old house, the mansion her kids had fallen in love with, was their home for life with all expenses paid. The words in the will kept running through her mind . . . *with the stipulation that my other granddaughter, Fawn, have a home for life in the main house, with a monthly allowance to pay expenses, to be garnered from the trust set up for that purpose, and that her bodily heirs shall have a home also, for the length of their lives, with the upkeep of the house coming from the bulk of the estate, of which my first granddaughter, Laura Worton, shall be executrix. . . .*

There was a lot more, but the rest of it was a jumble, and really had nothing to do with her. The old mansion was filled with antiques; they belonged to Laura and Antique Village. The more modern furniture belonged to the house, which, she understood, was hers to live in as long as she wanted. The kids would probably both be wide-eyed when she gave them a brief explanation—if she told them at all.

The tires of Laura's car whispered on the pavement, and the traffic moved by as they drove down Main Street and toward home. She saw familiar store fronts, but the people on the sidewalks were different. There were more of them now; the small town had grown to a small city.

"Want a Coke?" Laura asked.

Fawn almost jumped. "I don't think so." Then, "Is the old drive-in still there? Where we used to hang out?"

"No, there's a used-car lot there now, but we get our Cokes at the Spee-dee Mart out on Twenty-fourth Street, on the way home."

"You can if you want."

"No, that's okay, I just thought you might like a Coke for old times' sake."

Fawn didn't respond. She sat looking straight ahead, but from the corner of her eye she could see her sister.

Laura had always been the pretty one. A year older, taller, more outgoing, she'd had more friends, more everything. Maybe that was why it had been so hard to find Jim, her steady for two years, falling for Laura.

Even now, the pain seemed fresh again, as if the wound had only crusted over, with the blood ready to ooze at the slightest break.

Laura still had lovely dark hair, glistening in the sun with scarlet lights, as if there were fire buried somewhere in the natural curls. Back then it had been long hair, falling down her back almost to her waist. She had carried it off, her figure just full enough, just tall enough, her waist tiny and slim, everything about her perfectly proportioned.

In contrast, reflected in the windshield as if to taunt her, was herself—shorter, rounder, with frosted hair that naturally had been neither blond nor brunette. In the beginning she had been as blond as Susan, with straight hair hanging past her shoulders. Her looks had been in style in those days, and the boys had called her Blondie. People had said she was cute. But Laura was pretty. Laura was beautiful.

The street became rural as they angled out toward Harbor Road. It would continue through a wooded area seven miles to the lake, and just this side was a narrow paved road curving through virgin forest to Antique Village, an arrangement of early American cottages and buildings that housed millions of dollars worth of antiques. As a teenager, Fawn had worked there during the summer, when streams of visitors came from every state in the Union and from many foreign countries. She had dusted valuable antiques, swept walks after the visitors left, and even served soft drinks and made hot dogs at the one concession stand outside the main gates. She remembered the picnic tables out under the trees, near the parking lot, and the trash that people left, which had to be picked up by kids like her. There had been a lot of summer jobs there for a lot of kids.

"You're going to stay, aren't you?" Laura asked.

It was almost as if Laura had picked up on Fawn's thoughts. Just the way it used to be, before their friendship ended.

"I don't know. I have an apartment, a job. And if I don't hurry and get back, I won't have either."

"But isn't it harder there? Who takes care of your kids while you work?"

"Well, they're in school. Of course."

"Latch-key kids?"

It had a critical sound, although Laura's voice was soft, and Fawn knew she hadn't really meant it that way. Fawn shrugged.

"It used to be day care. I had to work." Fawn turned her face away and looked out the window. They were driving past houses that hadn't been there eighteen years ago. All set far apart on big, long yards, one or two-acre plots. Brick homes. In most cases, probably three or four bedrooms. The trees she had always loved hadn't been removed, though, and there was plenty of privacy. No trash, no litter, no gangs slumped against a corner. It was the kind of neighborhood she had dreamed of on cold Chicago nights, and had believed she would never live in. Not with her prospects.

"Do you know that I know almost nothing about you anymore?" Laura said. "We used to be so close, Fawn.

What happened? Suddenly one day you were gone, and I never heard from you again. Only through Granddad. Have you any idea? . . ."

Laura's voice broke, and Fawn looked at her and saw she was biting her lower lip, her eyes bright with tears ready to fall. Fawn quickly looked away. She wanted to say, I'm sorry I didn't confront you with my feelings, I'm sorry I never wrote or called. But she couldn't. Did Laura have no idea of her own pain? Even if it had been more a matter of ego than reality. She'd understood after a while that Laura might not even have known of Jim's growing interest in her. What did it matter now?

"I'm divorced," Fawn said. "It was a short marriage. He left when Susan was only a baby. I haven't seen him since, and don't even know where he is, or if he's alive, though I suppose he is."

"No child support, then."

Fawn laughed shortly. "No child support. That was one of the problems. He wanted to be the kid himself, forever. He didn't want kids of his own."

Kevin was like a distant dream now, not quite real. She hardly ever thought of him.

"My husband died," Laura said, her voice still soft, still on the verge of tears. "It was a boating accident. A bunch of guys had gone fishing, and I think they had beer with them, too much of it. There was a storm, and the boat capsized. Donny drowned. Donald Worton, remember him?"

Donald Worton? Fawn had a faint memory of watching a ball game in which the star was a guy named Don. He was a senior when Fawn was only a freshman. He had come up to the bleachers and thrown something to Laura.

"A paper rose? Or a poppy? Did he throw something like that to you after a game once?"

"Yes. I was thrilled, I remember, the first time he

looked at me. It kind of elevated me to queen status in school there for a while, remember? A sophomore noticed by the senior football king? Wow." She laughed. "I actually didn't start dating him until—well, after you left."

Fawn wanted to say, What about Jim—my Jim? But she didn't.

"I'm sorry you lost him," she said. She remembered in a yearly Christmas letter Granddad had said Laura's husband was killed in a boating accident. But Fawn hadn't let it touch her. It was different now, hearing it from Laura.

"Yes, it's hard. So that's when the board of Antique Village gave me a job as curator. I moved into the cottage out there sometime later, and I've been there ever since. You can work there too, Fawn. We need the help, and you'd love it. It's so beautiful out on the lake, even in the winter."

"Me? What could I do? Run the concession stand? I haven't even touched a typewriter since I left school."

"You could take a course at the local college. You were taking business when you quit, weren't you?"

"Yes, mainly."

"But you didn't pursue it in your work?"

Fawn snorted laughingly. Laura, she thought privately, had no idea of what the big cold world was like. No idea at all. "No," she said, trying to keep her voice gentle. Where had the harshness in her come from? When had it developed? "I found I needed more experience than I had. In order to eat, without sacrificing my virtue, I had to go to work in a hurry. I hit Kansas City with nine dollars in my purse. Can you imagine?"

"Then why on earth didn't you come home?"

Fawn opened her mouth, then closed it. She looked out the window on her right. Figures blurred, houses, trees, an occasional person.

"You had no reason to run away, Fawn, did you?"

Laura sounded frustrated and angry. It was almost like old times when a fight between them was brewing. But it would be Laura who would do the fighting, the yelling, the demanding of an answer from Fawn, while Fawn turned away, keeping her feelings and thoughts to herself.

Fawn shrugged. "It doesn't matter now."

"Oh, Fawn, sometimes you make me want to wring your neck." She reached out and squeezed Fawn's hand. "But I love you, and I won't pry if you'll just stay. Now, where were we? You were in Kansas City, nineteen years old and with only nine dollars. What did you do?"

"I went to work as a waitress. And I've been a waitress ever since. Sometimes in restaurants, sometimes bars. It turned out to be a kind of trap. Once the workday ended, I didn't have energy left for more study."

Or was it more a habit of taking each day as it came? Without planning for a future? The future had been put aside, left with Jim.

"Well, you don't have to go back. We don't want you to. The girls, Jill, Erin, and Kara, are so delighted to have cousins. They'd be crushed if you left. Kara fell in love with Susan. Of course, I suppose you'll have to go long enough to take care of your furniture. Maybe get a moving van? The expenses can be taken care of from the estate."

"No furniture," Fawn said. "Our apartment is rented furnished."

"Then you don't have to go back at all. Your personal things . . . could you get someone to send them?"

No personal things, Fawn almost said. Well, a few, maybe, the kind of things the apartment supervisor would put in a bag and send to Goodwill or dump in a trash can, more than likely. They had brought most of their clothes with them, because she had come with the idea of staying a month, even though it created a problem with school. But a month with Granddad, she had thought, would be better for the kids than a month at school.

Only Granddad was dead.

What had she expected of him, immortality? He had been ninety-four his last birthday. Yet it seemed impossible that he could be gone, that he had become one of the members in the small family burial ground in the far corner of the home property.

They rounded a familiar corner and came to the long driveway to the old mansion. From the road, the house looked almost ugly. The original part, which jutted out at the front, rose straight up for three high-ceilinged stories, with an attic atop that. The exterior was dark brick, the only bright spot the wide, red door beneath the overhang of a small roof. From the side you could see the new wing, which had been built onto the rear of the house and which contained a modern kitchen, utility room, sunroom, dining room, sitting room, and maid's room. It had been called the new wing longer than Fawn had been alive. Far longer. Built in the twenties, it was almost a hundred years younger than the rest of the old, tall house with its two floors of dark bedrooms and sitting rooms and a ground floor of parlors, library, and dining rooms.

Laura pulled the car into the driveway. The smell of the outdoor air changed, and became cold and damp. It was still another month before the trees would turn deep green, another month before Antique Village opened for the summer season.

Laura stopped the car at the front walk, but she didn't get out. "I feel drained, Fawny. I think I'll go on home."

Fawn looked at her, and saw a sadness in her face that hurt deeply. She started to reach out to her sister, for the first time since so long ago, but then the kids came running around the corner of the house toward the car.

And she remembered.

"Would you come in for just a minute? There's something I want to show you. I think you should see it."

Laura looked up.

Fawn explained, "The kids found it in the trash that was to be picked up the next day, after the funeral. Martha said Granddad had specifically ordered it thrown away. But I think you should see it."

"You're not going to tell me?" Laura smiled, getting out of the car.

"I want you to see it. Susan is crazy about it, and wants it terribly, but I told her no, you had to see it first, give your permission."

The kids hit Fawn then, Susan the hardest, with a hug around the waist. Andy grinned up at her. At eleven he was almost as tall as she. He was growing so fast it made her heart ache. Where had her chubby, cuddly baby boy gone?

She returned Susan's hug and patted Andy's shoulder. Susan went next to Laura and hugged her, calling her Aunt Laura, as if the name were sweet on her lips. Before now Susan had hardly known an Aunt Laura existed.

Had she done her kids a terrible injustice by keeping them away from the only family they had? But she had to stop regretting. The past was gone. Granddad was gone. And she was sorry, so sorry.

They went around the house to the side porch and into the bright sitting room in the new wing. The trunk had been left in the middle of the floor, a dark, antique metal object, in a bright and modern room. To Fawn, who had never been particularly fond of antiques, it seemed a blight. As if something gross had been brought into the lovely room.

Laura stopped and stared at it.

"Where on earth did that come from?" She knelt on the floor beside it, running her hands gently over the carved figures on the swollen, bulging, convex lid. "This must be at least a hundred and fifty years old. Look at those little cupids and the birds and vines. The art is probably from the early to mid eighteen hundreds. Maybe much earlier."

Martha had come into the room. She had been the housekeeper for as long as Fawn could remember and had been a kind of substitute grandmother to her and Laura. The older woman looked just as she always had. She wore flat, laced shoes and heavy stockings in both summer and winter; a print dress, always fresh and ironed; and a ruffled apron. She now had her hands in her apron pockets.

"It evidently was in the old shed all this time," Martha said, standing with Fawn, Andy, and Susan as Laura stayed on the floor at the side of the trunk. "Mr. Evans told me a few days before he died to have the shed cleaned out and everything put in the trash. He said to have some old chairs and things brought down from the attic and put on top of the trunk. He said under no circumstances to open it. 'Just throw it away,' he said. 'Don't bother it at all.' But the young'ns here, they found it. You know how young'ns are."

There was no criticism in her voice. Martha had been delighted to have kids around again, she had told Fawn, and Fawn felt it was indeed true. Martha had always been good with children.

"But why? Why would he throw it away?" Fawn asked. "With his knowledge of antiques . . ."

"It was in the shed all these years, Lord only knows how long." Martha drew her hands from her pockets and crossed her arms over her stomach. "You know how he would never allow anyone to bother that old shed. He didn't even give me the key until the day he said to have it cleaned out."

"I just don't understand."

"He meant to throw it away. It seemed to be very important to him, like it was the last thing he had to do in this life. Something he had to see was done. His mind seemed good, even right at the last."

"But something is wrong. Granddad throw away an antique such as this? We have only three old trunks at the village, and none of them in as good repair as this one."

Laura's fingers lifted the latch. "This looks as though it's been pried open. Is there anything in it?"

The lid came up, pushed by her hands, and she stared in silence.

The doll lay in the quilted interior of the trunk, its cream lace dress carefully arranged, unwrinkled. It was a large doll, at least thirty-six inches long, with real, golden hair, and was in mint condition. A valuable antique, Fawn now suspected.

"Victoria!"

Laura's voice was a hushed, astonished cry. She turned on her heels and looked up at Fawn, her face pale, a mixture of emotions on it that Fawn didn't understand.

Chapter Two

"Victoria?" Fawn said, clearly puzzled. Susan started to respond, but Fawn covered her mouth with one hand, to stop her.

Laura was transfixed by the doll in the trunk. She couldn't believe her eyes. This was Victoria, the most expensive doll at Antique Village, that priceless beauty on the dark blue velvet pedestal. Yet it couldn't be, because Victoria was still there, protected by fences, caretakers, attack dogs roaming free at night, and then by heavy plate glass wired with an alarm system. This doll wasn't dressed like the other Victoria either. This doll wore old lace.

She reached down and felt the ribbon that tightly held the doll in the trunk. She observed the quilted interior, a pale ivory with pink tones, as if once it had been pink. It was eerily like a coffin.

"Don't you remember Victoria, Fawn? That lovely doll at Antique Village, in the dollhouse, the one that stands on the most prominent pedestal? A very expensive, one of a kind doll, Granddad always said, and as far as I could learn, it was. But this—this doll is exactly like it."

Fawn had moved her hand away from Susan's mouth, and Susan now said, as if she couldn't hold it back any longer, "Millicent."

"What?" Laura looked at the little girl and saw her shining eyes, her obvious excitement.

"Millicent. Her name is Millicent, not Victoria."

"Millicent," Laura repeated. She took the wrist of the doll and found the same small gold identification bracelet that was worn by Victoria at the dollhouse. The engraving was in fine old English script and difficult to read, but Susan was right. Millicent.

Laura sat back on her heels, perplexed, feeling strangely betrayed. This doll, an exact copy of Victoria, had been in Granddad's possession all these years.

"Why?" she said aloud. "I don't understand."

"Becau—" Susan got out before Fawn shushed her.

"I just don't understand," Laura said, shaking her head. "Granddad himself said Victoria was a doll that had been especially made for his sister Victoria, and given to her on her eleventh birthday, December twenty-first, eighteen ninety-nine, just two days before her death. Don't you remember, Fawn?"

Fawn was silent a moment too long, and Laura looked up at her. She saw Fawn frowning down at the doll in the trunk, which had, for some unaccountable reason, been made into a coffin.

"Yes, I remember," Fawn finally said. "The doll Victoria is the one that stands on the blue velvet, on the highest point in the dollhouse, right? I used to like to look at all the dolls." She added, "And I used to dust them sometimes. They didn't seem so great then."

Laura untied the velvet ribbon that held the doll in its quilted satin bed. As she lifted it she noticed the eyes were open. Even as it had been flat on its back, the eyes had been open. The dampness, trapped in the trunk, she thought, might have rusted the mechanisms behind the eyes.

She lifted the dress, which seemed in oddly good condition, and looked at the body.

"Yes, it's a copy, obviously of Victoria. It's a French walker doll," she explained to Susan, who seemed fascinated by the doll. "The legs are jointed at the knees and ankles, the arms at the elbows and wrists. The head turns from side to side, the mouth is open. See those perfect, tiny teeth." She glanced back at Susan with a smile. "It's almost like she's smiling at you, isn't it?"

Susan nodded, her eyes eager and shining.

"See her shoes and hosiery," Laura said. "Perfect. This doll looks as if she hasn't aged at all. She'll be a beautiful addition to Antique Village's dollhouse."

Martha said, "You don't think it'll lower the value of the other doll? You'll have to change its standing, won't you? I mean from it being the only doll in the world of its kind."

Laura hesitated. Martha was right. Yet to leave this doll in hiding would be deceitful, dishonest.

She became aware that Susan was squirming, and she remembered Fawn had said Susan had fallen in love with the doll. She reached back to give the child a reassuring pat.

"There are other dolls, babe, still in the house. Lots of dolls. Not as old as this one. Some of my own dolls are still here. You'll find them in my old room, and you can have any of them you want. But this one, well . . ."

Fawn said, "I told her it was probably antique. I had forgotten about Victoria. Just slipped my mind, I guess."

Laura stood up, the doll in her hands. Its bisque skin glowed as if it were real. She smoothed the dress down. The glass eyes were sky blue, and seemed to have depth as distant as outer space. It was extraordinarily beautiful, and had none of the tiny hairline cracks Victoria had close to her cheeks. The long lashes were as silky and thick as her own Kara's, the hair as real, and as baby blond. Victoria's hair, as she remembered, was a bit darker. Since the hair of both was real human hair, it had probably been impossible to match the wigs completely.

She shook her head. "I still don't understand what Granddad was doing with this second doll. I don't remember ever hearing anything about it, do you, Fawn?"

"No."

"And the trunk . . ." Laura bent over. Dust, which had long been attracted to the lid, encrusted the carvings. It would have to be carefully cleaned. "Made into a coffin? It's almost as if someone buried this doll."

Martha said, "Maybe the little girl, Victoria, was given two dolls on her birthday. One named after her and one named Millicent, and maybe someone, her mother maybe, buried this doll when Victoria was buried. Maybe it was supposed to have been put in the cemetery."

"Then why was it in the shed? And why didn't Granddad ever say anything about it?"

"And why," Fawn said, "did he want it thrown away?"

"Yes, that is odd. Look, the doll even has pierced ears, just like Victoria. See the tiny earring, Susan?"

Susan nodded her head. The smile on her face seemed forced and sad, and Laura pulled the little girl to her for a quick hug. "Believe me, sugar, I know how you feel. I used to want Victoria so badly I once cried. But Granddad had no sympathy for me. He told me I ought to be happy with the dolls I had."

She felt within her the same disappointment she had felt then, when at the age of six she had been permitted into the dollhouse at the Village, and had gotten a really close look at the special doll that had belonged to Granddad's dead sister. There was something about the doll—she had felt then, and still felt—that was special. As if the little dead girl had given something of herself to the doll. As if the doll were more than the others that stood beneath her on their own pedestals and special stands. Ever after that Laura had felt that Victoria was special, a gentle, loving spirit that was beyond human understanding.

But this doll in her hands evoked a different feeling, she realized. It was even more perfect than Victoria, but there was something almost frightening about it. Was it because of the circumstances of its discovery, the coffin bed, its having been concealed all these years by Granddad, to whom antiques were almost everything? That he had insisted it be thrown away, destroyed by the trash truck, went against all that Granddad had been. Or so it seemed to her.

"Look at her hands," Susan suddenly exclaimed, and Laura almost jumped. "They're almost as big as mine."

Martha said, "Oh, yes. The hands of those dolls are made better than my own hands. I remember that about the Victoria doll."

"Yes, it's perfect," Laura declared. "I guess Granddad's parents paid a lot of money to have Victoria made for their daughter."

She placed the doll back into the trunk, with its head on the little satin pillow, but she didn't retie the ribbon. Just as she lowered the lid she looked at the eyes again. They were still open. The mechanism obviously was rusted. But maybe a little oil, she thought . . . and then drew in her breath. In a delayed action the eyes were closing, slowly, softly, as if the doll were going to sleep.

An eerie little chill snaked up Laura's backbone and into her scalp. With a sense of relief she closed the trunk lid.

"I've got to be going. Susan, I want you to come out to the Village and look at all the dolls. Maybe you can help me decide exactly how to display Millicent. Okay?"

"Okay," Susan said, the disappointment on her face

lessening only slightly. She hung back as the others moved toward the door.

Laura picked up the trunk. It was awkward, but not difficult to carry. However, Martha said, "Here, let me help you," in that definitive tone she could use, and took the leather handle at one end of the trunk.

They went out, across the porch and across the grass to the driveway, Laura carrying one end of the trunk, Martha the other. Andy rushed ahead to open the front door.

Fawn said, "I suppose she wants it in the back, Andy."

"No, that's fine," Laura said. "I think the trunk will fit on the front seat."

They slid the trunk in and balanced it so that it wouldn't rock or be in the driver's way. In having it sit there Laura realized she was humoring Andy in a way. The back of the station wagon was the logical place to put the trunk. She couldn't define her feelings about having it in the car at all. It was almost as if she were suffering remorse pangs for disobeying Granddad. She had to tell herself that perhaps Granddad hadn't been in his right mind at the last.

Yet that didn't explain all those years, since he was a child of four, since the day his sister died, that he must have known about this twin doll.

And that, Laura decided, was what it was.

Victoria's twin.

Millicent.

She looked back as she drove in a circle at the end of the driveway, and waved at the small group of people. Martha unfolded her arms from across her stomach to wave in return. Standing slightly behind her, Fawn waved. Susan, farther back, had a lonely, sad look on her face, and for just a moment, in an instant of impulsiveness, Laura almost braked the car, almost rolled her window down to call out to that little girl to come and get the doll. The dollhouse at Antique Village didn't need another star. Especially this one, which would take her place beside Victoria. But then Laura's eyes caught Andy, who had stooped to pick up some gravel from the driveway. As he threw it, his gaze met hers, and there was within it some undefinable expression that sent Laura on.

Later, she thought. Later, I might just let Susan have the doll. But first, it has to go to Antique Village, it has to be reunited with its twin.

Andy drew a long sigh of relief. For a while there, when he saw Aunt Laura looking back at Susan, he'd been afraid she was going to give her that weird doll. He didn't ever want to see it again. Even since he had found it, and he and Susan had taken it to the house, he'd had a bad feeling. Susan had gone silly over it, and had sat on the floor beside the trunk looking at the doll until he had asked their Mom to make her stop. That was yesterday.

"What am I hurting?" Susan had yelled, and Mama had asked at about the same time, "What is she hurting?"

"It's real old," Andy said, searching for an excuse they might accept. "Maybe the air isn't good for it." He couldn't say, "Look, I saw it open its eyes. Yesterday, when we found it, we opened the trunk lid. It was just layin' there with its eyes shut, and then it opened its eyes and looked straight at Susan." If he'd told his mom that she would have sent him to his room to rest. Too much excitement, she would have told him. He knew her. Every time he came up with something she didn't want to deal with, she'd tell him he'd been seeing too much TV, or playing too much ball, or getting too much excitement of some kind. "Go to your room and rest," she'd say.

Besides, he felt silly just thinking the stuff he'd been thinking about that doll. No, not thinking, actually, but feeling. It was as if another presence had entered his Great-granddad's house, and he could feel it, no matter where he was, how many walls or floors were between him and that trunk with its doll down in the sitting room.

His mother and Martha were going back into the house, up onto the porch and through the door into the kitchen. Susan dawdled on the porch, her hand on a post, looking down. But she wasn't looking at anything. It was almost as if she were in mourning, like his Mom had been after they had found out her grandfather was dead.

"Hey, Susan."

She didn't answer.

"Susan? Come on, Suse, let's go do something."

"What?"

Andy shrugged. "I don't know." He looked toward the shady grounds behind the house. How far was it to the fence? What all was back there? Where was the stream their mother had told them about? "Let's explore. Remember Mom used to tell us about a little creek where she'd catch crawdads under the rocks? Let's go see if we can find it."

Susan circled the post slowly, hanging on with one hand.

"Come on," Andy urged. Forget that damned doll, he wanted to say, but she'd probably only get mad at him because he couldn't understand why it was so important to her. And he didn't.

"I don't want to," she finally said, still making her slow orbit about the post.

"Aunt Laura said you can have all the dolls in her room."

"I don't want 'em."

"Well, you can't have that one!" Andy burst out. "I don't know why you wanted it anyway. That creepy old thing!"

"It was not creepy!" Susan yelled. "It was beautiful!"

He had her angry, and her hand came loose from the post and she was looking for a pebble or something to throw at him. He began to laugh and to run backward, taunting her, teasing her out of her bad mood, he hoped.

"Creepy old doll! Creepy, creepy!"

He ran, toward the back of the house, around the end of the big screened porch, down a pathway toward adventure.

Susan came running behind him. "You're creepy!" she yelled at him, still looking for something to throw. It didn't matter. Even if she found something and threw it, she couldn't hit anything.

"Hey, look, Susan! Look!"

"What? Where?"

She had forgotten to be mad, and was coming to see what he had found. When she reached him, he pointed on back toward the dark green of thick trees.

"I think I see the creek," he said, and then ran on before she could challenge him. He heard her coming behind him and he tipped his head back and breathed deeply of the cool, shadowed air.

It was great being here, especially now that the weird doll was gone.

Chapter Three

At the kitchen sink Fawn drew a glass of water and drank it. Through the window she could see the corner of the long back porch and the yard that once had seemed endless to her, a long wilderness that reached into mysterious and sometimes frightening places. Now she felt slightly uneasy as she watched her own kids running across that yard, even though she knew they would find little beyond it but woodland and a small creek, and at the line of the twelve-acre property a fence. She thought about calling to them, telling them not to try to go beyond the fence. Never climb the fence. Those were orders from Granddad, all her life. What was beyond the fence? Probably housing developments now, since the town had grown so much.

"Want a cup of tea or coffee?" Martha asked. "Some coffee cake? A sweet roll?"

"I don't think so, Martha, thanks. I believe I'll go upstairs and rest awhile. I feel like I've been through the old sausage mill."

"Well," Martha grunted as she sat down at the kitchen table and took the lid off the sweets container. "I know. I feel kind of like that myself, but something sweet and gooey always perks me up, and my coffee, of course. I don't have to worry about my figure anymore, like you young girls. It can go any direction it wants to, just so's I feel good."

Fawn smiled. In all her life she couldn't remember Martha looking much different. Perhaps her hair had been darker at one time, with less highlighting from the gray in it now, but if she had ever worried about her figure she hadn't said so.

"Enjoy," Fawn said. "I'll be down later. If my kids show up tell them to mind their own businesses for a change."

"Well if they had been minding their own business, that doll wouldn't have been found."

"I guess you have a point there."

Fawn left the kitchen and went into the hallway leading through the new wing of the house. At the end of it, a set of double doors closed off the main section of the house, and when she passed through them she stopped.

The old house seemed darker than she remembered, the ceilings higher, the silence more profound. The hall she stood in culminated in the center of the first floor, and her footsteps echoed faintly as she approached the stairwell. She stood at the bottom of the stairs and looked up. The distance seemed even more immense now than it had when she'd lived here, when she had been used to the old house.

The stairs took up the entire center of it, winding upward from first floor to second, to third. Although she couldn't see the gate from where she was, she knew it was still there. It closed off easy access to the third floor, which hadn't been used in all her memory. It was dangerous up there, Granddad had said. "Don't ever go past that gate unless I, or Martha, go with you."

Fawn climbed the stairs slowly. The wallpaper had a dark floral pattern, and pictures—photographs and paintings—of long-dead relatives, framed in heavy, ornate gilt, still hung where she remembered them.

She moved upward through the silence. Where the

second-floor landing branched off from one side of the circular stairway, she paused, looking up. Then on impulse she started climbing again.

A few steps up she came to the gate. Built of the same dark wood as the stairway, it kept children from going higher.

Granddad's sister, Victoria, had died in a fall from the third floor, she remembered. Her room was up there, and the playroom. And after her death Granddad was not allowed beyond the gate that was later built across the stairs.

For years, all she and Laura had known about the barrier was that they should not pass it. Not until she was thirteen or fourteen years old had Granddad finally told her about his sister's fall. It was almost as if he had put it out of his memory, or still couldn't bear to talk about it.

Perhaps, she thought, that was why he had never told her about the second doll.

She unlatched the gate and heard the rusty whine of hinges as she opened it. She moved upward on stairs that had not been vacuumed, her hand on a bannister not dusted in a long time. She knew that occasionally, perhaps once every two or three years, Martha had gone upstairs to vacuum and dust. But by the time Fawn had been old enough to go with her, she had lost interest.

Her footsteps seemed to be echoing, and she became aware of a strange discomfort, as if she were doing something wrong. She climbed slowly, pausing on each step, listening to the pulsing silence of the house, hearing faint creaks as she listened intently, as she looked upward into a shadowed third story.

The same wallpaper darkened this wall, and other old photographs of long-dead family members hung on it, carefully spaced a few feet apart.

She continued to climb, looking at the faces in the pictures on the wall against which the stairway was built, and when she came to the child she knew, without ever having been told, without ever having seen the portrait before, that this was Victoria.

She had fair hair, pulled back from her face in a center part, in the style of that period. She was as sober as the older ones, as if smiling had been against the rules then. But she had a nice face, and in the photograph looked to be about nine or ten years old. There was nothing of Granddad in her face, and no name on the nameplate, yet Fawn knew in her heart that this was Victoria, who had died in a fall from this upper floor just one day after her eleventh birthday.

There was something wrong with that brief story, Fawn thought, as she passed on by and climbed another few steps. The bannister was quite tall, the posts separated by perhaps sixteen to eighteen inches. She could understand why a small child would be unsafe up here, but an eleven-year-old?

She stopped again. There was something wrong with the arrangement of the pictures. The perfect distribution, the precise distancing between them, was flawed.

She stood back against the bannister to get a better perspective, and saw that one picture must have been removed, the one beyond it changed to take up the emptiness.

Fawn stared, frowning at the space, and then shrugged. What difference did it make? No one was ever up this far to see it. Whoever had hung the pictures must have gotten tired, or perhaps had simply run out of old photos and paintings.

She came out onto the third floor. The hall was long in both directions, the doors closed. She walked on, hearing a hollow sound beneath her feet, soft, but disturbing. She opened one door and saw a small bedroom, the mattress bare, nothing personal left on the dresser top.

She opened two more doors and found similar scenes. The odor of mustiness, of long-closed rooms, began to make her feel smothered, and she turned back to the stairs.

She stopped, feeling slightly dizzy. It seemed an enormous distance to the ground floor, a tunnel that went downward, dark and long and dangerous. At this moment Fawn was aware of the inadequacy of the bannister, and wondered why it hadn't been replaced.

She made herself look away from the long drop to the first floor, and with her hand against the wall, her eyes on the next step down, she descended, passed through the gate, and carefully latched it behind her.

Don't go past the gate, she thought to herself, and remembered she had not warned her kids.

From the second-floor landing she went down the hall toward the rear of the house. Her room was the third door, just beyond Laura's old room. Martha had put the kids in the spare rooms nearby, and when she went into her bedroom she left the door open so she would know when Andy and Susan came upstairs. She had to caution them about that third floor. She would tell Martha to lock it again and keep the key in her pocket, the way she used to.

Don't go past the gate.

Laura drove along Harbor Road more slowly than usual, taking the curves and corners in a drifting, almost absentminded way, much like Granddad had driven. There was little traffic at this time of year, since most of the lake resorts and homes were closed. The road passed several private lanes on its wandering path through the forest to the lake. Then a sharp left cut off from it under a large arch announcing the entry to Antique Village.

After she left the main road and took the winding

blacktop through the trees to the Village, Laura slowed even more.

The trunk on the seat between her and the passenger door rocked slightly each time she went around a curve, and her elbow brushed against the cold metal end. She found herself glancing at it and thinking involuntarily of the family graveyard and of the cold earth Granddad's coffin had been buried in. The trunk, made into a coffin with quilted satin and lace, was cold, as if it had long lain underground.

Laura passed the small restaurant that had been built a couple of years ago outside the gates of the Village. It opened during the season, and was now shuttered and closed. She rolled down her window. In the pale green, new grass at the roadsides small purple flowers grew, the first signs of spring. Song birds were beginning to arrive, staking out nesting places, their calls a marvelous blending without discord. But the happiness she had always felt with the arrival of spring was missing. She felt a dark weight, a burden that seemed beyond her natural grief at losing the person who had filled her life from childhood with love and care.

She thought of Fawn, as she had so often since her sister's arrival. Fawn had left in the fall many years ago, without saying a word to her or even leaving her a note. For years Laura had gone over and over those days before Fawn had run away, trying to find some inkling, some clue as to why she'd left. For six months they hadn't heard from her at all, then on Granddad's birthday a card had arrived. But it was the next Christmas before Fawn began to communicate with Granddad. Laura had written to her, but Fawn's answer had been through Granddad. It was as if Fawn had removed herself from her sister and wanted nothing more to do with her.

Laura reached the high, locked gates of the Village and stopped the car. She rummaged in her shoulder bag for the keys as she got out and went to the gates. Through the links of wire she could see the road angling on beneath huge trees, past picnic tables and a grassy parklike area, toward the parking lot. Old rail fences separated area from area, and a concrete pathway to the left began the narrow walks of the Village. Farther to her left, down over the slope, Laura glimpsed the sparkling water of the lake. Between her and the lake were the buildings of the Village, holding the millions of dollars worth of antiques that had come from all over the world, but mainly from early America.

The gates swung back, and two of the attack dogs ran to meet her, their tails wagging. Both German shepherds, and well trained, they knew they should not pass through the open gate.

"Hi, Mutt and Jeff," Laura said, and gave each dog a pat on the head. Whoever had named them must have chosen the names for some reason other than size, because they were as alike as twins. As alike as the twin dolls.

Two other attack dogs, not quite as friendly as these two, would be released after nine P.M. They were black dobermans, and hard to see in the dark. None of the four dogs would ever attack any of the family or the people who worked here, and privately Laura wondered how serious an attack would be launched on someone climbing the tall chain-link fences that surrounded the forty acres of the Village. Just the sight of the dogs through the fence, and the signs along it warning of attack dogs, must have been enough to discourage anyone from trying to steal, because there hadn't been a burglary since the dogs had become part of the Village four years ago.

Before that a couple of men and one woman had come in from the lake side, which had no fences. But the alarm systems had been enough to protect whatever they had been after. Laura would never forget the awful sound of the alarms going off at two in the morning. By the time she had reached the lake the motor boat was roaring away. The police had caught its occupants, but of course nothing had been done. They were guilty of no more than trespassing, so their lawyer had said.

Laura drove the car through the gates, locked them behind her, and then drove along the lane, through the parking lot, and on around to the cottage where she and her three daughters had lived for the past seven years. It was a small four-bedroom house, with a living room that looked out over the lake. The yard sloped down to the water, and in the rear of the property was the playground with the swing set and sandbox. The kids were all in school. She had kept them out for three days because of Granddad's death, and this was the first day of their return. Now that she was home she missed them.

She didn't go into the house. Her office was attached to one side of the cottage, at the end of the carport, and she went into it just long enough to get the key to the dollhouse.

The dogs had not come with her, and she wished they had. Through the trees she could see the cottages of Harry Blahaugh and Ivan Ellis, the Village's permanent caretakers, but neither they nor their wives or children were in sight, and she felt very much alone.

With the key to the dollhouse in her hand she returned to the station wagon and opened the passenger door. Overhead a mockingbird scolded her as it perched on a tree limb, one sharp eye tuned in to her activities.

"I live here too," she said aloud.

She pushed up the lid of the trunk, and felt a startled speeding-up of her heartbeat when she looked at the doll's eyes. They were open again, even though the doll was flat on its back.

Laura avoided looking into those eyes, though she felt

slightly like a fool, and lifted the tall doll from its coffin. A French walker doll, it probably could have walked beside her if she had held its arm and guided it just right. She could almost hear the reaction of the little girl for whom this doll had been made on the day the boxes containing the two dolls were opened. She probably had squealed the way Kara did when she was surprised by something. Or had she known they were coming? Perhaps she had waited in anticipation for the months it had taken to create these dolls, eagerly looking forward to the day they arrived from Paris.

But why order two dolls just alike?

And why had Granddad kept one of them hidden?

The narrow streets of Antique Village curved and angled, allowing room for small shops and houses of the Victorian era and earlier, the reconstructions donated by various people. She trod the wood sidewalks of Antique Alley, past the old barber shop with its antiquated leather chairs, straight-edged razors, scissors and other equipment; past the dentist's office, where she couldn't help but cringe each time, wondering at the courage it took for people to enter that horror chamber over a hundred years ago, with nothing but whiskey for anesthetic.

She followed walkways that passed between buildings, beneath the roofs, with glass walls on her right and left, colorful glassware on one side and copperware on the other. The windows were full of things people had used when the country was young—to wash clothes, grind sausage, and harness animals for work in the fields.

Every time Laura passed these buildings and saw the tools that were part of life then, she gave thanks that she had not lived until now.

She carried the doll in her arms, one arm around its body beneath its arms, the other holding its legs. It was an awkward load, and heavier than it should have been. It seemed to her as heavy as a child its size. Then she realized she had never lifted such a large doll before. Victoria had stood on her pedestal ever since Laura could remember, and she had handled her only to brush the dust from her, since it was never allowed to accumulate. Laura had always loved caring for Victoria, checking to see that this was still the most beautiful doll she had ever seen.

And here, now, was Millicent, to stand near Victoria on a pedestal of her own.

Victoria was no longer a one-of-her-kind doll.

Was that the reason Granddad had kept Millicent stored away? Because, as Martha had said, the doll might lower the value of Victoria?

No, never. Granddad was honesty itself. Whatever his reason had been, it was not that.

Laura entered the hallway that ran through the center of the building on one side of which was the dollhouse. The section on the right contained glassware, in all colors, cut glass, Flow Blue, Tiffany, Mary Gregory, and much more, in rising tiers. To her left, behind the same heavy plate glass that fronted all other display areas, were the dolls.

There were more than two hundred dolls, ranging from tiny wood dolls, Russian dolls that fit one within another, to the three-faced doll with the china head and the black papier-mâché dolls, and finally to sweet-faced Victoria at the top, standing on her blue velvet pedestal, one arm slightly raised, her fingers curved as if beckoning. Small teeth showed through the parted lips that gleamed under the overhead light. Shadows from her eyelashes lay on her cheeks. She was attired in blue, her dress made of organdy, and trimmed in fine lace. Her underwear was white, a long body stocking beneath the bloomers that reached to her knees. Even her shoes were white, in contrast to those of the doll in Laura's arms, which wore black, high-button shoes and black stockings beneath its pale lace dress.

"Hi, people," Laura said as she opened the door. She had started talking to the dolls the first year she'd been allowed to enter the house with her fine feather duster. Fawn had been with her often then, and at times they had giggled and carried on conversations with the dolls.

"Hi, Victoria," she said as she carefully climbed the wood tiers toward the top, stepping cautiously between dolls, keeping Millicent's feet high enough to avoid knocking one of the lower dolls off its private little pedestal.

"Remember Millicent? Well, here she is. Come to stand beside you. We'll have to have a pedestal built for her, but I thought I'd just see how she looks."

Laura reached the top and sat down on the rise, which was built on the order of stairsteps that stretched from one wall to the other. She placed the doll she had carried up beside Victoria and sat looking at them.

There were differences evident now, although Laura doubted they had been noticeable in the beginning. Now Victoria's soft hair looked dull beside Millicent's, and her clothing somehow seemed cheaper and less well made.

Laura examined the workmanship of both dresses and saw that the dress on Victoria had been handmade, probably by an individual who didn't make a profession of sewing dolls' clothes.

The lace dress Millicent wore was perfection itself, the lace collar gathered full at the throat. The sleeves were long, with ruffles at the wrists, the hem scalloped. It had not lost its ivory color. The coffin lining was also ivory, Laura remembered.

Their earrings were the same, except Victoria's was in her left ear, and Millicent's in her right. Each of them had only one, and in each case only one ear was pierced. The earrings were tiny gold circles.

The bracelets were identical too, except for the names.

But Millicent's eyes seemed a brighter blue, the glass as perfect as it had been almost a hundred years ago. Her hair was finer and lighter, her lashes darker and longer, her skin more perfect.

The tiny hairline cracks in Victoria's cheeks, just at the edge of the rouged area, seemed more pronounced with Millicent standing beside her.

"I can't do it," Laura said, and laid Millicent down. "I can't do that to you, Victoria. You've been the queen doll too long."

Upstaging Victoria seemed almost a crime. Besides, there really wasn't room for another doll in the dollhouse.

Was Millicent a much newer copy? She checked them again, going so far as to undress them and examine the joints of the limbs. On the back of each doll, she found, were identical numbers, with only two letters to differentiate them. *A* and *B*.

So they were twins, made at the same time, and probably for the same child.

She dressed them again, put Victoria back on her pedestal, and adjusted the supports at the waist that held her upright, although the doll could have stood without them since her feet and shoes were so finely made.

"Okay then, girls. You have met again, but I think we're going to let Millicent become a little girl's companion. Is that all right with you, Victoria? I thought so. You rather like being the queen, don't you? Besides, your subjects wouldn't know what to do. It might confuse them if there were two of you."

Laura picked up Millicent and carefully descended to the solid wood door, thinking of Susan, imagining the look on the child's face when the doll was handed to her. She stepped carefully from tier to tier, between the other dolls, careful not to accidentally knock one over. She paused briefly by a black doll. Some people objected to it because it was an old cloth nanny doll. She smoothed its black, braided hair.

Something, a strange feeling that she was being watched, made Laura turn back toward Victoria at the top of the tiers. The blue glass eyes seemed to be looking directly at her, and at first glance she felt she was looking into a stare filled with fear and warning.

Laura shrugged, then went on down to the door, carrying Victoria's twin in her arms.

Chapter Four

Susan followed Andy with little interest. Her feet were wet now because she had slipped off a rock and into the water of the shallow little creek, and she was afraid to go back to the house before they dried. Not that she had ever slipped into a creek before or been scolded for getting her feet wet. She just had an instinct about these things, as if she knew her mother wouldn't approve. She was wearing her good white shoes, with the strap and pretty gold buckles. She had put them on without permission, because they were so pretty.

She sat down on the mossy ground beneath a tree and gathered a handful of last winter's leaves to wipe her shoes, and then wailed aloud because along with the water on her shoes, she now also had bits of brown leaves.

"I want to go back to the house," she told Andy, her face squeezed up against the threat of tears.

"I'll dry them for you," he said, and went down on his knees in front of her. He pulled his shirt out from his pants and began patting the wetness from the white patent leather of Susan's shoes.

She could hear the water, several yards behind them. It made splashing noises as if it turned into a waterfall somewhere farther downstream.

Andy had wanted to go on, but she had spoiled his

day with her clumsiness. He hadn't yelled at her. Still she knew he'd wanted to, and he almost had. But then she'd wailed before he could get mad at her, and he had helped her back across the stepping stones.

Andy had crossed to the other side without any problem. And the worst part was, he had told her to stay on the side where she was until he found out what was across the stream.

It was the doll. She couldn't quit thinking about the doll and how great it would be to have her. Millicent. Under her breath, the name rolled off her tongue, like chocolate ice cream.

"I'll take you back," Andy said. "Maybe Kara will come and play with you after school?"

"How can she? She lives way out on the lake. At that place."

"Antique Village."

"She rides the school bus, she told me." Susan looked off through the trees and tried to imagine riding one of those big, long, orange school buses. "Will we ride a school bus, Andy? With Kara and Erin and Jill?"

"Who says we're going to stay here?"

Andy sat in front of her, his face down so she couldn't see his eyes, and wiped hard on her shoes, getting the tail of his shirt grimy and damp.

"Andy, you can be so depressing," she said.

He sighed and got up. "It's true," he said, shaking his shirt as if to dry it, stretching it to take out the wrinkles. "Nobody ever said we were going to stay here. Come on, follow me."

She had to follow him. All around her was nothing but trees, and she wasn't sure where the house was. She was all turned around in these big trees. She hadn't wanted to come out here in the first place, she remembered grumpily. She had wanted to stay in the house with Millicent. She missed the trunk being in the living room, where she could sit and look down at the doll and wonder at her eyes. Sometimes they were open, and sometimes they were closed. It was like sometimes she looked straight up at Susan with those lovely blue eyes.

And sometimes, when Susan sat by the trunk admiring Millicent, Andy would come by without her knowing he was around, and over her shoulder say, "Weird."

In these past two days since they had found Millicent, Susan had decided he wasn't such a nice brother after all.

But she had to depend on him to take her back to the house.

He was disappearing into the woods, and she had to run to catch up with him. He zigged and zagged, and she was beginning to wonder if he, too, were lost, if they both would be lost until searchers came looking for them, when she saw he had stopped and was staring at something.

She started to yell, to ask what it was, when she saw that he was holding the rusted iron fence that surrounded the graveyard.

Beyond him, she saw the pale tops of tall gravestones, silent as ghosts. Some of them were shaped like angels, or strange, frightening birds, because only the wings and heads were left. The features were blurred with time and the moss growing in the eyes and mouths.

One tall stone had a cross at the top, and another was peaked like a tall house, but the writing on them was filled with moss like the features of the angel or the bird.

Susan stood still. She didn't want to go closer. Even when Andy called to her to come on, she stood without moving.

"Come on, it's okay. It's just the cemetery where Mama's granddad was buried."

"I want to go back to the house."

"I'll take you back in just a minute. First I want to go

in here. You come and stand by the fence, you don't have to go in."

"Well . . ." She went slowly forward, to stand by the old, tall rusted fence and watch her brother open the gate and push it back. She heard the long wail of the squeaky hinges, and it seemed to be crying a warning to stay out. She held tightly to the cold iron of the fence railing and watched her brother approach the angel-bird stone.

Laura locked the gates of Antique Village. The dogs hadn't accompanied her back to the gate, and she looked for them through the trees of the picnic area, the parking lot, and the buildings of the Village. But she might have been alone in the world. The feeling was not pleasant. Alone, but for Millicent, who was back in her coffin-trunk on the front seat of the car.

She put her keys back into her purse and went around the car to the door. The day had suddenly grown cloudy, and the breeze off the lake was cold and strong, as if a storm was coming up. Even the birds were silent now.

Laura felt heavy hearted, as if sensing bad vibes, none of which she could define. She only knew the sun was gone, the wind was cold, and there was a chill within her.

Get this over, she thought to herself. Give the doll back to Susan, then head on home and get busy in the kitchen. Maybe a pizza for supper? The girls, on coming home from school in this cold wind, would love salad and a pizza.

She slid onto the seat and pulled the door shut. The car's interior felt cold too, and Laura rolled up the windows she had left down while the car was parked. She started the engine and put the car in drive.

The road uncoiled ahead of her, a bit faster than

usual, a lot faster than when she had driven in earlier. She was aware of heavy tree trunks growing close to the edge of the narrow, winding stretch, or sudden turns, of dips and rises as she drove as fast as she could and still handle the car. She wanted to get rid of the doll and go on to the cheerful lights of the supermarket.

At the highway she stopped and looked in both directions. A pickup went by, headed in the direction of the lake. When the road cleared she pulled out, twisted sharply to the right, and sped back toward town.

The station wagon moved ahead swiftly. Laura held the steering wheel with both hands and fastened her gaze on the two lanes of the road. At the top of a hill she met a truck that was filling his side of the road and part of hers, and she pulled to the right, barely avoiding the grassy shoulder.

"Damn," she muttered.

She was only half aware of a faint squeaking sound as she safely guided the car back into her lane and started down the hill on the other side. The hills out in this area weren't very high or very steep, but one followed another so that driving the road was like riding a roller coaster—up, down, up, down. Antique Village, built in an area perpendicular to the westbound road, stood on nearly flat terrain that gently sloped down to the edge of the lake. Before reaching town, the hills leveled off again, and the road became a series of long curves instead of hills.

Laura met two cars, both in the other lane, and she glanced into the rearview mirror to see them disappear over the hill behind her.

The lid of the trunk moved. She heard a faint whispering of rusted hinges, and her eyes jerked toward the sound.

Her breath caught in her chest, causing a sharp pain, a sudden tightening of her scalp. She could feel the skin on her cheekbones tightening, constricting painfully.

She was awake, yet she was in a nightmare.

The trunk lid was rising, the squeak long and rusty, as the lid moved slowly, slowly upward.

Laura stared, her hands gripping the steering wheel tightly, her eyes fastened on the rising lid of the trunk.

The doll became visible, the arm first, then the hand pushing against the trunk lid. And then the lid was back against the seat, and the hand was flexing, the long, precisely made fingers with the tapered pink nails looking horribly real. The fingers curled and uncurled, as if in some terrible sort of exercise that would enable them to reach out and grasp her and hold her forevermore.

This wasn't possible. This was a doll made in a factory in nineteenth-century France, a doll made with human hands.

Yet it was rising from its trunk, its coffin, and turning toward her. Its head was turning, and she saw the pink of its small perfect lips, the white, pearl-like teeth behind them.

And the eyes, with a depth of blue that seemed to hold the reaches of outer space. Or the dangers of bottomless lakes.

The right hand touched her first, reaching for her throat. She felt the sharp fingers, as hard and piercing as nails.

Somebody, or something, was screaming. It didn't seem to be her. Yet it couldn't have been anyone else.

She forgot where she was, that she was gripping the steering wheel of a moving car. Ahead of her was a pickup truck coming down the hill, and she went toward it, the scream in her ears, in her brain, nails in her throat.

Nails . . . fingernails . . . a doll that had risen from a coffin that had been made for her by someone who knew.

Someone who knew . . .

Roger Hamilton's worst fears were coming true. He knew that in the slow-motion second when he saw the car headed straight for him. He saw it cross the center line, the two yellow stripes that shouted in silence, *Danger—do not cross.* Yet the car was crossing, coming toward him, nose to nose, the woman behind the wheel a blur in his sight, the other person with her, the child, leaning close as if to stop her, or push her, or fight with her. *Clawing at her face!*

What in the goddamned hell were they doing?

He screamed out three words, "You're crazy, woman!"

He jerked his pickup to the right and thought of the load of furniture he carried, and how easily it might tip. He heard the crash of metal against metal and felt himself jerked sideways. The seat belt tightened on his chest as the automobiles spun together in a terrible crashing of metal and squealing of brakes.

Then both vehicles were falling, down over the side of the road, and rolling into the steep ravine, welded together, metal forged into metal.

He realized he was hanging head down, and he put his hand out and touched the top of the pickup just inches above his head. But to his right was an open space, and he saw that the door on the passenger's side had been partly torn off, and above the emptiness of that space was the pale green of young leaves.

He tried to find the seat belt release.

He wasn't dead. Maybe he wasn't even hurt. But he wondered about the people in the station wagon, and hated—dreaded—to know. How could they have survived? The wagon was beneath the truck, he knew that. He could feel the slight movement of the truck as it settled over the sinking car. He could hear the groan of metal, the ratchet sound of movement, of metal pressing into metal.

He heard the silence of the woods, except for the rasping of metal. No birds here, no frogs chirping in a pond, just the voice of twisting metal. No woman's voice, no child's voice crying out for help.

"Oh God, you crazy woman," he cried aloud.

And then a voice was calling.

"Hey down there! Anybody all right down there?"

He yelled back, just a yelp, a call that would let the man up on the road know help was needed. He heard a thrashing sound on the hillside, as if someone were coming down to help him, to see what could be done. He lifted his voice in a screaming demand.

"Go for help! There's a woman and a kid—somebody! Down there! In the car. Get help!"

He heard the sound of feet in grass and leaves fade as the person, whoever he was, climbed the hill to the road again, and prayed the man had a CB in his car.

Roger gingerly braced himself, then found the seat belt connection and pressed the button.

For a moment it seemed impossible to lift himself, to climb upward to freedom.

But he had to. He had to extricate himself and then see if he could help that woman and child in the automobile beneath his pickup.

He reached for the door above, heard metal grind into metal somewhere below, and groaned at the horror of knowing the two people beneath him would be further crushed with every move he made.

Lord, God, damn the luck! What had possessed that woman to drive right toward him? It was deliberate—or had she lost control because the kid wasn't in her seat belt? He had seen the little girl close to the woman, had seen a movement in the child that suggested a hug or a kiss, arms at the woman's neck or something like that. Horsing around. Playing in the car. Fighting? Not fighting. He couldn't imagine a kid of that age, not more than six, fighting with her mother. Or whoever it was with her. Mother and child, it must have been. But the child hadn't been in her seat, nor did she have her belt on. He had seen that much, clearly, in the seconds before the crash.

"Oh, God . . . oh, Jesus," he said again, wishing he could back up to the top of the hill and reverse the downward trip that resulted in this terrible thing.

He had to get out of his crumpled pickup cab and get to that woman and kid. There was no sound from them, only the creaking of metal settling even more, a crushed car becoming more crushed as minutes passed.

He struggled again to reach the door above him, put his hand into shattered glass. He drew back and saw the red gashes of small cuts, but felt nothing beyond regret over this last trip out of town.

Why had he chosen today to bring another load of furniture out to his new lakeside house? Why hadn't he gone on back to the shop to see how the guys were getting along with that new cabinet job?

Somewhere in the back of his head, Roger's past life flashed before him, one scene rapidly superimposed upon another. His brother and him swimming in the lake. His mother calling them. The excitement of going back up the grassy slope to the picnic table where he and his parents and his brother ate while camping on that two-week vacation his first trip to Harbor Lake.

At some time during that vacation Roger had made up his mind that this was where he wanted to live.

It was fourteen years before he made the move, he and his bride. But Gina hadn't liked it. Too much country. Fish all the time, she'd said, sit in that damned boat and just float around on the water, what's so great about that?

So they had moved back to the city.

When she had decided that wasn't so great either, especially with him, they had separated. Just one of those things, he told himself. A case of two people not liking the same things.

So he had come back to the lake, started a cabinet shop in town, and finally, after another ten years, had managed to buy a part of the lake shore, with a house on it he could really settle back and live in, a long screened porch across the back almost close enough to the water to hang a fishing line from, and a boat dock down below where he kept his twenty-four-foot bass boat. Not new, now, but shiny as a Las Vegas silver dollar.

He had planned to go fishing this afternoon, as soon as he got his load of furniture into the house. He hadn't even intended to arrange it. Just set it in there, and get his boat revved up for a trek upstream to the dam where fishing might be good today, although deep in his heart he didn't care about fishing that much anymore. Mostly it was an excuse to be out on the water, roaming around, nosing into little hollows and beneath bluffy areas along the borders of the lake. Getting away from the crowd. Finding his own little private world where there was no bad news, no crazy bastard gunning down a bunch of school kids, no NRA screaming their brains out about the right to carry arms. No bombs in airports or shopping centers. No drug trafficking across the borders.

He'd had no premonition that he might be involved in a car wreck that could have killed a woman and her child.

"Oh, Jesus, you crazy woman."

Above him the door that was left hanging to the cab began to make sounds. It was being moved. Metal screamed and glass fell, bits of it striking his shoulder and arm and clinging to the hairs on his arm where his shirt sleeve was rolled up.

"Can you give me your hand?" a man's voice called down to him. "Maybe I can give you a lift out of there. Think you can move? You okay?"

A face looked in at him through a hole in the shattered glass of the passenger door. Then the door was opening, being pulled upward and away from him, letting in fresh air, more light. And the face of a grizzled, ancient angel. He saw whiskers that had been growing for a few days and brown eyes as sharp and curious as the eyes of a young hunting dog. He wasn't sure if this was the same man who had gone for help.

"I'm okay," Roger said, reaching up, feeling strength in the hand that grasped him. "But I don't know about the woman and kid in the station wagon."

"Help's coming. Police, ambulances, fire fighters, rescue, whatever is needed." The man doubled his effort, one hand gripping Roger's wrist, his sharp eyes watching every movement. "I believe I know you. Ain't you the cabinet man? Roger Hamilton?"

"Yes." He saw then that the face above him was familiar. It became one of his former customers instead of an angel, making the change slowly as the man helped him out of his totaled truck cab. "Thanks . . ." But he couldn't remember the man's name, not now, at this moment, when his mind was still on the woman and the little girl in the smashed automobile beneath him.

"Charlie Young."

Roger nodded. "Thanks, Charlie. I don't know what we'd have done without you."

Above him on the side of the road, he could see two cars parked. Men were coming down through the broken brush and crushed weeds, and a woman stood on the edge of the pavement, amid bits of glass that sparkled in the light of a lowering sun that shone for a moment through a break in the clouds, her hands crossed over her mouth as if holding back a scream.

Roger understood her feelings. There was inside him a scream too, of remorse, of regret that he had been driving down that hill yonder as the woman had been coming down the next one, regret that they had met at the bottom of the two hills, with her coming straight into his lane.

"Oh, God, that crazy woman."

He wasn't aware that he had spoken aloud until the old man, who was still holding his arm, said, "You know her? You know who's in that car?"

Roger shook his head. "I only got a glimpse of her."

Sirens were swelling in the air, discordant as a dozen buzz saws but the most welcome sounds he had ever heard. A moment later the first police car appeared at the top of the hill and seemed to drop toward them. Behind it came the first fire department rescue team and then the first ambulance.

Roger looked at the station wagon. It was almost hidden beneath his pickup. Furniture—a chair, two occasional tables—were lying against the rear wheel of the wagon. It was on its top, and looked totally flattened. Roger groaned and turned away.

A wrecker was backing down the hillside now, into the ravine, getting ready to hook on to his truck and lift it off the car.

"You the owner of the pickup?" a voice said, and Roger turned to see a Texas-Ranger type of highway patrolman. He was in uniform, his trousers looking as if he hadn't even sat in them after someone had pressed a knife-sharp edge, his shirt as pressed as his pants, and his hat on just right. Roger felt scroungy and ugly beside the handsome man.

"Yeah, I am," he said, and gave his name and address, then remembered he had a new address, a lakeside address, but couldn't remember what it was. "I was bringing out a load of furniture to my house on the lake, and was coming down that hill when this station wagon met me at the foot. It swerved right into my lane. We hit head-on."

He moved back, to stand with the highway patrol guy and the old angel with the whiskers who had pulled him out of his cab, and watched the work of the wrecker. In minutes the pickup, looking like so many tinned cans squashed together, was pulled off and back up the hillside to the road. Traffic was beginning to pile up in both directions. Highway patrolmen were stopping cars and trucks, and rescue workers were already working on the smashed car. People from the stopped vehicles were beginning to gather and gaze down upon the tragedy in the ravine below.

"Who all's in that car? Did you see anyone?"

"Yes. A woman was driving, and she had a little girl in the front seat with her. The girl was close to the woman, with her arms around her neck, and the woman drove that goddamned car straight at me. I don't know why. She was looking at me, I know. I saw her look at me, but I guess she just lost control. The kid . . . horsing around . . . not in her seat belt . . . *Jesus.*"

A blow torch was being used to remove metal that once had been a door on the station wagon; then the torch cut away some of the roof, and two of the firemen pulled out a body, that of a young woman with dark hair and blood on her face and neck. Her arms hung limp as if they were boneless. For just a moment Roger saw her, as the medics rolled her onto the stretcher and ran uphill with her. Then she was gone, the ambulance screaming away, trying to find a path through the stalled traffic and the people who wondered what had stopped them.

The rescuers seemed to be pausing, and Roger felt like screaming at them.

"There's a kid there," he said, but no one seemed to

hear him.

"Take it away," someone yelled at another wrecker that had backed down the hill.

"No!" Roger cried out. "There's a child in there!"

The highway patrolman went closer to the wrecked car. "There's another person in there."

"No, there's not."

"I know frigging well there is," Roger yelled. "A kid. A little girl with blond hair. A beautiful little girl."

It seemed the men at the station wagon all paused to stare at him. None of them was trying to look deeper into the wreck to find the child.

Then one man turned back and reached down into the hole the blow torch had made in the metal.

He pulled out a doll. A tall doll with a sweetly perfect face and blond hair. She was wearing a lace dress and, oddly, old-fashioned black, high-button shoes. Beneath the dress black stockings were revealed for just a moment as the fireman handed the doll to his partner.

The doll smiled its fixed smile at Roger, and he saw blood on its hands.

"There's no kid in there. There was no one but the woman. And this big doll."

The doll's perfect face smiled upward into the treetops as the fireman climbed down from the smashed station wagon, the doll under his arm.

Chapter Five

"You okay?" An ambulance attendant in sloppy green clothes asked Roger. "Hadn't you better come along with us for a checkup at the hospital?"

Roger drew away from him and turned to watch the man with the doll climb the hill. He saw him intercepted by the tall Ranger-type.

"I know that family," the patrolman said. "I'll deliver the doll to their house."

"Hey, guy, you okay?" the attendant persisted at Roger's shoulder.

Roger hardly heard him. He had to get closer to the Ranger and tell him about that doll. He started to climb the hill, and stumbled. The ambulance man steadied him with a hand at his elbow. The hand remained firmly planted after Roger regained his balance.

"I'm okay," he said. "That Ranger, who is he? I've got to talk to him."

"The Ranger? You mean the patrolman?"

"Jesus, man, whatever. Who is he? Where's he going?"

"I guess he's going to tell the woman's family about the accident and deliver the doll."

"Well, I have to talk to him." Roger was desperate to catch up with the man, to tell him there was still a kid in the crushed car, or somebody was crazy and it wasn't him. He knew what he had seen. *He knew.*

"Name's Ruther," the ambulance attendant said. "James Ruther. The patrolman's name. Mine's Haywood."

"I've got to talk to him." Ruther was getting away, going up toward the crowd, toward the area where police were sending cars on through, trying to clear the highway.

The man behind him raised his voice and yelled, "Hey, Jim."

The tall patrolman paused and looked back.

"Guy here wants to talk to you."

Roger saw that Ruther almost went on, the doll in the crook of his arm; then his dark eyes settled on Roger.

He was going to wait. He even began coming back down the hill, hesitantly, impatiently, as if he had better things to do.

As Roger approached him from the downhill side, he had to look up at a man that even on level ground had a good four inches in height on him, and he began to feel intimidated.

"You okay?" James Ruther asked.

Roger put a hand to his face and felt it, wondering what he looked like since everyone asked if he was okay. He felt nothing out of the ordinary. A somewhat prominent nose, a cleft chin.

"I'm okay," he said. "Fine. I just wanted to say there's a kid in that car. . . ." He paused. The doll was being held so that its face was only inches away from his. Its glass eyes looked straight at him, the pretty little mouth smiled, the tiny teeth gleamed in the shadowed light.

It was the face he had seen in the station wagon, the same pretty face that had been close to the woman's. But he had seen movement then. Then it had been something other than an inanimate doll. He knew it. He had seen it. And staring into the doll's eyes he suddenly saw something that chilled him to the bone and caused his heart to pound. He felt the cold touch of fear. The doll looked at him, and its smile changed, became a smirk. He could see it, yet he knew the ambulance attendant behind him couldn't. The look of evil and hatred and triumph was meant for him only.

But . . . he was thinking like a crazy man.

He put a hand to his head again. Had he been struck? Without realizing it?

"You okay, man?"

He was goddamned sick of hearing those words. He had to get out of here.

But first he had to know. "Are you absolutely sure there wasn't a kid in that car?"

The patrolman touched his shoulder sympathetically. "No kid, Roger, just this doll. I figure you saw it and mistook it for a kid."

But he hadn't. Even though he knew that was the logical explanation, in this case it didn't cover what he had seen.

"I saw it moving," he said, and got the kind of looks he had expected. They thought he was crazy to begin with or he'd gotten a severe knock on the head. But now that he had started, he had to keep on. "It had its arms around her neck. I thought it was just horsing around with her. I saw it moving."

"The motion of the car. You said it was just a split second that you saw the station wagon."

"Longer than that. I saw it coming down the other hill. We met at the bottom. She pulled over into my lane at the bottom of the hill."

"He needs to be taken to the hospital," James Ruther said to the attendant. "Have you got family in town that should be called?"

Roger shook his head. A few friends, that was all. His

close relatives lived six hundred miles away, and he didn't want them disturbed about this. His mother would probably be out planting flowers, and his dad, who was retired now, would most likely be on the golf course. Or both of them would be in their camper headed someplace interesting. And his brother was busy with his work and his family.

But he had to get back to town. A ride with the ambulance attendant was as good a way to get there as any other.

He let the attendant hang on to his elbow as they climbed the hill, and even let him hang on until he was sitting in the back of the ambulance van. But he shrugged off the stethoscope and other stuff they wanted to use on him.

He sat with his head in his hands on the ride back to town, trying to make sense of what he had seen. How was the woman? Had she died in the wreck?

At the hospital they ushered him into the emergency room even though he kept telling everyone he was all right. Nurses smiled at him, then ignored his requests to be dismissed.

"There's nothing wrong with me," he finally said, the anger and frustration he felt coming out in his voice. "But I want to know . . . who was the woman and how is she?"

It was at least an hour before he got answers. By that time a doctor had checked him over and told him he was free to go. A nurse called a cab and told him, "The woman is named Laura Worton. She's thirty-eight years old and in intensive care."

"She's still alive?"

"Yes. But she's in a coma."

Roger let out a long breath. Alive. It was all he could think of at the moment. She was still alive.

Only later, when he was in the cab headed back to his

rented house, did he think of Laura Worton's family. Were there children?

Was the doll going to be delivered to them?

They were unsuspecting, innocent. They would be victims, as Laura was—as he was, in a way. It couldn't happen. He had to find Ruther and make him understand. The doll had to be put someplace where it couldn't get out.

Ah, he was crazy. Mad as a hatter, as the old saying went. He had cracked his head sometime during the collision, and it had thrown everything he had seen out of focus and made it seem like something it wasn't. The doll, most logically, had been leaning up in the seat against the driver, Laura Worton. And she had been suicidal, the way some people are, and she'd compulsively pulled her car head-on into his. A good way to commit suicide. Forget the other person in the other vehicle.

Hadn't she been screaming? She had looked as if she were screaming.

Or was that, too, just something his craziness had just made up?

He didn't want to go home, he decided.

"Take me to sixteen-forty Maple," he said. "To my shop."

"Yes, sir."

He would get one of the other trucks and one of the guys to help, go back out to the wreck site and pick up his broken furniture.

Anything to keep busy.

Fawn heard the old-fashioned bell ring just as she was starting down the stairs. She hadn't been able to take a nap, which didn't surprise her. At work she would get drowsy and think how great it would be just once to have an afternoon to herself, with nothing to do but take a nap. Yet now that she had one, she was wide-eyed as if she were without eyelids to close.

The kids were still somewhere outside, she thought, and then heard Susan's voice. It was a relief to hear those fine, musical, child's tones. Fawn smiled faintly to herself as she slowly descended the stairs. The person at the door wouldn't be coming to see her, she knew. She didn't know anyone in town anymore, it seemed, even though she had seen some of the people she'd hung around with years ago when they were all kids. It had been hello, I didn't know you were back, Fawn. And that was all. Except for Greta, who had said, "Come to see me before you leave, Fawn." Assuming she was leaving, assuming she knew Greta's address or last name or anything about her now.

Martha was at the door. Fawn heard voices, and something deep within her constricted. She paused on the bottom step, frowning inwardly, feeling suddenly smothered.

"Yes, Jim," Martha was saying. "For goodness' sake. How are you?"

And then, hidden from Fawn by the open door, Martha said, "Millicent?"

In the hallway, standing no more than ten feet away from the door, was Susan. She was staring toward the man at the door, and as Fawn glanced at her, a smile came to the little girl's face. A smile of delight and surprise. Susan started forward, skipping, as she did when she was happy.

"Millicent!" she cried.

"Is Fawn here?" the deep voice, the distantly familiar voice in the doorway asked.

As Martha stepped back, Fawn went forward. She had known in her heart who he was, yet she wasn't prepared for the man she saw.

He seemed to have grown, to have broadened across

the shoulders. He was incredibly handsome in the uniform he wore. Her nervousness at seeing him was suddenly reinforced by the uniform and the doll he carried. Laura had taken the doll to Antique Village. Where was Laura?

"What happened?" Fawn asked, going forward, close to him again, within reach for the first time in eighteen years. "Where's Laura? Where did you get that doll?" She heard her voice. It sounded shrill as if she were scared.

Susan had crowded against her, but she hadn't reached for the doll.

"Laura was in an accident on the road, Fawn. I'm sorry."

"She's . . ." *Dead.* Oh, God. No. This was her punishment for staying away so long. Losing Granddad and losing Laura. This was her punishment.

"She's not dead, Fawn. She's in intensive care. I'll take you to her." He leaned down and smiled at Susan, holding the doll out. Susan looked up at him worshipfully, as if he were a god delivering the greatest prize on earth.

"Is she going to be all right?" Fawn cried, relief making her feel faint. She was still alive. Laura was still alive. That was all that mattered at the moment.

"I'm sure she will be." As he carefully placed the doll in Susan's arms, Jim asked, "What's your name?"

"Susan."

"Would you like to take care of the doll for Aunt Laura?"

With only a smile in answer Susan clutched the doll to her breast. Its pale hair blended with hers as if it belonged, was part of her.

"Martha," Fawn said. And Martha nodded.

"You go ahead. The kids will be okay. I'll stay with them. Just call and let us know."

"Sure."

Fawn didn't think to get a sweater, her purse, money, anything. She just went with Jim to the patrol car that was parked in the driveway and got into the front seat. She sat trembling as he closed the door and went around to the driver's seat.

They had gone several blocks before he spoke. She sat hugging her arms against herself, tightly.

"It's good to see you again, Fawn. You haven't changed much. Were the two kids yours?"

"Yes, Susan and Andy."

"Any others?"

"No. What happened, Jim? With Laura?"

"It's kind of a mystery, Fawn. All indications are that she lost control of the car. She collided head-on with a guy in a pickup truck. Roger Hamilton. Do you know him? But you wouldn't, would you? It's easy to forget that you've been gone, now that you're back. Do you plan to stay?"

She suddenly knew that she would. She had been given another chance. Laura was still alive. That was all that mattered.

"Yes." She tried to relax. "How badly hurt was she?"

"She didn't look terribly injured. By that I mean she had scratches on her face and neck. But she was unconscious. The car was totaled."

"She must have lost control," Fawn said, beginning to see in her mind the scene of the accident. Tire marks on the road would tell the path of the car.

"She wasn't suicidal, was she, Fawn?"

"Of course not. She has three daughters. She would never do anything like that deliberately."

"I didn't think so."

"She was on her way out to Antique Village, to take that doll out to the dollhouse there."

"On her way . . . No, there must be some mistake. She was headed back toward town."

Fawn stared at Jim, seeing his profile against the passing scenery. "Back toward town? With the doll still in the car? I wonder why?"

Jim shrugged. "Roger Hamilton said he saw her driving straight into his lane. He said it looked like she was screaming, fighting, or playing with a child. But people sometimes get strange ideas after a wreck. There was no child, just the doll. Still, it is true that she drove her car into his lane. He couldn't have avoided her even if he had taken to the ravine. Where he ended up anyway. Both vehicles wound up in the ravine. Wreckers were hauling them away when I left. We'll be looking over the car, to try to see what happened. Of course, as soon as Laura can talk the puzzle will be solved."

Jim's left hand rested on top of the steering wheel as he drove, and Fawn saw he was wearing a gold band. Of course he would be married. Had she thought he might not be? But she had no feelings about it at all, except to hope it was a happy marriage. Perhaps the shock of Laura's accident made her numb to Jim. But she sensed that she would never feel anything more than friendship for him again.

They had reached the hospital. Jim drove into a slot in the large parking lot, but Fawn didn't wait for him to open her door. She went ahead of him, running to the sidewalk and up the wide steps into the lobby and reception room.

When she paused, lost, Jim was at her elbow, guiding her past the circular desk with a motion of his hand to the woman who greeted visitors.

"Intensive Care," he said.

They went through halls to the elevator and up to the top floor, and it seemed to Fawn that she had never ridden in a slower elevator or in one that had to stop for so many people on so many floors.

When they reached the reception desk of Intensive

Care, Jim asked that they be allowed to see Laura Worton, and a nurse's aide was assigned to escort them to her.

Through wide double doors, they entered a room that seemed to be filled with white figures and irregular beeping sounds. Then they passed curtained rooms and came at last to Laura, behind another curtain, in another room where the beeping sounds intensified.

Fawn almost lost control of her knees. They suddenly felt limp as if they were boneless. She could feel the color leaving her skin, the blood draining away.

Laura was propped up against a large pillow, tubes connected to every part of her body, it seemed. Her eyes were closed, her face crisscrossed with shallow, red gashes. Some of them were bandaged, but most had been treated with some kind of medication that increased their look of rawness.

"Laura?" Fawn reached for her sister's hand, her tears blurring Laura's features.

The attending nurse said, "She can't hear you, dear. She's in a deep coma. She's not aware of anything."

Chapter Six

She's not aware of anything.

No, no, that's not true! Laura screamed silently.

She knew pain and fear. She heard the sounds, the beeping of the many heart monitors in the Intensive Care Unit, the voices of the nurses and doctors and visitors. She knew everything that had happened except for those few moments of darkness as the two vehicles collided. In that last second, that one terrible glance, she had known she was going to hit him, whoever he was. She had seen his young-old face—too young to die, her age or less—and had seen the high cheekbones, the skin pulled tight across them as his mouth widened in horror and surprise.

She felt her own horror, again and again, like waves of intense cold, as she remembered the doll. That terrible doll with the strange, dark life of its own.

She felt its hands on her face, the sharp fingernails digging into her skin. She felt its hands at her throat, and knew in that moment when she lost control of the car that the doll was going to kill her.

She had heard Fawn come to her bedside, with someone she hadn't been able to see but whose voice had sounded familiar. And the nurse had told Fawn, "She can't hear you, dear. She's in a deep coma. She's not aware of anything."

The man had left after a few minutes, telling Fawn, "Call me here if you need me, anytime." And she had heard the rattle of paper as he'd written his telephone number. "Or contact the state police, here, and they'll reach me."

So Laura knew then he was with the police, but he was someone Fawn knew.

She heard Fawn weeping alone at her bedside, with the beeping of the monitors providing a frightening kind of background music. And Fawn's whispers.

"Laura, forgive me. Laura, I was jealous of you. I guess I always was. You were so pretty and so popular, and I couldn't handle it. I was a fool. God has given us another chance, Laura, please don't die. Come back, Laura."

No, Fawn. No. You were wrong, Fawn, it wasn't that way.

"I'm sorry I stayed away. I wanted to come home, but I guess I was too proud. Laura, forgive me."

Fawn, the doll . . . the doll, Fawn. Where is the doll?

"I'm sorry, dear, your time is up. Two members of the family can come back in for fifteen minutes in two hours."

Oh no, oh no. Fawn. The doll. Don't go, Fawn. Don't go.

She heard their footsteps, both soft, as if both women were wearing soft-soled shoes. She heard every movement Fawn made. She heard her go to the foot of the high, narrow bed and stand a brief time longer, felt those wide greenish eyes of Fawn's looking at her, and saw in her mind, as if her own eyes were open and she could see Fawn's face, the tears filling them, running down her sister's cheeks. She heard the crinkle of soft tissue as Fawn wiped her eyes.

Then the footsteps were leaving, and Laura struggled to leave too, to follow Fawn. To go home with her to Granddad's house.

Where was the doll?

What had happened to the doll?

Millicent. Not a doll. But Millicent. *What was it?*

To whom had the doll belonged?

And who was the young man in the pickup? What had happened to him?

Was he, too, in intensive care, or had he not made it this far?

Oh, God, forgive me, whoever you are. I didn't mean to cause you problems. I was only trying to get away—get away from the thing that came up out of the trunk.

Where was the trunk? Had someone put the doll back into it?

But what good would it do? The lock was broken.

Whoever had locked it in long ago had known what they were doing.

Who had created Millicent, made her into what she now was? Into a thing that had been shut into her own coffin by someone who had carefully quilted the material that lined it, as if laying her to rest in comfort, as if that person had loved her, had been unable to destroy her.

Had she killed before . . . or tried to kill?

Her keeper, whoever that was, had known of her, of the danger of Millicent.

Nurses entered Laura's room, and she struggled to make a movement, to let them know she was aware, that she was not in a deep coma. Something was wrong. She was unable to move, even to open her eyes. Yet she struggled.

A pair of doctors came in, a man and a woman, and Laura strained to reach them. She concentrated on moving her legs, and when that failed, on the movement of one hand or one finger. She concentrated on her right hand, her index finger, and her brain felt stressed to the point of exploding with the attempt to speak, to tell them, I can hear you. I'm not unaware. Help me, please.

"I don't understand this," the woman said.

There was a blank space, a silence with only the rustling of tubes being moved. Soft sounds that reached Laura's ears above the beepings from all areas of the dark vast world she now inhabited.

She felt pressure against the side of the bed, and a hand brushed against her.

"Normal," the male voice said. "Only slightly off. Well, something's right. At least we know she's not brain dead."

They were leaving and from her silent world, Laura screamed at them to come back, to help her.

But they went on, and she was alone again.

There were other people, other patients, in other rooms. She could hear the beeps of their monitors. But their voices were silent. She could hear the rustle of clothing as nurses went past her room, sometimes slipping in for a minute to check tubes and monitors. She could hear soft breathing and smell the antiseptics used in cleaning the floors and walls and windows. She could hear the soft whish of oxygen and feel it pressing into her nostrils, two forceful tubes of air. Yet no one knew she could hear any of these things, and she felt herself sinking downward at times, toward a long, dark tunnel from which there might never be a way back. She struggled with everything in her to hold herself from that fall into blackness.

What had happened to her station wagon? Had the police wrecker pulled it to the police station? Was the doll still in it?

Millicent.

Who was Millicent?

Why had Granddad kept the doll? Why hadn't he

had it destroyed long ago? Was it possible that he had not known what it really was but had been instructed by someone else never to open the trunk? He had told Martha to have the trunk destroyed. Do not open it, he had said. Have the trash truck take it away. Laura understood his thinking. The trash truck ground its load, destroyed it, reduced it to its smallest possible size, and then deposited it at the landfill where it was covered by a bulldozer.

But if he had known what Millicent was capable of, why had he entrusted her destruction to people who might have kept the trunk for themselves, or opened it as the children had?

Granddad, talk to me.

She was in a suspended world, between the living and the dead. If she couldn't reach the living, could she reach the dead?

Granddad, talk to me. Tell me what to do, how to reach my family and warn them about the doll. How to reach whoever has the doll and warn them. She's dangerous. Millicent is . . . deadly.

Outside her curtained window the wind howled and cried, and she heard fine, faint whistles, as if there was a crack around the window frame which the wind penetrated. Or was she hearing sounds from the other side? Of lost souls floating in an endless abyss. Of creatures like Millicent, in the world they inhabited, a world that had crossed over into her own.

"Mama!"

Oh God. Jill. She heard her daughter's sobs, and felt the cool, soft, young hands close over her hand and wrist. In her mind she could see Jill. Lovely at sixteen, with clear skin and glossy dark hair, long and curly and held back on the top of her head with a barrette. Today she had worn a barrette with tiny pearls along its length and a loose blue sweater over her blue jeans. But

Jill was feminine and at times wore skirts and blouses, or more often chose a dress, often one with the full skirt and the little ties at the waist that were presently popular.

Had she come here from school, or was it evening now, or night?

"Oh, Mama."

"She can't hear you, Jill." Fawn's voice.

I can, I can . . . listen carefully, watch carefully, please, please . . . listen to me. What did they do with the doll? With Millicent?

"Aunt Fawn, what happened? Mama had never been in a car accident before. She never even had a fender bender. The only scratch she ever got on the wagon came from somebody backing too close to her when she was parked! I can't believe this."

"I don't think anybody knows exactly what happened, Jill."

"What are we going to do? Without Mama?" Jill's voice was a soft wail, as if she were afraid Laura could hear and was trying to keep that from happening.

Laura struggled to cry out, to make her silent voice heard. But she felt her stillness, the total stillness of lips pressed softly together. She felt the tubes in her nostrils, and the needles in her wrists. She felt the catheter between her legs, and she was aware that something was pressed at various spots to her forehead, monitoring her brain waves. She could feel similar little suction cups on her chest, monitoring her heart. And through it all was the *beep, beep, beep*—everywhere, from all directions—her own louder than the others and faster than some. It was steady and even. Couldn't they hear it, see it, know that she was all right?

Jill and Fawn were talking softly, and Laura began listening again.

"You probably should stay with us, Jill," Fawn said.

"At least for a few nights. Laura's brain waves are almost normal, they told me, and she could come out of the coma any moment. She might be out of it by tomorrow. Her vital signs are strong, the doctor said. They can't understand why she hasn't awakened."

I am awake. Jill . . . Fawn . . . please.

It was as if she had been poisoned somehow by the terrible fingers of the doll. As if when the nails had penetrated her skin, the poison had entered her bloodstream and paralyzed her. But then Fawn was talking again.

"She has a concussion, they said. They don't know yet how severe it is."

"How long will she be here? In Intensive Care?"

"Nobody knows."

Tried to kill me . . . the doll tried to kill me. Listen to me, please. Listen.

"I still can't believe that Mama lost control of the car. It's so unlike her. Do you think she might have had a stroke or something? But she's so young. Do people as young as Mama have strokes?"

"Yes, it can happen. But there are a lot of strange things about the accident, Jill. She went out to Antique Village with a special doll my kids found in an old trunk. It was an exact copy of Victoria and—"

"A copy of Victoria?"

"Yes. And Laura was on her way with it, in its trunk, to put it beside Victoria in the dollhouse. Yet the police say she was headed back toward town, and she still had the doll with her."

"In the car with her?" Jill asked, as if unable to assimilate the information. "A copy of Victoria?"

"Yes. As if she had forgotten something, or had changed her mind and was bringing it back. A patrolman, James Ruther, brought it to the house and told us Laura had been in the accident."

Oh, God! No . . . no.

"Was the doll? . . ."

"It was perfect. Not even a nick, as Jim said."

Jim. Of course. She hadn't heard his voice for so many years. Yet now that she heard his name she knew the voice, remembered it. Soft, deep, low. He had returned the doll to Granddad's house. And Laura had a strong feeling that he had done exactly what the doll had wanted him to do.

The doll was in the house, somewhere, with Susan and Andy and Martha. It was out of its trunk, its coffin, at last.

Laura strained to move, to speak, to make herself heard. She struggled to reach them in any way she could, but felt her helplessness, her silence, the pull of the black hole beneath her. Tied to her bed with tubes and paralysis and silenced by something over which she had no control, she could only listen to the voices of these two she loved and feared for.

"Maybe we should stay with you," Jill was saying. "I guess I could run out to the cottage and get a few things for us. Our pajamas, something to wear tomorrow. We can't go to school, Aunt Fawn. How can we go on to school as if our mother were okay? I have to be here. Erin will want to come, too. And she can, can't she? She's twelve now. Won't they let her come in to see Mama?"

"I'm sure they will."

"Kara can play with Susan."

"Yes."

"We'll just leave the doll at Granddad's until Mama is well. I don't know what Mama was going to do with it, so we can wait until she tells us or does it herself, right?"

"Yes, sure."

"I'm sorry, ladies, time is up. You can come again at

ten o'clock, but after that not until eight tomorrow morning."

Laura felt Jill's lips touch her cheek. "Oh, Mama," she whispered.

She felt Fawn's hand, always warm, lie for a moment on her arm. And then they were leaving, their footsteps whispering on the floor, the curtain moving and rustling softly as they let it fall back behind them. They were leaving without hearing her scream.

Couldn't they hear her scream?

Couldn't they see her rising and coming with them, grabbing at their shoulders, their arms, crying at them to wait, to listen.

Don't go home. Don't go back to Granddad's old house, except to get the kids and Martha out. Don't leave without hearing me.

It will kill you.

The doll, Millicent, will kill.

It's not a doll. It's something else.

Something horrible, with a dark life that might go on forever if it isn't destroyed.

Couldn't they hear her screaming?

Chapter Seven

"I really don't think you should play with the doll," Martha had said when the man in uniform gave it to Susan and asked her if she wanted to take care of it for Aunt Laura.

That was after the tall front door was closed, and Mama had gone with the man. Andy stood back in the shadows of the hall and said nothing. He didn't even say, "Weird," when Susan walked past him with the doll cradled so carefully in her arms. It was so long that its legs hung down from the knees where they were jointed, just like a real little girl being carried.

"I'm not," Susan said, feeling half insulted. She knew now that the doll was worth lots of money, maybe even a hundred dollars. Maybe a million. And she wasn't going to hurt it. What did Martha mean by play? Susan didn't understand. She was only going to love the doll, look at her, talk to her, and just keep her close.

She hadn't known where to take it, not then. Up to her room? Back to the living room? She didn't want to let the doll out of her sight.

So she had taken it to the bright living room in the new wing of the house where she could look at it and fix its dress and straighten its stockings while she pretended to watch TV with Martha and Andy.

Then Kara and Erin came. The police had notified Jill at the high school, and she'd told them to come to Granddad's house on the bus instead of going home. They acted as if their mother had died, and Susan didn't know what to say to them.

Both Erin and Kara stared at the doll.

"What's Victoria doing here?" Kara asked. "Where'd she get that dress? And the black shoes?"

And Erin said, "That's not Victoria, is it?" She looked at Martha, at Andy, and then at Susan for the answer.

Susan was happy to oblige. As if it were her very own doll and she was telling them all about the way it came to be hers, she explained about finding it in the trunk and Aunt Laura's taking it out to the dollhouse to put it beside Victoria but having a wreck before she got there. She ended with saying the policeman had come and taken her mother to the hospital to see Aunt Laura, and he had asked Susan if she would take care of the doll for her aunt.

Kara and Erin looked at the doll, neither of them touching her, and Susan's concern that Kara, or even Erin, might try to take it away from her faded away. Erin was sad, and she went to the window seat and sat looking out at the setting sun.

It was not until the lights had come on, after they had eaten supper and Martha had mentioned getting baths taken for bedtime, that Jill and Mama came home.

"How's Mama?" Erin asked, and Kara, who had been sitting on Martha's lap, got off and stood at her knees, listening carefully.

Jill hesitated, then said, "She's not awake yet. But she will be. Maybe by morning. She's going to be fine."

"Can we go see her tonight?" asked Kara, and Erin answered her, saying, "She's asleep, Kara." But Susan could see the relief in Erin's face.

Jill, as tall as Mama, stood looking down at the doll where it sat so ladylike in one of the big chairs. As Erin had done, she stared at it for a long time and as Erin had, she looked sad.

She had a narrow face like Aunt Laura, with deep-set eyes that were dark, even though they were blue. Her lashes and eyebrows were dark, and her nose small and straight. She didn't look like Erin, whose face was round, like Mama's. And Susan liked to think that Kara, who was really neat, looked like her. They both had blond hair and blue eyes. Sky blue, not dark like Jill's. The color of Kara's eyes was almost as blue as the doll's eyes. Millicent's.

Sometimes Susan thought of the doll only as "the doll." And at other times she was Millicent, as if she were very, very real. Millicent sat like a lady in the chair, her hands down against the lace dress, her face smiling toward the TV as if she were watching the movements of the people on the screen.

"Amazing," Jill finally said. "It's exactly like Victoria."

"No," Erin said, turning from staring out at the yard light in the driveway. "It's not like Victoria."

Even Andy turned away from the TV. He sat on the floor a few feet away from it, his knees raised, his arms wrapped around them. Without moving, he turned his head and listened and watched.

"Well," Jill said, touching the lace dress at the hem, lifting it and letting it fall back. Susan resisted an urge to straighten it. Couldn't Jill see it was no longer lying flat on Millicent's knees? That she had left a wrinkle? Jill added, "The dress is different. The shoes are black. The hosiery black instead of white, but those are minor points. The doll itself is exactly like Victoria."

Erin said nothing. Susan expected Andy to say

weird, but he didn't. Kara stood at the end of the sofa where Martha sat, her hand on the sofa arm, Martha's hand covering hers.

Fawn sat down in a chair near Andy, and Susan heard her sigh.

Jill touched the ringlet that fell forward onto the collar of Millicent's dress and said, "Her hair is the same." She lifted the arm with the identification bracelet and looked at the bracelet. "The bracelet is exactly like the other. Millicent?"

Erin left the windows. Susan saw a streak of lightning behind her, in the black sky beyond the yard light that was always on from dusk to daylight. The line of white fire seemed to burrow right into the trees, back toward the graveyard, and Susan felt a long shiver trail down her back and arms. She was glad Mama was home.

"Looks like a storm coming," Martha said. "Why don't one of you kids pull the drapes?"

Erin turned back and pulled the draperies even as she began explaining why Millicent was different from Victoria. Susan didn't know what she was talking about. She had never seen Victoria.

"This doll is newer than Victoria." Erin walked over to stand beside Jill. She touched the doll's cheek with a finger. Susan saw her jerk back her hand, as if she had hurt herself, but she didn't explain the action. Susan watched her put her hand into the pocket of her jeans, as if to protect it from something. "This doll has none of those age cracks, like Victoria. And her hair is lighter and in better condition. And also, look at the mouth."

"What about it?"

"The teeth are larger. Victoria has a sweet smile. This doll has a . . . a . . ."

"Weird look," Andy said.

Susan glared at him.

But Erin right away said, "Yeah," as if Andy had said something great. "Weird."

"I don't agree," Jill studied the doll. "She looks just like Victoria to me. Except for the way she's dressed. And this dress looks just as old as the one Victoria is wearing."

"Is Mama going to put her beside Victoria?" Erin asked.

"I don't know. Aunt Fawn told me the police said Mama was on her way back to town. So maybe she decided not to put this doll there. Not yet anyway. Or maybe she just forgot something and came back to get it. Whatever, we'll wait and let her handle it."

"I hope she doesn't put it there. It would spoil the effect."

Erin sat down on the floor beside Andy, her knees drawn up like his. From the back they weren't a lot different. Erin's hair was cut as short as Andy's, and they were almost the same age. Erin was twelve, eight months older than Andy.

But Susan and Kara were almost twins, because Kara's birthday was in May, one month later than Susan's, and that made them almost twins even if they weren't sisters, but cousins. We even kind of look alike, Susan thought. She loved Kara, and was glad Mama had brought them here to live.

"Why do you think it would spoil the effect?" Jill asked Erin. "I think it would be neat. Twin dolls."

"I don't. There'd have to be a sign change for one thing." Erin held her hands up in the air, her fingers squaring off a sign. "Attention! Victoria, the most valuable doll at Antique Village, Victoria, one of a kind, made in 1899 for Victoria Evans, age eleven, now has a twin, hidden all these years in a trunk. Maybe, if we look through all the nooks and crannies at Great-granddad's old mansion, we'll find some more."

"Don't be ridiculous, Erin. Of course we couldn't do anything like that. It is odd, isn't it? Two of them when there was only supposed to be one. But what the heck. She's a nice doll."

Jill smiled consolingly at Susan, and the moment Susan saw that smile she knew she was going to lose Millicent. And just as she had feared, Jill picked up the doll.

"I think we should put her away, though, don't you, Susan?"

That left Susan with no choice but to nod her head. She couldn't speak because her throat was suddenly filled with sadness. She felt as bad as when her puppy, the only dog they'd ever had, ran out in front of a car and was killed. It hadn't helped for Mama to say, "But he died instantly, Susan. He didn't suffer."

She watched Jill pick Millicent up. Erin twisted her head around to frown at Jill.

"What're you going to do with it? You're not taking it out to the Village are you? Not tonight?"

"No. But I need to put it somewhere very safe. What would you suggest, Martha?"

Susan held her breath hoping Martha would tell Jill that she was supposed to take care of the doll, that she hadn't harmed it and never would. But Martha was not even looking at her.

"How about your great-granddad's room?"

"Yes, that's a good idea." Jill started toward the door into the old part of the house. "For the time being. Until Mama can tell us what to do."

Susan watched Jill go into the dark hall with Millicent in her arms. The face of the doll was turned back toward Susan, and she could see the shining blue of the eyes until the door closed behind Jill.

* * *

The lights in the old part of the house were controlled by little round buttons that had to be pushed, rather than switches. The wiring had been put into the house early in the century, Jill had been told, and she had always wondered why it hadn't been updated. Every time she wanted to turn a light on, she had to fumble and push and push again, and sometimes a button refused to work at all and she had to turn on a different light.

The hall was darker than she had expected. There was a light burning somewhere at the front of the house, either in the downstairs hall or on the stairs. Martha would have left a light on. Jill had heard her complain often enough about how dark the old house was. But the one light burning was little more than a glow in the distance, like a moon behind thin clouds.

Jill felt as if she were in a huge, strange house that had ghosts lurking behind every turn in the hall, every large piece of furniture, every doorway.

She ran her fingers down a row of buttons at the bottom of the long stairway and tried one. Nothing happened. In her left arm the doll seemed to twist. The hard body suddenly, for just an instant, became supple and turned, and Jill almost dropped it.

Her heart came up into her throat.

Bitter fear rushed into her stomach like gall; then reason saved her, and she knew her hold on the doll must have loosened just enough for the doll to slide sideways in her arm.

God, what if she did drop it, after taking it so that it would be safe? Safe from young hands that couldn't bear not to touch it, to handle it? What irony.

She got a better grip on the doll and pushed another button, and a light came on above, on the second-floor landing. She sighed in relief. Looking up into the darkness at Great-granddad's stairway was almost as bad as looking down into a deep, dark well.

As she climbed the stairs the thought that the doll had turned in her arms made Jill feel terrified and lost, as if she had crossed a boundary from the warm, safe world she knew to a place that only looked familiar on the outside.

She could swear she had felt the doll turn, just like a child squirming in her grip. The way Kara used to when she was three or four, and Jill had to get her out of something.

But the doll was large, and hard to carry because of the jointed legs and arms, she told herself. That was all. She'd lost her hold on it without realizing she had. The heaviness of its jointed arms and legs had pulled it sideways in her arm, making it seem as though it were turning voluntarily.

Even though Jill knew that was the only reasonable answer, that it was the real answer, she now carried the doll with a tightness, an urgency—a need to get rid of it.

On the second floor she hurried toward the front bedroom where her Great-grandfather had lived and died. She didn't pause to turn on another light. The landing light, a wall-hung lantern, showed her the way past the tall bookcase with the stained- and frosted-glass front, past the chair with the needlepoint seat, which had been made, he'd told her several times, by his mother. Long, long ago.

His door, the wood almost black in the dim light, was at the end of the hall to the left of the landing, the only bedroom at the front. Closed off beside it was a sitting room that he had never used. The room had belonged to his mother, who had died young, and had not been used since. It used to fascinate Jill, and she would occasionally slip into its silence and darkness. But she had not been inside it in years.

She thought about going into the sitting room with the doll, leaving it there on Maybella's dresser, but hardly paused in her hurried walk. She just wanted to get rid of it and go back to the new wing. That was the only part of the house she could stand, and she really didn't know why, now that she thought of it. Maybe because the old part was so high ceilinged, so dark, the windows long and narrow and so sparsely situated. She supposed the house had been built that way because windows were hard to come by in those days. Or maybe it was because they didn't have air conditioning, and this layout helped keep the house cool in the summer and warm in the winter.

She turned the knob of Great-granddad's door, heard the soft squeak of metal rubbing against metal, and felt a chill along her arms, the hair rising. At that moment she knew she couldn't stay the night there.

The faster she could get the kids and go home to the cottage on the lake, the safer she would feel.

Light from the distant wall lamp on the landing hardly penetrated the black of the bedroom. The draperies were closed, she knew. Even in the daytime there would be little light here. How had he stood it? But Granddad had been such fun to be around, such a bright and cheerful person that he had made any room he was in seem light and cheerful.

She felt on the wall for the row of buttons that controlled the lights in the bedroom and also in part of the hall outside. The first button she pushed wobbled sideways uselessly, so she tried the second.

A light high in the ceiling came on, a firefly glow that made the room seem filled with dark shadows.

Jill looked for an appropriate piece of furniture on which to set the doll, and decided on the bed. It was a high bed, antique, part of the original furniture, the kind that had a two-step stool at the side. The mattress was thick and soft. She had sat on it with Great-granddad a couple of times when he hadn't felt like getting out of bed.

She could almost see him there now, his white head propped up on the two thick pillows he had always used. The pillows were still there, in white cases that had crocheted trim.

Jill placed the doll against the pillows, her back at the very place Gran's head had lain the last time she saw him.

At the door, as she put her finger on the button to turn out the light, she looked back.

The doll's head was turning, had turned. It stopped the instant her glance touched it, so that she wasn't quite sure of what she had seen.

Jill stood still, staring at the doll, feeling strangely observed as it returned her stare, its glass eyes catching the light and glowing, almost like a fire. Blue fire. Cold. Deadly.

She had placed the doll with its hands down at its sides, its head straight, its permanent smile turned toward the big dresser across from the foot of the bed.

Yet now it was looking at her, at the door, as if watching for her to leave.

Creepy.

Crazy.

She only thought she had fixed the doll just so, she told herself. Obviously she hadn't.

She stepped out of the room before she pushed the button. The room suddenly was dungeon-dark, and she pulled the door shut quickly.

The laughter was soft and tinkling. A child laughing. A sound so nearly inaudible that it was like the turning of the doll's head, and after a pause in which her heart threatened to shake her to pieces, Jill told herself it was only this awful, crazy night. This terrible day, the most terrible in her life, even worse than the day her great-granddad had died.

It was this day, with the tearing up of their lives. Their mother being so still and looking as if she would slip away from them forever.

This day. This nervousness within herself, the quiet anguish that she had to keep hidden from her younger sisters.

She hurried downstairs, leaving the landing light on.

She had to face Martha and Aunt Fawn next, persuade them that she and her sisters must go home to the cottage.

She couldn't stay in this house.

Chapter Eight

After Jill came back from putting the doll in Great-granddad's room, they all sat together for a while and listened to the sounds of the storm as it drew near, and Susan slipped closer to her mother for warmth and security. Back home, storms had seemed so far away. Above their own apartment were ten more stories, so thunder and lightning didn't seem to belong to Susan's world.

They were going back to see Aunt Laura, Susan knew. She didn't want her mother to go out. The night beyond the crack in the curtains seemed too dark, even with the light in the driveway still on. Andy parted the draperies and looked out, and Susan could see the slanting rain. But the storm was softer now, as if the clouds had taken it into themselves and were cradling it for the night.

"You can't go out into this weather without something warm to drink," Martha said, and led the way into the kitchen with the rest of them trailing behind her.

This part of the house was bright and cheerful, even at night, even when it was storming. The kitchen floor tile was white with little gray flecks, and the tile on the counters was white. Susan liked the kitchen. At one end, by big windows, was the eating area, with table and chairs and a breakfront with lots of glass and pretty dishes. The kitchen was like two rooms in one, with no partition between.

Susan thought of the Pied Piper as she watched Martha leading them, and she giggled. Kara took Susan's hand and giggled with her, raising her other hand to cover her mouth and keep the laughter secret between them.

Susan was glad to see Kara acting like the cousin she had first met. They had come eye to eye, almost, the day they met, staring at each other, each seeing how the other looked, and it was like finding treasure. It was almost like opening the trunk and finding the doll for the first time.

Kara was her cousin, Mama and Aunt Laura told Susan. Kara was like finding you had a sister just your size, who even looked something like you.

At dinner that first evening Kara had said, "I want to sit by Susan."

And that sealed their friendship, because it was what Susan wanted too, but she had been too scared to say so. In this strange place, this big house, in a dining room that looked bigger than her whole apartment, at a table that was long and covered in white and had real china that looked as if it would break if she touched it, she had felt so timid. And then Kara had smiled at her, sat beside her, and everything was all right.

They had their snack at the table in the kitchen, or the breakfast room as Martha called it. But it really was only an extension of the kitchen, with the round table down by the double windows at the end, beside the screened porch. All the meals, except that first one, were served at this table. Susan liked it much better than the big, dark dining room.

They drank hot chocolate with marshmallows, and Martha put out a platter filled with a variety of cookies, sweet rolls, and brownies.

Kara took brownies for both of them, placing them just so on napkins and giving one to Susan. Jill was talking, and Susan began to listen, her heart sinking as she realized what Jill was saying.

"Our clothes are there. And it's getting so late. It would really be a lot more convenient if we went on home tonight."

"But, Jill," Martha said. "You'll be all alone out there, you and the girls."

"No, not alone. Harry and Ivan and their families are both there."

"And the dogs," Erin said. "It's perfectly safe. There's not a safer place in the world."

"But it's storming," Martha said. "I'd be scared to death one of those trees along the road would fall on your car on the way home, and it's such a little car, it wouldn't take much of a tree to crush all of you inside it like sardines."

"The storm seems to be passing," Jill said patiently. "I really would feel better if we . . ." Her face brightened. "Why don't we all go? Why don't all of you go out with us and spend the night?"

"Oh, no," Martha said hastily.

Kara spoke up. "I don't want to go," she said. "I want to stay here with Susan. Can I stay all night with Susan, Jill? Please?"

"Yes, please," Susan added, and in her lap she crossed the fingers of her right hand. It was a fabulous idea. She was delighted Kara had thought of it.

Jill argued with her for a while. There were reasons she should go home. "Clothes, Kara. For school tomorrow."

"But I can't go to school tomorrow."

"And why not?"

"Because of Mama."

"Kara, you can't go to the hospital."

"Why not? Why can't I go? I want to go too. Why can't I see her?"

"Because you're not old enough."

Fawn said, "I don't know why they wouldn't let her in for a little while, at least once."

Jill looked trapped. "I'm not sure it's a good idea. Kara, Mama is . . . well, she's resting. Sleeping. Very deeply. But she has tubes in her mouth and in her nose, and it's really a frightening sight. You don't want to see her like that, do you? And she doesn't know anyone is there. It's like she's very sound asleep. Or more than that—it's like she's under something that makes her . . . well, unconscious."

"Isn't she going to wake up?" Kara had pulled her hand away from Susan's, and she sounded as if she might start crying. Susan reached for her hand.

"Of course she's going to wake up. But—"

"I'm not going to school," Susan said. "Can't Kara stay with me?"

"Let her stay," Erin suggested. "A couple more days out of school, what the heck? She can make it up. She's no dummy."

"All right," Jill said. "Just one day. And then you have to go back to school. Mama would want you to."

"I will. And Susan can go with me."

"Yes," Fawn said. "I'll go tomorrow and enroll both Susan and Andy."

"Aww," Andy said. "So soon?"

Kara turned to Susan and squeezed her hand, and whispered, "I get to stay all night with you."

"Neat!"

Fawn got up from the table, as did Jill, and Jill said, "Erin, you come with us. We'll go see Mama at the ten-o'clock visitation, and then we'll drop Aunt Fawn off here before we go home. Okay?"

Jill came around the table to Kara and kissed her cheek, then she kissed Susan's.

"Both of you get to bed. Don't bother Martha. And don't stay awake all night."

Susan paused to hug Fawn; then she and Kara ran out. The halls of the old house seemed long and dark, with very high ceilings, but Kara knew where all the light switches were, and they left lights burning behind them at times, enough to show Andy and Martha the way upstairs. But then Susan remembered that Martha wouldn't be coming upstairs. Martha's room was down on the first floor, off the kitchen. It was a big room, and one end of it looked like a living room, with rocking chair and recliner, tables and lamps, and a television. There was even a sofa, squeezed in beneath double windows.

Andy would have to come upstairs by himself. Did he know the way? Of course he did. He had been all over the house, he'd told her, except past the gate that shut off the third floor.

"Kara," Susan asked as they climbed the stairs, "why is there a gate shutting off the third-floor stairway?"

"I don't know."

They went to the bathroom, and Kara borrowed one of the extra toothbrushes in the drawer. They giggled and brushed their teeth. Every time Susan looked at Kara, and Kara looked back at her, it was so funny they both doubled over with laughter. The toothpaste on Kara's chin looked funnier than anything Susan had ever seen. Then Kara drew toothpaste mustaches on Susan's face, and they nearly died giggling.

Then Martha looked in and told them to stop wasting toothpaste and get to bed, but she didn't look very severe. Susan even thought Martha smiled as she turned away.

"I'll be back in a minute to tuck you girls in, so you'd better be in bed."

They went into the room Martha had given Susan, where the bed was twice as big as her small bed at home. A double bed, Martha had called it. "All the beds in the house are at least double. Some larger. Even in the old days they built some beds wider though they weren't called queen- or king-sized then," Martha had said that first day they were in the house, when Susan still felt so shy.

The bed was high and soft, and Kara had to give Susan a boost up, and Susan collapsed, giggling. Then she extended her hands to Kara and pulled and pulled and finally Kara came up over the edge and they both collapsed, giggling.

At that point Martha came in and threatened to turn out the light.

"Can't we have a night light?" Kara asked. "You always gave me a night light when I stayed here."

"Oh, all right," Martha said, and left the room and came back later with a small light she plugged in.

She kissed both girls good night.

"If you need me, you know where I'll be."

For a few minutes after Martha left, the room was so quiet Susan thought Kara had gone to sleep. She could feel the warmth of her cousin's arm against her, Kara's fingers still curled loosely within her own. And she could hear soft breathing, almost like soft sighs. But over that she could hear the thunder. She saw through the drawn blind sudden, distant explosions of lightning, and she was glad Kara was there, so close to her. It would have been scary in the big bedroom alone.

Then Kara whispered, "Susan?"

"Yes?"

"Let's go say good night to Millicent."

"Hey!" Susan forgot to keep her voice down. The sudden excitement she felt almost brought her to her feet in the bed. "Could we? Could we really?"

"Let's do!"

"All right!"

Roger stood on his screened porch overlooking the lake and watched the lightning illuminate the landscape with its brilliant to pale white light, the suddenness of its coming and going leaving the world as black as a cave for a few moments. Then gradually the features of the lake shore became visible again, dim, distant. He could hear the wash of water against the bank below his house, one wave after the other. The water, clear in the daytime, was like black oil tonight.

The lake was not huge, as lakes go. It came from a small river on which the state had built a dam that reached from one hillside to another about ten miles south. When he was a boy and first visited the area, they had crossed the dam, which from the top looked no different from any bridge across any wide body of water. But then they had gone down into the dam, and it was like a city of offices and control rooms from which the outflow of the water was regulated. He hadn't been down into the innards of the dam since, but he had been left with a sense of stability, of man-made control.

And from his back porch, the lake might have been a natural production of nature.

Which in a way it was.

Natural man, building natural lake.

His thoughts kept going back to the afternoon. He had gone back to the shop and, with Adam Thornton, a young fellow of twenty-one who worked for him, and was learning cabinet making, recently married, he had returned to the wreck site and picked up the broken furniture and hauled it off. Thornton asked for one of the tables, saying he was short on furniture and his bride would love it. The table didn't need much work to be put in shape. The two men had then gone to the garage where the totaled pickup had been taken and had unloaded the furniture that had been strapped in the back of the wrecked truck. This they had brought out to the house on the lake.

When Roger and Thornton had gotten back to the shop, it had been past quitting time so Thornton had headed home to his wife. Roger, alone for the first time since the accident, had then driven the road out to the lake again, into a coming storm.

He had a batching outfit in the house. The stove and refrigerator were already in the kitchen, and over the past weekends he had stocked the freezer with food. In the bedroom was a mattress set on the floor. The frame and headboards were either in the junk or scattered down the ravine. In the living room were a chair, a couple of tables, and a TV he hadn't turned on yet.

Another room held a bunch of stuff not yet settled in permanent places. The sofa was there, as were the coffee table and, upside down on top of it, the ottoman that belonged with a chair broken in the wreck.

None of that really mattered.

What bothered him was the memory that kept returning. Again and again he saw that woman's face, her mouth pulled back in horror, and that . . . *child* against her, face turned toward the woman's face, hands digging at her neck and face. Slapping. Hands moving as if she were fighting with the woman, striking at her, scratching her. Both of the woman's hands had come up in defense, and the car had jerked sideways, its wheels turning, as if of their own volition. But the look on the woman's face, the horror, stayed in his mind like a nightmare.

Each time the memory returned the scene became more vivid, more detailed. Each time it replayed in his mind, he saw movements he hadn't registered before, in slow-motion detail.

She's going to cause a wreck.

Goddamned crazy woman.

She was pulling the car straight toward him.

No, her hands had lifted off the wheel to fight the child. The car was turning, as if its front wheels had been yanked sharply to the left.

And then he'd be standing on the hillside amid the wreckage, hearing the voice of the state patrolman. "There's no child in the car. Only the doll."

No child. Only a doll.

He tried to tell himself that what he had seen was the tall doll falling over in the seat, its hands and arms tangling for that one fatal moment before the wreck with the woman, blocking her view, startling her, causing her to jerk the car toward him, to take her hands off the wheel and use them to push the doll back where it belonged.

And then he knew damned well that wasn't what happened.

Either they had lied to him and there had been a child in the car, a child that had the face of the doll, or something was damned weird.

He had to find out about the woman.

He wouldn't be able to rest until he did.

She would know. If only he could talk to her, she could tell him what really happened.

He left his house, got into the shop truck and backed out into a steady rain. The driveway curved uphill to the street, and he pulled onto it and headed back toward town.

By the time he reached the only large hospital in

town the rain had lessened and become hardly more than a drizzle. He drew up in the parking lot that was by now mostly empty. Tall lights spotted the lot, as did the few big, old trees that had been left standing by the contractors.

Roger liked an appreciation of nature. There were few things that irritated him more than seeing a woodland bulldozed down to make a parking lot. When it would have been so easy to at least leave trees around the edges.

Her name was Laura Worton. It had been going around in his head all afternoon and evening. Even since he had learned such a person existed.

He was scared that she had died. He almost backed out on going in after he had climbed the wide steps and stood at the doors. What if she had died? A young mother. Thirty-eight years old.

He moved closer to the doors. They opened silently for him and he crossed an expanse of tile. A woman, sitting in a large reception area encircled by a counter, looked at him and watched him approach her. The lobby, with all its chairs upholstered in dull rose, was empty except for one young guy down at the far end who couldn't seem to sit still.

"Visiting hours are over, sir," the receptionist said. She was past middle age, her hair soft and white, her skin soft and wrinkled, but her eyes were sharp and alert.

"I . . ." He was going to lie, and he ran the tip of his tongue over his lower lip to make it less stiff and dry. "I have family here. I just recently heard. I need to know about her—how she is."

"What is her name?"

"Laura Worton."

The lady checked the files in front of her. "She's in the Intensive Care Unit." She looked up. "You're family?"

Roger softly cleared his throat. "Brother," he said.

The lady pointed with her pencil toward a hall to her left. "ICU is in that direction, top floor. There's one more visiting hour left tonight, at ten o'clock. You have a few minutes."

"Thank you."

In the hall he met two nurses, but they only smiled at him and went on. The first elevator he came to was on the basement floor and didn't seem to want to rise, so he went to the next and rode up alone to the second floor, where three nurses got in.

He was getting nervous. Would they let him in to see her? What would happen if he met her husband there? And he probably would. But then, wasn't it natural that he, who was part of the reason Laura Worton was in the hospital, would be interested in how she was?

He got off the elevator into another lobby, but he passed the desk without anyone paying him any attention. At the end of the hall he came to wide double doors that had the Intensive Care sign above them and a waiting room to both left and right. At the desk was another of the guards, this time a man, bald, big nose, heavy jowls, but with the same sharpness in his eyes that the woman in the main lobby had.

Two other people sat in chairs, he saw, a young woman with blond hair and a lovely heart-shaped face and a girl with dark hair and eyes, no more than sixteen or seventeen years old. The clock on the wall indicated two minutes until ten.

"Can I help you?" the man behind the desk asked.

"I'm here to see about Laura Worton."

He noticed the movement of the two women. Both of them seemed suddenly alerted, both pairs of eyes staring at him.

The blond woman stood up. She was wearing jeans

and a cotton pullover sweater, and he was not unaware of her curves.

"I'm Laura's sister," she said, the question in her voice asking, who are you?

He put out his hand and felt hers go into his in a trusting way that touched his heart. He felt the warmth of her hand, the softness. He was aware of the girl standing. And in the corner was someone else, not standing, but sitting, watching. There was also a much younger person, a boy or a girl, short hair, snub nose, alert eyes. Soft, full lips suggested it was a girl. She was dressed in jeans and a matching jacket.

Roger held the sister's hand, and fought back an urge to clasp it between both of his. He could see the sadness in her eyes, the questioning, and he dreaded telling her that it was his truck that had helped put Laura in Intensive Care.

"I'm Roger Hamilton," he said. "I . . . uh . . . I . . . I'm so sorry. Is she? . . ."

The man in the corner stood up, and Roger saw for the first time who it was. He was out of uniform, but it was the same good-looking face, the dark hair and eyes of the man who had carried the doll off to the family of Laura Worton.

Roger nodded a greeting at James Ruther.

"How're you doing, Hamilton?"

"I thought I'd come in to see how Laura is."

The sister said, "You're the man who? . . ."

Roger nodded. He felt a slight pressure of the woman's smooth fingers.

"I'm very glad to see that you weren't hurt. I'm sorry for what happened."

"I came to see about your sister," he said. "How is she?"

"She's in a coma," Fawn responded. "We just keep hoping and praying."

"Sure," Roger said, feeling out of place, uncomfortable, too aware of the sister, whose name he didn't even know.

Then the patrolman was saying, "This is Laura's sister, Fawn, and Laura's daughter, Jill. And her daughter Erin," he motioned toward the kid in the corner.

Jill gave him a slight smile and a nod of her head. "My mother's insurance company will contact you."

Then the man at the desk was telling them it was ten o'clock and time fore their ten-minute visit. "Only two family members are supposed to go in, but I guess it would be all right if the little girl went too, if you're very quiet."

Roger watched the two women and the girl go through the double doors and disappear beyond. For just a minute or so while the doors were open he heard the beeping sounds, a mixed bag of beeps, some fast, some slow, overlapping. He saw the beige tile of the floor, so polished it reflected the images of those standing on it, and glimpsed the curtains covering the wide doorways of each room. Then the doors closed.

"You doing okay?" the patrolman asked.

"No bones broken, no unexpected fractures. No knot on the head," Roger said, trying to make a joke of it and failing. He sat down a couple of chairs away from where the patrolman had been sitting, and the man took his chair again. Roger noticed a jacket hanging over the back of the chair.

"You were one of the luckiest guys I've seen in a while. Most people don't walk away from a collision like that."

Roger didn't answer. He was trying to figure out a way to understand what he had seen, a way to put it into words without getting himself put away.

"I've been thinking of what I saw," he said. "The . . . kid. The . . ."

He could feel the man's eyes, straight and unblinking.

Then the man was saying, "I had that car examined from one end to the other, for another passenger. Take my word for it, Hamilton, there was only Laura."

"And the doll."

"Well, yeah, and the doll."

The scene was before him again, as clear as if it were happening, a replay in slow motion of what went on in the front seat of that station wagon. The other passenger, the one with the angelic face, the sweet smile, the blond hair, turned and reached for the woman's face, her fingers curled as if she were deliberately trying to blind the woman.

He saw the woman jerk her head sideways, turning it, looking straight at him. He saw the horror on her face, her open mouth, the silent scream that came through the noise of the cars as they hurtled toward each other.

He saw the supple movements of the doll, the fingers gouging into the face and neck of the woman. He saw the red streaks of blood that appeared on her skin in that last instant before the crash.

But the patrolman wouldn't understand what he had seen.

He saw the fireman bringing the doll out of the car, its sweet face set in a permanent smile, its tiny teeth showing between painted lips, its glass eyes looking upward into the trees—and then at him.

Straight at him.

He had a chilling feeling there was some kind of recognition in that look. As if the doll were memorizing his features.

"What did you do with the doll?" he asked.

"I took it to Laura's grandfather's house, and gave it to Fawn's little girl, Susan, to take care of for Laura.

They deal in antiques, the Evans family. They own Antique Village. We went through the car from one end to the other. There was an old trunk on the front seat, but it had fallen down beneath the dash, and only had a little dent in the top—I knew they'd want that."

But Roger had stopped listening.

Somewhere in this town was a little girl who had the doll he had seen attacking Laura Worton.

Millicent moved. In the darkness of the room the silence was disturbed by the soft grind of long-still joints made of bisque and rusted wire, the wrists turning, the knees bending, the hands reaching. She left the room and went to the stairway and up. At the gate she paused. A latch held it tightly shut when she tried to open it. For long minutes she stood still. Then she began working carefully and patiently with the latch. The gate opened and she climbed the stairs to the third floor.

She went down the hall to the first door and opened it. In the total darkness she went unerringly to an old toy box and pushed up the lid. She stood for a long time, and then she went back out into the hall and headed from room to room searching.

She then returned to the landing and stood near the broken bannister, looking down.

Chapter Nine

"It's so dark!" Susan whispered, her head close to Kara's, their hands tightly clasped. Kara's steps were as jerky and hesitant as her own now that they were out of the bedroom and in the long hall.

"It's like a tunnel," Kara whispered in return.

Susan wanted to go back into the bedroom where there was a night light, but she wanted to say good night to Millicent too. Farther ahead of them, in the big emptiness of the stairwell, a light burned. She could see the glow on the bannister, and the shadows the supports cast. They looked like the black teeth of a monster.

Then something terrible occurred to her, and she stopped. "I don't even know where Great-granddad's room is."

Kara pulled her on. "I do. And there's a night light on the stairs. Come on."

She giggled, and Susan giggled too. But she was getting scared, and feeling as if they were in a great, dark world that held danger, there, beyond the wall, where the light beckoned.

"It's like a monster whose eyes shine in the dark," Kara whispered, "and it's going to eat us when we get close enough."

"Don't say things like that!"

They giggled some more, holding each other's hands in the darkened hallway. Somewhere in the house a door squeaked, and they ran, Susan back toward the bedroom, and Kara on toward the light of the stairwell, still holding hands. They fell, and got up and hugged each other, trying to keep their laughter quiet.

"It was only a door," Kara whispered. "Martha somewhere below, or maybe your mama came home."

"Yes, it was probably Mama."

"We'd better hurry."

Knowing that Mama might be in the house, Susan ran with Kara, braver than she had been before. They ran on tiptoe, paused in the open place of the stairwell and looked in all directions. Susan even looked up, and then wished she hadn't. The third floor, beyond the long stairway with the gate closing it off, was totally dark. No light at all penetrated the distant mystery of that silent and forbidden world.

She felt Kara tugging on her hand, and she followed. They crossed the landing and went into a hallway on the other side. Here, in the lantern light on the wall, the bannister supports cast long shadows. These were the teeth of the monster, at her feet, all around her, reaching into the halls, and falling far down to the first floor.

She felt now it was not her mother who had opened the door somewhere in the house. It must have been Martha. Or Andy.

They passed two closed doors; then the hall turned sharply and there was another door. Kara stopped.

"Here it is."

Susan wondered, Is this where he died? But she didn't ask. Great-granddad was a living figure in her mind, but distant and frightening. The granddad her mother had told her about did not fit the image she had seen in the coffin.

Kara opened the door, and they heard the squeak again, a slow, drawn-out whine so eerie it might have come from a horror movie, those shows Susan's mother wouldn't let her watch, not since she had come home late and found Susan and Andy still up watching one.

Susan shivered and looked at Kara, and Kara looked at her. Neither of them had to say anything. Susan knew. It was this door that had opened.

Susan pulled back, but Kara held on to her. The room beyond was as black as the third floor, and Susan felt anguish for Millicent's having to be in that terrible dark. Would it be all right if they took her back to their room with them?

Kara was feeling for a light switch. A moment later the ceiling light came on, and Susan saw Great-granddad's room for the first time.

It was large, twice as big as her own bedroom, and was filled with big furniture. There was a long, low chest at the foot of the bed, and heavy, dark red velvet draperies covered the windows on the opposite wall. Near the draperies was an area almost like a living room, with two chairs, a table with a lamp, and a magazine rack.

The bed was big, with fat pillows tilted up against the dark headboard.

The ceiling was very high, as were all the ceilings in the old part of the house.

There were chests of drawers and a big old dresser with a dim mirror.

But there was no doll.

Kara walked about in the room looking on the chest, in some of the drawers, on the dresser, even in the closet. Susan followed her, uneasy in this room, aware of the death that had occurred here so recently. The shadows in the corners seemed to move, to beckon to her.

"She's not here," Kara said. "I guess Jill put her someplace else."

Susan was glad to leave, to hear the whining cry of the door as they closed it behind them.

She was tired now, and sleepy. She wanted to go back to bed.

They returned to the bedroom quietly, and Susan wondered where Jill had put Millicent. She knew Kara was wondering too.

The rain had stopped when Roger drove slowly home. He had waited with Jim Ruther until the women came out of ICU, planning to follow them, to see where they lived. There had been no easy way to get that information out of the highway patrolman. Too many questions would make him look askance at Roger.

Still, he had found out a couple of things. There were no husbands. The husband of the woman injured in the wreck had died years ago in a boating accident on the lake. Could have been right below his porch, Roger wryly thought to himself. Life has a way of setting up coincidences that are unnerving.

Since then she, Laura, had worked and lived at the Village. She had three daughters, of which Jill was the oldest.

The other woman, Fawn, was a mystery. Ruther didn't seem to know much about her, yet he treated her as if he had once known her. She had two children, a little girl and a boy, and they were presently staying at the old mansion, Ruther had said.

Roger knew about the old mansion. He'd heard it mentioned a couple of times, but he hadn't been interested in it then. So he still didn't know where it was.

He had asked one question, "Is that where you took the doll?"

And Ruther had given him that look. It was a look that made Roger damned uncomfortable, as if the man were asking, "You lose a wheel out there in that ravine?"

So Roger had carefully kept quiet as the five of them went down in the elevator and out into the damp night. He had seen the ladies get into a small, blue car, and Ruther into a larger red car, a sedan. His own shop truck, bright red, not cherry red like Ruther's, would stand out even on a dark and drizzly night such as this, so he dared not follow the ladies to see where the old mansion was. He had a feeling the patrolman was watching him, and watching them. He also had a feeling there was something between the policeman and the woman, Fawn. But he didn't know what. She'd been living some distance away for several years, so it must be in the past.

He turned off the main highway without having met very many automobiles and proceeded on toward his street. The pavement was shining black in the night, the one stripe down its middle coiling away into the darkness, the only visible thing beyond his window other than the tree limbs that drooped over the road and were caught by his truck lights and then lost one after the other, like falling dominoes.

He thought he would feel relief at getting home, but he didn't. He left his keys in the truck, the garage door locked behind it, and went through the door that led up into the hallway, a utility room and half bath on the right, the kitchen on the left.

He made a cup of decaf coffee in the microwave and carried it through the living room and out onto the screened porch.

Below him the lake glistened in the pale light that

seeped through the clouds, collected in the atmosphere from the hidden lights of other houses on the lake shore. A cold wind drifted through the screen and sent long shivers down his arms.

He sipped the hot coffee, stared at the water, listened to it splash against the bank below him, and wondered what approach he could make. For more than one reason now he wanted to get better acquainted with Fawn.

She was one of the most attractive women he'd ever seen. The only one he'd had this interested, protective feeling toward since his wife had left him. It was a feeling he'd thought he'd never experience again.

But it was tinged with sorrow, as if he already knew nothing would ever come of it.

And although he'd never met her little girl, and might never meet her, he had a feeling of tenderness toward the child. He wanted to protect her, too.

He knew what he had seen, but he didn't know how to handle it. At times he had to admit that he might be nuts, that something might have struck his head during the terrible tangling of the two automobiles and their rolling fall off the road into the ravine.

He wanted to protect a child from something that might not even exist.

Laura Worton might never be able to talk to him about it.

Come back. Listen to me, please, please. Oh, God. Where are you? Fawn . . . Jill!

She struggled against her helplessness, her total paralysis. Mentally she reached out to them, begging them to listen, to listen. *Don't let the children be with the doll. Put the doll back into its coffin and nail it shut. Don't go without hearing me.*

Fawn!

They had stood at her bedside, one on each side, and she had felt their hands on hers. She had known by the touch of the hands that Jill was on her left, her daughter's hand thin and soft and light and cool, and Fawn was on her right, the hand larger, warmer.

They had been with her such a short time.

"Don't worry about your girls, Laura. They're fine. Jill feels she and Erin should go out to the cottage, all their things are there—"

Oh, God! Oh, thank God. But . . . the others . . . the rest of you . . .

"But Kara is spending the night with Susan."

No! No!

She had tried to reach them. She had struggled so hard to move one of her fingers that it seemed her brain would die with the effort, her blood vessels bursting, drowning her brain in its own blood.

She had tried to open her mouth, to make a sound.

But they had left her, their kisses soft on her forehead, their footsteps gone . . . so far gone now.

She had to get out of bed and follow them. She couldn't let them go without telling them. *The doll is deadly. That's why it was locked away.*

Why hadn't it been destroyed? Why had it only been locked into a metal trunk? Why had Granddad waited until he was on his deathbed to order it destroyed? Why, God? Why hadn't he told her about it? She could have sworn there was nothing important in Granddad's life she didn't know about. He had spent all his years at the mansion, in this community. There were no secrets. And yet . . .

The doll just didn't fit into anything she knew about Granddad and his family.

Victoria? Granddad's sister? Dead at age eleven, when Granddad was only four.

It had to do with her, somehow.

But it didn't matter now. All that mattered was that she rise from this bed and carry out Granddad's orders, before one of the children became a victim of Millicent.

She had to rise. The tubes could not hold her, the constant beeping of the monitors could not keep her here. She had to rise, to *rise*. . . .

The room was suddenly visible, light blinding her. The darkness she had lain in was lifted, and she could see! She saw the bed with its white sheets, and the woven cotton blanket that humped over her feet and showed the outline of her legs and thighs and was folded back at her waist. She saw her arms straight down at her sides, and the needles in the wrists, taped with white. She saw the tube running to the bag held at the side of the bed. She saw the tubes in her nose and throat.

She saw . . .

For a moment she froze in fear.

Her view was from the ceiling.

She was looking down upon the room, upon her body in the bed.

She could see her closed eyes, the white bandages on her face and neck. She saw the IV bottles hanging by the bedside, and then as she watched in a kind of still horror, she saw a nurse push the curtain back and check instruments, needles, monitors.

And then she knew.

She was floating in the air, weightless, beyond the physical. She had risen from her body, and she was free. Free!

She wished herself at the mansion, and in that instant she was surrounded by darkness, and she felt the flush of panic. What had she done to herself?

Then she saw a pale light. It became brighter, though still it was dim, as if it were candlelight.

She saw two girls, small, their heads close together. They were sitting on a floor, on which the dim light pooled.

Kara and Susan!

She moved closer to them and then realized they weren't her baby, Kara, and her niece, Susan. They were much younger, no more than three years old, and the hair of one was darker, a rich and glossy mahogany. It was held back by a striped satin ribbon. The other little girl had soft, baby blond hair, and the ribbon in her hair was pale blue.

Someone was coming along the hallway outside. The footsteps were slow, as if the person were old or tired.

The two little girls moved, their heads turning, and Laura saw their faces.

The face of the dark-haired girl was as beautiful as a flower. The other little girl paled in comparison, her eyelashes catching the candlelight like thin, fine silk, casting no shadows on her cheeks as did the long, dark lashes of the other child.

The only sound in this strange, dim world was the sound of the footsteps. The only movement that of the two little girls as they stood up.

Laura saw their clothes, and a sense of shock went through her. The one dress, with the tiny buttons down the long waist, and the long sleeves, the dress the blond child was wearing, was one of the antique dresses out at the Village. It now hung in a dress shop there, a replica of the eighteen hundreds. It was dark and heavy, a terrible garment for a three-year-old child.

The dress of the other child was unfamiliar. It, too, had a long waist with tiny buttons, and a collar trimmed in black tatting. But it was not among the antique clothing at the Village.

Their shoes reached up their small legs to their calves, and were buttoned as tightly as the dresses.

The door opened, the footsteps stopped.

The woman wore a black dress, as heavy and full as the dresses of the children. The bodice fit her plump figure closely. Her face was round and plain, her dark hair pulled straight back into a bun. She smiled. It was a distantly familiar face, as if Laura had seen it in an old photograph.

The dark-haired child ran to the woman, hugged her, and pointed back at the little blond, but Laura couldn't hear what she was saying. The blond child shook her head, but only once. The look on her face suggested she was near tears.

Laura's world became black again, and just for an instant she felt suspended in an emptiness beyond anything she had ever imagined.

Then sounds began reaching her. *Beep, beep, beep . . .*

Moonlight touched the small head as the figure moved from light to shadow and into the trees. Jointed knees whispered, like old silk rubbing against old taffeta. The jointed wrists turned and lifted as the doll pushed aside vines that grew on the side of the shed.

Millicent stepped up and over the high threshold and went into the shed. With unerring direction she went to the corner of the building and stooped, her unjointed body straight, as if she wore a tight corset. Her fingers touched a handle, half buried in the dirt floor. They curled tightly around it, and lifted.

She left the shed, and stood for a moment in the moonlight looking back toward the tall, old house. As she moved toward the door moonlight glinted on the dulled and rusted knob of a ballpeen hammer.

Chapter Ten

Andy lay in the strange bed, tense and stiff, on his back, looking up into the darkness. He was listening, listening so hard he couldn't go to sleep. He had heard the girls giggling, a long time ago, and yet it hadn't sounded like real girls, or real giggling. It had a weird sound, as if it came from the graveyard out beyond his long, narrow window. Or from the walls, like a memory embedded there from a long time ago.

He had heard doors squeak as they opened, and he had heard them squeak as they closed and then the soft thuds of their closing. And he had been hearing footsteps in the hall. Sometimes they sounded as if they might be his mother's, and his heart would gladden. He'd get set to run to her, and then he'd think to himself, if it were his mother she would come to him, kiss him good night, tuck his blanket around his shoulders.

He hadn't been afraid in this room the first few nights. He had looked at it, and thought about how his things would look here, on the dresser, on the walls. He had thought maybe his mother could get some new wallpaper, the way she had in their apartment, and together they would make the walls bright and cheerful.

He had thought about how great it would be to live here, to have all that wooded world behind the house and yard to play in. The little dam, the creek, the pool above the dam to fish in, swim in on a hot summer day. He had thought how great it would be to live in a small town and go to a new school, and maybe get to have a bicycle and ride on the roads and paths and sidewalks.

Then they had found the weird doll, and he had started staying awake a lot at night.

There was something about it.

He'd been so glad when Aunt Laura took it away. But having the policeman bring it back was like knowing you were trapped. If the policeman brought it back, it had to stay.

He didn't know where Great-granddad's room was, the place where Jill had put the doll.

And he wasn't really sure why he had shut his bedroom door tonight for the first time, even though he was shutting out the dim reach of light from the small wall lamp on the stair landing.

He lay in the dark and listened to the house move. He heard something scrambling in the wall, just a little sound of movement. A mouse, or a chipmunk, maybe. It was a comfort to know it was probably just a furry little animal, instead of dark fingers from long ago moving along the old, dreary paper at the head of his bed.

He heard the sounds of giggling again, and goosebumps rose in a wave all over his body.

He felt suddenly angry. Damn Susan and Kara. Why were they up and laughing at this time of night? If Mama were here she'd settle them down in a hurry.

But when Mama was gone, he had to watch after Susan.

It made him mad that the sounds he kept hearing were scaring him. He'd never give Susan the satisfaction of knowing that. She would most certainly giggle then, just to annoy and aggravate him.

He got out of bed and moved through the dark in the direction of the door. There was no outline of a door in the dark room, but as he blinked and stared he could see the black edges of something that might be the tall chest at the side of the door.

As he went toward it he heard footsteps outside in the hallway. Small feet on thin, old carpets. Carpets as dark as the walls. The steps were small and quick, and came in pairs, it seemed, not in rhythm, not like soldiers, but *tap-tap, tap . . . tap*. It was like they were running out in the hall.

Andy came to the black edge and found it was the chest. His hands touched the cool, slightly sticky finish of the wood, and he felt past it to the wall and found the door.

As his fingers touched the knob he found it was moving, and he froze, too terrified to pull his hand back or make a sound, to feel for the button light switch and put an end to this awful black world in which he stood. Beneath his fingers, the doorknob slipped, first in one direction and then in the other, as if whoever were turning it didn't have the strength to pull it open. He was suddenly reminded of Susan trying to open a door when she was younger, two or three. When she was too short to really reach it and had to stretch up with both hands and try to pull it open.

The knob stopped turning. His fingers barely touched it, feeling that it had been released.

Then the footsteps started again, and he could hear they were leaving his door. But this was no pair—only one.

Susan?

But why hadn't she yelled at him, as she usually did? And why hadn't she been able to turn the doorknob far enough for the latch to click.

Was she only teasing him?

He could picture her running back to Kara and the two of them giggling together.

He jerked the door open.

He stood blinking, looking at the door of Susan's room. It was closed. There was not even a crack showing.

The light in the hall was very dim, and trailed away to blackness behind every piece of furniture. To his left the hall was like a dark tunnel. To his right it opened out onto the stairway landing and another hall to the right leading to the front bedrooms. Places where he had never been. The glow of the light on the landing was like moonlight shining on the roof across the alley, yet darkness surrounded his feet and seeped out of the room behind him.

He stood on the threshold and stared at Susan's closed door.

The house was very quiet now. There were no footsteps, no giggles, not even any mice in the walls.

Andy had started to pull back into his room when he saw the face in the shadows.

It was a pale round spot against the big, old bookcase across the hall. She was standing back in the corner made by the bookcase and the wall, as if she were trying to hide from him. She must have been hunkered down, because her face was lower than it would have been if she were standing.

"Susan," he said, and waited for a burst of giggles. Where was Kara? Was she on the other side of the bookcase?

"Susan, what are you doing? Mama's going to be mad as hell at you if you don't behave and go to bed and to sleep like she said."

Even if Susan wanted to tell on him about his cussing, she'd be afraid to, because then he'd tell that she had been up long past bedtime.

But why wasn't she answering him? This was the cue to come out giggling and jumping around, both of them.

A strange coldness, accompanying the goosebumps spreading over his body, dug into his scalp. He could see the face better now, and it seemed smaller and rounder than Susan's. He could feel its stare was directed toward him, but there was no movement, no sound.

Then footsteps were in the house again, heavier, slower, coming up the stairs.

Mama?

He waited, his eyes changing direction, going past the dim face in the shadows and toward the open end of the hall and the bannisters beyond.

His mother came into view, outlined against the dim light. He felt such relief at seeing it actually was her that it seemed his bones melted. He held to the door and waited.

She was halfway down the hall toward him when she stopped and stared.

"Andy," she said. "What are you doing up?"

She was standing almost even with the dim face beside the bookcase, and Andy knew at that moment that it wasn't Susan, or Kara. It was something else. Just a round blob that was lighter than the dark around it, maybe.

"I heard footsteps," he said.

She came to him and hugged him. "Go to bed now."

She started to turn away, and he added, "And giggles. I heard giggles."

He hadn't meant to tattle on Susan, not if she apologized for acting like a nut and running up and down the halls and giggling and turning his doorknob to scare him. But it had slipped out. He needed to have his mother to check on Susan.

"Oh, no," Fawn groaned, but not as if she were losing patience. "The girls must be awake too."

She started across the hall, and then stopped, and

stood in silence. Andy knew she had seen the face in the shadows.

She turned back, and said in a low voice, "Where are the lights in this place, anyway?"

She opened the bathroom door, down the hall from Andy's room, and turned on the light, leaving the door pushed widely back. The light spilled out into the hall and spread both ways, illuminating the dark roses on the thin carpet, outlining the bookcase and the face beside it.

Andy's heart gave a frightened lurch, as if he had fallen off a cliff.

"Millicent!" Fawn said.

Andy stared at the doll. He saw its round, rosy-cheeked face with the red lips and the tiny white teeth and the perpetual smile that looked not quite friendly. It was like Erin had said, weird. Eerie. As if from outer space.

His heart settled down to a heavy pounding.

The doll was just standing there, leaning back against the corner made by the bookcase and the wall, one arm bent, the fingers of the hand reaching out, the other arm down, fingers against the cream lace of the dress.

Fawn went toward it, her shadow falling ahead of her, long and thin in the hallway.

"Who put that doll there?" she said, not really asking Andy. It was a question he couldn't have answered anyway. He watched his mother pick the doll up. She went down the hall with it. "I thought Jill put this doll in Granddad's room. Go to bed, Andy."

But Andy couldn't move.

He listened to his mother's footsteps go past the rising circle of the stairway and then down the hall toward the front of the house. He heard a door open, and a moment later close. He felt in his bones the long, thin whine of the door as it moved. Then her footsteps were coming back.

He saw her come to Susan's door and open it, and beyond the door he saw pale light and stillness. The house seemed filled with silence now.

His mother stayed in Susan's room only a moment, and when she came out and closed the door she smiled at him.

"Sound asleep, both of them," she said softly. She came to him and kissed him. "To bed with you."

He stepped back into the dark of his room and pulled the door shut. He stood still for a while, and then felt on the wall for the light switch.

His room was transformed. The dark and bulky pieces of furniture stood out against the dim figures on the wallpaper. His bed looked big, halfway down the wall, the tall headboard reaching almost to the pictures that hung high on the wall.

He climbed back into bed and pulled the covers up to his chin.

And then he stared at the doorknob.

Fawn took her robe and nightgown and went back to the bathroom. She locked the door and turned the water on in the tub. Nothing had changed in the bathroom. The mirror was still small and old, and the only light bulb was on the ceiling. The wash basin, one of the earliest made, was standing in its peculiar old cabinet, and the water running into the big old cast-iron tub made a rumbling sound that caused Fawn to cringe for fear it would wake every sleeper in the house.

She let the water run so hot it steamed, and filled the tub almost to the overflow drain. When she turned the water off, silence drooped around her like the steam from the tub.

She stripped and stepped cautiously and slowly into

the water and settled down, her hair pulled up into a plastic cap. The old tub was far more comfortable than the more modern ones. It was sloped just right for reclining, and its length allowed her to stretch out. She laid her head back and closed her eyes.

Laura.

God, how sad, how terrible, to see her sister lying there, face and neck bandaged, helpless, unconscious. Tied to her bed, and to life, by tubes and monitors.

Even though she kept telling the kids that Laura could wake at any minute, any second, Fawn felt in her heart that Laura would never wake. It was like having her sister dead, or dying, and it was hard even to try to pray, as if it would do no good. If there were a god to direct Laura's life, the decision had already been made, and that Power had withdrawn to let nature carry out its duties.

Oh, God, where are you? She had asked the question, in her mind and heart, so many times that it now had a hopeless ring. And yet the sun would rise, and she would lift her head and her eyes, and know she was not alone. Hope still lived.

She thought of Jim. Seeing him again had been, at first, a shock that had hit her full in the stomach like a fist. And then her feelings had remained numb. She had looked at his face, even more handsome than it had been when he was a teenager and had been the most important person in the world to her, and had felt nothing.

It's Laura, she thought. If Laura was well, then Fawn's feelings for Jim might return, the thrill might come back. When her emotions weren't so strained by sadness.

She had seen in his eyes that he was glad, or at least surprised, to see her. But she knew nothing about him anymore. He probably had a menagerie of wives and kids.

Tonight when she and Jill and Erin had reached the waiting room he'd been sitting there, wearing civilian clothes, looking as if he had been waiting for some time. But almost instantly her heart had told her he was waiting more for Laura than he was for her.

He had risen to meet them, his eyes holding hers, and had taken her hands in his and pressed them closely together between his. It was a habit she remembered. But the warm firmness of his hands had been that of a stranger.

The man who had come up later kept returning to her thoughts as she got into bed. Roger Hamilton. She felt sorry for him. He had seemed so uneasy, so worried. He was several inches shorter than Jim, but he had one of the best builds she had ever seen. She was shocked at herself for even noticing. His face was ordinary, with light eyes, blue or green, and hair that probably had been blond when he was small. It was sandy brown now. Still, there was something very appealing about him. She was glad the wreck hadn't hurt him. Was he afraid he was responsible in some way? She knew he wasn't. Even Jim had told her that. The tire tracks had shown, Jim said, that Roger had pulled his truck to the right to try to avoid Laura's car, but the skid marks showed she had kept coming right into his lane.

There was a sound in the hall outside the bedroom, and Fawn's attention was drawn to it.

A footstep?

Andy still unable to sleep?

Fawn lay still, waiting for the door to open.

Then the footsteps were going back toward the stairs, and sounded older, somehow, than Andy's.

Fawn slipped out of bed. Martha, she thought.

The only telephone was downstairs.

Dear God, not Laura. Not the hospital calling to say Laura had died.

Fawn pulled the door open.

There was no one in the hall, or on the landing of the stairs.

Fawn listened.

It was as if the footsteps had existed only in her room, in the dark of her mind.

Jill tied her robe securely at the waist and slipped on her shoes. The cottage, as they had always called the four-bedroom house on the lake, seemed so oddly empty and lonely without Mama. It was the first time in her life that Jill had spent a night in it without her mother, and she just couldn't sleep.

Martha had been right. Aunt Fawn was right. Even Kara. They should have stayed at the mansion, she and Erin. It was really silly not to stay there. They would have been seven miles closer to the hospital and to their mother if the hospital called them.

All night, ever since she and Erin had gotten home and gone to their separate rooms, she had lain awake listening for the phone to ring. Telling her their mother had died.

Mama had looked as if she were already dead, and it scared Jill so much that her tears were trapped within her, swelling, filling her chest and throat with great lumps that choked her when she tried to sip water to relieve the dryness of her mouth.

The hall light was on, and she walked through the light and out into the shadows of the living room and across to the small front porch with the steps down one side onto the walk that led to the driveway.

The storm had passed. At midnight she had seen lightning from her window, distant, the thunder no louder than the water lapping against the shore a hundred yards down the slope of the yard. Now the moon had come out, thin and pale, like a sliver of silver. New moon, old moon, she wasn't sure. She didn't know the signs very well, even though she and her friends played some with astrology. She saw it was a slanted moon, tipping as if it were a cup tilted to pour its contents on the earth.

She stood still as a black, sleek figure separated from the shadows at the end of the Village and ran toward her. Stand still, Ivan, who handled the dobermans, had told her. If you come out at night when the dogs are loose, just stand still. When they recognize you, they'll back off.

She loved dogs, even the dobermans, who were less familiar to her than the shepherds. But she always felt a tingle of apprehension when they came rushing at her after she came in from a date at night, or from just being out. Her dates always had to say good night at the big gates, and so far none of them objected. Especially after they saw the shadows of the dogs on the other side of the high fence. It could get really funny, and her feelings of annoyance at having these restrictions had so far all been overcome by her amusement.

The dogs allowed her to leave her house and walk freely on the grounds at night, if she wanted to. But she had never been out of the house so late before. The cuckoo clock in the kitchen had peeped three o'clock just before she'd gone out the door.

The dobermans' names were Pete and Pip, but she didn't know which was which. They were both black, and unless she could see them in light, they were totally identical.

The other dog was standing on one of the narrow streets of the Village, and she felt more wary of him than she did the one who had rushed at her. He was staring her way.

She let the dog near her smell her hand, and he

turned and walked at her side as she approached the street. The other dog came toward her then, casually trotting, and she put her hand out to him.

Accompanied by both dobermans and then the two German shepherds, Jill took the walk that went down the slope to the lake. The grass was neatly trimmed, and flowers had been set out in the beds. Around her, shrubs were blooming, and their fragrances reached her in the night, sweet and fresh.

She stood for a few minutes, looking out over the lake. On the distant shore she could see the lights of homes, yard lights that burned all night as did those in Antique Village.

The image of her mother, with face and neck cut so terribly, with the bandages and the tubes, floated in front of her eyes wherever she looked. She had wanted to stay at the hospital, but the nurse had said it would be better if she went home and they would let her know as soon as there was any change.

She climbed the hill again, going up the walk past the tiny church. As she started to pass the structure she stopped and went to the door.

The church was called the cathedral, though it was hardly large enough for half a dozen worshippers. She opened the double doors and looked in.

The interior was dark, but the outlines of the pews gradually became visible as the light from the street lamp and the faint light from the stars and moon entered the dark little building. Through the stained-glass windows a dim rainbow of colors fell across the lectern.

Jill wanted to pray, but she couldn't put her feelings into words. She heard the snuffling of the dogs as they investigated the steps and the shrubbery outside the tiny cathedral. Then she backed away and closed the doors.

She went up Lakeview Street, climbing steps and the rising walk, and entered the shadows of the buildings.

Lights were on in most of the shops and beneath the roofs and overhangs. The walkways between buildings, narrow streets that were more like hallways, were always lit, night and day. Yet there was a different feeling tonight as she walked these familiar paths in the Village. It was as if the Village held its breath. As if it waited for something. Daylight? The people? The crowds who would surge through it during the open season?

With two of the dogs still with her Jill entered the street that passed the Civil War building. There were muzzle-loading guns behind the glass wall, and cannon balls, scarred and dented. Uniforms, both blue and gray, hung on the walls and outfitted mannequins.

Walking faster, she passed buildings, not pausing before them. Overhead lights glinted on cut glass and the stones in the mineral collection. Then she came to the street that led into the dollhouse.

The board walks creaked beneath her feet as she entered the passageway between the plate-glass front of the dollhouse and the toy room.

Signs, asking that the glass not be touched, stood at each end of the building, and a wood railing separated walk from glass. She stood with her hands on the railing and looked at the dolls.

Victoria stood on the top tier, the tallest doll in the collection. She had one hand raised waist high as if offering it for a kiss, and the other higher, as if waving. The smile on her face was the sweetest of all the dolls of any doll Jill had ever seen. The face was perfect. From the railing outside the plate-glass window the tiny cracks around the edges of her cheeks weren't visible.

She was wearing white shoes, but they were high-button shoes like those of the doll that came out of the trunk. Victoria's stockings were white, too, now turned a dull gray. Jill knew that the clothes were occasionally removed and washed; still, they had turned, as Mama had once said laughingly, tattle-tale gray. Jill had suggested getting Victoria new clothes, but Laura had been horrified. "New clothes on Victoria? On an antique doll? Bite your tongue, girl." Slowly, throughout the years, Jill had learned that you do not mess with antiques. To try to improve them is to destroy them.

Something had been bothering her, and now she began to realize what it was.

Millicent.

She had to know more about Millicent.

So many things seemed to have changed with the discovery of the doll in the trunk. The trunk that had been made into a coffin.

In the office, her mother had books and papers on antique dolls, Jill knew, as well as on every other imaginable art or craft that early Americans, especially, ever thought of. But would they tell her anything about Millicent?

No, she was sure they wouldn't.

Nor could Victoria tell her.

"If only you could talk, Victoria," Jill said softly, and it seemed that Victoria's eyes turned, just slightly, the light catching the blue glass and reflecting from it as the doll looked down at Jill.

"If only you could talk . . ."

She turned away and went across Memory Lane toward the street back to the cottage. Only one dog was with her now, the shepherd named Jeff.

At the door she patted him good night.

It would be a while before she would walk again with him in the moonlight, because tomorrow she and Erin were moving to Granddad's house to stay until Mama could come home with them.

Chapter Eleven

Laura stared into the darkness and listened as night became day, as day became night. She felt as though she were holding her breath to listen, and her terror grew. Her head throbbed with it, her muscles strained to move, to communicate, but it was as if she were isolated from those who moved around her. As if she didn't exist.

She heard the nurses as they came and went. She felt the tug of tubes against her body, in her nose, in her throat, between her legs. She felt the needles piercing her wrists, even her ankles. The pain of her face, of the cuts the nurses talked about as the bandages were changed, was nothing compared to that terror.

"Lord," said a nurse whose face she had never seen, whose name she didn't know, to another invisible nurse, "Isn't it terrible? She must have run her face into the windshield. And so pretty too. What a shame."

"I expect most of the cuts will heal without problems, if she survives. I'd say the cuts are minor, compared to the coma."

"Well . . . but she was so pretty."

"She's still pretty. A few scars."

"I wonder if she was wearing her seat belt?"

"Obviously not."

Yes.

"Glass can do a lot of damage."

Not glass, it was the doll. Her hands, her fingers, hard, sharp, deadly. Listen to me, please. Get my family out of that house. Help us.

But the nurses were not aware of her anguish, nor were Jill or Laura.

She might have slept, she wasn't sure. The time seemed endless, the dark everlasting.

She felt Kara's hands touch her arm, knowing the touch of her youngest child, her baby. She tried to rise to put her arms around her child, and could not. Kara said nothing, until Jill told her it was time to leave, then Kara's small voice said, "Mama?"

I'm here, sweetheart. I can hear you.

She tried so hard to move, one finger, one eyelash. Then she heard their footsteps going away again.

Time dragged by. The nurses came and went, and once in a great while a doctor came by.

"Strange," one of them said. "Perfectly normal." Then to her surprise she felt his breath on her cheek and his voice came so loudly in her ears that she sensed the tightening of her muscles as her heart seemed to leap. Yet she had learned to listen to the monitors, and she heard that her heart had not registered her surprise.

"Mrs. Worton," the doctor yelled near her face. "Laura. Can you hear me?"

Yes, yes, yes.

For a moment there was only the *beep, beep* of monitors, and then he said in a normally soft tone, "No change. Notice that? No change in the heartbeat or the brain wave. She's out of it."

Laura felt the tears of frustration collect, somewhere at the back of her eyes, hot and burning. And then she was left alone as the footsteps faded away.

Later she was aware she must have slept, or drifted on a black cloud away from everything, from the hospital, perhaps the world. Fawn's voice woke her.

"The kids have gone back to school, Laura. I enrolled my two, and they went today for the first time. It strikes me a little . . . strange that they are going to schools I attended at their ages. Westside hasn't changed at all. It still has the same old monkey bars on the playground. Kara will help Susan adjust to the strange school, I know."

Laura concentrated on lifting her right index finger. Maybe, she thought, I didn't concentrate hard enough on just one finger. Maybe the struggle to rise, to be seen or heard as being conscious, had been too diffused. Maybe if she concentrated only on one finger . . .

Then Fawn was telling her something that made her forget everything but the safety of her children.

"Jill and the girls have moved to the house in town. She brought in enough clothes to last a couple of weeks. She wants to be closer to you. She'll be in this evening after school. She said she knew you would want her to keep up her schoolwork."

Millicent. What did you do with Millicent?

"Do you know Roger Hamilton, Laura? He's the guy in the pickup truck. The other car, you know. He keeps coming to see about you. So does Jim. But Roger seems really concerned. And he came to the house once, but I had gone to the market. Martha said he wanted to know about the doll. She said he acted strange, and she wasn't sure about him. He was too interested in the doll, she said."

Oh, my God!

He had seen something. In those moments before the crash, Roger Hamilton had seen Millicent attacking her. Was that possible?

His face was before her again, in that instant when she had looked ahead and seen the hood of the pickup truck, so close to her, the gap between them closing rapidly. For just that instant she saw the shocked eyes, the stonelike face, the grip on the steering wheel.

He had been looking at her. He had seen something in Millicent.

She hadn't thought of him. She was sorry, but she had forgotten the other driver.

Thank God he hadn't been injured.

"He told me something once," Fawn was saying. "When I met him in the lobby downstairs, he said he thought he had seen a child in the car with you. And he asked me if there had been one. It seemed he didn't believe the police."

So he had seen Millicent attack her. Roger Hamilton had seen. She didn't know him. Where did he live? How could she reach him?

"I have to go." Laura felt the lingering pressure of Fawn's hand as she said goodbye. "We'll be back this evening, Jill and I. We love you, honey."

Fawn.

Fawn, see, I'm moving my hand. I'm trying so hard to move my hand. Fawn.

She couldn't even weep. Her emotions, thoughts, and fears were trapped inside a body that wouldn't respond.

She cried silently for Fawn to wait, to listen, but the footsteps, as soft as the nurses', faded into the sounds of the Intensive Care Unit.

Laura changed the direction of her concentration. She had left her body before. Perhaps she could do it again, and follow Fawn, somehow persuade her to contact Roger Hamilton. He could help her. He was the only one who knew.

She struggled to lift herself, to burst forth into the light again, to see the room from the ceiling, with her body so straight and prone in the bed. But the darkness clung to her, taunted her.

She felt herself drifting away into exhaustion. Sometimes she slept, she knew, because the sounds would fade away, and the frustration would lessen. She didn't want to go to sleep now. She couldn't go to sleep. She had to find Roger. She had to go to Granddad's house and locate Millicent, and somehow try to throw a shroud around her.

Laura was in the light again, suddenly, as if she had just awakened. At first she didn't know where she was. She had never before seen the dark green background of the wallpaper, or the maroon flowers and leaves that trailed vinelike toward the ceiling. There were voices in the room. Children's. Fine, flutelike. She tried to understand what they were saying, but it was like hearing a distant chattering. She saw a cradle against the wall, but it was small, and it held a doll, not a child. She realized she was in a playroom. As the room became more visible she saw a large toy box, open, and the toys that spilled from it were the toys that now were protected behind heavy glass at the Village. Tiny wagons and trains, made of iron, pulled by iron horses. Men made of iron sitting on the wagon seats. Wooden dolls, and child-sized tables and chairs, made of wood. And in the corner a dollhouse. Victorian, with Victorian furnishings.

"It's mine," the dark-haired child screamed, and there was a cry as the other child fell backward onto the floor. The aggressive child snatched toy furniture from the other child, clawing it out of her hand.

She could see the children now. The brunette beauty and the delicate little blonde. The blond girl was lying on the floor. As Laura watched, wanting desperately to reach out and help her, the little girl got up. She was crying. The dark-haired girl stood over her, taller, stronger, and as soon as the smaller girl regained her feet the other child pushed her again.

Scream, Laura tried to tell her. Call for help. Get away from the damned little bully.

"Mine! Mine! Mine!"

With each exclamation, the larger child reached out and shoved the smaller, and Laura saw the pipestem legs of the more fragile child when she fell again and for a moment her long dress came above her high-topped shoes.

These were the same two children she had seen the other time, she now realized. She was back in the old mansion. But she was on the third floor, and this was the playroom, before the paper had faded and changed the intensity of its color.

The door opened jerkily when the little blonde reached up for the knob and tugged. Tears ran down her cheeks, and her tiny body heaved with sobs. The larger girl kept pushing her, on and on, out into the hall, down it toward the stairs.

"You can't tell," she said, reaching out again, her hand flat against the back of the smaller girl. "You can't tell. Mama won't believe you. It was mine. Mine, not yours."

The blonde didn't answer. Sobbing, she began to run faster, the girl behind her jostling her forward with hard pushes against her back.

Turn around and let her have it in the face, Laura wanted to shout, but she could only watch, as invisible as she was helpless. She tried to grab the child with the mahogany hair, and found herself close enough to the child to see in detail the tatting on her collar and the tiny flowers in the material of her long dress. But the child did not know she was there.

Laura knew it was a scene from the past she was watching. Somehow, in her out-of-body experience, in trying so desperately to return to the old mansion, she had returned to another time. She didn't know who these children were, if they had lived before Granddad's time, if they were related to the family. She didn't know why she was here, seeing a scene long dead and one over which she had no control.

A scene as vivid as if it were now happening.

The little girl had reached the bannister of the stairwell, and then both hands of the larger child went out, palms flat, against her back, and shoved hard.

NO!

The blond child fell, her head striking a bannister post. For just an instant she lay still, crying, her hand to her head, so close to falling through the bannister supports that Laura held her breath in fear. And then she started to rise. Her tear-filled eyes looked at the other girl.

"Don't, Milly," she pleaded.

The larger child's face was set in cold, evil determination. Though her face was no older than the small blond child's, it held an evil as old as time. With both hands she pushed, and pushed. The blond child screamed, and her hands clawed at the supports of the bannister. But then her tiny body was slipping through, and her feet were dangling over the long drop to the first floor. Only one hand clung to the bannister.

The dark-haired child carefully and intently pried her fingers loose.

Laura heard the long, frightened scream as the small blond child fell through the hollow distance to the first floor.

Then she heard the silence.

The dark-haired girl drew away, no longer looking between two of the supports, and Laura saw a smile on her lovely face. Then, as if she were an actress, as footsteps sounded far below and adult voices cried out, the child's face crumpled into tearless crying, and she went running down the stairs.

Laura was alone on the third floor. For a brief moment in time she saw downward, the distance long, as if she were looking into a vertical tunnel.

Two women had rushed to the crumpled figure on the floor. The little twisted doll-like figure that was so silent.

Darkness blotted out the scene, and Laura heard the beeping of the monitors.

Erin lay on her bed reading. It was past midnight, and she knew she should get into bed and go to sleep, but her books had been even more important to her since her mother's accident. She was reading *Call of the Wild* again, her favorite book of all time. Except, when she had reread *The Secret Garden,* she'd thought it was her favorite. And the same with *Black Beauty.* The only trouble with *Black Beauty* was it made her want a horse so badly she could hardly stand it. She also liked *Heidi.* She had read that book twice also. But she didn't care much for *Alice in Wonderland.* It was too weird, as Andy would have said. Like the doll, Millicent.

Twice that evening, she had run Kara and Susan out of Great-granddad's room. She had heard them in there, talking, and had gone to see what they were doing. As she had suspected, they were handling the doll.

"That's an antique," she had told them, and had taken it away and laid it across the top of the chest. "You're not supposed to play with antiques."

Later she had caught them there again, and again they had the doll. That time they weren't really in the bedroom, they were just outside it, just over the threshold. And she couldn't believe what they were doing.

Susan was on one side of the doll and Kara on the other, and they were walking Millicent along, of all things. The doll's legs were swinging forward almost like those of a toddler learning to walk.

"What are you doing?" Erin had yelled at them. Where was Aunt Fawn, or Jill or Martha? she silently complained. Didn't anyone ever watch these kids? But she knew Aunt Fawn and Jill had gone to see Mama, and then they were going to the supermarket. They had even asked her if she wanted to go, but she had said no. She couldn't bear to see her mother like that. So . . . like, dead.

"Nothing," the girls said to her, so innocently.

"Nothing! What do you mean? How did you get that doll down off the chest?"

The chest was so high Erin had had to stretch to put it up there.

"We didn't."

They talked at the same time, almost like twins, Kara and Susan, saying almost the same things.

"Liars," Erin accused, and took the doll away from them again. She went back into the bedroom, put it back up on top of the chest.

The girls followed her.

"We didn't lie," Kara said adamantly. "We found her out there in the hall. She was sitting in the needlepoint chair."

"Oh, come on." In school Erin had learned a really neat way to sneer. She had learned it from her best friends. And now she used it. The curl of her lip said, I don't believe one word you're saying.

"It's true," Kara yelled, and looked to Susan for backup. "Isn't it, Susan?"

Susan nodded her head, up and down, up and down, her blue eyes as guileless as those of the doll, it seemed to Erin.

"Sure, sure, sure," Erin said as she ushered them back out into the hall and shut the door of the bedroom behind all of them. "Now leave it alone, or I'll tell Jill you were playing with it."

She left them. When she looked back from the other side of the stairway landing, she saw them standing there staring after her, Kara's eyes as big and innocent as Susan's. She couldn't believe how much alike the two girls were. Kara was a lot more like Susan than her own sisters. And, for that matter, Erin and Jill weren't alike.

Erin was supposed to go to bed at ten o'clock. She had to get up at seven, so her lights were supposed to be out by ten. That gave her nine hours of sleep. But she had lain on her bed reading and the time had slipped by. When Jill had opened her door at ten-thirty and told her to get to bed, Erin had nodded her head.

Then she became part of the frozen north as she moved through *Call of the Wild.* She forgot the time. Just one paragraph, one more page, one more chapter.

She heard the footsteps before she really began to listen. Two little girls were running, their steps felt as much as heard. Then it occurred to her that the steps were louder than they should have been, as if the girls wore shoes with heavy soles or heels, as if they ran, or walked quickly, on uncarpeted floor. Then it seemed to be only one, not two.

Erin paused in her reading and listened. And something very odd about the sound finally dawned on her. The steps were distant, fading and then becoming louder. Where were they? As far as Erin knew, there were no bare floors in the house.

Then she realized the footsteps were somewhere overhead.

They were lost again, faded away, and although Erin listened intently, she did not hear them again.

It was late, and the girls were somewhere upstairs? They weren't even supposed to go upstairs! They knew they should not pass through the gate on the stairs that led up to the third floor, and yet that was where the footsteps had been.

Lord, what would they think of doing next? Honestly, Kara had never been this much trouble before Susan came along!

Erin got off her bed and went to the hall.

All the doors along it looked closed, the shadows heavy against dark wood. The bathroom door stood open a couple of inches. As she passed it she reached out and pushed it farther open with her fingers.

She stopped on the landing and looked up. Sure enough, the gate to the upstairs was open.

In all her life, she had never before seen that gate unlatched. She remembered when she was about four years old, and was at Great-granddad's for Christmas dinner, she had come up the stairs to this gate and had swung on it. When she'd been found she'd almost gotten a spanking. Everyone, every kid in the family, knew that gate was not to be opened or gone past without an adult. Once, later, Erin had gone up to the third floor with Martha, when Martha was cleaning, and she had been allowed to go into the old playroom, but there was nothing much in it now. All the toys that had belonged to Great-granddad and his sister, who had died when she was eleven years old, had been put in the toy room at Antique Village. The other rooms on the third floor were either small bedrooms or storage rooms. Once she'd seen them, Erin had never again had a desire to pass the gate. What for? Nothing was up there but dust—and distance from the lower floors.

She looked back down the hall toward the bedrooms. With the only light on the landing, the hall drew darkness as if it had a curtain separating it from the light.

She thought about going back to Jill's room or to Aunt Fawn's, but she was sure they would be asleep.

The house was so quiet. If she hadn't heard the steps and listened carefully to them, she would have thought it was just her imagination.

But Kara and Susan were up there, she knew they were.

She could feel the presence of someone, as if she was being watched from the cover of darkness on the third-floor landing.

She went up the stairs slowly, her bare feet silent on the steps. She went through the small gate, pushing it closed behind her, though she didn't latch it. With her face tilted upward, her eyes catching the shapes of the solemn faces in old dark-framed photographs, she climbed the stairs.

Darkness went with her, settling deeper around her with each step upward. Her steps became slower, more hesitant.

When she reached the top-floor landing she stopped, a strange nervousness coming over her. It occurred to her that there was no light up there. The little girls wouldn't be up there in such darkness. Didn't they have a light burning in the room they shared, night and day?

Erin was unsure of herself now, and she turned to go back downstairs. If they had been up here, they had run back to their room before she had left hers. Yet something was wrong with that assumption, and she felt it in the cold tension of her skin, in the pull of her hair at the back of her neck.

She realized she was afraid of the dark up there, of the long hall stretching away past old bedrooms and storage rooms and the playroom not used since Great-granddad was a child. She was afraid of something that still lingered in the old house. Something that she had never known before, that seemed to have just recently been resurrected from its grave.

As if in burying Granddad, they had freed something else.

As she started back down the stairs, she saw the figure. Small, still, it stood to her left, beyond the corner of the wall.

It had a round face and fair hair, and even in the shadows in which it stood she could see the little red smiling lips and the white teeth.

The frown was in her mind, the question, the puzzle. Why would Kara and Susan bring the doll up there and leave it standing against the wall? Why? . . . And she knew they hadn't.

Terror curled through her stomach like hard, cold fingers made of bisque.

She heard the slight creak of movement as the doll lifted both her arms, heard the light footsteps on the bare floor of the hall, and she remembered suddenly, the upstairs was not carpeted. The steps she had heard, she now suspected, stunned and with growing horror, had been the steps of the doll.

Running like a child. Back up the steps and toward the playroom. Where once it had lived, Erin knew. And where once . . . it had been put into its coffin.

As Erin watched, stunned with horror, unable to move, her legs heavy with fear, her feet melded to the floor, she watched the perpetually smiling doll walk out of the shadows toward her.

The arms creaked faintly at the jointed elbows and wrists as Millicent raised them toward Erin.

There was something in her right hand. Shadows hid whatever it was. Erin could see only the shape of something several inches long. But perhaps it was only the deeper shadow at the right side of the doll.

It was . . . as if she held a weapon.

The arm swung up, and down, a thin, harsh sound cutting through the air.

Chapter Twelve

Fawn, stirring restlessly in her bed, fragments of dreams returning to her like shattered visions, sat up suddenly to listen. She had heard a cry, and footsteps overhead, running, colliding, stopping. Scuffling sounds. And the cry, short, aborted.

But no one was ever in the third story, not at this time of night, not even in the daytime. She listened and heard the sounds of her own body in her ears, heart thudding, blood flowing.

The cry had come from her dreams, as had the footsteps, as had the broken visions that left her feeling as if she had just escaped a terrible nightmare. She scrunched down into the bed and pulled blankets over her, pressing them against her ears and eyes.

Erin had backed up as far as she could. Behind her she felt the hard supports of the bannister. She was aware of a dim light far below on another landing—and the long drop to the floor. The doll was between her and the top step, as if it had the intelligence to know her thoughts, to know she would try to reach the stairs.

The smile was still on the doll's face, but Erin saw it now as a mask covering something unbelievably horrible and deadly. A perfect, lovely mask. Almost perfect. The thing she had first noticed, the difference between this doll and her twin, Victoria, was lost in the shadows, the darkness of the third-floor landing. Moving away had been difficult, even turning her eyes from the doll to find the stairway down was an effort. Her brain felt frozen in horror and disbelief. She refused to believe she had seen a doll, even an eighteen-nineties French walker doll, move without being touched.

The doll stood still now, blocking the stairway, its face shadowed, its tiny, lovely features reduced to small blobs of white in the dark. It hadn't moved now for several minutes, it seemed. Erin stood with her hand gripping the bannister, waiting, preparing herself for a dash past the doll.

Could she have imagined it all? Could the doll, having been leaned against the wall, somehow have fallen out at her? All the things she had thought she'd seen, the raising of the arms, the reach, the movement toward her, her own rushing retreat, could it have been something she'd imagined?

Her mouth was dry. Something within her refused to believe.

The doll was standing on its own, unsupported.

It had happened, and she was terrified. She wanted to call out for Aunt Fawn, for Jill, just one floor below; but her mouth was so dry and her tongue so thick and wooden that she could make no sound.

She had to try. If she could just reach the top of the stairs she could curl herself into a ball, her head protected, and roll, if she had to. She had learned to do that in gymnastics. For protection of the head when in an accident, curl up like a mealy bug, with legs and knees drawn in, head protected by the knees, arms around legs, and roll.

She had to try.

It was only a doll, she tried to tell herself. What could it do? What did it want with her?

And then with the shock of lightning striking she thought of her mother, in the car with Millicent, and she knew. The doll had not been in its trunk. Why had none of them thought of that? The highway trooper had brought the doll to the house and left it, and then later Jill had gone to the police station and brought home the things that had been taken out of the station wagon. A few maps, a box of tissues, a box of Wipe-ems, a mashed candy bar, the little plastic bag of tools kept in the glove compartment. And the trunk.

Why had none of them thought of that?

The doll had been out of the trunk.

And Erin knew: the doll had moved, it had risen from the unlocked trunk. She saw in her mind the bandages on her mother's face and neck, and she remembered something. Blood on the doll's hands, in the creases. Someone had cleaned off the blood, but it had darkened the creases at the edges of the fingernails and in the palms of the hands. Dark stuff. She hadn't thought before about it being blood, but now she knew.

With each flash of understanding her terror grew. She had to move, to act fast. She had won races with all her friends, and even on the girls' team at school. She had even outrun some of the boys. Why was she so afraid she would never get past the doll to the stairs?

She glanced behind her, down the long hall of the third floor. It was black and endless. No wall, no door was visible. But doors were there, in closed bedrooms. If she could reach one of the rooms she could barricade herself.

If she could call out, Aunt Fawn might hear her. Aunt Fawn's bedroom was the closest to the stairway landing.

"Aunt Fawn!"

Her voice was a squawk, low and hoarse.

The doll moved suddenly, leaping toward her. One bound, straight at her, as if Erin's voice had activated whatever there was in the doll that caused movement.

Erin heard her voice again, a short cry, involuntary now, as she instinctively ducked her head, putting her arms up for protection. Then she was running, dodging, feeling the sharp dig of the doll's fingers on her arms as it turned with her, poised in the air beside her, made another leap upward toward her face. Erin flung her hands out, and felt the back of her wrist strike the doll. She felt the hard, unyielding surface of the head, as hard as a hockey ball.

Then in cold horror she saw in the dim light from the floor night light below the glint of something in the doll's hand. She was holding it up, prepared to swing it forward. A hammer?

God no. The doll was coming at her with a hammer raised over its head, to strike her, to crush her skull.

She tried to coil her body, to fling herself toward the stairs, but the sharp pain in her head as the hammer struck pulled her sideways.

The doll's fingers were in her hair, holding her, pulling her down to its level and back toward the dark hallway toward the bedrooms, the old playroom. She heard the hammer against her skull, a strange, terrible, dull sound. The pain seemed nothing compared to her fear, her terror. She felt the shattering of her skull. She saw it, as if she were looking into a splintered mirror, and behind her was the perfect, small, smiling face of the doll.

Erin screamed and lunged sideways.

She heard the splitting of wood, and felt the bannister yield as it broke.

She heard her long, terrorized scream, and saw far below the hard surface of the first floor.

Then she was falling. She saw unbroken bannisters and reached for them, her fingers feeling wood for just a moment. But the winding bannisters slipped past her, flashed in her eyes, and were gone.

She felt the floor as it welded into her body. But pain was secondary to fear. She had stopped falling, and she was looking upward. There was no breath left in her.

She tried to cry out again, even as she heard the running steps along the lower hall. She knew Martha was coming. She had to tell Martha . . . tell Martha . . .

High above, a white round ball in the darkness of the third floor, beyond the broken bannister, the face of the doll looked down.

She had to tell Martha. . . .

The doll . . . was going to kill them all.

The long, thin, animal-like scream resonated throughout the house, penetrating walls, reaching some of the rooms like a distant whisper, part of a bad dream. Kara stirred and moaned, her head buried in the thick pillow, but didn't waken. Susan opened her eyes, like a sleepwalker, and turned over and closed them. Like a small animal in its den, she burrowed deeper into the big soft bed. Andy sat up and listened. But the scream was an echo now, part of a nightmare he'd been having, and he wasn't sure it had been real. Jill woke, terrible dread in her, anxiety causing her heart to quiver in her chest. The house was so silent. She lay still a moment longer, then sat up and slid out of the high bed and started looking for her house slippers.

Fawn woke, chilled at the ending, the sudden drop of the scream. In her memory it had started far away, at the cemetery perhaps, and had drawn nearer, as if it were coming through the house. It had passed her bedroom door, loud and piercing, and then had faded away again, and at the end was the hard thump.

She was running, her robe and slippers left behind.

Oh, God . . . one of the children . . . had fallen.

Martha had been walking through the house when she first heard the scream. Restless, she had been unable to sleep. There was something wrong in the house. She'd been feeling it since the day Mr. Evans died. Or perhaps the day he was buried. Yes, she thought, it started the day he was buried. She had felt uneasy, she remembered, as if something terrible was going to happen. Then when Laura had had her accident, she'd thought that was it; her premonition that something bad was going to happen had come to pass.

But the feeling didn't go away.

So, sleepless, she had been walking about when she heard the awful scream. At first she couldn't tell where it was, but instinct had sent her running toward the central part of the old house, where the stairs rose.

Something fell almost at her feet, not ten feet away.

For one moment, in the silence after the fall, the sudden ending of the scream, she had been unable to move.

Then hardly knowing she had moved, she was kneeling at the side of the child, and she saw it was Erin.

She started to put her arm under Erin's head, to lift her, but stopped herself, knowing it was better not to move the injured child. Her heart exploding in her chest, her muscles limp rags, unable to speak or voice the prayer in her heart, Martha sat at Erin's side.

She saw the blood ooze from Erin's nose, mouth, eyes. Saw Erin trying to speak, her mouth working.

And she saw that Erin was staring upward.

Martha looked up.

Far above she saw the broken bannister, and in the dark hole behind it she saw a small, white something. She might have thought it was only a spot before her eyes, a blemish in the distance, if it hadn't moved.

At first it seemed to come nearer, as if it were leaning through the broken bannister. Then it moved sideways, and she knew what it was. One of the younger children was up there, still up there, on the third floor!

But no, she was wrong. Nothing moved in the dark above.

Jill ran, hearing footsteps outside, a door slamming back, then another door opening. Her ears seemed acutely aware of every movement in the house. She heard something rustling nervously in the walls, as if it, too, had heard and been disturbed by the scream.

She ran out into the hall and toward the landing. Andy almost collided with her, at his door. Aunt Fawn's door was open, and the footsteps that sounded as if someone were stumbling on the stairs and attempting to retain balance, were hers. When Jill reached the landing, Fawn was already at the bottom.

"Call emergency," Fawn was crying out, "Call! Hurry! My God, what happened?"

"She fell," Martha said, her voice breathless.

Jill ran to the landing and down, and sensed Andy behind her, a blur of movement in the shadows at the corner of her eye.

Erin was lying twisted on the floor, her eyes staring upward. Blood streaked down her face, coming in rivulets from her eyes, her nose, her mouth.

Jill stopped and turned away, her hands covering her face. She couldn't bear to see this, her sister bleeding, dead.

Dead, yes.

The eyes stared too steadily upward for there to be any life left.

Jill sank to the floor, unable to stand.

* * *

Martha's hands shook so hard she had trouble dialing 911, and she choked up while requesting help and giving the address. After she hung up she wasn't sure she had done it right, so she called back again to make sure.

"Yes ma'am," the voice said. "An ambulance has been dispatched."

She could hear Fawn, crying out, questioning, calling out to God, to herself. Martha hurried back toward the front hall.

"Someone needs to go up and get that other child," she muttered as she went back to Erin, to Fawn who was at her side, and to Jill who was slumped against the bottom of the stairs. Andy stood against the wall, silent, his hands behind him as he stared first at Erin and then upward.

"Someone needs to—"

"Did you call?" Fawn asked.

"Yes."

"God, what happened? *What happened?*"

Martha sensed that Fawn was becoming hysterical. Fawn had always been too sensitive, too quick to react. It was something Martha felt but had never put into words, not even with Fawn.

She put a hand on Fawn's bent shoulder. "You go, Fawn, see about—about the kitchen . . . something."

"Oh, God. It's no good. She's dead. What happened?"

Martha saw that Andy was still looking upward, as Erin had, his eyes staring through the dark above as steadily as Erin's had. And she again thought of who had been up there, where Erin had fallen through the bannister. But she saw no one now.

"I don't know what they were doing up there," Martha said. "I can't imagine what. She fell. Erin fell. It's a long drop. A dangerous fall. Why anyone built a stairway like that, I don't know. That bannister was old, brittle."

It seemed forever, and the ambulance wasn't coming, not in this lifetime, not for Erin. She couldn't just lie there like that, her arms flung out, her legs twisted, her face white as paper beneath the streaks of blood that now were turning black in the small amount of light.

Martha went back to her bedroom and brought a clean white sheet and started to spread it over Erin, but Fawn stopped her.

"She won't be able to breathe, Martha, she won't be able to *breathe.*" Fawn's face was twisted like Erin's body, the features distorted.

Martha stood holding the sheet, hearing the siren in the night, its scream adding to the unreality of this horrible hour.

She went to the door, the sheet draped over her arm, and stood back as the medics entered.

Later, hours later it seemed, though it was still night, the darkness hanging like a shroud in all the rooms and halls, Martha went upstairs. Erin's body had been taken away. The medics had called the police. Accidents, they said, required notification of the police.

Jill, Andy, and Fawn were in the living room at the back of the house, waiting, when Martha climbed the stairs, carrying a kerosene lamp. She checked on Kara and Susan, sleeping together in Susan's room, sharing it as they had wanted. They were both asleep. Martha frowned thoughtfully. She'd thought she had seen one of the girls above on the third floor when Erin fell. But they had slept through the scream, the sirens, the noise the medics made when taking Erin's body away.

It was just as well.

Martha went on toward the third story. When lights had been put in on the first and second floors back in the early part of the century, the third floor hadn't been wired. Too dangerous, Mason Evans had once told Martha. There had been no point in having electricity up here because the third floor was closed off, no longer used.

Martha entered the third-floor landing. She didn't touch anything. She stood well back from the broken bannister and stared at it, shuddering, wondering why Erin had been up there in the dark of the night. Why she would come up there at any time.

She had found the small gate open, unlatched.

The children all knew they were not to open it.

Except, perhaps, Fawn's children. Had anyone told them?

Was the face she had seen up here Susan's? Had Susan, scared, gone back to bed and pretended to be asleep? Martha didn't really know Susan. Was she that kind of child? Now Kara knew better than to go upstairs even with Erin or Susan.

But so had Erin.

It was, Martha thought for the first time, a blessing that Laura was in a coma. That she didn't know, and perhaps would never know, what had happened to Erin.

The pain in Martha's heart seemed insurmountable, as if it enclosed her in a tight cocoon. Then came the numbness again, the protection. She mustn't think about herself, her own feelings.

She went down the hall past two bedrooms. Her house shoes whispered on the bare floor, and old boards creaked as she walked on them. The hall here was narrower than on the second floor, the bedrooms smaller, darker.

She opened the door to the playroom.

Erin had known where it was. Martha had let her come along once when she was cleaning, and Erin had looked into the playroom with her. It was the largest room on the third floor, but there was nothing much in it.

Martha stood on the threshold, the yellow glow from the kerosene lamp falling dimly into the room, leaving shadows in corners creating dark lumps of the few remaining pieces of furniture and the empty old toy box.

But in the shadows there was a face, small, round, white.

At first Martha thought it was the face of a child, a very small, very young child. A ghost of the child to whom this room belonged, perhaps, the long-dead little Victoria. But then, as she moved the light, and the flame flickered and brightened, she saw it was the doll.

Millicent.

She stared at the doll for a long moment. It was sitting on the floor at the end of the old toy box, smiling sweetly.

Now she knew what Erin had been doing up here. She had brought the doll up. Probably to keep the little girls from playing with it.

But why had she brought it in the darkness of night?

On her way downstairs Martha locked the gate securely.

Chapter Thirteen

The accidental death of Erin Worton, age twelve, did not warrant television or radio coverage. At Roger's shop work went on as usual, the saws buzzing like oversized bugs and the men yelling at each other at times over the noise. Between the saws came the sanders and the smell of paint or varnish. Roger was back at work, giving estimates to builders, seeing that the cabinets went into the right places—kitchens, bathrooms, storage rooms, garages, offices, bedrooms. In his shop the suddenly popular entertainment centers were being built, some of them large and elaborate.

His employees talked, worked, laughed, took ten for coffee. The sun rose and set, mostly behind spring clouds and drizzly rain. And through it all Roger wondered about Fawn and Laura, about their children. And he constantly envisioned the doll, smiling at him from the state trooper's arms as it was carried up from the ravine.

At times he dreamed of it. A dream like a picture or a painting, with no action, no movement. The doll would be in front of him with its perpetual smile, its perfect little face, and he would wake with a cry as if he were ten years old again.

Then in the newspaper he read the obituary, and cold shock washed over him. Erin Worton, twelve. Laura

Worton, surviving parent. The obit didn't say how the child had died, only that it was accidental. It didn't say that her mother was in a coma in ICU at the hospital.

It gave the time of the funeral and the place, a local funeral home. Burial was to be in the family plot.

Roger sat at the back of the shrouded room in the funeral parlor. He heard the organ music, the strange and terrible silence. The family was secluded behind a velvet curtain in another room.

He had sent flowers—a large arrangement on a stand, a wreath of white daisies and yellow roses—and a sympathy card that was inadequate but all he could find. He had seen the child only once, but he mourned for her. And the face of the doll kept coming between him and the huge flower arrangement around the coffin at the front of the building.

After the services, as he stood outside in a misty rain that was getting wetter and heavier by the minute, he saw that Jim Ruther was in the crowd.

Roger went toward him.

He was dressed in a black suit, and stood, like Roger himself, in the rain without a hat. Roger saw the hat he held at his side. He faced the rear of the funeral home, where the hearse was parked, waiting for the casket to be brought out, waiting too for the family.

For Ruther that was acceptable. He had known the family a long time and would probably join them at the family burial ground. But Roger didn't feel he should intrude.

"Hamilton," Jim said, nodding solemnly.

Roger stood beside him and watched the pall bearers bring the coffin down the steps of the funeral home and put it into the hearse. He had to ask a question of Jim, but he waited until the doors of the hearse were closed and the crowd began to disperse to their cars to follow it to the cemetery.

"Jim," Roger said, "the paper said this was an accidental death. What happened?"

James Ruther hesitated. "The old mansion," he said, his eyes absently following people as they walked past, "has a central stairway. The whole thing is open all the way to the top of the house. The ceilings are high, so it's a forty-two foot drop from the top hallway to the bottom. She fell the other night, about one-fifteen in the morning."

He started to walk away, to go to Fawn and the rest of the family who were now coming down the steps and going to a waiting limousine.

Then he stopped again and looked at Roger. Roger saw a perplexed, worried look in his eyes.

"The strange thing is, the third floor of that house has always been closed off. I used to be in that house a lot. Fawn and I dated for several years when we were teenagers, and I hung around there most of the time. There was a gate closing off the top story. There aren't even any lights up there. Nobody knows why Erin went up there at that time of night." He paused, then started on. "Or why she would go up there at any time. The city police who investigated assumed she fell against the bannister, or leaned on it too hard, maybe to look over, and it was old and rotten and broke off at the base." He tugged at his tie. "You coming out to the cemetery?"

"No," Roger said. "I don't want to intrude."

"I'm sure you'd be welcome."

Roger shook his head.

He went to his car and sat until the funeral procession had pulled away, and then he drove to the hospital.

As he went upstairs to ICU he tried to picture in his mind the old mansion. He had put aside, these past few days, any idea of trying to talk to Fawn or Laura or anyone else about the doll. After several sleepless and puzzled nights, he had come to the conclusion that he had seen the doll fall over in the seat beside Laura as she came downhill toward him, and had only imagined it tangling with her as she jerked the car over. The gashes on her face, the blood, must have come from something on the doll's arms or hands. He didn't know. He only knew that appearances must have been deceiving.

So he had tried to catch up on his work, and forget about the doll.

But today, he had to see Laura. This was his chance, maybe, to get into ICU.

The woman at the desk in the ICU waiting room smiled at him and asked who he wanted to see. It was one minute before four o'clock, and the family was out at the cemetery.

"Laura Worton," he said, hoping he wouldn't have to lie again and say she was his sister. But he would if he had to.

"You can go in," the woman said.

Roger went through the double doors along with the people going to see other patients, but he felt lost and alone and out of place. He had no idea where Laura's room was, or very little idea what she looked like.

He had to stop and ask the nurse behind the long white division, the one who watched monitors on all sides of her, where Laura Worton was. He was afraid she would challenge his right to see her, but she only smiled and motioned to a half closed curtain three rooms down.

He walked on, slowly, aware of the time ticking by. He had ten minutes, but he wasn't sure what he was going to do with it.

The face on the white pillow was partly bandaged, and he could see the scratches, deep, healing, where bandages had been removed. And suddenly he was thinking something that hadn't occurred to him before. *The wreck had saved her life.*

If he hadn't been coming down the opposite hill, if he hadn't been there to stop her car, to roll into the ravine with her, what would have happened? If the police hadn't been called so quickly, Laura wouldn't be alive now.

She would be lying dead in the cemetery, where her daughter was being buried at this moment.

The doll would have killed her.

Crazy, he told himself. He had made himself stop thinking that way. He had given up on ever talking to Laura.

He stood at her bedside looking down at her. Dark hair, naturally curly, had been brushed back from her high, white forehead, but it curled in tendrils from beneath the white cloth laid over the top of her head. Although a tube entered there, her neck was most heavily bandaged, as if her throat had been cut. *Gouged open with sharp, hard, knifelike fingers.*

Stop it, he told himself.

Her eyes were closed. Her arms were carefully placed at her sides, and her legs straight; but a pillow lay to one side of her as if she had recently been turned onto her side and propped there by the thick pillow.

"Laura," he said, "you don't know me."

She didn't recognize the voice. She waited for a hand to touch her, but felt nothing. She held her breath, listening, waiting. Say something, she wanted to shout at him. Who are you? What do you want with me? Where are Fawn, Jill? I haven't heard from my children in days, months, years maybe. I don't know how they are. Ask them to bring Erin and Kara to see me. Please.

She listened intently. Had he left? She listened for movement, for his voice. She at last heard an indrawn breath. Then his voice came again. Low, pleasant, but sounding hoarse with emotion, hesitant, as if he were holding back.

"You don't know me," he said again. "I'm Roger Hamilton. I saw you once before. Maybe you saw me. I don't know. I'm the guy in the pickup truck."

Roger Hamilton.

Oh, my God.

She struggled to speak to him, to ask him what he had seen that day. *Millicent. Millicent. The doll. Did you see the doll? Roger, did you see the doll rise up from the trunk, the unlocked trunk, did you see her push the lid up and rise from it and lean toward me with her sweet face, her horrible face, smiling, smiling. Like a snake flicking its tongue, its cold, unfeeling eyes coming closer, closer. Eyes made of blue glass, colder than the eyes of any living snake.*

Did you see her hands come toward me, Roger?

The sting of the nails on her face, the digging of the nails into her throat. She could feel it still. Her pulse throbbed and the pain was with her again as sharp and piercing as it had been that day. And the surprise, the fear, the feeling of unreality.

She tried to lift her hand, to let him know she could hear him.

"I've been wanting to talk to you," Roger said, and she heard him swallow hard. "This is . . . my first chance. I saw . . . I thought I saw a little girl in the car with you. Playing or fighting you. But Jim Ruther said there was no child."

Help me, Roger. Go to the house and ask about the doll again. Tell them to put it back in its trunk and strap it tight, then take it out to the Village and put it in the storage building. Roger, please, help me. Before something terrible happens.

My children are in danger. Fawn's children, too. Was the doll given to Susan? I would have given it to her. God, I didn't know. Nobody is safe with the doll out of the trunk. Not even Fawn or Martha are safe there.

"I'd better go, Laura," Roger said. "I don't know why I came up here in the first place."

Roger! No!

The children aren't safe there.

Andy stood just outside the door of the screened porch at the back of the new wing of the house, looking toward the family graveyard. The funeral was over, all the people gone now.

He had gone back to his room just long enough to take off his suit and tie and hang them in the wardrobe, that big chestlike piece of furniture in all the bedrooms he had been in, that took the place of closets. They hadn't built closets back in the days when the mansion was built, Martha had told him. It didn't matter. The wardrobe was all he needed to hang his two suits, one of them black, for funerals. He guessed for funerals, because it had been bought for Mama's granddad's funeral. And now it had been used for Erin's.

He was really sorry about Erin. It scared him to think that someone only twelve years old could die like that.

He had hardly been able to sleep or eat since he had stood in the hall that night and looked at Erin on the floor. When he slept he dreamed of her face, and the blood.

And he also dreamed of a small, white face up in the darkness behind the broken bannister, looking down at him.

Nothing scared him like that face.

Nothing.

He adjusted his jeans and pulled his knit shirt down over the waistband. Then he pulled up the hood of the dark blue windbreaker his mom had bought for him at Wal-Mart's and put his hands in the pockets.

He was almost getting used to being alone, to not being followed around by Susan. She was with Kara all the time now, and he supposed that was all right. They did girl things together, like playing jacks on the cement steps or walks, or playing with the dolls in Aunt Laura's old room.

Since Erin died he hadn't seen or heard anything about that big antique doll, Millicent. Sometimes he wondered where it was, but he didn't ask. He thought it was upstairs. He thought it was the doll's face he had seen in the dark behind the broken bannister. Yet he wasn't sure he had seen anything there. Spots in front of his eyes. The image of Erin's white face, wherever he looked all that night and every night since.

He walked into the damp grass of the back yard, past the bird fountain where the water hadn't been turned on yet for the summer. Beneath the fountain was a small pool with lily pads and a few goldfish. He stood for a couple of minutes watching the fish, then strolled on.

After the funeral his mother had made him leave the cemetery, though there were some old stones that drew him. He had been going over to read the names when she'd pulled him away. The gate had clanged shut behind him, closed and latched by the tall man who was once a friend of his mother's. Jim Ruther.

Andy passed behind the spruce trees and looked back at the house. Only the roof was visible now, the trees thicker, closer together, taller, it seemed. And so quiet. Water dripped in large drops from the branches, gathered there from the mist.

It was beginning to look dark beneath the trees and around the edges of the cemetery. He could see the rusted iron fence, the spikes at the top that kept kids from climbing over.

But the gate wasn't locked. And what difference did it make if he went in and looked at the old stones?

The gate screeched as he opened it, and he stood with

it halfway open and waited, as if he might be heard and scolded and made to come away again. But there was no sound now, except for the soft drip of rain.

He entered the cemetery plot.

Great-granddad's stone was large, and there were two names on it. The soil where he had been buried was still fresh looking and mounded up. The other grave was flat, and the short grass was beginning to turn green. Her name had been Sarah Myrna, and she died in 1951. She was Mama's grandmother, Andy guessed.

Erin's grave didn't have a stone. Nobody had expected her to die. Andy stood with his toes at the edge of the mound of fresh earth and felt regret deep in his heart, the ache sharp as knives in his chest. He had liked Erin. Maybe they would have had lots of good times together this summer. He wondered if Aunt Laura would be buried here beside her. Would they have a double stone like Great-grandad and Mama's grandmother who died so long ago?

But it was getting darker, and rain seemed to be coming heavier on the hood of his windbreaker. A chill went over him. Goosebumps covered his arms. There wasn't much warmth inside the windbreaker.

He moved on toward the back of the cemetery where the stones became crowded. He looked at the tall angel stone, and saw the name and date.

Victoria, angel in life, angel in death, born December 21, 1888, died December 23, 1899.

He knew who this Victoria was. She was the owner of the doll he had heard about. Victoria. The most valuable doll at Antique Village.

Leaves rustled suddenly in the shadowed corner of the cemetery plot, and Andy looked up, heart racing in fear. Yet his instinct to run was overwhelmed by curiosity. He had glimpsed something light in color, something moving. It was small, close to the ground, like a small child.

And he had a feeling he would be able to see the ghost of Victoria if he stared long enough, hard enough.

He went forward slowly. During Erin's burial he had seen something back in this corner that he'd wondered about. It was the emptiness here. The rest of the back of the graveyard was crowded with the stones of relatives, going way back, back two hundred years or more he guessed, but in that one corner where the trees shaded the fence and the ground, there was nothing.

And it was there that the ghost had moved.

But it couldn't have been a ghost, Andy told himself. Ghosts don't make noises in leaves when they move. Ghosts are silent. He didn't know how he could be so certain, because he'd never seen a ghost before. It was something he was just born knowing, he guessed, as if once he had been a ghost too.

He was no longer afraid, just curious.

He went around the tall angel stone, past two others he didn't pause to read, and came to the edge of the bare corner. It was as barren as it had looked from the front of the cemetery, where the graves were new. In an area of about the size of his old bedroom at the apartment, ten by ten feet, there was one small stone. But it was lying down, broken off at the base, and half covered by leaves and dead grass. This area of the graveyard wasn't tended, it looked to Andy. Maybe it had never been tended, because there were briars growing here in the corner by the fence, and vines ran in a dark green tangle among the leaves and grass.

Andy went to the stone. Moss filled in the shallow depressions where the name was. The carving was shallow and uneven, as if someone who had never carved a stone before had chiseled the name of the person buried here.

Andy sensed the neglect, the unfairness. Here, a stone gathered somewhere, not one of beautiful marble like the angel stone or most of the others. Here, a stone with the name chiseled by someone no better than himself at printing.

He picked up a small twig from the ground and dug at the moss in the letters on the stone.

And then, as the first three letters began to reveal themselves, he drew back.

M I L

He sat still for a long minute, on his heels, staring down at the stone. Then hurriedly he cleaned the rest of the letters, though he now suspected what the name was. He cleared the date of birth and the date of death, and again he sat back on his heels and stared at it.

Millicent
Born December 21, 1888
Died Feb. 13, 1900

Chapter Fourteen

Andy ran. He bumped into a stone, the sharp edge tearing a small hole in his jeans. Groaning, bending to one side, he held the bruised place on his thigh, but he kept running.

He swung the rusted iron gate farther back and heard the long squeak of the hinges. He ran past trees, dodged bushes, and came to the shed at the back of the mowed part of the yard. His feet clattered on the walk that ran from the patio at the corner of the house to the fountain in the middle of the back yard.

Lights were on in the house, yellow and welcoming beyond the curtains. His hair was damp from the light drizzling rain, the hood of his windbreaker now hanging down his back. He started to go around to the living-room porch, but dodged again to the side and went to the screened porch instead.

He burst into the kitchen.

Martha, at the sink, said something to him, but he didn't listen.

"Martha! Mom! Jill!"

"Whoa!" said Martha.

"Where's Mom and Jill?"

Fawn and Jill came in from the living room even as he was asking, their faces reflections of each other's wonder edged with fear, as if they dreaded knowing. At the table, which was set for supper, Kara and Susan colored, sharing one coloring book between them. They looked up without speaking.

"I found it," Andy wheezed breathlessly. "It's out there." He pointed behind him, toward the door he had left standing open, and the cemetery far out under the trees.

"You found what?" Fawn asked.

"Her grave."

Jill put her hands to her face and cried softly, "Oh my God."

Andy looked at her, and felt guilty and sorry. But he had to tell them. Even though Erin hadn't been dead long, and her grave was still fresh, he still had to tell them what he had found. It was important. He could feel the urgency building in him. Was his mom going to make him stop talking about the cemetery? This soon after Erin's burial?

Fawn put her arms around Jill and held her, and Andy stood quietly watching them.

Martha began moving about again, taking to the table a bowl of salad. Lots of other food was still on the table, and part of it had been there all afternoon. Andy had seen the bowls and dishes of food brought in by neighbors and friends and relatives. There were a lot of relatives he had never heard about, and some of them, it seemed to him, not even his mother knew very well.

Lots of people who hadn't come to Great-granddad's funeral had come to Erin's. But for Andy it was a gathering of strangers.

"Food will make you feel better," Martha said. "Sit down and eat something, Jill. Fawn. Andy, you too. Better wash your hands?"

She looked at his hands.

"Have you been digging in the dirt?"

"It's important," he said.

Jill was not crying after all. She just looked sad and tired when she took her hands away from her face.

"Whose grave, Andy?" Jill asked.

"Millicent's."

All of them stared at him. The two little girls at the table lifted their heads and stared at him too, as well as the others. For a while the only sound was the clock on the wall, ticking slowly and lazily.

Then Martha said, "Millicent's?"

And Kara asked, "The doll's?"

"No," Andy said. "A real person. She was born the very same day as Victoria, but she died February thirteenth instead of December twenty-third. That was the only difference. Except Victoria has a big marble stone with an angel on top, and Millicent's gravestone is small and fell over a long time ago. And it's partly covered with old leaves and dead grass and briars and stuff."

"Well," Martha said, "let's sit down and eat."

"But it's important," Andy wailed. "Don't you see? She was the owner of that weird doll. The twin."

"Millicent isn't weird," Susan cried. "Mama, make him stop saying Millicent is weird!"

Fawn stood in the middle of the room, between the kitchen and the dining area, looking at the back door. Then she was walking toward the door.

"It isn't dark yet. I think I'll go out and see it."

Andy ran ahead of her, opening the screen door and holding it back. Behind his mother came Jill, Martha, and then, running, both of the girls.

Andy led them out of the short, green grass of the back yard into the trees, past the shed and toward the thicker growth of trees behind the house.

They went toward the cemetery and the yard fence on the left, and the narrow little service road. He led the way through the cemetery, going around the fence this time and straight back to the untended corner. It was no darker now than it had been a few minutes ago when first he had discovered the stone.

He bent over it and brushed it with his hands, trying to clean it better so they could see in the dying light.

Fawn and Jill and Martha bent to read the stone, their heads together.

Fawn straightened and pushed her hair back out of her eyes.

"She must have had a twin sister. Victoria—where is her stone, Andy?"

"The angel."

"There are several angel stones."

"The big one. The tall one."

He led the way again, back through the cemetery toward the middle, stopping beside the marble stone.

"This is very odd," Fawn said. "Why would Granddad keep secret the one sister? The date of birth is the same."

"Could have been a distant relative born at the same time," Martha said. "A cousin. Maybe she was illegitimate. In those days illegitimate children weren't acknowledged."

"What's illegitimate mean?" Kara asked, but no one answered her.

Andy hadn't thought about the other girl being a cousin or just a relative. Since the dolls were just alike, so they said, he figured the two girls were too. Millicent and Victoria. Though their names didn't rhyme, or anything like that the way twins' names did sometimes.

"It's going to be dark soon," Martha said. "We'd better get on back to the house."

"Even if Millicent was a cousin to Victoria, they must have been raised together. Until their deaths," Fawn said.

"What makes you think that?" Martha asked. "The dolls?"

"Right. Granddad said Victoria received her doll for

her eleventh birthday, an especially made doll for that special date. And she died two days later. He never seemed to want to talk much about her. He would talk for hours about his dad or grandparents or uncles or aunts, but when we'd ask about Victoria, and we were fascinated because of the doll, he just didn't say much." She added, "But she had fallen, too. That's why the gate was built on the stairway."

They were walking toward the gate. When Andy turned to close it behind everyone he noticed that Jill was still back in the corner, standing there, looking down at that small, fallen stone.

Something was wrong. Something terrible had happened, and Laura knew it. They had stopped talking to her. Even Fawn, though she came every day at most visiting hours, had stopped talking. Laura knew her footsteps and the touch of her hand. Sometimes Fawn would ask the nurse, "How's she doing today?" And the nurse would answer, always in a cheerful voice, "She's just great. Everything stable. All her vital signs are good."

She could hear Fawn's sighs, and her footsteps going away.

It seemed to Laura that no one stayed as long as they once had, and she wondered if they would eventually stop coming to see her. But of course they wouldn't, she tried to reassure herself. Of course they wouldn't.

Jill came in the evening, alone. Fawn's steps weren't with Jill's. The quick, hurried walk of Jill was slowed, so that at first Laura wasn't sure who it was. Then Jill's warm hands clasped her arm and held on tightly, and she wept.

What is it? Laura screamed inside her brain. *What's wrong?* Where are the children? Let me see my babies! Erin, Kara! Where are they? Where are Susan and

Andy? Bring them all to me and let me know they're all safe and well.

But no one heard her, and only Jill and Fawn came, each alone now much of the time.

Twice there were the footsteps of a man, and she wondered if Roger had come back again and looked in on her. And once she knew it was he, because she heard, beyond her curtain, his voice asking someone, "Do you think she can hear yet, or respond?" As if he still wanted to talk to her. To have her talk to him. But the nurse said, "Oh no. Not at all. She's still in a deep coma."

I'm not, Laura tried to scream. I can hear. Talk to me, tell me what's wrong.

She could tell when deep night came. Although the monitors kept beeping, there weren't as many footsteps beyond the curtain. She knew a curtain hung between her bed and the main room containing dozens of monitors, because sometimes a nurse would push it back and the rings on the bar above would tinkle like chimes, the fabric of the curtain would swish back and forth before it hung still again.

In the dark of the night she felt her body lift from the bed, as feather light as a soft breeze stirring the air, and the light blinded her again, the bright fluorescent white-hot in her eyes.

Then the room was gone, and she was sinking through another ceiling, and she recognized the mansion.

It was here she always came. Always the mansion. And she willed herself to go to the second-floor bedrooms to see if her children were safe.

But it was not night here. The light of day seeped through the curtained windows and made shadows in the end of the hall.

She saw the tall bookcase with the beveled glass insets and the stained-glass corners. It held within it the same books bound in leather, old books now called classics, and beside it was the chair. But the seat was different. Instead of the needlepoint done by her great-grandmother, it was covered in a dark tapestry.

She had failed again to reach her own time, her own family. She felt the heaviness of failure within her and wished herself gone. She was afraid. Did this returning to a former time mean she was dying? That she would be caught in a kind of time-warp, forever invisible to others, nothing of substance to her?

She heard voices. A man's deep voice, words she didn't understand, floated beneath a woman's more penetrating answer.

"I won't even consider it. My child will be taught at home."

The door opened, and a woman, full of figure, her waist cinched by a corset whose bones showed beneath the dark material of her full-skirted, ankle-length dress, came out into the hall. The man's voice followed her.

"Children, Maybella. You have *children,* not just a child. Think of Victoria. And Mason."

The woman stopped. When she looked back at the bedroom, through the open door, Laura saw her face. The same dark eyes, the high, arched brows, the faint dark line of fine hair growing on her upper lip. It was the woman she had seen enter the playroom once before. The woman in the photograph, now hanging on the wall of the stairway next to the framed image of her husband, John. Granddad's parents.

"Mason is hardly old enough to go to school! I don't want to hear anymore about this, John."

The woman spun on her heel and went on down the hall and across the landing into the back-bedroom hallway. A little girl came running out of a bedroom, and the woman bent and kissed her. It was the dark-haired beauty, and Laura saw her faint resemblance to the woman. The same diamond-shaped face with the deep dimple in the chin. But the child's eyes seemed more luminous, her lashes longer, her eyebrows less arched.

"Have you been helping Victoria?" the mother asked, her voice softening, her adoration obvious in the way she smoothed the child's hair.

"Yes, Mama."

Innocent eyes looking up. Guileless eyes. Outwardly as pure as heaven, as willing to please. Without conscience. She was older than when Laura had last viewed her. She had been three or four when she had pushed the little blond girl through the bannister. Now she was seven or eight or more. There was a slow clumping sound in the hallway, and both dark heads turned to look. The door of the pink room was pushed back. The pink room was at the end of the hall, Victoria's room it had been called for all of Laura's life. None of the child's things were still there though. At Antique Village was a reproduction of Victoria's room called the Pink Room, complete with bed, dresser, chest, cedar chest and even the pearl-handled mirror and hairbrush set. Everything that had belonged to Victoria had been moved to the Village.

The child came slowly into view, crutches slowing her.

She was several inches shorter now than the dark-haired girl. Her legs, broken in the fall, had healed badly and had failed to grow as they should have. Laura stared at her. The little girl still had long, blond curls, tubed as if someone had carefully curled each one. She had a hunch it was not the mother. The mother stood with her hand on the other child's shoulder.

Victoria stopped several feet away and stood looking at them.

"I helped you with your dress, didn't I, Victoria?"

"Yes. She helped me."

The mother patted the shoulder beneath her hand. "How sweet of you, Millicent dear. You're my good girl."

There were footsteps behind them. Victoria's face

lighted and became the sweetness of the doll Victoria, which Laura knew the child would receive for her eleventh birthday. She now knew who the artist had patterned the faces of the two dolls after. Victoria herself. Why hadn't she seen that before? One old photograph of Victoria, framed in gilt, hung in the Pink Room at the Village, and Laura hadn't really looked at it in years. But the resemblance was there. When Victoria smiled, and hurried forward on her crutches, Laura saw that the smaller of her legs was dragging. On that foot was a smaller shoe than on the other.

Did the parents know Millicent had pushed Victoria?

"Papa," Victoria cried, going around her mother and Millicent.

The tall, bearded man grabbed up the child, letting the crutches clatter to the floor. He swung her high above his head and then cradled her in his arms.

"How's my princess?" he asked. Her arms curled tightly around his neck.

Another child entered the hall and bent to pick up one of Victoria's crutches. It was a little boy, in short pants and long socks that reached just below his plump knees.

When he straightened Laura's heart tripped in tenderness. Granddad. Even at age two or three he had the same round face, the round, curious eyes, the sweetness and gentleness of his sister, Victoria.

The scene before Laura took on a stillness, a distance, like a still-frame from a film, and the figures grew smaller. She knew she was drifting away and she tried to stop herself. She willed herself to return to the mansion, to wait, to try to reach someone, in her time or theirs, but the scene was leaving her.

Millicent.

It was as if Granddad had forgotten she had ever existed.

Laura still didn't know who she was, though John had

called her Maybella's child. And the resemblance made that true.

"Who is this?" Laura had asked Granddad once, long ago when she had first become interested in the large, framed photographs on the stairway wall. It was a picture of a dark-haired woman, hair pulled back from her face. Her cheekbones were prominent, and there was a deep dimple in her chin. She had arched eyebrows, very dark and heavy.

"It's my mother," Granddad told her. "Her name was Maybella Louise. And the man there, with the beard, is my father. John."

Millicent had been, must have been, Granddad's sister as was Victoria.

But he had never mentioned her name.

And there was nothing in the mansion or in the Village that had ever belonged to her.

There was only the doll, Millicent.

Chapter Fifteen

Jill stood at her mother's bedside, looking down at her. Tears no longer blurred her eyes as they had in the beginning when looking at Laura with the tubes and the bandages had been so heartbreaking. Now there was a dryness in Jill, a hurt that just wouldn't go away. But there was an acceptance, too. A waiting. A constant dread. When would she enter this room to find Laura dead, the monitors no longer beeping?

When would she have to see the ground opened again at the family cemetery to receive her mother?

She hadn't said anything to Laura. What could she say? Mama, Erin is dead. It doesn't seem possible, but she is. It seems like she's in school, with Andy, with her friends. I think of her like that. It makes it more bearable.

"Oh, Mama," she whispered, the tears almost coming, but stopping instead just behind her eyes to burn and sting. "Please wake up, Mama. I need you so much."

It was noon. She had left school and come to the hospital at this time because she knew no one else would be here. Aunt Fawn had said at the breakfast table that she would visit Laura at ten o'clock and then do the week's grocery shopping.

"Mama," Jill said, "we found Millicent's tombstone. It

had fallen over, back in that old untended corner. You remember how Granddad had always said leave it alone? I can remember him saying that one time when we went out to show the gardeners how to clean it up; he said forget that old corner. It's too damp in that corner, he said, for it to ever be used. Too dark and shaded. Do you remember that, Mama? I think I was about seven then. He said the quail and the rabbits need a place to call home too, and they could have the corner."

When they'd left the cemetery that warm summer day, Great-granddad had told her to stay away from the cemetery unless she was accompanied by an adult. She had never gone back, not until she had entered with her mother to show the grave diggers where the new grave was to be dug, where the double stone was, where Great-grandma had been buried. Great-granddad's name was already there, carved years ago when his wife had died. His name and his date of birth. His death date had been carved in that last day, the same day they dug his grave.

"I'm going out to the Village, Mama. I just remembered something last night. I couldn't sleep. There's the old family Bible in the room of Old Books. Remember? There's something strange about Millicent, Mama. Granddad never mentioned her, did he? Yet the odd thing is, her birthdate is the very same as Victoria's. Did you know that, Mama? As Erin used to say, I can smell the fish in Denmark."

Jill leaned down and kissed her mother's cheek. It felt warm to her lips. A lot of the bandages had been taken off now, but the cuts were still visible, pink and raw in some places, healing.

" 'Bye, Mama."

Used to say . . .

Jill, come back. Jill, please, how is Erin? Bring Erin to me.

Jill, what has happened to Erin? Jill!. . . Jill . . .

But the footsteps were fading away. Jill leaving, going out along the side of the curtain, her soft-soled sneakers making a whispering squeak with each step on the polished tile or linoleum floor. Laura knew how well polished this floor was. Every night the cleaning lady or man came in with shoes that squeaked like Jill's sneakers, and used mops and fresh-smelling waxes.

Laura sank into hopelessness. More and more the hopelessness came on, as did the periods of silence within her, of sleep, perhaps, she didn't know. There were no dreams, just awarenesses. Just the vivid out-of-body experiences that were in a way frightening and terrible, and in another way oddly exhilarating. They were her only freedom from a body that no longer responded to the commands from her brain.

But they did not occur voluntarily. There were times when she struggled to release herself from her physical body, but nothing happened and she was left in the darkness of her coma.

She prayed for release. She struggled mentally to rise and follow Jill. Her brain felt as if it would burst as she sought the light and freedom. But darkness pulled her in and held her.

It was called skipping school, just as it had been in her mother's day. In Great-granddad's day it had been called playing hookey. Jill smiled faintly as she drove. "You have to go to school," he'd told Jill, holding her on his knee. She had leaned against the comfort and security of his belly, which came halfway between his thigh and his knee when he sat down. But still he wasn't so big-bellied that he couldn't hold his great-grandchildren, he had told her many times as he'd picked her up to bounce her on that piece of lap.

"You have to go to school. That's just one of the requirements of life, don't you see? If you don't go to school, you'll be a dunce. Do you know what a dunce is? It's like a clown in a corner with a tall hat on. And everyone stares at and laughs at a dunce. Of course, it doesn't hurt to play hookey once in your school years." And he whispered in her ear, "I used to play hookey now and then."

Playing hookey sounded like a lot of fun then, when she was in the second grade. Now it was something she felt an urgent need to do, today, not next Saturday. Now she'd give anything to put her life back where it was a month ago, with Mama well and at home, with Erin . . .

With Erin.

Alive.

Jill didn't know why, but she felt something terrible had come over her family, settled about them like a nuclear cloud, and if she didn't find the reason for it and dispel it, the cloud would destroy everything. Whatever it was, it had something to do with the unknown Millicent.

Skipping school was very easy these days. Her teachers knew her mother was still in ICU, unimproved. They knew Erin was recently buried. And her great-grandfather. They also knew why, at this time, she couldn't be the student she had always been.

She was in the last semester of her junior year of high school. In a few more weeks, school would be out for the summer. Her grades were made. The teachers were more understanding than her friends. Just yesterday, Sean, a guy she had dated more than any other, had asked her to go to the prom with him. He was graduating this year and going on to college; she didn't know where. He had invited her to the prom, and then, before she could answer, he had said, "Oh hey, I'm sorry. For a minute I forgot." And he'd walked away, leaving her standing with Samantha and Caroline, with no date for the prom.

But she hadn't thought about the prom since her mother's accident. And especially since Erin's death. She knew she wouldn't be going. Not this year. Maybe not even next year. She felt as if she were in limbo.

And perhaps she was, as her mother was. Maybe all of them were. The world they had known had slipped away when they weren't noticing. Everything had changed. Though the trees were getting greener, just as if it really was spring, and the grass was growing, and motor boats were beginning to stir the waves on the lake, it only looked normal. The world was really in limbo.

Jill drove up and down the hilly area out Harbor Road toward the lake. All traces of her mother's wreck had been removed by now, she noticed as she approached that fateful spot. The bushes at the side of the road in the upper tip of the deep ravine had straightened again. The scattered pieces of wood—broken furniture—had been picked up or covered by the growing vegetation. Jill drove past the spot without slowing, her stomach doing a little lifting and settling as the car dipped through the bottom of the hollow and rose again toward the top of the next hill.

Three miles farther on she put on her left-turn signal, slowed, waited for a truck and three cars to go by, then turned down the paved lane to Antique Village.

She drove more slowly, though the road no longer dipped into hollows or rose over hills. It wound along the ridge down toward the lake, passing beneath oak trees two hundred years old. In the woods the dogwood were blooming, great bouquets of white among the shadows and spring green, and Jill felt tears sting her eyes. Lately, the tears came involuntarily and unexpectedly. She would be talking, or even laughing at something one of the kids at school said, and then, like a hysterical person, she would be crying.

Erin, who had never gotten hysterical about anything in her life, had loved the dogwood. "Well, thank God," she'd said last year, Jill remembered, "Life is returning to the earth. The dogwood are blooming. Finally."

Jill pressed harder on the accelerator and the trees whizzed by. Since she wasn't going to stay at the cottage, no matter how much she would have liked to, she parked outside the gates. She followed the walk down to a smaller gate and unlocked it. There were signs of life at the small restaurant, which was outside the gates. A van was parked in the back. Someone was probably getting it ready to open.

As she entered the Village grounds, she could hear mowers at work. The caretakers, Harry and Ivan, were also getting ready to open. Tears threatened again behind her eyes, and she stared wide-eyed into the trees until they receded. This would be another first, opening without her mother. Thank God for Aunt Fawn, who had been coming out to do Mother's work.

Jill went through the narrow and winding streets of the Village and across the park to the cottage. The key she needed was among those in her mother's office.

The office, which had a separate entrance, smelled as if it needed airing. Jill opened the door into the house.

There was a quality of unreality about the house now, as if no one had ever lived there. She decided it needed airing too.

She walked through the rooms, opening windows. The lake side of the house held a narrow band of sunshine in the southwest window. The tree outside it hadn't grown leaves large enough to provide much shade. She could hear the sound of the water and felt comforted, as she always had. The movement of the water against the shore, below the house, had sung her to sleep almost all of her life, through most of her memory.

In her own bedroom, where the windows looked out

into the trees at the west end of the house, she opened curtains and the window and sat for a moment on her bed, looking out. Then she got up and went down the hall.

Erin's things were just as she had left them. All her clothes were in the closets, as her mother's were in the big corner bedroom. Jill almost closed the door, leaving in the room that lack of air, that lack of aliveness that permeated the whole house. Then she changed her mind, crossed to the windows, and opened them. And when she left the room she left the door open.

Jill returned to the office and the collection of keys. She looked through all the labels. The various colors meant nothing to her, although she knew her mother would have been able to pick out the key she wanted just from the color code.

The Barber Shop . . . Post Office . . . Bank . . . Log Cabin . . .

The Pink Room.

Victoria's room, with all her things. A replica of the bedroom she'd had back at the mansion, Jill knew, with all her favorite toys and dolls except the large doll, *Victoria.*

And finally she found the key she wanted, the key to the house of old books and documents and newspapers.

She went down Antique Alley, passing several buildings of Odds and Ends, as they were called. These contained every imaginable small item used by early Americans in their daily living.

Halfway through the street the two German shepherds found her, and came trotting up with their tongues lolling and tails wagging. They looked very happy, as if they had been following the mowers at work over in the park.

She let herself into the brightly lit Old Books and Newspapers building. There newspapers laminated onto flat boards dated from an almost unreadable issue printed in 1844, the date so faded and cracked as to be practically indecipherable, to clearly legible print from a World War Two era paper.

But the book Jill wanted was the old Bible, its heavy, dark brown leather binding now cracked and peeling, the decorations of textured gold dim with age. Great-granddad had told her the Bible had belonged to his grandparents, and had been used when he was a child. But Jill had never opened it.

It lay on a table near the back of the room, tilted slightly so it could be seen but never touched, a thick book with pages edged in gold.

She made her way between newspapers and old, carefully maintained display books. She passed an old school desk on which a kid named Charlie had carved his name and had added the date, April 10, 1844. It was a funny-looking little desk with an attached stool that had no back.

She stood looking down at the Bible. Dusting the books in this room had been done by very dependable workers with feather dusters. Just moved the dirt around, Jill thought, from being settled on a book to floating through the air, and then settling again when it was left undisturbed.

Still, the heavy plate-glass window, the lack of open air kept most of the dust out.

She felt afraid to touch the Bible. All her life, it had been one of the forbidden items in the Village. Her early curiosity about it had drifted away, and she hadn't even thought of it in years.

But she knew the only records of earlier births and deaths were kept in these old family Bibles.

The leather creaked as she lifted the cover. She felt it would split away in her hands, break from the spine, separate forever from the pages. She lifted it slowly, as she would have opened a rusted, forbidden door.

Then it was open and unbroken, and she held it carefully as she lifted the first page, the tissue-thin, gold-edged paper.

There was a list of names. They might intrigue her if ever she became interested in genealogy but she read now only for knowledge of Great-granddad's family, the Evanses. On the third page she came to the wedding date of Johnathan Evans and Maybella Morningstar. August 1, 1875. After that came a long list of infant names, dates of births and deaths, sometimes on the same day or within one week.

Jill reread them, shocked. Eight babies, dead either on the day of birth or within one week? Great-granddad's brothers and sisters? Julianne, Mary, Joseph, Andrew, Ira, Lily, John, Solomon. Brief names, as if they were identified by only one name in those lives that in some cases could be counted in hours, not days or weeks.

It must have been terrible, Jill thought, and for a moment she saw the hardship of life a hundred and twenty years ago, of babies born at home, dying at home.

For the first time it occurred to her that Great-granddad's parents had only one child who had lived to become an adult.

With her finger moving gently down the long list of names she came at last to Victoria, born December 21, 1888. And died, December 23, 1899.

Millicent.

It was there, beside Victoria.

Millicent, born December 21, 1888.

There was one more.

Mason Charles, born July 10, 1895.

Great-granddad.

And then she noticed. For all the other children and for Maybella, the mother who died June 20, 1900, and Johnathon, dead November 17, 1912 when Great-granddad was seventeen years old, there was a date of death. But for Millicent, there was none.

There were no more entries.

Great-granddad had not used this Bible for his own small family of one wife, one daughter.

After the death of his father it had been closed.

Victoria and Millicent.

Twin girls.

How happy they must have been, Maybella and Johnathon, to have, at last, two healthy children.

And then to lose Victoria at age eleven.

And Millicent also . . . but why wasn't her death written in the family Bible?

The old tombstone said she died on February 13, 1900. Less than two months after Victoria. Just a few months before her mother.

Then Great-granddad must not have remembered his mother very well. Jill had never thought of it before, but he was only four, almost five, when his mother died.

When Victoria and Millicent died.

Jill left the House of Books, wandering the hallways between plate-glass fronts, and came at last to the Pink Room. On the wall at the back of it, where even the floral carpet was authentic, hung the large, framed photograph of Victoria.

Kara could have been the girl in the faded picture, if her hair were pulled back. It could have been Susan, for that matter, or Erin, or even Jill herself when she was that age. A softly defined face, rounded eyes, a sweet upturn to her lips though she wasn't smiling. Smiles, it seemed, were not allowed in those days. Or perhaps they were impossible to maintain, since taking a photograph was not a matter of having your picture snapped. Jill had a momentary vision of a photographer, a black cape over his head, standing in front of an apparatus on a tripod and saying, "Hold it, hold it please, don't move, sit very still. Please, stop smiling, it's turning into a grimace, hold it, *hold it.*"

By the time the photo was completed everyone would have been exhausted.

Why was there no photograph of Millicent?

Perhaps there was, in the attic at the mansion, or in the shed. Or perhaps Millicent hadn't been well? Considering the early deaths of so many children, maybe neither of these girls was healthy. After all, surviving to the age of eleven was not exactly being long-lived.

She would have liked to go into the Pink Room, but didn't have the key. She stood looking through the plate glass, seeing for the first time the life Victoria might have lived.

There were a couple of older dolls, one of them made of cloth. A rag doll. It looked worn, the embroidery of the face worn through in places, the little red mouth faded to light pink in one spot and completely missing in another.

On the dresser was a hand mirror and brush, with bits of the natural bristles missing.

On the bedside table, beneath the elaborate old lamp with the tassels on the glass shade, was a small pile of books.

The pink bedspread looked hand crocheted, and Jill turned back to reading the sign to learn that it had indeed been made by Victoria's mother, Maybella.

Had she crocheted one for Millicent also? And if so, where was it?

Jill looked for a sign, any sign, that indicated Victoria had a twin sister. But found none.

If it hadn't been for the doll in the trunk, Millicent would have been just another of the dead children whose births were listed in the Bible, names unread.

It struck Jill as being very sad.

And it was also puzzling, disturbing.

She would have to look elsewhere for Millicent.

Chapter Sixteen

Fawn stood at Laura's bedside, looking down at her. Her sister was on her side, a pillow behind her back to keep her from rolling. Her arms were lying loose, and there were no signs yet of drawing in, of tightening of the muscles in the hands and arms.

Fawn didn't know what to say to her anymore. Not that it mattered. Laura couldn't hear, the nurses assured her. Except for one nurse, an older woman who looked as if she had been in the business a long time. "Don't you believe it," she had whispered after a pair of doctors had assured Fawn that Laura was probably not aware of anything. "They're just telling you that because they don't know. There's a lot about the human brain nobody knows yet. Some of these coma patients come out of it not remembering anything, that's true. In fact, most of them. But once in a while . . . well, you just never know."

But every time she visited Laura, Fawn had a dreadful feeling that Laura was gone. Irretrievably lost.

"It's two o'clock," Fawn said. "The . . . the kids are in school. It's a sunny day, for a change." She opened her mouth to say more, thought of nothing to add, and closed it again.

This was the first time she had mentioned the kids to Laura. It had been so hard to visit her sister without talking about Erin. At the beginning she had almost asked

Laura about the funeral arrangements. Did she want her buried in a special color? Her casket to be made of some specific material? That beautiful, polished oak? Or did she prefer the steel? Yet it was all so macabre, and Fawn couldn't voice her questions.

As it was, Jill had chosen pure white for both, the dress Erin was buried in and the coffin. Even the veil was white, and the family flowers were mostly white.

Laura lay on her side as if she were sleeping, her eyes closed, her hands clasped together, palm to palm.

Fawn leaned down, kissed her cheek, and silently left the room to walk past other rooms in which patients were awake, their curtains drawn back, sun shining through the windows.

She went out into the waiting room, into the noise of daily activity. She hardly noticed that someone separated himself from the magazine-reading people sitting on various chairs and benches, rose, and came toward her.

"Hello, Fawn."

She saw Roger's friendly, concerned face, and could have hugged him. She hadn't realized her need to be with someone else, someone to talk to, walk with.

"How is Laura today?"

Fawn shrugged. "There's no change."

"And how are you?"

He didn't take her arm, but he walked close beside her so she could feel his presence. She was comforted by it and felt a need to keep him with her.

"I'm okay. And you?"

At the elevator he took her arm, his fingers warm through the thin sleeve of her blouse. The elevator was crowded and he pulled her against him, both hands on her upper arms. They stood in silence together. He was just the right height for her. She could have laid her head on his shoulder, and she had a strong urge to do just that. She controlled it with difficulty. She hadn't realized before her need to be held and babied.

When they left the elevator, she deliberately pulled away from him so that his hands were no longer touching her. She didn't feel like making a fool of herself, and she was afraid she would if she continued to feel the warmth of those strong hands.

They talked about the weather on the way across the parking lot. Fawn stopped by the old Buick she was driving.

"That's a classic," Roger said, looking at the mint-condition car admiringly. "What is it, a sixty-three?"

"Sixty-four, I think. I don't know. It belonged to Granddad. Sat in his garage without being driven for several years. He had a station wagon a year or so old, but Martha had to use that today, so I thought I'd see if this one still ran. And it does. On this car I learned to drive a long time ago."

"Not so long ago," he said.

"Yes. Twenty years."

"You dated Jim Ruther then," he stated, surprising Fawn, causing her to pause

Finally she responded, "Yes, I did. But I don't know him well anymore. He's wearing a wedding ring, so I guess he's married." She tried to laugh, but it came and was gone again in the flicker of an eye.

"I hope he is," Roger said. "If that would make a difference."

She felt his eyes on her and was unable to meet them. Her heart was racing, as disturbed in rhythm as it had ever been.

She shrugged. "It doesn't matter." He said nothing, and she suddenly realized how many ways her answer could be taken. Swiftly she looked up into his eyes and saw something she hoped was not irreversible disappointment in her. Her laughter now was honest and spontaneous, even though it was brief.

"What I mean is, there's nothing left of my feelings for him. I don't care whether he's married or single. I hope he's happily married."

They smiled at each other for just a moment. Roger touched her hand, then pulled away.

"Want to come out to the house for coffee?" Fawn asked. "Where are you parked?"

Roger motioned to the vehicle several rows away. "One of the trucks. I just thought I'd drop by the hospital after lunch to see how Laura was getting along."

"You don't need to feel responsible for that wreck, Roger. It wasn't your fault."

He looked down. Then suddenly he looked up again and touched her shoulder. "Thanks for the coffee offer. I'll follow you."

Fawn watched him hurry through the parked cars toward a blue pickup. She liked the way he walked, his shoulders moving, almost with a swagger, swaying just enough for it to be a natural movement. She liked everything she saw about him, she realized.

And he was attracted to her. She saw it, sensed it, and was attracted to him. He had been entering her dreams lately, the better ones, the dreams not filled with frightening images and feelings. She felt a twinge of guilt for finding something in the present horror of her life that gave her pleasure.

She drove slowly through town, not really trusting the old car even though its engine sounded as soft and velvety as it ever had. In the rearview mirror she watched the hood of the blue pickup, and the face behind the windshield.

She speeded up when she came to the street out of town and the traffic fell back. She came to the mailbox and the edge of the yard and signaled a turn. The blue pickup followed.

She drove the car on into the garage and saw that Martha was still gone. Jill's car was gone too, of course. She wouldn't be home from school for another hour.

"No wonder they call this The Mansion," Roger said, joining Fawn outside the detached three-car garage, looking up at the height of the old house.

"You've heard that?"

"Yeah. One of the oldest houses in the area. Or maybe the oldest?"

"It could be, I don't know. I do know that the people who built it bought up a lot of land, and so did some other settlers who came along at about the same time. Several houses were built here in the early eighteen hundreds. But I think this is the tallest, with the highest ceilings, even if it isn't the oldest of the old places. It was, I believe, Granddad's grandfather, or maybe his great-grandfather, who built the house. Laura is the one who knows the history of the place and the genealogy, as well as the authenticity and value of the antiques. I don't know that much."

They went onto the porch of the new wing and into the living room. The house was quiet, but the smell of freshly baked bread lingered in it.

"Martha baked this morning. It makes us all feel better," Fawn said.

"Martha?"

"She's . . . I think she's a distant relative of Granddad's. Anyway, she's lived here as his housekeeper since she was in her thirties. She had been married, but her husband died so she came here. Laura and I were small then. She was our substitute mother. She's been here ever since. And Granddad left her well taken care of, so she can now afford to retire. But she doesn't seem to want to, and I'm glad. We need her so much."

They went into the kitchen and drank coffee, and talked about themselves. Fawn learned that there was no one in his life now, and hadn't been for a year or so. For the first time she felt as if she had come home. She was glad she had and suddenly knew she would stay. Even if Laura got well and no longer needed her.

She offered to show Roger the rest of the house, and they went through the lower rooms to the stairwell. She saw him look up. The gap in the bannister far above was a deadly reminder, ends of broken woods still hanging in air, raw and splintered.

"Is that? . . ."

"Yes." Fawn motioned to a new area rug on the floor. "The rug has been replaced."

"The fall killed her."

"Yes."

Roger frowned. "It doesn't seem like it should have. How far is that? Forty, fifty feet?"

"I think the ceilings are twenty feet high."

"Fifty feet at the most then. I suppose if her head struck at a vulnerable . . ." He seemed to become aware that he was thinking aloud, and he touched her apologetically. "Sorry, Fawn."

She said nothing. She could hardly bear to pass this different rug which Martha had brought down from the attic. Passing it was to remember the blood that had spilled from Erin's splintered skull, trailing in rivulets onto the hardwood floor and the tasseled edge of the former rug.

"That should be repaired," he said, looking at the broken bannister far above.

"No one goes up there. There's a gate; I'll show you." She led the way up the stairs to the gate. It was now locked, a padlock sticking out from it like a growth. "The kids know they are not to go past it, and never, never to climb over."

Roger shook his head. "Don't you know how kids love a challenge? The bannister should be repaired."

"I think Martha tried to get a carpenter, but they

couldn't, not for a while."

"I'll do it, no charge. Do you have the key? I'll go up and take a look at the kind of lumber needed. When I'm through no one will be falling through that balustrade."

Fawn went back down to the kitchen for the key. Martha had hung it with the others on a nail in the pantry, and had said it was not to be touched. Meaning, Fawn knew, by the children. Anyway a child would need a ladder to get the key or would have to climb the pantry shelves. She trusted her two kids. They knew what had happened to Erin, and they understood they weren't supposed to pass the gate.

"Fawn," Roger asked when she gave him the key, "what happened to that doll that was in the car with Laura?"

"The doll . . ." It was the first time in several days Fawn had even thought of it. "It was put away."

"Here? In this house?"

"Yes. Why?" Martha had told her, she remembered, that Roger had once shown unusual curiosity about the doll.

It seemed he was about to tell her something. He held the key in his hand, looking at it, turning it as if he wanted to keep his hands busy. Then the outside door opened and Jill was calling out, "Anyone home?"

"Just us, Jill. You remember Roger? He's going to take a look at the bannister, and repair it."

"Oh. Do you do carpenter work?"

"Sure do. If you girls will excuse me . . ."

He went through the kitchen door into the hall, and the door swung closed behind him. Fawn almost followed, then Jill began talking to her again.

"I didn't go to school this afternoon, Aunt Fawn."

"Oh?" What could she say? Hey, you gotta go if you don't want to wind up like me?

Jill poured a glass of milk and took it to the table. Fawn sat down with her.

"I've been searching through old records, that sort of thing. I went out to the Village and looked in the family Bible. She was Victoria's twin sister, Aunt Fawn."

"Millicent?"

"Yes. Why do you suppose so much was made of Victoria's things, even to her room being preserved, and nothing of Millicent's?"

Fawn sat frowning, unable to assimilate the reality of Millicent. Victoria had always seemed so real, a tragic little girl who had died a terrible death. But Millicent? How strange that she was never mentioned. It didn't seem possible that she had really existed.

"I have no idea. Are you sure about this? There really was a Millicent?"

"Didn't Great-granddad ever mention this other sister?"

"Not to me. Evidently not to Laura or Martha either."

"What?" Martha's voice accompanied the closing of a door.

Martha came into the kitchen carrying a sack of groceries, and Jill again explained what she'd done that afternoon. Martha put a few items in the refrigerator, left the rest sitting on the cabinet, and sat down at the table with them.

"I went to the courthouse," Jill said, "and looked through the old records there, but do you know no records were kept back then, not to speak of? Only on real-estate taxes and sales. And there are records of burials in cemeteries, but not of ours because it's a private one. I mean, it's down on the map, but the people buried there are not recorded individually."

"There's one person who might have some information," Martha said. "Mason has a cousin still living. Madeline Northrop. She's about his age, and didn't come to the funeral. I don't think she leaves her house anymore. Do you remember Madeline Northrop? She lives in the old Northrop place over in the east side of town. I don't remember the address anymore. I used to drive Mason over to see her once in a while. And there's somebody else who might remember. The old man in the shack next door. He lived there a long time." Martha motioned westward, toward the trees, in the direction of the lake. "I don't know how old he is, but I know he's been there since I've been here, and once I talked to him when I was picking wild blackberries in the patch down the road, and he said he was born here."

Jill rinsed her glass and put it into the dishwasher. "I'll be back later," she said.

"Jill." Martha motioned as if to stop her, but Jill was gone, the door closing on Martha's words. "I don't know if she should go there alone. He's strange. He might be the kind of guy to meet her with a shotgun."

The wood was old and rotten, the supports too far apart for a bannister this far off the ground floor. Roger measured the length of the bannister from the wall of the upper floor back to the landing. The lower bannister, which protected the outer edge of the stairway, seemed solid enough.

He stepped back, looking down the long, dark hall. The blind was drawn on the window at the end. The whole house, since he had left the kitchen and the cheerful living room in the newer wing, had a silent darkness that did not appeal to him at all. He couldn't imagine growing up in a place like this.

He stood with his hands hooked into his back pockets and eyed the broken bannister. Parts of it had been left hanging over the edge. He had ripped them off and put them into the small pile of broken supports that someone, probably a policeman, had laid back against the wall.

He had been hesitant to ask Fawn about her niece, not wanting to bring up something so painful. But he had asked others, and probably knew as much as Fawn did. The girl had been up here, where there was no electricity no lights of any kind, at one o'clock in the morning. Why?

And she had fallen through this bannister to her death below.

It didn't wash.

She wouldn't have been up here alone and just fallen unless she'd had a seizure or something of that nature.

He looked down the hall again, and then walked as silently as he could on the uncarpeted floor. Most of the doors stood open, but one, the first door on his left, was closed.

He opened it.

It was a large room, and in the shadows he saw what looked like an old wooden toy box. There were a few more pieces of furniture: a rocking chair, a child's table with a broken leg, part of one small chair, some empty bookcases, and a small desk.

He stood in the middle of the room, looking around.

There was a feeling here he couldn't identify, but it almost seemed that the room were still filled with the life it held many years ago. It was a playroom, yet it had not been a happy place.

This was the first time Roger had ever given credence to the word *haunted.*

He started to leave the shadowed, silent room, then paused. Walking gingerly, he crossed the room to the toy box.

In the bottom a few old items were piled, as if they were litter left by someone who had removed the better toys. He saw a broken jack-in-the-box whose clown dangled permanently out of it and a tiny ladder with a broken rung. There was one small doll, no longer than seven inches, that once had had hair. It looked as though the hair had been brutally yanked from its head.

In the corner, almost buried beneath odds and ends, old things, was something made of iron. It had a round, rusted knob and looked familiar and very out of place. He picked it out of the litter.

It was a small ball-peen hammer.

He turned the hammer in his hand, looking carefully at it, wishing he had better light. The peen was oddly darker than the rest, as if it had been coated at one time in a dark substance. It had now rusted to a deep brown, but there seemed to be something moist and fresh within the crusts of the rust.

He laid it back into the toy box, placing it gingerly on top of the jack-in-the-box.

What was a hammer doing in a child's toy box?

Chapter Seventeen

The old man's name was Charlie Adamson, Old Charlie to the people in the neighborhood. Jill had seen him twice, once years ago, once when she'd been with her great-granddad. She had gotten the impression then that Old Charlie was very grouchy. He had hardly spoken to Granddad. And he had stared at her until she'd pulled away and hid on the other side of her great-grandfather to get away from Old Charlie's piercing eyes.

Later, when she was about twelve years old, she had climbed the fence of her great-grandfather's property, following a squirrel that kept running a few yards and then looking back at her as if wanting her to pursue it. And she had inadvertently found herself face to face with Old Charlie, realizing too late she was on his land.

He had said a strange thing.

"You still here?"

She stared at him a long moment, then turned and ran. Oddly, his question had not seemed cross, only pointless, because she had never been there before.

Jill drove her small car into the almost trackless little road onto Old Charlie's land, and followed it as it wound through virgin forest. The timber here looked as if it had never even been pruned by man. The trees were as old and large as those out at the Village.

The road ended in a small clearing. In the open space was a cabin built of logs, the kind of cabin the Village would have paid a lot of money to acquire. It was probably at least as old as the mansion.

Behind it was a vegetable garden, and Jill saw a bent old man working there, pulling up the young, new weeds that were growing between his neat rows of vegetables.

An old, fat dog came only as far as the corner of the log cabin and puffed at her. But two younger dogs raced right up to her car, barking at it, circling around it, and sniffing at the wheels, their tails wagging madly. It was obvious none of these dogs had ever been mistreated, and Jill's remaining fear of Old Charlie lessened considerably.

There were cats about also, as fat as the dogs, stretching themselves, coming toward her from somewhere behind the cabin.

The old man came next, picking up a hoe from the ground as if for protection. Jill got out of the car but left the door open, her hand on it.

She felt more at ease when she saw that Old Charlie was using the hoe as a stick on which to lean.

"Mister Charlie," she said. Then, wondering if she should have used his last name, said, "Mr. Adamson, I'm Jill Worton."

She started to add that she was Mason Evans's great-granddaughter when he said, "Well, I see you're still alive."

Whatever she had been going to say was lost in surprise. It completely left her mind. She had run through several different approaches as she'd driven in from the road, and now they were gone.

"Your sister, though," Old Charlie said, "she wasn't so lucky."

Jill said nothing. She felt more confused than she ever had.

Old Charlie continued. "Evans, he had nothing to do

with that. He was already dead himself."

Jill wished she hadn't come. He hadn't drawn any closer. He had stopped at the hood of the car and was leaning on his hoe. The dogs milled around him, their tails still wagging, smiles on their faces. Jill felt something touch her leg and she jumped and looked down.

"Only one of the cats," Old Charlie said. "They won't hurt you."

It occurred to her the old man's voice was kind. Just as it had been that day he had found her on his land following a squirrel. And she thought now, for the first time, that the squirrel had been his pet. Had this old man lived here all these years with no companions but the animals? She didn't know if he'd ever had a wife or children of his own.

"Mr. Charlie," Jill said, "I've come to ask you a question, if you don't mind."

"Don't mind at all. Fire away."

"We have found that Granddad – my mother's grandfather, we girls always called him Granddad too because it was so much easier to say – we have found, since his death, that he might have had twin sisters. We knew about Victoria. She died at age eleven. But there might have been another sister. We wondered if you might know – "

"Millicent," he said, interrupting her, leaning more heavily on his hoe.

Jill felt her heart beat heavily a few times before it became unnoticeable again. "You knew her?" she cried out impulsively.

"Well, not me. I wasn't borned then, you understand. Your grandpa was a few years older than me. Nine or ten. The girls, both of them, were already dead before I was borned. They died about the time my older brother came along, I reckon. I arrived in nineteen hundred and five, right smack dab in the summertime. In fact, my brother was borned about the time their mother died. Mason's mother."

He moved over and leaned against the car. He seemed almost nothing but skin and bones inside the loose, hanging overalls so many older country men wore. It looked to Jill as if he fed all the food to his animals.

"But I know the story. My own mother warned me many a time. Stay away from Mason Evans."

Jill frowned. Stay away from Mason Evans? As if there were something wrong with him? Her well-educated, intelligent, gentle great-grandfather?

"I don't understand," Jill said, half on the defensive.

"No, I don't expect you do. It was the girls, you see, and the story was hushed up so very few people ever knew about it. I expect I'm the only one left who does know. You can bet your life, missy, that it's not recorded anywhere."

One of the cats leaped up onto the seat of Jill's car, and with trembling hands she lifted it out and then shut the car door. She almost wished she hadn't come. Old Charlie sounded as if he knew some horrible secret about the Evans family, and she wasn't sure she wanted to hear it.

"The first girl, Victoria," Old Charlie said, "she died in what they said was a fall, you know. First of all, she fell from the top of them eighty-foot stairs when she was only three years old, and was crippled from then on. My own mother saw her many a time, always on crutches."

Jill was shaking her head. Not eighty feet. That's wrong. But she didn't stop him.

"My mother herself saw them stairs in that old mansion, as it's called. She said it was like someone tried to build stairsteps to heaven, only I guess they built them to hell instead."

Jill said in a small, defensive voice, "Not eighty feet. They're not but sixty, or less. Fifty, maybe."

Old Charlie seemed not to hear her. "She used to go

over there to do washing and ironing. The Evanses, they had money when they came here from the east. Pennsylvania oil people, it was said they was. Anyway, they could afford a woman to work, and my mother did. And that's how she knew."

Charlie spit brown, thick tobacco juice onto the ground. He then shifted into one cheek the wad he'd kept hidden somewhere while he'd talked.

"So, the little crippled girl died from another fall, even though the stairway had long been blocked off. My ma said there was a gate built there, the fanciest gate she ever seen, and it was locked. But somehow the girl got upstairs, and she fell. And this time it was worse than just being crippled up." He paused and looked at Jill, and she remembered how piercing his eyes had been. "I hear your little sister fell from up there too."

Jill only stared at him, unable to answer. A terrible pattern was beginning to form, but she didn't understand it. It was like the complexity of DNA, confusing to a high-school student. Yet she had a feeling the old man was not wrong, that nothing he was telling her was wrong.

"But I reckon you asked about Millicent, eh? My ma said she was pretty. The prettiest thing you ever saw. And as sweet as she could be. Pretty and sweet. She looked like her mother. They didn't look much alike at all, the two girls, even though they were twins. My ma said it's that way some of the time. Twins can be born just alike or as different as if they came from two different women. And that was the way with Victoria and Millicent.

"There was times when the girls didn't get along real well. I reckon that's normal. The Victoria girl, seems she was always crying. The girls would be playing somewhere, and then Victoria, she'd be bawling. Millicent would try to comfort her, it seems, but Victoria cried a lot. Ma figured it was because she was a cripple."

Victoria a cripple? Jill thought of the Pink Room, of

everything she had ever heard from Granddad about Victoria. There were no crutches preserved in the Pink Room, nothing to suggest that what Old Charlie was saying was true. And yet . . . Jill found she wasn't doubting him.

"But the surprise, the big surprise," Old Charlie said, "was not the death of Victoria. Ma said she probably got sick and tired of not feeling good and went back up them stairs deliberately and jumped from that eighty-foot landing and killed herself."

"Not eighty feet," Jill corrected again, "Fifty." But her voice was thin and small, and she knew Old Charlie didn't hear. She wasn't sure of the height of the stairs, she realized. All her life it had seemed impossibly high and scary to that dark third-floor landing. She wouldn't correct or interrupt him again, even though he seemed not to hear.

Old Charlie was locked into a past he never knew, a story he must have heard hundreds of times.

"But two months later, after Victoria died, Millicent died. And she was killed. Murdered. Hammered to death."

His sharp eyes held Jill's and he was silent, as if waiting for her to adjust to knowing the truth about a great-aunt she hadn't even known existed until recently.

"That pretty girl, her brain hammered in. She was out in the shed in the back yard — that old shed, probably still there — playing with Mason. Just her and Mason out there. The door shut. It couldn't have been done by anyone but the little boy, Mason."

Jill stared into those hard, bright eyes. Was he calling her granddad a murderer?

"Their mother reached them first. But right after that, my ma, who was on the back porch doing a washing, said she saw Mrs. Evans just standing there, staring into that shed, and she knowed something was wrong. So she went running. And there was pretty Millicent, dead, and the bloody hammer was there. And the little boy. So you see," he added more gently, "it had to have been done by Mason. There was nobody else in the shed with Millicent."

"I don't believe this," Jill said. "Mason—Granddad—was only four years old."

Old Charlie nodded, and then nodded again. "Yep. That was why nothing was ever done. The story was just hushed up, that's all. Then everything changed around there. The mother, she got sick. She was never well again, and she died in the summer. My brother was born then, so my ma stopped working for the Evanses. But she always told me and my brother, stay away from Mason."

Jill found she was shaking her head, over and over. She opened the door to her car and picked another cat out as it jumped in ahead of her. She stroked its head automatically before putting it down. She was trembling hard, all over. It wasn't exactly from anger, more from a terrible sense of unfairness. All these years there were people living next door who thought such a terrible thing about her great-grandfather? She couldn't believe it. She didn't believe it. And yet as she looked into Old Charlie's eyes, she saw he believed it.

"He's dead now," Old Charlie said. "I reckon he never did do no more harm. Me, I was never around him. Except just to see him at the store and places. When I went to school, first started, he was already passed on to the next school, and then he went away to higher learning and I didn't. I stayed right here, where I was borned. Had a couple of younger brothers and a sister, and they moved on. But I stayed. My oldest brother, he died from the flu when he was only fifteen. Me, I was never sick in my life." He leaned into the car as she started it. "I'm glad to see you got growed up."

Now she understood what he had meant that day when he had asked, "You still here?" But she couldn't answer him.

As she drove out the long, winding lane to the street, the trembling ceased somewhat and was replaced by fury. What nerve, to tell her that Granddad was a murderer. To tell her he, at age four, had hammered his pretty sister Millicent to death.

At the street she stopped, even though no car was in sight in either direction. She sat still, staring into the yard of the house across the road.

And yet . . . Millicent had been hidden all these years. Even her doll had been hidden, in a trunk made into a coffin. And at the end of Granddad's life he had ordered Martha to have the trunk destroyed, unopened.

Something was definitely not right.

But she would have to go home and tell Martha and Aunt Fawn that she had learned nothing from Old Charlie. Never, never could she tell anyone that Granddad was thought to have killed Millicent.

Still one other person might know something that would refute what Old Charlie had said. What was her name? The elderly distant relative Martha had told her about . . .

Jill checked the notes she had made and found the name. She pulled out into the street and headed toward town.

Fifteen minutes later Jill sat in her car alongside a telephone box in the shopping center, the receiver in her hand, the feminine voice still echoing in her mind even though the lady at the other end of the line had hung up.

I'm sorry, didn't you know? Madeline Northrop died two years ago.

Jill replaced the receiver and rolled up the car window. The air was getting cold, the sun sinking down behind the trees to the west. She sat gripping the steering wheel. The only person who could have said "Mason a killer? How ridiculous!" was herself dead.

And Jill was left with only Old Charlie's version of what had happened in the Evans family.

Mason Evans, at age four, had bludgeoned his sister Millicent to death.

But that didn't explain why Millicent was then wiped out of the family records as if she had never existed.

Chapter Eighteen

Andy stood on the second-floor landing, looking up. The gate that closed off the upper stairs was unlocked, and someone was on the third floor. In the driveway as he came in from school he had seen a pickup truck with a sign on the door saying HAMILTON CABINETS. Now he knew why. Some guy was going to rebuild the broken bannister.

Andy looked around. Susan and Kara had gone on to the room they shared, and Martha and Mom were still down in the kitchen, he guessed. They were probably cooking supper by now.

Just to make sure, he leaned out over the bannister and took a good look below. The foyer was empty. He looked up, then down the hallway. All clear.

He began to climb, slowly. A strange thing happened when he passed through the forbidden gate. The hair on the back of his neck rose. He could feel the tingle. It caused him to turn his head and look behind him, but no one was there, no one was watching. Only the faces in the old pictures on the wall eyed him critically, the men and women from another century.

He climbed more quickly, keeping close to the wall.

When he came out onto the third-floor landing he put his hands into his pockets and stood there, looking around. A thin, fine whistle began pushing at his lips.

It was pretty dark up here, he saw, and the hall was narrower than downstairs and seemed to go off into long tunnels. There was a guy up here somewhere, because he could hear hollow footsteps, as if the floor he walked on were built over a deep cavern.

Andy tested his own footsteps, and they sounded hollow too.

He went closer to the place where Erin had fallen through and peered over.

The drop seemed a long way. The furniture in the foyer below looked oddly small, like furniture in a dollhouse. There was an eeriness about it, about being up here so close to the broken bannister. The hair on the back of his neck rose again. The hair on his arms tingled too, and he took a firm grip on the small penknife in his right pocket, the rock in his left.

"Hi there."

The voice was almost at his shoulder. Andy jumped and whirled. The man was standing at the mouth of the shadowed tunnel on Andy's right, the hallway that seemed to stretch to infinity.

"Hi."

He was pleasant-looking, his eyes friendly, his smile showing white teeth. He didn't look at all critical, and when he spoke again, he didn't sound critical.

"Don't you think you're standing a little close to that empty space?"

Andy backed up, getting away from the last place Erin had ever stood. When he thought of that, he wanted to run. He almost wished he hadn't come up there at all.

"You going to fix it?" Andy asked.

"Yes, I am. We'll build a new balustrade down at the shop and just bring it up here and stick it in, but when we're finished it'll be solid as a rock." He touched a post at the corner. "The balusters will be closer together. No one else will ever fall from here."

"She was my cousin," Andy said.

"Are you Fawn's son?"

"Yessir."

The man put out his hand. "My name's Roger."

Andy put his hand into Roger's. "Mine's Andy."

They grinned at each other, and Andy was aware of the warm feel of the man's hand, the strength of it, the gentle way it surrounded his. For the first time in his life he had an oddly warm thought: I wish he was my dad.

He had hardly ever thought about a dad. He had never known his, had never wanted to know him. He knew his mom and he and Susan had been deserted when Susan was just a baby, and he considered the guy who hadn't wanted them to be just a stranger. Not needed. Nor had he ever seen any other guy he had wanted for a dad. His mom had dated a man for several months, and both he and Susan had been afraid she might marry him. He had black greasy hair, and when Andy and Susan were alone with Freddy he was cross and short-tempered. When Mom had gotten tired of him and he'd faded away, they'd been glad to see him go.

But this guy, this Roger, was something else.

Andy listened carefully as Roger told him what was wrong with the construction of the old bannister, or balustrade, as he called it.

"The balusters are too thin and too far apart. It's all too insubstantial. And now the wood is getting old and fragile. The whole bannister probably should be replaced, although I guess it's considered an antique. I don't know much about antiques."

"Neither do I," Andy admitted. "My Aunt Laura, she's got a whole village full of antiques. We went out there one day. It's really neat. Do you know they lived out there? Aunt Laura and Erin and Jill and Kara? Right on the lake, right there in the Village."

"Oh yeah?"

Andy remembered, and flinched. "Erin, though. She won't get to go back. And maybe Aunt Laura won't either."

Roger put a hand on Andy's shoulder, and Andy felt its warmth and leaned into it as much as he dared.

"Sometimes things change," Roger said. "We can't stop the changes; we just have to do the best we can."

Andy nodded.

"Do you use the old toy room very often?"

"What old toy room?"

Roger looked at him.

Andy said, "We're not supposed to come up here by ourselves. I heard you up here, so I thought it'd be all right. Where is this toy room? I'd like to see it. That's where Victoria used to play, until she died, I guess."

"Right there, first door."

Andy started to go into the room. He stood on the threshold and saw a wooden box, a bit scarred, with figures painted on it, faded now. Ducks, birds, plump and roundfaced children. He saw an old rocking horse that leaned to one side, one rocker broken.

"Maybe you'd better not," Roger said. "I didn't know it was off limits. I might be getting you in trouble."

"It's okay if I'm with a grownup," Andy said, not at all sure he spoke the truth. But the playroom drew him, suggesting hidden treasures in the old toy box.

Then, as if she had materialized from the shadows along the long hall, a voice was shouting in his ear.

"What on earth are you doing up here?"

It was Martha. She was still on the stairs, coming up toward them, not down the hallway as it had sounded. She looked more dangerous than Andy had ever seen her. With a few more steps upward and several fast ones along the hall, she was gripping his arm.

She shook him. "Don't you know better than to come

up here? After what happened to your cousin, you still came on up? You shouldn't be bothering this man. And what're you doing so close to those broken bannisters?"

"It's my fault, I'm afraid," Roger said. "He probably wouldn't have come up if I hadn't been here. And I'm sure he won't ever come up again without an adult, even when the new bannister is in."

Andy glanced up at Roger with gratitude. Then he saw that Martha was pale and trembling, and he was sorry—well, almost sorry—for what he had done.

"I was careful, Martha," he said. "I won't do it again. I just wanted to see—"

"Yes, well, you come on down now. You be careful, hear?"

"Yes, ma'am."

Roger rewound a tape measure and put it into his back pocket. "I'm finished now. We'll go down together."

Martha stopped on the second-floor landing and watched the pair go down the stairs and out of sight. Andy was chattering like a chipmunk as they descended together, and Martha thought it was a pleasing sight, the man and the boy, especially with the boy needing the man the way she figured most boys needed a dad.

She shrugged, turned away, and went down the hall toward the girls' room. There were rooms aplenty on this second floor. Kara could have had a room of her own, but those girls wailed like two motherless monkeys when she suggested separate ones.

Martha understood. She had shared a room with her sister once, and had missed Rita horribly when she'd married and moved away.

The girls' voices came to her faintly through the door. Chatter, chatter. Just like Andy talking to Roger Hamilton. Martha knocked lightly.

"Better get ready for dinner, girls," she called through solid oak.

"Okay," one of them said. It was impossible to tell which with the thickness of the wood between them.

Martha started back downstairs, but on the landing she paused and looked up. The gate was unlocked. She had come down last, and she was the culprit. She went up to it and started to close the padlock, then paused and looked up.

Pulling the gate closed behind her, still unlocked, she began to climb.

In the quiet and dim world of the third floor was a feeling she didn't like, an atmosphere not quite definable. The bannister gaped open like broken teeth in a mouth widened in a silent scream, and the edge of the floor seemed fragile and dangerous, as if it might collapse under a person's weight.

She gave it wide berth and, staying close to the wall, went on down the hall to the playroom.

She pushed the door open and went in, her eyes instantly finding the toy box and the place at the end where the doll had been sitting the last time she'd been in the playroom. Where Erin had placed it, she figured, for reasons of her own.

Martha blinked and stared. Even in the dim light of the room, she could see that the doll was not there.

She began searching through the room, even opening the drawers of the old chest that stood against the wall and looking into the jumbled mess in the old toy box. She saw a small, odd-looking hammer lying on top of a few broken toys. It had one rounded end, and one regular flat striking end. For a moment it seemed she had never seen one like it, and then she remembered. There had been one out in the old shed. Lying on the ground beside the trunk.

She had stood looking around the shed that day, the

first day in her life she had ever entered it. Mason had given her the key. "Go," he'd said in his weakening voice, holding out to her his knotted hand. "Take this and open the shed, Martha."

She'd put out her hand and he'd dropped a key into it. The key was old, as most of the mansion keys were, long and heavy, with a loop at one end and the clawlike opener at the other. It had felt oddly cold in her hand, even after being held in Mason's.

"Open the shed," Mason said, his face pale even against the white pillow, his skin loose and folding, line upon line. He had lost so much flesh these past six months, the plumpness gone now, death near. "Open the shed. In the center you'll find a small trunk. It's locked. Don't open it. Take it out of the shed and put it with the trash, and be sure the trash man picks it up. I want it destroyed."

"Destroyed?" A trunk from the shed that hadn't been opened in all the years she had worked for Mason?

"Yes!" For just that one word his voice strengthened. Then she'd seen his chin quiver. "I can trust only you, Martha. You must listen to me. Put the trunk with the trash and see to it it's destroyed."

Martha had nodded. "Of course, Mason."

She stayed by his bedside. Death is imminent, his doctor had said, it could happen at any moment. She hadn't wanted to leave him. But even though his eyes were closed now, he had known.

"Go," he had said. "Do it now. Come back and let me know."

"Yes."

She had left the room and gone downstairs and out into the back yard. The shed was half hidden beneath a wild and unfettered growth of vines, behind shrubs and trees that had grown up around it. Mason never allowed the gardeners into that part of the yard. Martha remembered his saying a few years ago when new gardeners had been hired, after their faithful old worker had died, "Leave that part of the yard alone, men. That's my jungle. I like it that way." He laughed then, his belly jiggling. He always reminded Martha of the Saint Nick in the Christmas poem, except, of course, he was of medium height. She always loved him as if he were her own father, instead of a distant cousin. And he knew she would carry out his wishes.

She made her way, on that cold, cloudy day, into the jungle where the shed was slowly becoming a part of the vegetation. The key was difficult to insert, and it took several minutes, but finally there was a click and the door opened.

Martha looked into a world of blackness. As she blinked at it, a room perhaps sixteen feet by sixteen, she began to see that it was nearly empty. It was not filled, as she had always suspected, with a bunch of junk that just came up short of being antique.

She could see, though, that she was going to need a light. In no way was she going to enter a shed that had been closed for at least thirty years that she knew of, in which all kinds of strange creatures might have taken up residence, without a light to guide her.

She went back to the house, got a flashlight from the kitchen drawer, and returned to the shed.

As she entered that building with the dirt floor, she shined the light around. On the walls hung such things as old broken harnesses and neck yokes with the stuffing falling out. From one hook a chain, thick and rusty, was suspended. An old gray chest, the boards falling off the ends, stood back in one corner.

But in the middle of the floor, as Mason had said, was a trunk. Martha shined the light over it. The trunk was a masterpiece, it seemed to her, as old as any at the Village, with a convex lid on which were carved cupids and vines and birds and flowers, the colors still there, though faded now. It was a small trunk, as trunks went in those long-ago days, perhaps forty inches long by twenty high.

The ground in the center of the shed was bare. If even a mouse had walked here in a half-dozen decades, it didn't show.

Except for one thing.

Martha outlined it with the beam of the flashlight. A kind of hammer, it was, with one round knob and a flat striking surface. She didn't remember ever seeing one like it before.

After sweeping the light around the rest of the shed and seeing nothing the vines growing through the cracks in the walls couldn't have, she put the light into her pocket, the beam angling upward past her face, and bent to pick up the trunk.

She took hold of the leather handles at each end of it and lifted. It came up easily from the floor, almost upsetting her. For some reason, she had expected it to be heavy, but it felt as if it might be empty, or at least lightly loaded.

With some difficulty she carried it out of the shed and back toward the garbage cans by the gate at the service road. It seemed to grow heavier with each step she took, and twice she had to put it down and rest. She turned off the flashlight, and stuffed it back into her apron pocket.

When she reached the garbage pickup area she took one last look at the trunk. And understood why Mason had said he could trust only her. If Laura saw this trunk, she'd confiscate it, saying—Martha could almost hear her—"Granddad must not be thinking clearly, Martha. You know as well as I do that in his right mind he would never throw away a trunk like this."

Martha turned to leave, then turned back once again, looking at the trunk. Impulsively, she lifted it again and shook it, listening for something within to make a sound.

Any sound.

And for a moment it seemed she did hear something almost like a gasp. She stood with the trunk against her chest and frowned into the trees, her ear against the rounded top. And then she put the trunk down and snorted at her own foolishness.

She went back into the house, left the flashlight in the kitchen drawer, and climbed the stairs to Mason's room.

He was asleep, lying just as she had left him.

She had sat beside him for perhaps ten minutes when she realized he was not asleep. He was dead.

She held his hand and found it cold.

For another hour she stayed with him, weeping, holding his hand, her head lying on his arm. He was the father she had loved, the only father she had ever known. Gone long ago was her own father, dead before she was seven years old. And now she was losing her father all over again.

For one hour she stayed with him, and then she went downstairs to the telephone to call Laura and the doctor.

It was as if the moving of the trunk had been all that Mason had waited for. His last duty on earth.

Martha didn't understand that, but she had accepted it.

Now she stood looking into the old toy box at the hammer she had seen in the shed, and for a few minutes she forgot the odd disappearance of the doll, of Millicent.

Who had brought the hammer up here and put it into the toy box?

And where was the doll?

"Good Lord, what in thunder is going on around here?" Martha muttered under her breath as she looked around the room as if the doll would materialize right under her nose. As if the hammer would somehow leave the toy box and go back to the shed floor.

She looked again at the end of the box, but the doll still

was not there. She looked again in the toy box, and the hammer hadn't moved.

Who was doing these things?

Couldn't anybody be trusted anymore?

It had to be the kids. That boy, Andy, he had probably been snooping around the shed . . . and the girls, especially Susan, she had probably looked for the doll. . . .

But Martha was getting very fond of Andy and Susan. Especially Andy. She didn't spend much time with Susan. Susan and Kara were always together. But Andy was alone much of the time, wandering around, looking past her arm when she cooked, going in and out the back door. Of course he was curious. Young and curious. She'd ask him about the hammer.

But first she had to attend to the doll.

The worst thing, she thought as she passed the broken bannister, was the danger. She didn't care if Andy played in the shed. What could hurt him there? But she didn't want him coming up to the third floor. They had already lost one child.

She was careful to close the padlock on the gate after she went through. She pushed until it clicked, and then tested it with her hands. Of course, she had to admit, if the children wanted to get over the barrier, they only had to climb. And that is what they must have been doing. Not only the little girls, but Andy . . . and Erin too.

Feeling half sick with dread, Martha went down the hall toward the girls' room. Just as she reached the door, it opened, and both girls squealed in surprise as they clutched each other and faced her in the doorway.

Martha marched past them into the room and stood with her hands on her hips, looking around. Dolls, plenty of them, sat or lay or sprawled here and there. Most of them had belonged to Fawn and Laura when they'd been kids, and they had all been in their old bedrooms until recently. But there was no Millicent in sight.

"All right, girls, what did you do with her? Don't you have enough play-pretties without bothering the antique doll?"

They stared at her. Two sets of wide, blue eyes, as innocent as the dawn on a June day.

"Well?" she demanded.

Kara said, "Well, what?"

If this wasn't innocence, it was such good acting that Martha found herself doubting her suspicions. She didn't know about Susan, but she would swear on a stack of Bibles that Kara wouldn't lie.

"I'm looking for the doll," Martha said more gently. "Erin took it upstairs, I reckon. It's the only reason I know she went up there in the first place. She left it in the old playroom, where your great-granddad and Victoria used to play. But now it's gone. Did either of you girls take it?"

They shook their heads in unison, their wide eyes watching her.

Susan said, "I thought it was in Granddad's room."

Her voice was small and timid, and reminded Martha of Fawn's when Fawn was this age. Gentle little Fawn, so easily hurt, so sensitive, and so precious to her.

Martha pulled both children to her and hugged them, then gave them gentle pushes. "Go on, wash up and go downstairs."

She left them in the hallway. As they went into the bathroom, Martha went downstairs. But by the time she had reached the kitchen she had decided to put off talking to Andy. He wasn't in the kitchen, and through the windows she saw Fawn, Roger, and Andy all standing near Roger's truck. Roger was getting ready to leave.

Martha had a sudden urge to leave too. While the others ate dinner, she decided, she would put on her hat and go to the hospital to see Laura.

She began busying herself now, getting the kitchen

table set, and taking the food out of the oven and the refrigerator. She looked at the clock. She would have to hurry to get to the hospital for the six-o'clock visit.

Laura wouldn't know she was there, Martha realized. But she had to talk to someone about all the things that were bothering her, and who better to talk to than Laura? Dear, precious Laura, who couldn't hear anything said to her.

Chapter Nineteen

Martha adjusted her hat as she rose from the chair in the waiting room at the hospital. She wore the hat only to church or to funerals. Only on the most solemn occasions. It gave her a kind of comfort, a feeling of doing something right.

"You can go in now," the man behind the desk said, smiling at her. She was the only one in the waiting room. Dinnertime, he had explained when she had come in. Most people are eating now. They need this time of relaxation after spending all day here waiting to see a loved one.

She felt a little guilty. She had left the final preparations for dinner in the hands of Fawn and Jill. Because of the little ones, dinner was eaten at five-thirty, and Martha had told them she wouldn't be there. She had to go out. Then, when she had come out with her hat on, Jill had asked, "Are you going to church?"

"No, I thought I'd go up and sit with Laura for a while."

Jill had returned from her trip very quiet. "Well, did you find out anything?" Martha had asked as she carefully sliced the angel food cake for the family's dessert.

"No," Jill had replied, and she'd gone off to another part of the house, returning to the kitchen just a couple of minutes before Martha had taken off her apron to leave.

As Martha sat in the waiting room, she thought of Jill. She had been too quiet. Martha had the feeling that she was hiding something.

She walked hesitantly into the large Intensive Care Unit, utterly lost. Noises came at her from every side, it seemed, beeps and wheezes and buzzes, while white-clothed men and women were everywhere, none of them seeming to be doing anything but looking at wavy lines on small computerlike monitors.

"Can I help you?" one of the nurses asked.

"Please. I'm looking for Laura Worton."

Smiling, the nurse pointed out a cubicle with a half closed curtain, the foot of a hospital bed visible. In a room filled with such sick people, this woman could smile? Martha didn't think she would be able to.

She had visited Laura twice before, with Fawn, during school hours, but she couldn't have found the right cubicle again on her own if her life depended on it.

She had been aware of many tubes and monitors and a sleeping Laura then, and she saw that nothing had changed. Laura was positioned on her right side, her body in a curve, a pillow at her back. She would have looked peacefully asleep if it hadn't been for all the tubes leading to all the noisemakers.

Martha stood looking down at Laura; then the tears came. With one hand holding a handkerchief to her eyes and the other clasping Laura's limp wrist, she wept, sobbed, her voice catching as she talked.

"It's all just fallen apart, Laura. It's like being on a big slide and not being able to stop. There's this hammer I found in the toy box. It was in the shed, beside the trunk, the day I opened the shed and took the trunk out. I didn't bother the hammer. I left it there.

"But then, when I went up to the third floor to get Andy down this afternoon, after he and Roger had gone, I looked in the room where Erin had put the doll the night she fell, but the doll was gone and the hammer was there. I don't know where the doll is. Susan and Kara swear they haven't seen it. I was too upset to ask anyone else. I just felt like I had to talk to someone, and you're the only one.

"I know you can't hear me, Laura. Bless you. I pray for you night and day. We need you to get well."

Martha wept harder for a few minutes. This was the only time she had given in to tears since the day she had gone back up to Mason's room to find him dead.

Then she dried her eyes, leaned down, and kissed Laura's cheek. "I reckon my ten minutes are about up, Laura sweetheart," she whispered. "Jill did the best she could with Erin's funeral. It was the most beautiful thing you ever saw. Well, I have to go. I'll hunt up that doll if it kills me. It'll be found when you wake up, I promise. And I'll keep it under lock and key in my own room."

Martha adjusted her hat again. It didn't seem to fit as well as it had when she'd bought it ten or fifteen years ago. She started to leave, then stopped and stood there, looking down at Laura. She saw a tear edge out from beneath Laura's lashes, and she touched her handkerchief to it and wiped it away.

At that moment the curtain was pushed back and a nurse looked in.

"Nurse," Martha cried in a hushed but excited voice, "Laura is weeping. Is it possible that she can hear? . . ."

"Oh no. Those tears are just reflexes."

Martha drew in a deep breath. She wanted Laura to wake up, to hear, to talk, to live again. But if she had known Laura might hear, she wouldn't have told her about the hammer and the doll, or about Erin's funeral. Not yet.

Laura felt her tears wiped away. The nurse had remained with her. She could still hear Martha's fading footsteps, but she was no longer sure if she really heard them or if she was clinging to the sound in her mind.

Erin dead. She had known something terrible had happened to Erin. And now Martha had told her enough for her to see in her mind what it was. Erin had not taken the doll upstairs as Martha, and perhaps everyone, believed. Erin would not have passed the gate just to carry a doll to the third floor. The doll, instead, had somehow caused Erin to go up.

Beautiful funeral.

Laura wept in the silence of her private hell, feeling tears down her cheeks unhindered. The nurse, too, had gone, the curtain having been pulled shut again.

Hope began like a light at the end of her dark world. If she had been able to leave her body and return over almost the span of a century to ancestors she had never known, was it possible that she might go back to the night Erin died and change what had happened? No, not that. That would never change. But could she perhaps—*please, God*—find Erin. Erin, her second child. Another miracle in her life.

Erin had always been less impulsive than Jill, less playful than Kara. Erin was . . . dependable. Even-tempered, sweet, good. Erin wouldn't have believed what she must have seen. Had the doll, Millicent, been lying or sitting on the stairs above the gate? Erin would have gone through to get it. If the doll had then moved upward, she would not have believed her own eyes. She would have persisted in following, in finding out what was happening.

Laura struggled to turn over, to move her legs, her arms, even her eyelids. And finally, almost exhausted, she willed herself to leave, to rise, to find Erin.

To die.

The light blinded her. She saw the room below, her body on the bed, and she felt that now the end of her physical life had come. The body she looked down upon seemed to belong to no one, to be an abandoned shell.

She was free.

The light faded and was replaced by sound, at first distant. Tinkling sounds, happy sounds. Voices of woods creatures . . . or perhaps children.

Laura suddenly hoped she had reached the boundaries of heaven, that Erin was one of the children and she would find her again.

Then she realized she was in a room and was looking down from a high ceiling. The room had familiar proportions, its long windows covered in dark, velvet draperies. The dining table was lighted by candles, and their light flickered on the faces of two adults and three children. She recognized the faces with a sense of failure.

Victoria, older than when Laura had last seen her, smiled into the light. Her soft, golden hair was pulled back and held with a pink ribbon. On the plate in front of her was a piece of partly eaten cake, a small, pink candle lying to one side of the plate on the cream lace tablecloth. The wick had been burned and was now black.

At her side sat Millicent, taller in her chair, her dark hair catching the light of the candle and returning it in a hundred gleams of dark gold and firey red. On her plate were only crumbs. The burned candle was carefully set beside her used fork and knife, on the edge of her plate.

At the ends of the table sat the adults, the parents, and on a higher chair across from the twins sat a round-faced little boy, his eyes gleaming with excitement. Granddad, Laura thought with warmth. He was perhaps four years old now. Another thought, cold and depressing, entered Laura's mind. This must be Victoria's—and Millicent's—eleventh birthday. In two more days Victoria would die.

"And now, for the surprise," their mother said, rising from the table and taking from a servant a long box. "This one is for Millicent."

Millicent took the box and pushed away from the table. "Oh, Mama. What is it?"

"A surprise, isn't it Papa?" her mother said. The candlelight softened the woman's lovely face, and Laura saw how much she resembled Millicent in coloring and features.

Victoria cried eagerly, "Open it. Oh, open it, Milly. Whatever it is must be *huge.*"

The man who sat at the end of the table said, with a playful grin, "It must be an umbrella."

"Oh, Papa," Millicent chided, the curving smile never leaving her lips, her hands tearing at the satin bow on the box. "We have umbrellas everywhere."

"A parasol, then," he teased. "With tassels."

Millicent shrugged one shoulder. "I would like that."

Victoria said, "But you have a parasol with tassels; it must be something else."

"Aw, Victoria," Millicent said, "must you always be so serious?" She pulled the paper away from the box, lifted the lid, and then gasped softly.

Lying on blue tissue paper was a doll, wearing a cream lace dress and black shoes and stockings. One arm was turned so it lay across her middle, and a bracelet gleamed on the wrist.

"A French walker doll!" Millicent cried, lifting the tall doll from the box. "I never dreamed! Just what I wanted. Oh, Mama, Papa!"

She hurried around the end of the table to them, the doll in her arms, and kissed their cheeks. The candlelight danced on the pleased and smiling faces of her parents.

Millicent set her doll on the floor, holding her by the arms, moving her forward. The knees bent, the feet took obedient steps. Millicent's face glowed with pleasure as she looked up at Victoria, who sat smiling in silence in her chair.

"She can walk, Victoria, she can actually walk! She has

jointed knees and elbows, even jointed wrists. Look, Victoria."

"Look at the bracelet," the mother said.

Millicent lifted the doll's wrist and read the name aloud. "Millicent? But what does that mean? That's my name. I wouldn't name her that."

The mother was smiling, and she motioned to the servant who stood back in the shadows. The woman moved forward, bringing another long box, this one done with a pink satin bow.

"And now," the father said, "it's Victoria's turn."

"Me?"

Millicent stood with her doll and watched, the smile on her face not reaching her eyes.

Victoria's hands trembled as she untied the bow, removed the wrapping paper, and lifted the lid. Another doll, exactly like the first, but dressed in pink lace, with white shoes and stockings.

The smile left Millicent's face. She stared at the second doll as Victoria lifted it from the box.

For a time Victoria was speechless, gazing at the lovely doll in awe, her lips parted.

"But," Millicent cried, "it's exactly like mine!"

"No," their mother said. "It's dressed differently, and look at its bracelet."

"Victoria," the blond Victoria read. "It says Victoria. That's so we'll be able to tell them apart?"

"Yes," Papa said. "They're twins, don't you see? Just as you two are twins."

"I love her," Victoria said softly. "I just love her."

Millicent stood in silence, her doll on the floor at her side, standing like another child in the flickering shadows of the room.

The light dimmed and changed, and Laura felt the slow movement of time. The candlelight of the small birthday party was gradually replaced by a different kind of light, a grayness, winter daylight penetrating lace panels at a window.

Laura was now in a distantly familiar room. She saw first a tall double bed, its fat feather mattress covered by linens and a crocheted spread. This was the pink room, Victoria's room. The voices in it weren't happy. As the light became penetrable to Laura's eyes, figures emerged. Victoria, on the floor, sitting, crutches at her side, the doll in her arms.

"But how can you handle a French walker doll?" Millicent was asking petulantly. "You can't even walk yourself without your two crutches. Why don't you let me have the doll?"

"No, she's mine. Papa had her made for me."

"Then let me have her dress. I like the pink dress. You can have this colorless dress my doll is wearing."

"No, pink is my color."

"No more so than it's mine!"

Millicent reached down and grasped the front of the doll's dress and yanked, and beneath Victoria's cry the dress ripped, so that in Laura's ears both sounds were tortured wails of distress.

"You tore it!" Victoria cried, getting to her knees, the doll in her arms, the front of its dress gaping and hanging open, the white of underwear showing through.

Millicent then began grabbing for the doll, pulling at its dress, ripping, ripping. Victoria struggled to get away, futilely trying to protect the doll. At last it fell from her grip as she tried to get to her feet. She reached up and grasped the foot of the bed, pulled herself up and then reached down for the doll. But Millicent snatched it away and ran with it, leaving her own doll standing against the wall.

Weeping, Victoria reached down for her crutches and, with them under her arms, swung her shortened and useless right leg forward as she hurried after Millicent.

"Milly! Millicent! What are you going to do with her? Bring her back, please. I'll give you the dress. I'll give you the shoes. Just bring her back, please."

The second floor echoed with her cries.

Laura saw her swinging her useless leg along, down the hall to the stairway landing, her crutches thump-thumping on the bare floor between the occasional rugs. As if she followed behind the young girl, Laura saw her. She saw her pause at the bottom of the stairs and look up.

The gate that closed off the third floor was open.

Above, looking down dangling the doll over the bannister at the very place where Victoria had been pushed through six years before, Millicent stood.

"Come and get it. I dare you!"

"I can't!" Victoria was crying again, her face turned upward toward her sister and the dangling doll. "What are you going to do with her?"

Millicent didn't answer. The doll slipped in her hand, dropped another inch into empty space. Victoria cried out and started forward.

No, don't go up there. No, Victoria.

She was destined to die. This young, sweet child. On December twenty-third, two days past her birthday. Where were the parents? Where was a servant? The house seemed empty, hollow and huge, the third-floor balcony dangerously distant. It was from there Erin, too, had fallen, Laura's Erin. If she could only keep Victoria from going there, perhaps somehow that would reverse Erin's death too, and she would wake to find that all of this was only a nightmare.

Don't Victoria. Don't go up there. Don't climb those stairs!

The light faded suddenly, and the figure on crutches became dim. Laura reached out, but found nothing.

As she drifted away she heard Victoria's voice say, "All right, Milly, you win. I'll trade dolls with you."

Chapter Twenty

Susan went slowly along the lower hall. Although she lived here now, she never walked this hall alone. Especially after the lights were on in the evening. It seemed so dark, with a light only at each end, and she was scared. But where was Kara?

"Kara?" she called, her voice timid and weak.

There was no answer. Her mother, brother, and cousin Jill were in the new-wing living room. She knew the television was on, but she couldn't hear it from here. Where was Kara? Kara was acting strange. She had hardly eaten, and she hadn't touched her angel food cake. She had slipped away when Susan wasn't noticing. Then, in the living room, no one seemed to notice she was missing.

"Kara?"

Susan began to climb the stairs. She heard her own footsteps, but she felt like someone was following her and she looked over her shoulder again and again.

The stairs seemed awfully dark. Up above, on the landing, was the light that always burned, but it seemed as far away as a star.

"Kara?"

She reached the landing and went a few paces down the hall toward the bedroom. Had Kara come up to the bathroom? No, the door was open, the room dark. Susan passed it gingerly.

She walked softly, so she wouldn't hear her own steps and think someone, perhaps a ghost, was behind her. She knew ghosts made sounds when they walked, because Andy said so. He had heard ghosts walking around on the third floor, he'd told her. In the night he could hear them.

Susan ran the last few steps to her bedroom door, and opened it to see that a low light was on. The little shaded lamp on the dresser was burning, its glow spreading like gold out onto the floor.

Kara sat huddled down in the far corner of the room, her face buried in her arms atop her knees. She was all drawn up, like a knot, just the way she slept lots of times.

"Kara?"

Susan went to her and found she was crying. Susan felt the spasms of sobs as she touched Kara, before she heard the soft gasps. Instantly Susan was on her knees at Kara's side, her heart aching for this new cousin she had found.

"I'll help, Kara. Really I will. What's wrong?"

Kara kept sobbing.

"Kara, Kara?"

Susan sat with her, feeling miserable. She looked around for something, anything, that might make Kara feel better. She saw dolls and toys piled in the corner and sitting on the bed. But none of them would help, she knew, because they had already been there when Kara began to cry.

"Kara, a show is on," Susan said, trying to make her voice cheerful, though she, too, felt like crying. "We could go down and watch TV."

Kara shook her head. In a voice so low and so jerky that Susan could hardly understand her, she said, "I w-want my mama."

Susan sat still with Kara for a few minutes, trying hard to think of something that might help. She finally said, "My mama is here, Kara. She'll help you."

Kara shook her head.

Then Susan remembered, the most beautiful thing in the world, the most precious gift anyone could have. Would Aunt Laura really mind if Susan gave Millicent to Kara? If it would make her feel better?

"I'll be back," Susan promised, and ran from the room.

All her fear of the dark, of the long hallways and empty rooms, was gone. She faced the third floor with only a little bit of fear. Hadn't Martha said the doll was up in the playroom? And Andy had told her the playroom was the first room past the landing. He had been up there and had looked at the broken bannister with Roger, who was going to make new bannisters.

But as Susan stood at the gate, she saw how dark it was on the third-floor landing. The light behind her illuminated the big gap where there was no bannister, and left blackness beyond.

The gate was locked, the padlock cold in her hands as she worked with it, trying to open it.

She turned suddenly and ran downstairs, down the hall to the new wing and into the bright living room. Jill sat curled in a chair, one hand playing idly with her hair, a magazine on her lap. She was quiet this evening too. She wasn't even looking at the television.

Andy lay on the floor, watching the show part of the time and drawing in a notebook.

Susan went to her mother and shook her arm to get her attention, to draw her gaze away from the screen of the TV.

"What, Susan?"

"Mama, can I give Millicent to Kara?"

Everyone looked at Susan. Jill stopped curling her hair around her finger.

No one answered. They only stared at Susan.

"Kara is crying," Susan explained. "If I gave Millicent to her, maybe she wouldn't miss her mama so much."

Jill uncurled herself from the big chair. "I'll go see about her. Where is she?"

"But why can't I take Millicent to her?" Susan cried, disappointment sharp as needles in her heart. "I wanted to give her the beautiful doll to make her feel better."

"I don't even know where Millicent is," Fawn said.

"Martha told Kara and me that she's upstairs. In the old playroom. She said Erin took her up there. But—" Susan suddenly slapped her hands against her mouth. She removed them to add, "But then she came and wanted to know what we had done with Millicent because she wasn't in the playroom anymore. I almost forgot."

Both Fawn and Jill were frowning at Susan. Andy was still listening, but he had started drawing again, his attention partly on the notebook.

Fawn got up. "Jill, I have an idea. I could get down the old rag doll that Laura always loved more than any other. Shall I?"

"Yes."

Susan trailed behind her mother and Jill, going down the hall and up the stairs. She heard footsteps behind her again, but this time it was Andy, she saw, several steps back.

In the hallway she waited outside the bedroom door. She heard Jill go to Kara in the bedroom. Their voices were low and murmuring, and Susan tried not to hear, to eavesdrop. Then her mother came with a funny-looking old rag doll, and Susan frowned at it as Fawn went past her. How could anyone prefer a doll like that to Millicent?

She would never understand grownups.

Andy knew where a flashlight was. He had found a drawer in the kitchen with three in it, and he had asked Martha if he could use one of them. He had kept the flashlight in his room because of the sounds he heard at night.

And because of that weird doll that always seemed to be in strange places. For several days now he hadn't seen the doll or heard about it. Since before Erin's death, he hadn't heard a word about the doll. Now, again, its trail had sort of come back to him, and he'd learned things he hadn't known before. Erin had taken the doll up to the playroom the night she had died. Martha had said so, according to Susan. And he knew Susan didn't make up stories. Then Martha had gone up to get it, he guessed, and it was gone.

Neither Jill nor his mom had said anything about putting it away again, so he guessed they hadn't. They were both in the bedroom comforting Kara, and Susan had gone in with them. Andy stood in the hall alone.

He could see through the long window at the end of the hall that it was now dark outside. Martha was still gone. He couldn't go to her and ask about the doll. He had to look for it himself.

He went into his room and got the flashlight out from under his pillow.

In the hall he stood still, wondering which way to turn. There were so many unused rooms in the house, so many places for the doll to hide.

For her to hide.

It was beginning to seem that way to him. As if she moved about in the house without help. But what would anyone say if he mentioned his fears out loud?

First, he would look in Great-granddad's old room. Granddad was the one person who had known about the doll being in the trunk. The doll might be back in his room now, either put there by someone, or . . .

He had never noticed so many dark places in the hall. Even when he turned on extra lights, shadows lingered behind the furniture along the walls and back in odd little corners. The house wasn't built with straight hallways like other places he had seen, but with twists and turns, some rooms set farther back than others, as if allowing for small sitting rooms in the hall. There was always more furniture in those places, even a settee in one and an old lamp with tassels. And Andy had once tried to turn it on and had found it useless. It wasn't even electric. Martha had told him it was gas.

He opened the door to Granddad's room and shined the light in. He saw the high bed, so high you needed a little stepladder to get into it. The dark, old spread came all the way to the floor.

Although he turned on the electric light at the door, he didn't turn off his flashlight. He circled the room cautiously, shined the light behind the heavy draperies that rested in folds on the floor, and got down on his knees and looked beneath the bed. There was enough room down there to hide an elephant, he thought as he crawled under and out the other side.

But Millicent was nowhere in the room.

He left the bedroom and the odd, strangling smell it contained and went into the next room. It was a strange place to him, but it looked like one of the other sitting rooms scattered over the mansion. He had explored one at the other end of the hall. This one was filled with furniture, the air was dusty smelling and old, and he felt if he touched the draperies they would fall apart in his hands.

He heard a sound, a faint squeak, as if a board had been stepped on.

He stood still, his heart thudding heavily behind his breastbone. It seemed the only sound in the whole world, that single squeak, somewhere near.

Then he heard faint footsteps, running. Quick, light, and then silence. Then again the squeak.

He looked up. The sound was overhead. Cold chills radiated over his body, and his chin hung down as he stared upward at the high ceiling, almost lost in darkness.

Susan and Kara were in their bedroom, and so were his mom and Jill.

There was only one . . . *thing* that could be upstairs.

Walking. Running. Without help from anyone.

"Andy!"

His mom sounded angry, as if she had been shouting at him for some time. He hurried to the door. Fawn was standing several yards down the hall, looking all around. When she saw him, she put her hands on her hips the way she always did when she was mad at him.

"What on earth are you doing in that room, Andy?"

He turned off his flashlight and pushed it down into his hip pocket. As he went past her, he said, "Never mind." What would she do if he told her? Punish him for making up crazy stories? Not let him ride the bike or watch TV or roam around the woods?

"It's bedtime, Andy, so take your bath and go to bed."

"Okay." Later, he thought. Later, he'd go upstairs and look for that old doll.

What would he do then? After he found it? An idea occurred to him, one he hadn't thought of before. He'd put the doll back in the trunk, where it belonged. In the trunk that was a coffin, especially made by someone just for the doll.

And then he thought of something else that made him weak and cold with terror. Erin had gone upstairs. She hadn't taken the doll up, he figured, but she had gone up to see about it just as he planned to do. And she had died.

Fawn grabbed Andy just before he closed the bathroom door behind him, and he found himself folded into her arms. He sunk for a moment against the security and warmth of her, breathed in the sweet smell of her cologne, her skin.

"Good night, sweetheart," she whispered.

"Good night, Mom. Is Kara okay?"

"Yes, she's in bed now, with her mother's old rag doll in her arms. Susan's going to bed, too."

"Are you?"

He'd feel better, safer, if he knew she was in her room.

"Pretty soon." She gave him a push, and he was alone in the bathroom.

He stood still, listening. But the only footsteps he heard now were Jill's and his mother's as they passed out of hearing.

Martha let herself into the house. Lights had been left on for her in the kitchen, but she could see through the doorway that the living room was dark.

It was late, for her. She was usually in bed by ten o'clock. After visiting Laura, poor Laura, unconscious in that high, narrow bed, she had felt so terrible that she had gone for a drive. Something she hadn't done in a long time. She had driven out to the lake and sat, watching the moon rise over the water. She had even allowed herself to remember when she was young and she and Jack had sat there in his car, looking out over what was then only a river. Forty years ago. It was that night he had asked her to marry him. They had made great plans. They would have four children and live in a vine-covered cottage.

It hadn't worked out that way. No children were born, and Jack had died after only a few years. She had never known what it was that sickened him and finally killed him. One of those mystery diseases, she guessed, that doctors didn't know about at that time.

She sighed and started removing her hat as soon as she'd closed and locked the kitchen door. She had to search for that doll. One of the kids, or maybe even that man who had been up there measuring for the new bannister, had taken it. She had to find it and put it away again. This time she'd put it where she could keep an eye on it. It was far too valuable to just be lying loose around the house. What would Laura think if she regained consciousness?

Then as Martha turned she realized someone was at the table at the other end of the long kitchen.

"Thought you were lost," Fawn said.

Both Jill and Fawn sat at the kitchen table, glasses in front of them. Martha felt oddly guilty.

"Oh," she said. "You waited up for me?"

"It's not as though you're that late," Fawn said. "It's not ten o'clock yet. We would have been up anyway. But we'll have to admit we were getting a little worried."

Martha laid her hat and purse on the kitchen counter and went toward the table. "I should have called, maybe. I know it's unusual for me to be out at night. But . . . I just felt like it. Did either of you go in to see Laura at eight?"

"No. How was she?"

"No better that I could see."

Jill got up as Martha sat down. "I'll get you something."

"No, thanks, Jill. I was only going to sit a minute. Well . . . on second thought, maybe just a glass of water, please."

"You sure?"

"Yes."

Fawn said, "Jill has been waiting for you. She has something she wants to tell us."

"What on earth is that?"

"I don't know," Fawn said, "She wouldn't let me in on it yet." She smiled. "It's some great dark secret, I suspect."

Jill came back to the table, but she wasn't smiling at her aunt's attempt to tease, to make light of something Martha hoped was not very serious. Martha didn't feel like handling any bad news that night.

Jill sat down, put the tips of her fingers together on the table in front of her, and watched them as if trying to accomplish something by precisely positioning one fingertip against another. She began talking slowly and carefully.

"I told you I didn't find out anything this afternoon.

Actually, I found out a lot, and I don't have any way to disprove what I heard. It seems that Millicent was murdered. She was hammered to death out in the old shed in the back. Millicent's mother found her. Old Charlie's mother worked here for Granddad's mother then, doing laundry and housework, and she went out there right afterward when she saw Millicent's mother just standing and staring."

Jill paused, moistened her lips, and folded her hands. The clock on the shelf ticked lazily and loudly. A faint wind whined beneath the eaves of the house. It seemed to Martha that no one breathed.

"In the shed with Millicent," Jill said, "was only one person—and the bloodied hammer. It was Granddad."

"Granddad!"

"Mason!"

They spoke together, Fawn and Martha, both of them leaning forward. But it was Fawn who spoke again. Martha's thoughts had gone to crazy Old Charlie. What did he know!

"But Granddad was only four years old!"

"That's right. And that's why it was hushed up, Charlie said."

Martha said nothing. The clock filled the silence again.

"I don't believe it," Fawn said. "Granddad? He never hurt a thing in his life. Even the bugs. He used to say, when a fly got in the house, put it out if you can, it can't help what it is. It's just like the rest of us, trying to live. Granddad kill his sister? I don't believe it."

"I didn't either," Jill said softly. "Then I got to thinking. Little kids don't know when they're hurting someone. Kara hit Erin once with a rubber hammer. But—"

"But she was only two," Martha said. "Two-year-olds aren't responsible. But at four years? I don't believe it either." Still, Martha felt an odd sense of doubt growing.

"And why, if Mason killed Millicent, was Millicent wiped out of the family records? Why was she treated as if she never existed?"

"I don't know," Jill said. "I can't figure it out either. Unless . . ."

They waited. Martha heard the wind, and looked at the window. The draperies hadn't been drawn, and the glass reflected the interior of the room. She saw her image, distorted, broken by the edges of the small panes. The darkness beyond the glass made her uneasy. A house that had been happy had turned dark, become a haunted place where things moved in the darkness.

"Unless?" Fawn urged.

"Unless it's because she was murdered. In those days it created such a stigma, perhaps, that the family reacted in that way. After talking to Charlie, I tried to get in touch with the cousin you told me about, Martha, but she died several years ago."

Martha murmured appropriately, shaking her head. "I didn't know. I thought Mason was in touch with her. Maybe not."

"And then," Jill said, "I went back through all the records I could find. Nothing. None of the old newspapers at the library go back that far. I haven't looked at the Village yet, but—"

"It won't be there," Fawn said.

"No," Martha agreed. "It won't be there."

They separated after a few more minutes, Jill and Fawn going into the front hall and upstairs, Martha remaining behind to turn out the kitchen lights.

When she went into her private rooms on the ground floor she remembered the doll. She should have asked Jill and Fawn if either of them had taken it out of the toy room upstairs, but the news of the murder of Millicent had made her forget all about it.

Chapter Twenty-one

Martha couldn't get what Jill had told them about Mason out of her mind. And Millicent, the poor child. It seemed so odd that someone who hadn't existed in Martha's mind had now taken on such qualities. Yet something was wrong. It was as if a terrible gloom had moved into the mansion, penetrating even to her bright room in the new wing.

She changed her clothes, put on a long robe and soft-soled houseslippers, and then sat in her chair by the window, with the blinds carefully drawn, and stared at the wall. Thoughts swirled in her mind. Laura. Mason. Erin. The funerals of Mason and of Erin. Laura. Millicent. A doll that had belonged to Millicent put into a trunk that had been made into a coffin.

Was that doll's coffin intended for burial too, when Millicent herself was buried? If so, why hadn't that been done?

When Mason had sent her to see that the trunk was destroyed, why hadn't he mentioned the little girl to whom it had belonged?

The hammer.

Lord a' mercy!

The hammer. That hammer she had seen in the shed. With the rounded end.

Ball-peen.

Suddenly she knew. It had slipped her mind, the name of that kind of hammer. A small ball-peen hammer, rounded and rusted on one end, a striking surface on the other.

It was that hammer, it must have been, that had killed Millicent.

Mason had used it to kill his sister.

Was that why he never mentioned her to anyone?

Martha leaned her head back against the top of her chair and wished she could close her eyes and sleep forever. She couldn't handle all this.

But she had to. Laura, helpless in her bed, with three children—no, two now. Two living children needed her. Needed her to stand up and be useful. And one of the things Martha had to do was see to it that an antique doll was put in a safe place.

Unimportant, considering everything else; still, it was something she could do.

She started to light the kerosene lamp, and then stopped to think. The light was not easy to carry, and sometimes required both her hands. If she was going to carry a large doll downstairs, she would need a smaller light.

She went to the kitchen drawer for a flashlight and chose one that had fresh batteries and a bright beam.

As she entered the dark front hall, the old grandfather clock in the foyer struck twelve.

Martha paused. No matter how she had tried to outgrow it, she still had a feeling about the midnight hour. In her mind it connected with the coming alive of the dead, with witches and black cats, and with things moving in the dark.

"Nonsense," she said under her breath, and turned on the big light in the foyer. It would help her find her way up the stairs, with the little lantern light on the second-floor landing and her flashlight.

She moved as quietly as she could. She didn't want to awaken anyone. Even though she couldn't help her uneasiness, she wanted to be alone. She didn't want any of them, even Fawn, to go upstairs where the bannister was not yet repaired.

When she reached the landing she looked down the hall. All was quiet in the area of the bedrooms where the children and Fawn slept. It wasn't likely the doll would be in any of those rooms. Other than the bedrooms occupied by the girls, Andy, and Fawn, there was the pink room, where Victoria had lived, now stripped of everything but the wallpaper, and Laura's old room. But, Martha now thought for the first time, one of those rooms must have belonged to Millicent.

Unless she had slept in a bedroom on the third floor, or at the front of the house.

No, the gate across the stairway had been put in after Victoria's fall, Mason had said. Years and years ago. Too bad, Martha reflected, that she hadn't quizzed him more about it. He might have told her something.

Truth was, Mason had never talked about the past. He'd lived in the present, a chuckling, happy man. The only sadness in his life seemed to be Fawn, her leaving without saying goodbye, her staying away without coming home. Her lack of confidence. Her thinking she wasn't as pretty as Laura, or as smart. And her pride. Only her letters to give him hope. Martha had read most of them. Mason had always said the same thing, "Read it to me, Martha." "But haven't you already read it, Mason?" "Yes, but read it aloud. Maybe I'll understand it better." And then, the same observation he'd made on the day she had left, "Maybe it was something she had to do. Maybe someday she will see that she's valuable to us, just as she is."

Fawn's letters, saying she would be home as soon as she could find the time. And then never coming until it was too late.

No wonder the girl had wept so hard when she had held that cold, dead hand. Her heartache must have been almost more than she could bear.

"Why?" Martha had asked her once, only once, after her return. "Why did you leave? Why didn't you come back?"

Fawn had sat with head lowered, and then, tears glistening on her thick lashes, had said, "Foolish pride, Martha, it's all I have for an excuse. Just stupid, foolish pride."

Martha didn't know exactly what she was talking about, and she hadn't asked her to explain. It was something only Fawn understood, and perhaps not even she. Martha knew that a young person could do a lot of foolish things, make a lot of mistakes and then be too proud to admit it. Perhaps that was the way with Fawn. She did know, but had always kept it to herself, that Fawn had felt a lot of rivalry with Laura. Maybe that had had something to do with it.

And she'd also known that Jim had started hanging around Laura a lot back in those crucial days.

Well, she was hunting for a doll, not trying to uncover problems that no longer existed. Whatever had sent Fawn packing was now settled somehow. Had been settled since the day she'd returned, Martha felt.

She went around the corner of the bannister and down the hall to Mason's room. After entering and closing the door, she turned on the light. Perhaps Jill had brought the doll back here. Maybe Roger had brought it down, and . . .

But why wouldn't he have said something about it? And Andy . . . they had been talking, Andy and Roger, like two men, or two boys, yet neither of them had the doll. Andy had come downstairs with her, and so had Roger, she now remembered. So the doll must have been moved afterward.

It wasn't in Mason's room or in the sitting room or in the other rooms that were empty of all but leftover furniture. Martha could feel that it wasn't here, but she looked, shining the flashlight in rooms where she didn't bother to turn on a light.

She went back out into the hall and to the gate to the third floor.

That hammer . . . up in the toy box. She'd have to ask Andy about that. Who else would have brought it up? Girls aren't interested in hammers.

Only boys . . .

She shuddered, remembering that it had been used to kill Millicent.

She had only Old Charlie's word for that, yet she didn't doubt it. It was as if the truth were written on the round knob of the ball-peen. As if the blood had crusted there.

She wished she had brought something to wrap it in, a towel, a cloth of some kind. How could she handle the thing?

From her robe pocket she took the key to the padlock. The sound it made as it turned the lock seemed magnified in the silence of the house. Yet, as she listened, she realized the house wasn't silent. The movements were soft, whispering. Wood squeaking, so faintly, as if someone walked lightly. Wind whistling, through cracks in old brick and beneath old window frames. A movement as of something huge breathing. The house . . .

Nonsense.

Martha pulled the gate shut behind her, but left the padlock dangling open. Surely none of the kids would be up and about tonight. What was wrong with her? She hated being one of those old women who eyed every movement a kid made and suspected everything that went wrong was being caused by one of the kids.

She turned the flashlight on as she climbed the stairs.

She heard creaks beneath her feet as she moved upward and found the sounds increasing her discomfort.

The light flashed from step to step ahead of her, leaving great areas of darkness, blacker than if she had had no light at all.

She reached the third-floor landing.

A shadow moved at the edge of the circle of light, and she stopped, then threw the beam nervously toward it. She saw a doorway, gaping, black. She started toward it, then stopped, reluctance holding her back, afraid to move into that dark room. Who had opened that door? All the doors up here were closed by her own hand. Who had stepped back into that darkness?

Nonsense. Nothing was there, only her own spooks, those in her own mind. She wasn't up here to shut a bedroom door that had been opened on the opposite side of the hall, she was here to get that dreadful hammer out of the playroom. And to look for the doll.

Feeling as if something horrible and unknown were about to grab her by the back of the neck, she set her path for the playroom. She crossed the threshold, and aimed the light at the end of the toy box where she had last seen the doll. Of course it wasn't there. What did I expect? she asked herself. That it would reappear? Like a ghost doll, that could be seen at times? And not seen . . .

Nonsense.

She was acting like a child, scared of shadows beneath the bed.

She crossed the room to the toy box without trying to silence her footsteps. The sound of her softsoled shoes on the hardwood floor reminded her of the sound she had heard a bit earlier, of footsteps somewhere here on the third floor.

She picked up the hem of her robe, to use around the handle of the hammer.

The strong, white beam of the flashlight illuminated

the box, the littered interior, the open lid. Martha stared. The hammer was gone.

She stopped and dug through the broken old toys and bits of junk in the bottom of the box, but uncovered nothing like a hammer.

It was gone. Pure and simple. Gone. Someone had taken it.

For a moment she felt frustration and anger. She felt invaded, as if too many people were trying to do her work. As if someone had cleaned her kitchen and had put everything in a different place.

Andy?

Her anger faded. If he had brought it up, could he have taken it again?

A cold fear eased down over her body. It seemed the earth had turned, and all warmth had been leached from it.

She slowly cast the light beam around the room, following it with her eyes, aiming it at last toward the door and holding it there. She stared at the doorway and wished she were back downstairs.

Why had she come up here tonight? What was so important about finding the doll, about taking the hammer back to the shed, that it couldn't have waited until daylight?

She took one step, and heard an echo. Then a soft slithering of steps, like those of a running child. A child who had seen her move and was hurrying away before it was seen.

It was the child who had stepped out of sight into the dark room across the hall, Martha knew. And now it was running somewhere in the hall, perhaps to get down the stairs before Martha saw her.

Yet Martha couldn't speak to demand that the child stop. An uncontrollable fear had frozen her, almost paralyzed her. She would not be calling for the child to stop, to make herself known, to answer for any of her actions. *It.* She didn't know that it was a girl or a boy. She only heard its presence, and she was terrified of it.

She moved slowly across the room, and for one moment had an urge to pull the door of the playroom shut and stay there, her back against the door, until daylight fogged the single window.

But she crossed the threshold, the light beam chasing darkness down the hall in both directions, driving it back into the open room across the hall. All the doors were open, she saw, but it wasn't important now. She knew the child who had hidden from her was the one who had opened them. Still, it didn't matter. She was going downstairs, and then, on the safety of the second floor, she might be able to think clearly.

She passed the broad, gaping hole in the bannister, and reached the landing. With a great sigh she started down the stairs. They were wide, she realized for the first time, but steep. She felt as if she were struggling to keep her balance on a mountainside, wanting to hurry faster than she dared.

She had almost reached the open gate when she saw the child.

It was a small girl, standing in the shadow of the gate.

Martha threw her light full on the face, and her heart did a strange jerk. Weakness spread through her limbs.

The doll. Not a child, but the doll.

She knew, in a second's thought, exactly what had happened. It was Susan who had done it all. Susan who had been upstairs, who had been interrupted by Martha herself, and had hidden in the bedroom. She had been up to get the doll. In the terrible dark of the third floor. And now, being followed by Martha, she had gotten scared and left the doll standing in the corner between the gate and the wall.

It had to have been Susan doing these things, because

Kara never would have.

Was Susan so fearless she would go into a dark, strange place?

It was a thought Martha pushed aside as quickly as it came.

She started to reach for the doll, then stopped, her thudding heart dripping ice into her veins.

The doll's right hand was raised slightly, her elbow bent. But the long, supple fingers were closed like wires around the handle of the hammer.

Martha stood with her light full on the doll. Its shadow fell onto the wall behind the gate. It smiled up at her, its lovely face set in a permanent loveliness of smiling lips, little pink tongue, white teeth, blue glass eyes with long lashes.

Martha stood staring, unwilling to move toward it, to take it with the hammer in its hand to the safety of her room.

She swallowed. The light trembled. She could leave the doll here until morning, she thought.

But I have never left things undone until tomorrow, and I'm not going to start now, she told herself, dredging up nerve from some deep source.

She took another step downward, and icy fear slapped her in the face. She stopped again.

The doll had moved.

She could swear the doll had moved.

"What's going on here?" Martha whispered aloud, her voice a sibilant hiss in the silence.

The doll smiled at her, smiled, smiled, the hammer lifted in its hand.

Martha stood unmoving. She didn't understand any of this she was seeing, but thoughts flipped through her mind.

Mason . . . the shed . . . the trunk. "Don't open it. Destroy it." Laura. The doll. Bringing it back from the

Village instead of leaving it there. For some reason, bringing it back. The wreck. The doll not even marked. Out of its trunk. Nothing said about the trunk. Roger Hamilton . . . asking, asking about the doll. What had he seen?

Footsteps in the hall, running. A child's.

The hammer appearing mysteriously in the toy box, and then being gone. Now in the doll's hand.

Martha moved again, taking one deliberate step sideways, away from the doll.

It moved. Took short, quick steps toward the gate.

Martha stared into its glass eyes. Its face no longer looked lovely, but horrible. Hideous. The loveliness of its surface could not hide the hideousness of it.

Martha's fear was oddly in control beneath the cold layer of this reality.

She knew the danger now, understood what must have caused Erin's death. Head wounds. Not from the fall, not from the broken balusters. From the hammer instead. Held in this doll's hand.

Martha searched for choices. She had to get this doll out of the house first, before she attempted to destroy it.

The shed.

She had to get it into the shed.

With a fast sideways movement Martha lunged through the gate, her light on the doll. She saw the instant response, the raising of the hand with the hammer, the hurried but awkward steps following.

Martha stood on the second-floor landing, the doll two steps above her, just out of reach. Her hand, holding the light, had begun to shake, and the beam wavered like candlelight, throwing long shadows behind the doll on the stairs, causing them to move in a puppetlike dance.

She took a firmer grip on the flashlight, glanced quickly down the hall toward the bedrooms, a silent prayer in her heart. *Dear God, keep them there. Asleep. Keep them safe.*

Martha took a step backward, feeling for the steps down to the first floor. With both hands she steadied the flashlight and held it on the doll.

As she moved, the doll moved, one step, another, Martha going backward, the doll following.

Martha edged to the wall, her shoulder against it for balance as she walked backward down the steps.

When she reached the bottom she realized she'd been holding her breath. The doll was still following, and in the quiet of the night Martha could hear the squeak of antique joints long unused. Metal moving against bisque, the interior construction, whatever it was, old and rusting.

Yet the doll kept coming, its sounds like something out of hell itself.

Martha moved backward through the downstairs hall, reaching behind to open the door into the kitchen, leaving it open.

In the kitchen she fumbled behind her for the light and turned it on. Something within her half hoped this horror would change, that the doll would become just a doll, with nothing in its hand.

But the doll stood in the middle of the kitchen, its hand raised, the hammer poised above its head. As Martha stared, the other hand began to lift, the elbow bending, the sound of the movement caused rasping in the silence.

Martha reached behind her and unlocked the outside door, then, turning her back to the doll for the first time, she ran across the porch and almost fell down the steps. She steadied herself with a hand against the porch steps' railing and turned. The doll was less than three yards away, poised just as it had been in the kitchen, hammer lifted.

Panting, struggling for a breath that didn't feel like knives in her lungs, Martha threw a glance toward the shed. It was some yards away, but the doll was out of the house.

She geared herself for the run. It was following her wherever she went. She did not doubt that she could get it into the shed. Then all she had to do was step out and snap shut the padlock that hung on the door latch.

She again turned her back to the doll, and threw the light toward the trees and vines that surrounded the shed. The light fell on the grayed wood of the front of the old building, and Martha saw with a sense of accomplishment that the door was standing open.

She ran, her robe tangling around her legs. With one hand she pulled it up and kept running, the beam of the flashlight jabbing ahead of her.

But at the shed she forgot the high threshold, the board beneath the door.

Her foot caught on it and she fell, sprawling face down. The flashlight fell out of her hand and rolled across the dirt floor, lodging beneath the base boards. It went out, and a heavy darkness filled the shed.

Martha felt a sharp pain in her head. She rolled to one side, her arms up for protection. She was aware of odors, the faint stink of old clothes, old metal, of things made a hundred years ago and kept locked in a coffin made from a trunk.

Then the doll was on her, like a small log, hard and oddly heavy, and the sound of the hammer striking Martha's head, again and again, drifted away from a roaring that filled the world to a dull, dead nothing.

Jill stirred restlessly in her sleep, disturbed by a sound. Then she grew still and her mind began arranging a dream around the sound. She was in a dark, close place from which she couldn't escape. There was a hammering on the wall, on the outside, and the sound of it, on and on, hurt her head, her ears, her existence. She put her arms up around her head to protect it from the sound.

Fawn heard the hammering as she woke. It had a far-away ghostly sound, as if it didn't really exist. At first, in that second of waking, she was puzzled. And then she remembered. Jill had told her about Granddad. He had hammered his sister to death.

It was as if she were hearing it now, except it sounded as if it were in the walls of the mansion.

In the darkness of the shed the doll moved, needing no light. She stooped, and rubbed the ball-peen of the hammer in the dirt, rubbing, rubbing, until the thin cracks in the rusted crust that coated it were filled with a mix of blood and dirt. She rubbed and rubbed, and then let the hammer drop.

She went to the body on the dirt floor and lifted its feet and began to drag it, slowly, her long, steel-like fingers curling around the ankles.

She dragged the body over the threshold and onto the dew-dampened grass, beneath the trees and shrubs and back beyond the shed, to the gate that opened onto the service road.

Moonlight touched upon the body lying in the narrow road, facedown, mouth filled with blood and dirt.

Moonlight touched the golden hair of the doll as it went up the back steps to the house, gleamed for just a moment on the round knob of the ball-peen hammer clutched in the doll's hand.

Chapter Twenty-two

Crack, crack, crack . . .

Laura became aware of the sound. Someone, somewhere on the intensive care ward, was hammering something, a horrible sound, a sound that tore distantly through Laura's consciousness yet seemed to be deep inside her, destroying some vital part of herself.

She made an effort to move and realized she was not on the ward. She was somewhere else, somewhere. . . .

Light gradually took the place of sound, and she saw Victoria moving awkwardly, quickly, down the stairs. The light in the foyer was dim, but Laura recognized the old settee that now was part of a parlor setting at the Village.

The scene had changed little from the last moment of Laura's awareness.

On the third floor, holding Victoria's doll over the bannister, Millicent stood. The doll dangled back and forth in her hand.

"You think you can catch her when she falls?" Millicent called down.

Victoria reached the foyer and stood leaning on her crutches, her head tipped back, looking upward.

"Please, Millicent. I said I'd trade with you."

"Why should I trade? I never said I'd give you my doll,

Victoria. You're very stupid, do you know that? You're ugly and crippled and stupid. What makes you think you deserve a doll like this? Why should you have a doll just exactly like mine?"

Victoria slumped. Her head tipped forward for a moment, her chin almost on her breast; then she lifted her head again.

Don't talk to her, Victoria. Leave. Go find your papa. Tell him. Tell him.

"Aren't you coming up?" Millicent called down, her voice echoing in the depths of the house and the stairwell.

Victoria tipped her head back and looked up. "No!" She began turning, a slow movement, on one crutch. She was headed toward the hall and somewhere away from Millicent. Laura urged her on in silent fervor.

Leave. Leave, Victoria. She's dangerous.

"Where are you going?" Millicent shouted, her footsteps loud on the stairs as she ran down.

Victoria didn't answer. A double door, closed across the hallway, stopped her progress to the rear of the house. She struggled to open the doors, her crutches under her arms. As one door edged away from the other, a crutch clattered to the floor. Behind her, Millicent's footsteps pounded on the floor of the lower hall.

In the foyer, the doll lay sprawled, dropped carelessly to one side when Millicent reached the bottom step.

Victoria stooped to pick up her crutch, but Millicent grabbed it and ran back toward the foyer.

"Come and get it!" she shouted. "Catch me if you can!"

Victoria began to cry, tears running freely down her cheeks as she struggled to walk with only one crutch.

"Milly, please. What do you want me to do? Give me my crutch, please. I need it." She slowly made her way back toward the foyer.

"Come and get it, if you dare!"

Millicent was halfway back up the stairs to the second

floor, looking down, holding the crutch above her head.

"What do you want, Milly?" Victoria stood with one hand on the newel post at the bottom of the stairs. "I told you I'd trade dolls with you."

"I'm not giving you my doll!"

"Then you can have both of them. Is that what you want?"

Millicent lowered the crutch. "You'd tattle."

"No, I wouldn't."

"Yes, you would, just like you tattled and said I pushed you through the bannister a long time ago."

"I didn't. I didn't tell."

"You'd tell Papa, and he'd make me give the doll back to you."

Victoria turned away from the stairs and lowered herself to the floor beside the doll Millicent had dropped. One of its hands was turned aside as if broken, one leg was bent awkwardly. Weeping silently, Victoria straightened the turned wrist and leg, worked with them for a moment to see that they hadn't been broken. She then began to pull the torn dress together.

Millicent disappeared onto the landing of the second floor, and a few minutes later reappeared with the other doll, the one dressed in cream lace and black shoes and stockings, the one that wore the bracelet with the name "Millicent" engraved in old English script.

She held the doll at her side with one hand and it moved, stepping down one step at a time at Millicent's side. They came slowly down the stairs like two children, one tall and slender, the other smaller, just learning to walk.

"Look, Victoria," Millicent cried. "She can walk. Did you know I've been teaching her to walk?"

"Yes."

"Why don't you teach your doll?"

Victoria said nothing.

"Oh, excuse me," Millicent said with heavy sarcasm. "I'm always forgetting. You can hardly walk yourself, so how could you teach a large doll to walk?"

Victoria sat in silence adjusting the torn dress. Her tears had dried, but her hands trembled.

"That's why I don't understand why Papa got you a French walker doll. You can't handle her. I can. I can teach her to walk. See how mine walks?"

Victoria looked up.

Millicent, one hand held out of sight behind her, led the doll with her left hand across the foyer and back, in front of Victoria. Laura began to have a feeling of horror about the hand Millicent kept behind her.

Get up, Victoria, get up and leave. Leave your doll. Get out of the house. Hide. Lock yourself in a room. Anything. Get away from her.

Victoria sat still, her doll across her lap. Then, as if she were hearing Laura's pleas, she put the doll aside and started to get up.

Millicent said, "Look, Victoria. I've taught my doll to do something else. She can hold things in her hand."

Millicent brought from behind her back a ball-peen hammer and put it in the right hand of the doll, curling its fingers tightly around the handle.

Millicent and the doll swept abruptly round, bumping against Victoria, throwing her off balance.

With her hand tight around the hand of the doll, Millicent then brought the hammer down on Victoria's head. Laura heard the crunch of Victoria's skull bursting, saw the blood reddening her golden hair. Victoria's cry was terrified and pain-filled as she tried to crawl away.

"I hate you, Victoria! You've ruined my life! I wish you'd never been born!"

The hammer came down again and again as Victoria crumpled, turning, her hands up, trying to defend herself. Blood ran in rivulets down over her face, into her mouth and eyes.

With the hammer tight in the doll's hand, Millicent struck, again and again. Her teeth clenched, she cried, "Kill her, kill her, Millicent. That's a good doll. Kill her."

On the stairway, propped in a sitting position on the bottom step, the doll Victoria watched.

Millicent stood looking down at her sister Victoria, now still and silent.

She shrugged and murmured aloud, "I didn't do it."

The scene dimmed and grew distant, as if Laura were watching it through tears. The actions of Millicent grew silent.

Laura watched her lay her doll aside, take the hammer out of its hand. Holding it gingerly by the end of the handle, she went down the hall, out of the house, and to the shed at the side of the back yard.

Millicent went into the shed and, a grimace of distaste on her face, rubbed the bloody round knob of the hammer in the soft dirt of the floor. Then, looking around the nearly empty shed, she chose a place in the corner, and carefully tucked the hammer beneath the edge of the wood foundation.

She looked down at her dress, and rubbed dirt into the tiny spots of blood that brightened the brown of the material.

Then she went out into the yard and stood waiting, wandering about, looking, looking down the road.

A carriage came into sight, pulled by two white horses. It turned and came into the driveway.

Millicent began to cry and to scream. She ran toward the carriage and it stopped, the horses tossing their heads at the hard pull of the reins.

Two adults and a round-faced little boy alit and came running to Millicent.

"She fell!" Millicent screamed. "Victoria fell! I told her not to go back up those stairs, Mama, really I did. I told her, Papa. But she went. She fell, and now she's dead."

Millicent collapsed in a faint at their feet.

As Laura drifted away she saw, as from a great distance, the tiny figures in the side yard of the mansion. She saw the mother running toward the house. She saw the papa pick up Millicent's limp body and carry it, running with it.

The little boy stood still, as if frozen, in the driveway.

Fawn dreamed of sound and darkness. She searched through the thick darkness for the sound, and as she drew nearer to it she realized it was hammering. It frightened her. The sound was drawing nearer and nearer, coming toward her through the dark, and she had to escape from it. She tried to run, away . . . away. . . .

She woke, the terrible, distant sound of hammering still in her ears. A memory returned. Of nightmares she'd had when she was a child, from which she woke screaming, and a vague recollection of a world in which there was nothing but darkness and the frightening sound of hammering.

"Night terrors," Martha used to say, comforting her, as she and Granddad stood at her bedside. "They'll pass in time."

And they had, until now.

Yet she could still hear the hammering. It sounded as if it came from somewhere deep in the house, past many walls, perhaps past the high ceiling that separated the floors. She could hear it, yet she had a feeling it was not real. No more real now than it had been when she was six years old.

Jill turned restlessly, pulling her pillow over her head to shut out the noise. Then, waking, she frowned as she listened. Someone was hammering at this time of night?

Andy pulled the flashlight out from under his pillow and turned it on. The bright beam made tracks across his room as he pointed it toward the window, then swung it to the door. With the light on the closed door he sat up in bed, listening intently.

It sounded like someone was building something. Yet it didn't really sound like hammering on wood but something else. Something more solid than a board.

He shined his light on the face of the alarm clock on the dresser. Two-thirty. A long chill went down his arms, then shot back up his spine and into the back of his hair. He listened. The hammering was fading away, so that even as he strained to hear where it was, what it was, it faded. Not as if it stopped, but as if he could no longer hear it.

It was like the ghostly footsteps overhead. They would sound so close, and then fade as if overtaken by fog and darkness.

Then suddenly the footsteps were not ghostly and somewhere above his ceiling but outside his door. It sounded like his mother, her steps soft and slow on the floor, more felt by him than heard.

He threw his cover back and ran to the door, the light beam racing ahead of him. It caught Fawn full in the face when he opened the door wide.

She frowned, blinked, and put her hand up to shadow her face. She was starting to say something when another door opened and Jill came into the hallway.

Andy angled the flashlight beam downward. Light from the landing threw long shadows past the chairs and china cabinets in the hall.

"Did you hear something?" Jill asked.

"Hammering," Fawn said.

Jill nodded, looking around, toward the landing, her eyes round and dark and shadowed. Andy kept the flashlight turned downward.

"I heard it too," he admitted.

"I thought I was dreaming," Fawn said. "But . . ."

"Could it be Martha?" Jill asked, starting toward the landing.

Andy followed, his thumb on the button of the flashlight. But he wasn't ready to turn it off yet. He saw that the door of the girls' room was open, and Susan stood there, her nightgown wrinkled.

Fawn went to her, and Andy saw them go back into the bedroom. He followed Jill.

They stopped on the landing. The stairway looked as if it led upward into a black tunnel, but the broken bannister still was visible, like a hole into endless darkness. Andy shined his flashlight up.

"No," Jill said. "I think it came from downstairs. Let's go see if Martha is fixing something."

Fawn came down the hall, hurrying to catch up. Jill led the way down the stairs, and Andy kept the beam of his flashlight at her heels. He only half listened to her and his mom's speculations on what the hammering could have been.

But he heard his mother say, "When I was a child I had night terrors a lot, and the only thing I could remember about it was the sound of hammering. Whatever it was, it always terrified me. I'd wake screaming, and Granddad would come to comfort me, or Martha. Although now I wonder how she could have heard me from her room. Maybe she had a room on the second floor too, when Laura and I were small."

She paused, and then said something Andy didn't understand. "Then tonight, after hearing about Granddad—and Millicent—it, well, it gives me a terrible feeling just to think about it."

Jill said nothing. They were in the bright light of the kitchen now, and Andy could see the pinched look on her face, her rounded eyes, still dark and large as if she were not only worried but scared.

Jill went to the door of Martha's private rooms and called in, "Martha?"

Andy stood with the beam of his flashlight on the open kitchen door. The light fell out into the darkness of the back porch.

"Andy," Fawn asked, "why don't you turn that light out?"

"This door's open," Andy said, but Fawn seemed not to hear.

Jill was returning, and her voice had a curious emptiness when she said, "Martha's not in her rooms. She hasn't been in bed. Her lights are on, but she's gone."

"She went outside," Andy said, pushing the flashlight beam ahead of him as he went to the kitchen door. "She left the door open."

They followed him.

He went down the back steps and into the cool open air. Somewhere back in the trees a whippoorwill called, called again and an owl joined it, crying in the dark night. Andy stood barefooted in the cold, damp grass and swept the light around the yard. Shrubs were larger, darker, hiding deeper shadows. Trees had grown to an enormous size, it seemed to him with his feeble light.

And deep in the trees and vines, with no path to its door, the old gray shed was ghostlike. Andy outlined the open shed door with his light.

"There," he said. "She went there."

"How do you know?" Jill asked.

"Well, let's see." Fawn took a few steps into the grass then called, "Martha!"

There was no answer.

Andy waded through the dew-wet grass toward the

door and stopped several yards away. It seemed to him there was a path in the grass, a path toward the shed, and then curving away from it, a darker path where someone had walked through grass glistening with dew.

"Don't you see," he said, shining the light along the darkened, narrow trail. "Don't you see, someone walked there."

"Let me have that a moment," Fawn said, and took the flashlight from him.

She walked briskly to the shed door, the hem of her light robe trailing the top of the grass. She shined the light in and around making a quick sweep.

"No, of course she isn't here. Why would she be here in the dark?"

Andy and Jill stood behind her, and he felt the cold dampness of the night begin to penetrate his pajamas, his skin.

"Something terrible has happened," Jill said. "I can feel it. I think we should call the police."

"I'll call Jim," Fawn said.

Somewhere close by, in the trees, near the old cemetery, an owl screamed. To Andy it sounded like a voice of the undead.

The doll placed the old hammer back into the toy box, deep in the debris, and then pulled the lid closed.

She went out into the long, dark halls, where once her mistress had taught her to walk . . . and to kill.

Chapter Twenty-three

Jim leaned on one elbow in the bed and listened to the voice on the telephone. For one moment after the first ring, when he had picked up the phone, still half asleep, it had seemed he was dreaming. Time had dropped away and he was seventeen years old again and hearing the voice of Fawn, his steady girlfriend.

"Who is it?" Catherine asked, rolling over against him sleepily.

Jim reached back and patted the hip of his wife, but didn't interrupt Fawn to answer.

"Something terrible must have happened, Jim," Fawn said. "Martha isn't in her rooms, and the back door was open—she was always so careful to lock the doors at night, you know."

Yes, he knew. Martha was always right there to lock the door behind him when he left the house, or she'd tell him, "Make sure you lock the door when you leave, Jim."

"I hate to disturb you this time of the night, but I know the police would say wait until morning, and if she hasn't come back, they'll look into it. Or they might even say wait twenty-four hours, like they do in Chicago. So many people just get tired of things and walk off for a few days. But not Martha."

"Could she have gone out for something?"

"The cars are all in the garage. Would you come over and help us look for her?"

"Yeah, sure. I'll be there in a few minutes."

He hung up the phone just as Catherine asked, "So who was it?" She sounded as if she were talking in her sleep. When he turned the light on, he could see that her eyes were closed. But she was listening, he knew that. There was nothing she didn't hear if it concerned his going out at night.

"Those people who've been having all the problems lately, at the Evans place. You remember the car wreck I told you about. Laura Worton. And then the death of her daughter, falling from the third floor—"

"That tall old monstrosity you call The Mansion, right?"

"Yes. The cousin, the housekeeper, is missing, and they're worried. I guess I'll go look around."

He didn't tell her about Fawn, that once he had dated her, from the time he was sixteen until he was twenty. It was just one of those unimportant facts of the growing-up years. Not that Fawn had been unimportant to him at the time, but his love for her had nothing to do with his more mature love for his wife and kids. In thinking of the kids now, safe in the house, two boys and a girl, he felt sorrier than ever for the family fate had introduced him to again.

For years he hadn't even thought of Fawn or her sister Laura. Then he responded to the call of a collision between a pickup and station wagon on the lake road and found Laura, bloody, comatose.

Beside her, unscratched, was a tall, beautiful doll, and he could tell by looking at it that it was old. A valuable antique. He had been out to the Village a number of times through the years, had even worked there some during his teens, and knew Laura wouldn't want to lose that doll. So while she was being transferred to the closest hospital, he took the doll to her granddad's house.

Not until he parked in the driveway of the mansion, did he notice the blood on the doll.

There were a couple of darkened spots on the lace dress, but they looked old, somehow, as old as the doll. Had they dried so fast? Or was it something else? But there was blood on the doll's hands and arms, and he used his own handkerchief to wipe the blood off.

Then he carried the doll to the front door of the mansion, the first time he had gone up that walk since the day Laura told him Fawn was gone.

Fawn was there, again, much like she'd always been. At first he couldn't believe his eyes. Time had dropped away. She was better looking than ever, though she still had the dimple in her chin and the widow's peak, giving her face a softness that was still childlike.

He had been glad to see her.

And anytime she needed help, she knew he would come and help her if he could.

She was right about the city police. They would probably tell her to wait. Especially since the missing person was an adult, probably sixty years old. Martha was old enough to know what she was doing, and had probably been so worried about all the things that had happened lately she'd just gone out for a walk. There was a little creek in the woods, Jim remembered. She might have gone back there. The moon was out, fat and round, and although it wouldn't be shining much in the woods, Martha probably wouldn't be afraid. She'd go, leaving the door unlocked, planning to return soon.

Yet as Jim drove into the driveway of the mansion and saw all the lights on from the second floor down to the yard lights, he had a feeling it wasn't that simple.

Fawn, Jill, and Andy were waiting on the porch, the brightness of the porch light extending out into the yard, and the yard lights all turned on, pushing back the darkness into the trees, the shrubs. The big, almost boundless grounds of the old mansion had always been filled with groups of things growing, of shrubs that bloomed at special times—spring, summer, fall—grouped together purposely. Mason Evans had loved flowers and trees, he remembered. His memory picture of Mr. Evans was of a chubby old guy wearing overalls, out in the yard with his pruners or clippers, pulling behind him a small cart loaded with gardening tools.

Fawn and the kids came down onto the walk to meet him.

Their faces were reflections of each other, wide-eyed, pale, worried. The boy, Andy, reminded him of his youngest son. He looked as if there were something he was bursting to say, but his eyes darted about, from Jill to Fawn to the dark beyond the lights, and every time he opened his mouth someone else started talking so he closed it again.

"We've looked through her room," Fawn said, "and in all of the closed rooms downstairs."

"No car is gone," Jill said.

Andy said, "I think—"

Fawn ignored him, turning to walk back toward the fountain. Jim and the kids followed her. "The back door was open, so she must have gone out that way."

Jim looked into the dark toward the back of the property. As he remembered it, the distance back to the creek was perhaps an eighth of a mile. Probably one-half of a twenty-acre plot.

"Aren't there ten acres to this property?" he asked.

Fawn stopped and looked back at him. He could see the puzzled look on Jill's face.

"Yes, why?"

"I was thinking she might have walked back to the creek."

"At this time of night?" Fawn cried.

"The moon is shining. . . ." Jim paused. What he needed to do was talk them into going into the house, so he could move about more freely. "I tell you what. If you'll wait in the kitchen, I'll take a light and look around. If it looks like we might need help, I'll call for assistance. Give me thirty minutes, okay?"

Andy said, "I can show you—"

Fawn put her hand on his shoulder and edged him back toward the kitchen. "Jim knows the way to the creek, Andy." She turned to Ruther. "We'll wait for you, then."

Jim went to his car and took a high-powered flashlight from the trunk. Its beam was like a small searchlight, and it shot through the darkness into the trees ahead of him.

As he left the mowed area of the back yard he looked back. They hadn't gone into the house. They were standing on the porch again, sharply outlined beneath the light. That was okay, just so he didn't have them on his tail.

He moved more slowly after passing the yard boundary at the back. Trees were closer together, but still not left in the natural growth of a forest as they were near the creek. Occasional mowing was done in some of the wooded parts, he could see. And over to his left was the service road and the cemetery.

He swerved left toward the cemetery and shined the light into it. The fresh dirt of the new graves. Earthy mounds where nothing grew, would ever grow.

How sad that near the grave of the old person, whose death was not only inevitable but probably a blessing, was the grave of a child. Erin Worton. So young. The age of his baby boy. She should be like his Toddy, with the world ahead of him, but few things more interesting than his Nintendo.

Martha was not there, as he hoped she might be, a silent wraith walking among the stones, perhaps come to say a last goodbye to two people who must have meant a lot to her.

He walked on through the woods, swinging the light in an arc before him, seeing trees, mostly, but occasionally the frightened leap of a rabbit or some other small animal. Deeper in the woods the whippoorwills called, their voices loud and beautiful. The whippoorwill was one of the most lovely of songbirds, to his mind.

He yawned. But he was waking up, the night air seeming colder, coming through the sleeves of his uniform as if they were made of net.

He had reached the creek. He stood still, listening, but heard nothing beyond the sound of water running over the stones in the creek bed, and the whippoorwills. He was reminded of nights long ago when he and Fawn had walked out here, hand in hand. And of one night in particular when they had necked on the bank of the creek and had accidentally rolled into the water. It had cooled both of them off in a hurry, and they had run home laughing. Martha had been waiting on the porch that night, and now her words came back to him as if she stood behind him at this moment.

"What on earth were you two kids doing out in the woods and down at the creek in the dark of the night? Don't you know you could run into almost anything out there? Bears, wolves, hyenas even. And look at you. Fell in the creek, I'll bet my bottom dollar! Well, it serves you right, chasing around in the dark like there was nothing out there that might eat you alive!"

And he knew. Martha would not have come out here, not at night, probably not even in the daytime. To her woods were places where man-eating creatures lived. If Martha was not in the house, then she was close by it.

When Jim turned back he had a bad feeling.

He could hear the owls now, and their cries grated down his backbone like a fingernail on a blackboard.

He walked swiftly back, and went along the side of the cemetery. When he came to the fence beside the service road he stopped and shined the light over it. Beyond the road was more unfenced property, but he thought it belonged to someone else. At least, part of it did. He knew an old hermit lived on land to the west, but he had never seen the man that he could recall.

He noticed the service gate. There was a padlock hanging loose on it. He took a close look, but saw it probably hadn't been locked in a long time. The padlock was rusty. Why it was there in the first place had probably been forgotten by everyone, because there was no fence at all at the front of the long yard. So if anyone wanted in, all they had to do was go to the front of the main property.

He swung the light down the little service road, suddenly stopped moving it, and focused it on something white lying on the grass strip at the center of the road. A moment later he was running through the gate, toward the figure on the ground.

Susan stood at the window watching the movements of the dark figures in the yard below. Her mother was out there, and so was Andy, she thought, because one of the people was small. Jill was there too, and a tall policeman. She had gone out onto the landing of the stairs and heard him talking; then her mother had seen her and motioned for her to go back to her room.

She turned and looked at the big, soft bed. Kara was asleep, her arms around the old rag doll that had belonged to her mother. Kara's cheek was pressed to the doll's flat cheek.

Part of the eyes and mouth were gone, the black embroidery thread picked out or worn away. The dress it wore was wrinkled and faded. How could Kara like the doll so much? Millicent would have been so much better.

Susan looked out the window again, pushing aside the lace curtains that hung between the heavy draperies. She put her face to the glass and tried to find the people who were looking for Martha, but all she saw now was distant, flickering light, off through the trees, beyond the old shed. Back toward the cemetery.

Were they looking for Martha in the graveyard?

Susan felt cold, and started back to the bed to get her robe when she was stopped by a noise.

Footsteps, soft and distant, somewhere in the house. It was at first like someone testing a step, to see if it would squeak, and then the person was running. But it wasn't a grownup. Grown people didn't sound like that when they ran. These were quick, light steps, followed by silence.

Had she only thought Andy was out there?

She looked again at the bed, but Kara was still asleep, huddled into the shadows made by bedposts and blankets.

Susan looked out into the hall, but it was silent and vacant. She guessed she had heard Andy running out, although he hadn't slammed a door.

She went back to the window and pulled the lace panel aside. A much larger light was burning now, pointing back down the little service road, and as she squinted to see better and moved as far left as the window allowed, she saw it was a spotlight on a police car. It seemed she could hear sounds, a cry, voices. And then again it seemed there was nothing but a terrible silence and the cry had come from an owl somewhere in the trees.

But something was going on, and she wanted to know

what it was.

She went out into the hall again, and stood listening. There was nothing. No one had come back into the house that she could hear. No one was down in the foyer.

Kara was asleep. Susan felt as if she were alone in the whole world.

Then she heard the squeaking board again, the sound faint as a mouse's movement. But someone was on the stairs.

Susan went down the hall to the stair landing and looked down. No one was there after all. With disappointment she turned to go back down the hall, and then a movement on the upper stairs drew her eyes upward.

In the almost dark rise of the stairs to the third floor she saw a figure. Standing beyond the gate.

And the gate was open, not far, just a few inches.

Never go past the gate.

But Andy had.

Susan started to yell at him, and then she saw it wasn't Andy at all. It was smaller, and in the deep shadows against the wall looked almost like Kara. Then she saw who it was.

"Millicent!" she whispered the name.

The next moment she had forgotten all the instructions she had heard about never going past the gate, and she was running up the wide, steep stairs. She pushed the gate wide open and went to the turn in the stairs where the doll was leaning against the wall.

"Millicent!" she said aloud, smiling, looking down at the beautiful doll. It smiled up at her, its blue eyes gleaming in the shadows as if there were lights behind them. The doll's tiny red tongue peeked out from beneath the five tiny white teeth, and her arms were lifted.

Susan felt a great and overwhelming thrill, as if the doll were a real little girl and was lifting her arms because she wanted to be picked up.

Susan lifted her, hands on the firm body beneath the uplifted arms. She hugged the doll, and felt the doll's fingers in her hair. They tangled, and pulled, and it hurt. Susan reached back and released her hair from the doll's curled fingers, then pulled Millicent's arm down.

With the arm lowered, the wrist turned, drooping downward, fingers still curled, bits of Susan's hair caught in them.

Susan felt an odd little trail of fear. It was as if the doll had turned her own hand. But of course Susan knew better. The wrist was jointed, and the hand was heavy and had been pulled down by its own weight.

What would Kara think when Susan took her the doll? She would be so happy, Susan knew. The beautiful Millicent was so much better than the rag doll.

Susan went down the stairs, walking slowly and cautiously, carrying the doll. She didn't take a deep breath until she was through the gate and had pulled it shut behind her. The gate wasn't locked. She didn't know how to lock it, or unlock it. Martha, she thought, was the one who kept the key.

Susan hurried down the hall, afraid Jill or someone would come in and see her with the doll and take it away again. Maybe Jill wouldn't take it away from her own sister.

With the bedroom door safely shut behind her, Susan stood with the doll and looked at Kara. She was sleeping, her cheek still pressed against the old rag doll. Susan wanted to wake her, but hesitated.

Finally, she took Millicent and stood her in the corner, leaning back, her smiling face turned toward the bed where Kara would see her the first thing tomorrow morning when she woke.

Then Susan went back to the window and looked out.

More cars were coming into the driveway and going back down the service road. She could see the beacon lights on top of police cars, and a boxy white van with red lights on the top. An ambulance?

She ran out of the room, remembering to close the bedroom door softly, so it wouldn't wake Kara, and then she ran downstairs and out to the porch. She stood in the chilly night air, waiting for Andy to come back and tell her what had happened to Martha.

Kara woke. It wasn't a gradual waking, but sudden and intense, as if someone had called her name.

She didn't move. The house was quiet. She couldn't hear the water of the lake.

Then she remembered. She was in Granddad's house, in Susan's room, and her mother was in the hospital, and Erin was dead, and . . .

Her gaze dropped from the high, shadowed ceiling to the corner and stopped. A quick frown touched her forehead and she stared, a startled leap in her heart.

Victoria.

What was the doll Victoria doing here? . . .

No, not Victoria, the other one.

Kara stared at it, feeling afraid to take her eyes away, afraid to sit up, afraid to speak Susan's name. She felt hesitant to move, to reach over and see if Susan were on her side of the big, soft bed.

She stared at the doll, felt it staring at her. Why did its smile look so fixed and forced? Why did the shadows from the tall dresser throw that darkness across it and make it look so different from the lovely doll she remembered?

"Susan?" she whispered.

There was no answer. Slowly, Kara reached out her arm beneath the warm blankets and felt for Susan. The covers on that side of the bed were thrown back, the pillow cold. Kara drew her arm back and hugged more tightly the warm old doll that had been her mother's. That was still her mother's.

She snuggled deeper into the blankets, pulling them up to cover her head.

The footsteps were soft across the room, coming closer to her bed, like bare feet on the old rug or the soft leather soles of the antique high-topped shoes the doll wore.

She was afraid to look, to see if Susan had come into the room.

Chapter Twenty-four

Susan came running across the grass toward them. Andy knew his mother had told her to stay in her room, yet here she was, getting her feet wet and cold from the dew. And worse yet she might see Martha, with her head all bloody and terrible, her dark hair gummy with blood and dirt. Her face twisted, mouth open, as if she'd been trying to scream. Andy himself was still shaking so hard he could feel his teeth clicking together. What would Susan do? He had to stop her from going closer to the place where Martha was still lying on the ground, bright lights from the police cars shining on her.

He tore loose from the small group—his mom, Jill, and a couple of police officers—going toward the kitchen, and ran to Susan.

Before he could turn her around, their mother had spotted Susan.

"Susan! Go back to your room. Go to bed, please. Andy, take her up to her room."

Susan kept trying to ask questions. "What happened? Where's Martha? What are all the? . . ."

Andy put his hands on her shoulders and turned her toward the house, pushing her along in front of him. At first she resisted, but after he whispered, "I'll tell you later," she let him take her back upstairs.

On the stairs going up he felt her small hand knotted in his. Her shoulder bumped against him as they climbed.

"Andy?"

"Martha," he said, the shaking coming over him again. His teeth clicked and rattled, and his chin shook. "Somebody killed her, Susan."

His little sister was oddly silent, then she asked, "She's dead too, like Erin?"

"Yes, only . . ." He started to say Martha was murdered. She hadn't fallen like Erin. But he said nothing.

He felt Susan pull back. "I want to go to Mama."

"No. Mama said to go to bed. She'll be up pretty soon."

"What's she doing?"

"She has to talk to the policemen."

"Why?"

"I don't know. They're trying to find out who killed Martha."

"But Mama doesn't know!"

"Go to bed, Susan!"

He pushed open the door to her room and went in with Susan, her hand in his. The room was only dimly lighted, and dark shadows hung from the ceiling like huge spider webs. He saw Kara was just a little knot under the blankets.

He took Susan around to her side of the bed and held the covers while she lay down, then he pulled them up to her chin and tucked them around her.

"Go to sleep. Mama wants you to go to sleep."

He heard Susan draw a long, shuddering breath.

"Leave the light on, Andy?"

He nodded.

Walking softly, he started to leave the big, shadowy

bedroom. Then he saw the doll.

It was leaning against the wall near the head of the fourposter bed, not far from where Kara slept beneath the blankets.

So they had found it after all, that weird doll, and had brought it to their room. Susan hadn't told him.

He picked the doll up, carrying it by one arm, and went out into the hall.

Andy stood, looking down the long hall toward Granddad's room. That was where Jill had put the doll in the beginning. But he felt reluctant to go there now. The little girls would only get it again.

Where it belonged was in the trunk, back where someone had put it a hundred years ago.

And he knew where the trunk was. Down in a closet in the new wing.

He went down the hall carrying the doll.

Beside him its feet bumped the floor with soft *thump-thumps* as if it were trying to walk. He remembered that even though to him it was creepy, too big for a doll with funny-looking joints in its wrist and elbows and knees, to Aunt Laura it was something special. He shouldn't be dragging it along the floor by one arm.

He stopped on the landing, looked carefully all around. He knew his mom and Jill and some of the police were down in the new wing, but their voices didn't reach him. He looked up and saw in the dusky distance the gaping hole in the bannister on the third floor. The stairway going up jutted out of the wall, getting darker with each step. The gate was closed, as always.

For a moment the doll stood at his side, then he slipped an arm around its waist and started down the stairs.

The foyer was lighted by the big lamp at the end of a

funny-looking settee that nobody ever used, but the shadows at the ends of the furniture seemed deeper and darker than ever.

Martha . . . lying on the ground, as if someone had straightened her, pulling her robe down around her ankles. Or as if she had been dragged, her robe held at her ankles. His mind's eyes flashed on, off, on with the sight of her. It didn't seem possible that she could be dead. And yet somehow it didn't surprise him. Hadn't Erin died? Wasn't Aunt Laura dying, perhaps? And Great-grandfather. The dying had started with him. Andy had a feeling it was going to go on until all of them were dead.

He had almost told the police that Martha had been dragged, and he knew where from. He had seen the dew-wet path into the shed and out of it again, leading away into the trees toward the service gate. But when he'd tried to tell, his mom had told him to keep quiet, go on back to the house where he'd be safe. There was a killer out there somewhere, in those trees.

"Old Charlie," Fawn had said, softly, to Jill. "I remember him as a strange and unfriendly man. Though he lived on land next door, I saw him only two or three times in my life. Do you suppose? . . ."

Jill, so white her face was like a ghost floating above her dark clothes, shook her head. Then, after a long pause, as they stood watching the lights outlining Martha's body on the ground, after the flashing of strobes as police photographers began to take pictures of the scene, she said, "I don't think so. He's frail. He's got animals, and he's good to them. Why would he want to hurt Martha?"

"Do you have any idea who might have done this?" one of the men asked them as he edged away from the brightly lighted scene.

Jill and Fawn shook their heads. No one asked Andy. If he had been asked he would have said, "No, I don't know who, but I think I know where. Martha went out to the shed. There was a path made in the dew, I saw it, and another leading away, and the other one going away was wider. Like she had been drug. He silently corrected himself. Dragged.

But no one asked him. It was like he was invisible until they reached the house and his mother sent him to take Susan back to her room.

Now he didn't want to see any of them. He had a mission. He was going to put the doll back in the trunk.

He was halfway down the stairs to the foyer and suddenly he was falling. He bumped down the steps, one hand out to grab the balusters, to try to stop his fall. With his left arm he hung on to the doll.

He sat up on the foyer floor, feeling as if he had fallen down a mountain. One of the doll wrists was turned almost backward, and he guessed what happened was her hand had caught on one of the stairway posts.

He wanted to cry. He hurt in one shoulder and his right leg, but the main reason he felt his face twisting was the senselessness of it. He had run up and down those steps a hundred times without falling. Something like this made a guy feel like a damned fool.

He got up, limping, and looked all around, up toward the landing above, across the foyer to doors that were closed on rooms never used. He looked down the hall toward the new wing. The house was as quiet as if it were on the moon.

With a couple of groans, he got a better hold on the doll and went down the hall toward the big closet where he had seen the trunk.

He had gone into this storage room with Martha a couple of times, and knew where the light switch was. But with the doll so awkward under his arm, he almost dropped it trying to reach the switch.

The light came on at last, a dim, single bulb dangling like a fat little spider on its one-strand web from the high ceiling.

Shelves at each end of the room held all kinds of things that might be interesting to investigate at another time. In the corners were vacuum cleaners, some of them real old looking, others new. There were brooms, brushes hanging on hooks, and even a small leaf rake. "This is just like a garden shed," Andy had told Martha the first time he'd followed her in. "Almost," she had said.

He couldn't believe Martha wouldn't be talking to him anymore. Wouldn't have cookies and milk ready for him when he got home from school. She had been the one waiting for him, like a grandmother, maybe. His mom was always gone for her four o'clock visit at the hospital to see Aunt Laura, and Martha would be down at the end of the driveway waiting as the bus stopped, looking to see that he, Susan, and Kara all got off safely.

They'd walk back up the driveway together, all three of them trying to talk to Martha at the same time, and Martha never once telling them to talk one at a time. She'd listen to all, as if she had three ears instead of two.

He felt the twisting of his face again, the almost crumpling into tears. But with a hard blinking of his eyes he could see again, and he saw the trunk was still there, sitting to one side in the room, the last item placed in storage.

The doll twisted suddenly in his arms, the heaviness

of its arms and legs pulling it away from him. He felt the hard punch of its foot against his sore leg as it rolled across the floor.

He grunted as he went down, his leg knocked out from under him. As he tried to get up he saw the doll lying on the floor, its wrists twisted oddly, its hands splayed, fingers arched like claws.

He stared. He had never noticed it looking like that. Had his falls ruined it? Maybe broken the wrists? Lord, he hoped not.

As he started to get to his knees, the doll rolled again, going from its side to its face. Andy stared, seeing the slow movement of the roll, the hands flat against the floor.

Then, as if with nightmare slowness, the head turned toward him, the jointed neck squeaking faintly, and the eyes stared directly at him. As if it could see him.

Andy sat up slowly, rising to one knee, one leg straight out as if he were on the track at school getting ready to run.

The doll's head had turned because it was heavy. Logic, on the surface of his mind, told him that. But a primitive fear, deep inside where there lived no logic, made the hair rise on his neck and arms.

The doll had turned from its side to its hands and knees, as if preparing to rise. *It had turned its head to watch him.*

The door was behind Andy, half open. He could walk out of the room backward and slam the door behind him, be safely away from that crazy doll.

But there was no lock on the door, and the doll would be loose in the room.

He swallowed hard, a dryness in his mouth like old dirt on a shed floor. He was scared to move, as if it were a standoff between him and the doll. If he moved, he was afraid that it would move too.

He wanted to yell for help, for his mom, for the police. But he could imagine their faces at the door, looking down at him. And think their thoughts. *Poor kid, seen too much death lately. Imagining danger in everything, even a doll.*

Tomorrow, he'd talk to Roger. Roger would listen. He knew, as well as he knew his own name, that the only person in the whole world who would listen to him was Roger.

He had to put the doll into the trunk.

That was why he had brought it down here.

I'm not afraid of any old doll. It's just a dumb old doll.

Slowly he got to his feet. The doll didn't move, but it seemed to him those glassy blue eyes watched him, moved as he moved, the head turning so slowly it was like magic, the sound of the squeak no louder than the beat of his heart.

He edged past it to the trunk, walking sideways, and reached down blindly and fumbled with the broken latch. The trunk lid lifted under his hand, the squeak of its hinges loud in the small room.

The interior of the trunk reminded Andy of the interior of Erin's coffin, except this color was not pure white. But it was soft and satiny and quilted, and there was a tiny pillow for the head of the doll. As if she were a real person.

The doll had not moved. Andy reached down cautiously and got it by one arm. He felt the cold material of its composition beneath the lace sleeve of the dress. The ugly joint of the wrist stuck out below the ruffled lace at the sleeve's wrist, looking gray and metallic.

Had he caused that when he fell with it?

The doll felt stiff in his hands as he carefully lifted it

and put it down into the trunk. It lay on the satin in the same awkward position it had lain on the floor, its legs up, its arms lifted, the head still turned with the eyes now staring at the wall of satin a few inches from its smiling face.

Andy stood looking down at it, feeling a little puzzled. For a few minutes it had seemed the doll was moving, almost moving, on its own. But now it lay stiff, its legs and arms in odd positions.

He went down on his knees beside the trunk and reached in to straighten the doll. He put its legs down straight, and turned its head so that its eyes looked upward. Its little teeth glistened in the dim light from the bulb in the ceiling. The sides of the trunk threw shadows on the side of its face. It had a nose like a baby's, tiny and perfect.

He reached in to push its arms down, to straighten the wrists that looked as if they were broken. They were turned awkwardly, the left wrist almost backward. The fingers arched, like claws, he thought again. The fingers were ugly, long and thin, like the hands of some women he had seen only much worse, the tips of the fingers long and pointed and painted pink, like long fingernails.

He didn't see the movement, but suddenly the fingers of the left hand were around his wrist, closing like metal wires. The hand jerked him inward, toward the interior of the coffin. The room's high ceiling echoed his startled cry, his terrified and shocked half-scream. Frantically he tore at the fingers around his wrists, prying them away, feeling the skin on his wrist peeling off beneath the force of the doll's fingers as he fought for release.

With his left hand he jerked the trunk lid down. The doll was rising, its body coming stiffly up as he pulled away, as he dug at the tight fingers on his wrists.

He was free. The trunk lid slammed down, and he saw the pink tips of the dolls fingers between the lid and side of the trunk. Then they were gone, pulled back into the darkness of the trunk.

Andy stood panting, holding the lid down with both hands.

It had happened. The doll had grabbed him.

No, it hadn't. The fingers were already curled, and they just caught on him.

No. It had really happened.

Inside the trunk he heard it. Soft thumps against the quilted satin sides. He could feel the thumps against the lid as the doll tried to push it up.

Andy opened his mouth to scream for help, but no sound came out of his throat. In the logical part of his mind he could see them, the policemen, Mom, Jill, running to the closet door to find him holding the trunk lid down. He could see the exchange of glances when Mom and Jill explained to the policeman that an antique doll was in the trunk.

Andy looked around for something to put on top of the trunk and saw a heavy old upright vacuum cleaner not far away. With an awkward twist of his body he put one knee on the trunk lid and then reached, stretched as far as he could, and finally got hold of the vacuum bag.

Inside the trunk the thumps became faster and harder, and he could feel the lid rise slightly with each one. He pulled the vacuum cleaner closer, and then onto the top of the trunk. It moved as the trunk lid lifted, moved a fraction of an inch, then more.

With terror cold in his heart, Andy looked for more heavy things to pile on the trunk. He pulled a box down from the shelf, holding items he had never seen, and anything he could pick up and make stay on the top of the trunk.

He realized as he piled things on the trunk that no sounds existed in the room but his own. His breath, gasping; his heart thumping. The trunk was quiet.

Andy stood on the threshold of the room and looked at what he had done, but when he backed out and closed the door behind him, he went with a nightmare sense of unreality, of danger behind the unlocked door, in the unlocked trunk. It didn't matter that it was piled with everything that he could stack on it.

Danger was there, in something that looked like a doll.

He stood in the hallway, wanting to tell.

I know who—what—killed Martha, he wanted to tell the police.

I know.

Hesitantly, he went down the hall toward the new wing and through the doors.

He crossed the lighted hallway between the living room and the kitchen and went through the swinging door.

His mom and Jill sat at the kitchen table, and the two policemen were between the table and the door, as if they were getting ready to leave.

None of them saw Andy. He tried hard to say, *Listen to me.* But he couldn't. One of the policemen glanced at him just before the outer door closed behind them.

The room was silent.

Then a chair moved, scraping on the floor, as Fawn stood up.

"Jill," she said, "Try to get some rest. Take a long, hot bath, or . . ."

Fawn saw him then.

"Andy, why are you up again?"

He looked at his mother and Jill and wanted to say, *Help me, please.*

"Come on." She put her arm across his shoulders and guided him out of the new wing and into the old, shadowy hall.

They passed the closed door of the closet where the doll was in the trunk, and Andy said nothing.

Susan hid behind the tall armoire in the foyer and watched her mother, Andy, and Jill. Even when all the lights in the foyer but one were turned out, she stayed hidden. She watched them go up the stairs and disappear at the turn of the landing.

Then she slipped out of hiding and moved down the dark hall, touching the wall with her hand to find the door to the closet. She didn't know what Andy had done with Millicent, except that he had left her in the big closet.

When her hand touched the raised wood of the door frame she felt for the knob and pulled the door open just enough to slip through. It was a dungeon, as black as if she had her eyes tightly shut.

She listened. Outside, muffled by walls, a car eased along the driveway beside the house.

Here in the storage room, somewhere, was the sound of a soft thumping, of movement. Something in the walls perhaps. Susan raised her hand and felt on the wall for the switch. She and Kara had played in this big closet, using it for a playhouse, and she knew she had to stand on tiptoe to turn on the light.

Her hand found the button and pushed it, and objects took shape beneath the light. Deep shadows filled the corners. They seemed to move as she moved, searching through the room for Millicent.

Then Susan saw the things piled on the trunk, a box, an upright vacuum cleaner, brushes, brooms. With frown lines between her eyebrows she began to remove the stuff from the trunk.

"What'd he do this for?" she whispered aloud. Something thumped hard on the floor when she pushed it off, and it seemed she heard an echo from inside the trunk. She shoved the heavy vacuum cleaner aside.

Susan lifted the lid, and saw the doll lying on the satin, one wrist turned sharply, fingers arched, the other arm across the doll's chest just the way Erin's arms had been laid across her chest.

"Why did he put you in here?" Susan spoke in whispers to the doll as she lifted her. "I saw him take you out of the room, and I followed. I saw him bring you here to the closet and stay a long time, and then I saw him shut the door. But why did he put you back in the trunk?"

Susan stood the doll on the floor beside her, holding one arm. She pulled, and a leg swung forward. Hadn't someone called Millicent an antique French walker doll? Because she could walk. Susan smiled. This long, dreadful night, with Martha gone, with the police coming and finding her dead, with all the bad things, drifted away like a bad dream. Millicent was walking beside Susan, one step after another, toward the door.

But then Susan stopped and looked back at the trunk. It sat with its lid up.

"Just a minute," Susan told Millicent, and left her standing by the door.

She rushed back to the trunk, put the lid down, and piled it high again with all the things Andy had placed there.

When she stood back and looked at it she said, "He'll never know."

She looked over her shoulder at Millicent.

The lovely face of the doll was smiling, tiny white teeth like drops of snow in the light, little tongue so red that at first glance it looked like blood.

Chapter Twenty-five

Waking, in Laura's dark world, was a changing awareness, a changing of the realities from dreams, from fragments of dreams, to the harshness of the Intensive Care Unit. Sounds took the place of images; feelings of sadness, of helplessness, of terrible despair replaced the peacefulness of dreams. Now Laura woke to voices, somewhere on the periphery of her world of darkness. Two women were talking. Her first rush of hope that it was Fawn and Martha ended in a plunge to cold reality.

Even with all the people in the ward, she was alone. Almost all the time, Laura remained alone. She wondered if she was beginning to sleep more, to drift more into unconsciousness, if she was missing the visits of her family. Where was Martha? Where were Fawn and Jill? Where were her babies?

Erin . . . dead.

Oh, Lord, take me out of this. One way or the other, take me out. Make it all hallucinations, a bad dream.

"Did you hear about that housekeeper?" one of the women said to the other, her voice hushed but close. Laura could make out the whish of mops now and knew they were cleaning women.

"What housekeeper?"

"The one that was murdered."

"Oh, yes, out at the edge of town. Awful. You don't think of things like that happening out in the country."

"Well, do you know who she was?" The same woman continued without waiting for an answer, her mop wiping the floor beneath Laura's bed, her voice close, "She was this woman's housekeeper. This is Laura Worton, you know."

"I thought she was her cousin. Didn't she used to be the companion of the old man? Out at that old place some people call The Mansion? Laura's grandfather? Seems to me one of the nurses said so."

"May be, but isn't it awful all the things that are happening out there? I mean with these people. First, that awful wreck and this poor girl just lying here like a vegetable. Probably be a vegetable for the rest of her life. And then the death of her daughter. And now the murder of the cousin, or housekeeper or whatever she was." The woman breathed heavily as she mopped, breathless with talking and working at the same time. "She was found in the—in what the paper said was the service road. Beaten to death. The morning paper said a blunt instrument. To her head. Last night. No suspects, paper said."

"Hmmm." The voice of the second woman was farther away, her words now a jumble, meaninglessness.

Laura tried to open her mouth, to let out the scream building inside her. The voices of the women drifted away as they left her room and worked along the hall. She heard them no more.

Martha dead, murdered.

It was happening. Laura knew what had killed Martha, what had killed Erin. She knew who had killed Victoria, with the hammer held in the hand of the doll. What had Millicent, the real Millicent, left behind in the form of a beautiful doll?

Oh God get me out of here!

She struggled to make her body respond, but the effort brought blackness to her mind, as if for a moment she had fallen unconscious.

In sharp awareness she listened for footsteps. Why didn't Roger Hamilton come to see her again? Only he could help. She had to reach him somehow.

She tried to picture his face in her mind. She recalled a man behind a steering wheel, an expression of shock frozen on his face. He had sandy brown hair, a clean-shaven chin that looked sharp as it dropped when his mouth opened. It was not a handsome face, but not a homely face either. She seemed to recall high cheekbones. But what predominated was the look of astonishment, of disbelief, on his expressive face.

Roger Hamilton.

Help me.

In the first instant of freedom, of the lifting away from her body, she was surrounded by darkness. The lights she usually saw were missing, and at first, in this suspension, she wondered if at last she had entered that long dark tunnel with the great light at the end, the entrance to death.

But she saw no light. She was aware of no tunnel, only of the floating freedom of her body.

Then the darkness lightened and became gray, a place of twilight, not of time but of atmosphere, filled with shadows, a place with small dimensions, with walls and a ceiling built in a V with rafters showing. A place with a soft, silty dirt floor.

She heard the voices of children.

They became visible. A girl with long, shining dark hair, and a little boy, sitting on the dirt floor.

They were in the shed. Laura saw clearly now the

neck yokes on the wall, the leather harnesses that belonged to the family horses.

Millicent and Mason were playing in the dirt of the floor. Mason had made a small mountain of dirt, with roads, and was guiding a small iron horse pulling a tiny iron wagon.

"No," Millicent said. "That's not the way to build a road. Why don't you go out under the trees? You can make much nicer roads there, and it's not so dusty."

Millicent knelt beside Mason, her skirt carefully lifted aside so that only her stockings rested on the dirt floor. "Let me show you a better way," she said then. "Why do little boys like to play in the dirt?"

"What's wrong with my road?" Mason asked, sitting back, his plump hands on his thighs.

Millicent patted the top of the dirt mountain with both hands as if she were forming a loaf of bread.

"You just don't know how to make a real road, that's all. Roads don't slope off to one side. How could the horse ever stay on a road like that? It has to be flat, see?"

Two dolls leaned against the wall behind the two children. The one with the white shoes and stockings, whose bracelet had the name Victoria on it, was wearing a new blue organdy dress with ruffles at the wrists and on the skirt.

The doll in the black shoes and stockings stood smiling, her arms lifted, as Millicent must have left her when she had brought both dolls into the shed.

Laura's attention focused on the doll to the exclusion of all else, as if somewhere within her consciousness a light pierced the doll. In silent horror she watched it.

The arched fingers on the right hand began to straighten. So slowly it was like the opening of a terrible flower. Then the head turned and the body leaned away from the wall.

It moved, silently and slowly, away from the wall, behind the backs of the two children.

Laura saw them all as if she were part of the rafters above. In a silence she couldn't break she watched them all. The children. The doll Victoria leaning as she had been placed against the wall. And the doll Millicent, walking now on her own—one step, another. She was going to the side of the shed.

Mason had built a mountain of roads in the soft soil of the shed floor, and he was propelling an iron team of horses pulling a tiny iron wagon. Millicent went down on her knees beside him and, with one swipe, knocked his mountain down.

"That's not the way to build roads up a mountain, dummy. Don't you know the road has to be back and forth instead of straight up?"

Mason objected. "It can be any way I want."

"No, it can't. Your horses will fall off, your wagon will roll down the mountain."

"Not my horses. Not my wagon."

They didn't see the movements of the doll.

They didn't see it reach down and pull from beneath the wood foundation of the shed the hammer that Millicent had hidden there after killing Victoria.

In horrified silence Laura watched the doll's long, supple fingers close around the handle of the hammer. She watched it move, more quickly now, as if walking were easier, a fluid movement, a natural condition. The doll was within reach of both children.

It lifted the hammer high.

Laura tried to scream, to cry out, to warn the unsuspecting children.

As if alerted, they both turned, their mouths open in silent wonder.

Millicent lifted her arms above her head, her voice a sharp, low cry. The hammer came down, again and again, into Millicent's rich dark hair. She fell, her blood splattering the walls of the shed, and splattering Mason, who was like a frozen statue, staring.

The doll circled her victim and moved to the little boy who hunched in silence, his hands still on his legs, his feet beneath him. He watched it, unable to move. Even when he saw the hammer descending toward his own head, he sat, helpless as a small, terrified animal.

The door of the shed opened suddenly, and the mother stood there, staring.

The hammer in the doll's hand poised, ready to strike the little boy's head.

The doll slowly turned her smiling face toward the woman in the doorway, the hammer held high, blood dripping from its peen.

Laura saw the mouth of the woman open, saw the distortion of her face as she screamed, and screamed again. The hammer dropped from the hand of the doll, and the doll fell.

It lay still on the other side of the flattened mountain Mason had built, the mound onto which Millicent's body had sagged. It lay just outside the pool of blood forming around Millicent's head.

The hammer lay against Mason's knee.

Another face appeared in the doorway, that of a young woman whose hair was pulled severely back into a knot. With one long stare she took in the entire shed, the harnesses on the wall, the one doll leaning upright and the other lying flat within reach of Millicent's outflung hand. After she had looked hard at the little boy with the hammer at his knee, she took the screaming mother and led her out of the shed.

The scene began drifting away. As it had come, in a

world of darkness, it now left, going from gray in which shadows loomed to the total darkness of the netherworld in which Laura existed.

The darkness remained. As Laura expected to hear the beeps and sounds of the ward, silence filled this terrifying world.

And then the light was returning.

With it came the sense of a change of time.

She first saw the shapes of furniture. A small sitting room. She recognized the second-floor sitting room that had belonged to Granddad's mother. Closed when he was a child, it had been left closed, the furniture undisturbed. She saw the framed print on the wall of a dog standing in snow, its muzzle pointing toward the sky, a child crumpled at its feet.

She saw Mason, small, his round face sad, slowly opening the door and peeking in. He came in only far enough to stand on the small rug in front of the door, his hand still holding to the door frame.

The woman sitting in the chair looked up.

Her dark hair had streaks of gray that must have appeared almost overnight. All light had gone from her eyes, leaving deep, dark sadness in them. She was sewing.

At her feet sat the trunk, its lid open. All of the lining was already in the trunk. She worked now only on a fringe of lace to add to the tiny pillow.

Mason said nothing. His mother did not call him to her, but she looked up at him again after she had attached the lace to the pillow and bent to place it in the trunk.

"You can't understand, Mason," she said softly, "but I lost everything when I lost Millicent. She was like me, you understand. She was my . . . my life."

The little boy took a step farther into the room. His

voice was so low the woman must not have heard.

"You've got me, Mama," he said.

The mother moved, rising from her rocking chair. She went to a dresser drawer, took a key from her pocket and unlocked it. She pulled it open. Inside lay the smiling doll wearing the cream lace dress and the black shoes and stockings. The gold identification bracelet read *Millicent.*

The little boy stared at the doll, drawing back against the door. Fear sharpened his face.

The mother lifted the doll and carried it to the trunk. She laid it carefully within, arranging its clothing as if she were about to lay to rest a beloved child. She looked up at Mason.

"How can I expect you to understand when I don't understand? But this, Mason, is *Millicent.* We knew, we suspected, she killed Victoria. But how could I ever accuse her? How could your papa? After all, she was his daughter too. Millicent. She was special to me. Right from birth. She was the firstborn. I've buried her once, put her into the cold ground. This time, I'm only putting her to rest. I've made her bed. A beautiful bed. Even though it's a casket, it's made especially for her. Every stitch my own."

She closed the lid and locked it, and then she got up and came toward the door, tall and straight, her long skirts brushing the tops of her shoes as she walked.

When she reached Mason she pushed him gently out into the hall, and then she put the key to the trunk into his hand.

"Don't ever open it, Mason."

He stood with tears in his eyes and watched her go down the stairs to the first floor and out of sight toward the back of the house.

At the distant sound of a closing door, the little boy

began to run.

He ran downstairs and out onto the screened back porch, then stopped.

His mother was going into the shed. She pulled the door shut behind her.

The little boy stood staring at the closed door.

Shadows filled the air, heavy clouds were overhead. Silence suddenly.

The gunshot was loud. An explosion that caused Mason to jerk convulsively. The shed seemed to reverberate with echoes of the shotgun blast.

Mason was running again, as silence descended once more over the world of trees and grass behind The Mansion.

He pulled open the shed door and stood trembling.

His mother lay on the dirt floor, the gun beside her.

Her head was gone.

Blood, bits of bone, flesh, brains lay sprayed across the floor and onto the rough board walls.

Mason crumpled on the high threshold of the door, the key to the trunk held tightly in his hand.

Laura fought against the beeps of the monitors. She struggled within to return to that little boy whose mother had shot herself almost in front of him.

Suicide. There was no record of it in the family history just as there was no record of Millicent.

She struggled to return to that motherless little boy who had seen his sister killed by a doll who had been used to kill before.

That child who seemed like her own, rather than the boy who one day would grow up and become her grandfather.

She heard the soft footsteps of a nurse, felt the comfort of hands touching her, turning her again to a different position.

Tears of helplessness and frustration and sadness for all the things she couldn't change eased from beneath her lashes, and the nurse gently wiped them away.

Chapter Twenty-six

Andy stood with his hand on the closet door. The hall was empty in both directions. The double doors closing off the new wing were both closed. His mother hadn't awakened him that morning to go to school, and he knew it was because of Martha. For three more days now, after her death, they would not go to school. It had been that way after Erin died.

He had to see that the doll was still in the trunk, but he was afraid he would find it standing there in the dark, waiting for him.

He thought of Roger. If he could only get to him, he could talk to him about what he knew, and Roger wouldn't think he was crazy. He knew that about Roger. Something inside him said, You can trust this man. This man was meant to be your dad, and maybe . . . maybe he will be.

Andy swallowed the knot in his throat, and turned the doorknob.

He heard a soft step behind him and jerked around. Susan and Kara had come into the foyer off the stairs and were standing side by side, holding hands. Both of them watched him.

Their presence gave him a sudden burst of courage. It was them he was protecting, although they didn't know it. He pushed the door inward.

The small room was filled with darkness, but outlined in the shadows at the center of it was the trunk, still piled with stuff, just as he had left it.

"What are you looking for?" Susan asked.

Andy pulled the door shut. It seemed to him there was a tiny smile at the corners of her lips. But it lasted only a moment.

They went past him, two little girls almost the same size, with hair almost the same color. They opened the double doors into the new wing, and he hurried to follow before the doors closed again.

He didn't feel like eating, but his mother made him drink a glass of orange juice.

"Can I go outside?" he asked.

"No," she said.

"Why?" There was almost a whine in his voice.

"Because, Andy." She sat down at the table. She looked pale with no makeup of any kind, not even on her eyes. With one hand she rubbed her cheek, and her eyes looked off into a distance that Andy couldn't see. "Because, Andy, you know what happened to Martha. You saw her, unfortunately. I don't want anything to happen to you."

He shook his head. "There's nothing out there to hurt me, Mom."

"You don't know that," she cried, almost in tears. "*Someone* hit Martha with something, and . . . Out there. You can't go out."

Kara asked, "Where's Jill?"

"She went to see Laura. For the eight-o'clock visit."

There was a moment of silence, then Kara asked, "Is Martha dead?"

"Yes," Fawn said softly, her eyes down.

Kara's face contorted as if she were going to cry, but tears didn't come. A moment later she asked, "Can I go see my mama?"

"Yes," Fawn said. "I'll take you for the ten-o'clock visit. Maybe Jill will be still there. Maybe we can have lunch downtown, or something."

"I'm not hungry," Kara said faintly.

"Me neither," Susan said. "Can I go with you when you go to see Aunt Laura?"

"Of course. I wouldn't leave you here alone."

Andy got up and went to the window and looked out. A police car was easing quietly along the driveway and into the service road on the other side of the long garage.

He hurried to another window where he could see out back, past the shed, into the trees toward the cemetery, toward the gate where he and Susan had found the trunk. And the doll.

He saw tops of other cars back there, through the undergrowth of greening vegetation. Not all of them were police cars with beacon lights on top.

"Mom, the police are still out there."

"Yes. They're still looking around."

"Then why can't I go out?"

She drew a long sigh. "We have to get ready to go. It's past nine now. By the time we're ready, we'll just have time to reach the hospital by ten."

"I don't want to go, Mom," Andy said. "Do I have to?"

She turned her head and looked at him. He tried not to let his feelings of horror show on his face, but the hospital, Aunt Laura in that awful bed with all those tubes connected to her, gave him the most awful feeling.

"She wouldn't care, Mom, if I don't go," Andy pleaded.

Fawn released another long sigh and her body sagged. "Okay. You can stay here. But you've got to promise me something."

"Sure. What?"

"Do not go outside."

"But the police are out there. Can't I go as far as the fence?" They might listen to me, he thought. If I told them I thought Martha had been killed in the shed and dragged away through the brush and grass, they might believe me.

Besides, he wanted to look in the shed.

If he could find a clue there, then they'd have to believe him.

"Mom, please? I promise I won't go out of the back yard."

She made a sound almost like a humph. "The back yard seems to have no boundaries this side of the creek."

"I mean the part that's mowed. I won't go out of the part that's mowed." Except, he'd have to follow the path made through the brush, if it were still there. But he couldn't tell his mother everything.

"All right," she said.

He rushed to her and put his arms around her neck and kissed her several times on the cheek. She really was the greatest mom in the world, and he was glad, so glad, she was sitting here in the kitchen chair, instead of . . . like Aunt Laura.

She smiled and patted his hand. "Go on. But don't bother the policemen, okay?"

"Okay."

"I'm not sure just when we'll be back, Andy," she called as he went out the back door.

"That's all right," he called back.

He hung around the porch, watching for cars for a while. Then he went to the fence that separated the back yard from the service road and looked over. But the police cars blocked his view. He could see there were at least three men walking around, looking for something. He occasionally heard their voices, calling to one another, but nothing they said had meaning for him.

He wandered back to the house, looking at the shed, but he wanted to be sure he was alone when he started hunting for clues on his own.

His mother called from the porch, and he went closer. He saw she was dressed in a blue and white suit, and the girls were wearing dresses. They waved at him.

"Remember now," his mother said. "We'll be back this afternoon. If the policemen leave, you go into the new wing and lock the doors. Jill might be home earlier."

"Okay, Mom."

He stood waiting until the car backed out of the garage and turned. He waited a bit longer, listening for it on the street as it sped toward town.

The shed seemed shrouded in vines. Like a large mushroom it huddled beneath tall, overhanging trees whose leaves had almost reached summer growth now. The green of foliage glistened around the shed, and even the shadows had a greenish cast.

The voices of the men on the service road beyond the shed became a source of comfort for Andy. He had to hurry now and see if he could find a clue, so he wouldn't be calling them for nothing.

The path he'd made out in the wet grass last night was gone now, the blades having sprung back as the sunshine had dried them. And the path that had led beneath the trees and on toward the service gate was gone too.

Andy searched the area around the shed, ducking beneath low branches, pushing aside heavy, evergreen vines. He found nothing that revealed anything had moved through there.

A sudden sound in front of him caused his stomach to revolt against the unwanted breakfast of orange juice, but then he saw it was only a bird with nesting material in its mouth. He laughed a little in relief.

The unpainted outer wall of the shed was within reach, and he put out a hand and touched the old grayed boards. They had an oddly cold feel, as if sunshine had never touched them, even in wintertime when the trees were bare.

He found his way out of the brush behind the shed and went around to the door. It stood half open, pushed outward. Unlike most doors, including the one on the closet where he had put the doll back into its coffin-trunk, this door opened outward.

Hair rose along Andy's arms and up the back of his neck when he stepped over the shed's threshold. In the interior was a strange twilight with a greenish tinge, and darkness hovered deep in the corners and around the few boxes and old broken chairs and things that were spotted against the walls.

The entire center of the floor was bare, but even in the dim light Andy thought he could see that the silty dirt had recently been disturbed. Without moving from just inside the door, he looked around. No obvious clue was visible. He was disappointed to see no weapon lying in plain sight, or even pushed back against the board foundation. But something might be there, hidden in the dark.

"Gotta have my flashlight," he said aloud, in very low tones. But as soon as the words were out of his mouth he backed out the door, the hair stiff on the back of his neck, as if something hiding in the dark corners had heard him.

He turned and ran toward the kitchen door. On his way up to his room to get his flashlight, it occurred to him that the police had probably searched the shed.

They had been looking everywhere. Two of them had even come into the house, at least on the first floor. He knew they had looked for a long time in Martha's rooms, but didn't know if they had gone to any others.

They might search the whole house before the day was over.

His footsteps clattered along the second-floor hall, loud between the rugs. He entered his room, inadvertently slamming the door behind him. He shuddered, hunching his shoulders against his mother's scolding. *Don't slam the doors! How many times do I have to tell you, don't slam the doors!*

The silence in the house reminded him that he was alone. His mother, Jill, and the girls all gone to see Aunt Laura.

He felt suddenly intimidated by his aloneness, and stood listening, aware of the big house so empty all around him, above him, beneath him. He had grown up with apartments above him and below him, but they were never empty.

The flashlight was under his pillow. He had made the bed, pulled up the bedspread. But there were lumps where he hadn't straightened the blankets. That was okay. It didn't bother him. His mother hadn't been checking on his bedmaking lately.

He missed Martha. Sometimes, when he had come in from school, he had found his bed smooth and all his dresser drawers tightly shut, and he had known that Martha had straightened up his room. If it had been his mother who'd looked in to see if the job was done right, she would have left a big note on the bed telling him to do the chores over again.

The sun wasn't shining now, he noticed as he crossed the room. He usually could look out his window and see it shining on the roof of the new wing below. But today, as if in accord with his feelings for Martha, for

Erin too, who hadn't been dead very many days, there was no sunshine. The sun had gone into hiding. It was like the continual lump in his stomach, closed in by sadness.

He upended the pillow and found the flashlight.

Overhead a series of footsteps ran along a hallway, *pit, pit, pit,* quick and light, and in some way gleeful.

Andy stood clutching the flashlight, still leaning over the bed, his ears alerted to those unexpected sounds above.

He waited, the cold fear of midnight with him, the terror of ghosts heard, not seen, above the ceiling of his room.

Night after night he had heard those same steps and he had lain frozen in his bed, staring upward at a high ceiling lost in darkness.

Who was up there, to run about at night like a child playing? *What* was up there?

In those first days here when he had heard the steps, he had told his mother. She had looked at him for a long time without answering. Then she'd said, "Old houses have a lot of strange noises. That's why they have the reputation of being haunted. Just try not to . . . to hear them."

It had seemed to him at that time, looking at his mother, that she was just as afraid as he was. He never mentioned those ghostly steps to her again. But once he had told Martha about the steps, when he stood at her side watching her mix brownies to bake. She had snorted and laughed. "You're getting just like your great-grandfather, Andy. He got to imagining he could hear what he called *them* playing in the halls overhead. He'd say to me, Martha, hear them? They're not supposed to go past those gates. They're not supposed to play on the third floor. Be careful of them, Martha, he'd tell me. Be careful of them.

"That was when he was half out of his head, mind you. He never said who it was I was supposed to be careful of. But he'd say things like, hear it? It's walking. She has taught it to walk, Martha. Be careful."

Andy froze, remembering Martha's words. For the first time understanding what they had meant. Martha hadn't understood then. She had thought Granddad was out of his head, and perhaps he was, but Andy thought now that Granddad was remembering. That in his mind he had gone back to his childhood, and he was hearing exactly what Andy now heard.

With the flashlight clutched hard in his right hand, his mouth hanging open in astonishment at how meanings could change once you understood, and his ears sharpened like a fox's to hear sounds that weren't ghostly at all, but real, he listened.

Silence. Something tiny moved in the thick walls, rustled, squeaked faintly, and was still. Sounds from outdoors did not penetrate the walls and ceilings of the old mansion.

Andy slowly opened his door, turning the knob so carefully that not even he heard it. He pulled the door open just as slowly, and looked out into the long, dim hall. A window at the end opened onto the sloping roof of a porch, but the light the lace panels let in wasn't enough to dispel dark spots and dreary shadows. He wasn't afraid of the shadows in the second-floor hall. The thing he was frightened of lived on the third floor.

Walking on tiptoe he went along the hall to the landing, where anything standing on the third-floor stairwell or landing could see him.

He stared upward into that perpetual twilight world and saw the gaping hole of the broken bannister. How much longer would it be before Roger came with the new one? It seemed so long ago that Roger had been here, talking to him, taking measurements. But it was only yesterday. Only one day ago. Had Roger heard yet about Martha?

Later, after he had done what he had to do, Andy would call him. It would be all right if he did, he felt sure. If his mother said, Andy, don't bother Roger, Andy could say, but I wanted him to know about Martha.

And I want him to know about . . . it.

After a long look toward the third floor, he went down the stairs to the foyer, walking softly, pausing to look upward over his shoulder toward the top floor. At times he thought he saw something there, back in the deep shadows, but he could never find a distinct form, a round face, a small figure.

In the foyer he hurried. At the door to the closet he turned on the flashlight, even as he opened the door and peeked in. The light beam pointed ahead of him to the trunk.

It was still there, as he had left it, with the vacuum cleaner, the box, the . . .

Something was different.

He turned on the room's light and went to the trunk, the flashlight still on, the beam a round white circle blending uselessly with the light from overhead. Something was different about the way the things were piled on top of the trunk. One of the boxes he had put right on top was on the floor, not as if it had fallen off but as if it had been put aside. Then he saw that the vacuum cleaner was not lying flat across the top. It was crosswise.

None of the things on top the trunk were the way he had placed them.

Someone had opened the trunk, and then put everything back to make him think it hadn't been opened.

The doll had gotten out.

Andy dropped his flashlight on the floor, and saw

from the corner of his eye how it rolled in a half circle, the beam spinning into the shadows behind a pile of boxes. But his hands dug at the stuff on the top of the trunk, pulling it off, letting it clatter noisily to the floor.

He opened the trunk lid.

The coffin-trunk was empty.

He stared into it, then slowly got to his feet and turned to face the open closet door.

Had the doll pushed the lid off and then rearranged the stuff on top to fool him? Somewhere in that molded head did there exist some kind of intelligence that would allow the doll to think about doing *that?*

No, he didn't think so. It was a weird doll, a dangerous doll, with something in it that made it move. But it didn't have a brain. It didn't have enough sense to *think,* did it?

Feeling uneasy and unsure, he retrieved the flashlight from the floor and held it in his right hand, leaving it on even though he went out into the hall and up the stairs where he didn't need the beam.

With his head tipped, his eyes turned upward toward that third floor, he climbed.

When he reached the gate he paused. For the first time he brought his stare away from that distant third-floor landing, from the broken bannister, from the parts of the dark halls that he could see.

The gate, he saw, was not locked. It was shut, but the padlock was not hooked through the ring on the railing.

Martha had unlocked it. She was the only one with the key.

Sometime, then, before she died last night, she had unlocked this gate.

He listened, but heard nothing.

He pushed the gate back and went through, took another step upward toward that dim and forbidden third floor.

Go get the police.

What is it? they would ask him. What's on the third floor that you're afraid of?

A doll. The doll is up there.

And they would look at him, and they would smile, and they would look at each other.

Call Roger.

Andy took another step upward, then another. He climbed close against the wall, aware of the growing height, the distance from the foyer below where he had seen Erin lying.

The flashlight beam angled upward along the wall, and lit the eyes of faces in old paintings and photographs. He carefully guided it away, toward the upper landing, toward the dark tunnels of hallways.

A noise from somewhere in the house stopped him.

A door had closed, so softly, somewhere in the distance. His heart raced, and he looked down, toward the first floor, hoping his mother had come back or a policeman had come into the house.

He waited for a voice, and heard none.

"Mama!" he shouted, and was shocked at his own voice, loud and echoing. He hadn't even known he was going to yell for her.

The silence that followed his shout seemed to be tensed and waiting.

Then he heard the footsteps. Along the hall, fast, quick little steps. On the third floor.

He had to see.

He switched the flashlight to his left hand so he could balance himself with his right on the wall, and he climbed, higher and higher, and came out on the third-floor landing. He stopped.

A door closed again, louder this time, as if it had been slammed, then footsteps were running and another door closed, then another and another. It was on the third-floor hall, doors closing all along the hall, one after the other. Or . . . the same door, opening, shutting, opening, shutting.

Andy walked out onto the balcony, staying carefully away from the open hole on the bannister. He saw in the wandering and searching beam of his flashlight the playroom door moving.

Opening. Swinging. Almost as if a child were swinging on the door.

The face appeared suddenly in the round beam of his light, smiling, the blue eyes reflecting the light in a strange, lifeless way.

The doll looked out at him as if she were inviting him into the playroom.

The light in the shadowy third-floor hallway had the perpetual dimness of a room where the blinds were always drawn, but the flashlight beam outlined the doll. Its shadow lay long in the playroom behind it.

The awful face looked up at him, wide, glassy blue eyes, smiling lips, little teeth, and red tongue. The jointed neck showed more than Andy had ever noticed before, above the lace of the dress collar. The left arm was up, the hand on the door. The right hand was out of sight behind it, or beside it, hidden behind the folds of the full lace skirt. The little black shoes showed beneath the skirt.

It's only a doll.

He had put it into the trunk before, and he could do it again. Susan, he thought suddenly. Susan had let it out.

"Susan did it, didn't she?" Andy said aloud. "She let you out."

He was talking to a weird doll, as if she could answer. He stared at the smiling face that silent, terrible face.

Get the police.

The doll moved, taking a step backward, pulling the door farther open, as if insisting he enter the playroom. As if inviting him in to play.

Run, call Roger.

"You wouldn't have sense enough to make the trunk look like you were still in there," Andy said. "You don't have any sense. You're just a dumb old weird doll."

It stared at him, its head tilted a bit sideways. Wasn't it straight just a moment ago?

"You killed Martha," he said. "I don't know how, but you did."

The doll stepped backward one more step into the playroom, releasing the door. Its left hand was still reaching out, palm up, as if motioning him to enter.

For a brief glance Andy looked beyond it, shining his light at the toy box back against the wall. Its lid was open too, he saw, like that of the trunk in the closet downstairs.

He was in a nightmare, he felt. A dream that seemed real, that was all. Martha wasn't dead, because this strange doll standing on its own feet in the playroom couldn't have done that horrible thing. He was only dreaming.

It moved again, a sideways step.

Andy put the beam of the flashlight full on it, and saw the long shadow behind, falling across the floor and up onto the toy box.

And it was there, in the shadow, that he saw the outline of the thing in the doll's right hand. As he stared, the shadow of arm and hand, and the thing it held, detached itself and became real. So real that Andy couldn't breathe, or move.

A hammer.

Its shadow outlined against the toy box.

A hammer in the hand of the doll.

Now he knew what had been used to kill Martha.

Get the police. Call Roger. Run.

He turned, aware of a slow-motion sense of being in the nightmare, of having his feet mired in quicksand.

He reached for the hall, for the stair landing, for the steps downward. Then he was falling, his arms flinging outward. He felt something at his ankle, tight and wiry. He twisted, and heard inside his skull the strange sound of something cracking, inside or out, he wasn't sure.

It might have been a gunshot somewhere far away.

Or it might have been the hammer, striking his head.

Chapter Twenty-seven

As soon as Roger heard that Martha had been found murdered the night before, he got into his truck and drove to The Mansion. All night he had stayed awake or dozed restlessly during attempts to sleep, feeling a growing urgency. That kid, Andy, was something special. Fawn's kid. A kid he could love like his own. The boy was there, in the old mansion. So were his little sister and a couple of cousins, and Fawn and the woman who ran the house, Martha. It had been hard for him to stay away last night, as if he knew, deep in his unconscious, that something horrible was happening there.

He had gone to the shop early, long before the rest of the guys, and had started working on that bannister. Get it ready, he told himself, and then you'll have an excuse for going over there. You'll have an excuse to hang around, because you can take your time installing it. How will any of them know how quickly an installation job can be done? Two of his men could take the bannister over and put it in and secure it, make it look like it had been there from the beginning, in half a day. But he, alone, could stretch the job out three days if he wanted to.

Then, a couple of hours after the guys started arriving at work, the news of Martha's murder reached him.

They had begun talking about some old lady getting bludgeoned to death.

"Odd how trouble, runs," David said. "First that woman had the car wreck; then her daughter died falling from the third floor. The same woman who ran into you, Roger."

Roger had been only half listening. He stopped work and lifted his head.

"In the house? Was the woman killed in the house?" he asked, cold horror crawling over his body from his scalp to his feet. He felt only a slight relief when one of them told him no.

"She was out in a driveway of some kind. Probably ran into a burglar."

As Roger turned his truck off the street and into the driveway at the mansion, he met a state police car, and saw that James Ruther was driving. Ruther was alone in the car. Ahead of Roger, down the driveway that curved past the house, out around the garages, and continued on into a small trail into the trees, a city police car was slowly proceeding along.

Roger rolled down his window.

Ruther said, "Nobody here. They went to the hospital to see Laura."

"I've got some repair work for the bannister," Roger told the man in uniform, glad he'd had the presence of mind to throw a few balusters into the truck. "Do you know when they'll be back?"

One of the men from the city police vehicle got out and walked up to the pickup.

"Could I ask your name and purpose for being here?" He had a notebook in his hand.

"This is the guy who was in the wreck with Laura," James Ruther said, and the city policeman lowered the notebook.

Roger had a feeling, from that movement, that the

police already knew everything there was to know about him.

"I'm doing some repair work on the bannister of the third floor," Roger said, relief making him feel weak. They were all safe, then, Fawn and the kids. All gone to the hospital.

James Ruther said, "I don't know when they'll be back. You may have quite a wait. We've done all we can here; we're pulling out."

Then the man from the city police force said, "The kid is here. The boy. He can let you in."

The exchanges from that instant on were meaningless to Roger. In front of him, three hundred yards away yet, secluded among tall trees, was the cold and ugly front of the old mansion, and somewhere within that many-roomed structure was a little boy, no more than ten years old.

With him, in that house, was the doll.

Roger fought an urge to leave his truck idling right where it was, and get out and run. But the men in the police vehicles were moving finally, edging past him in the narrow, paved driveway.

Roger gunned the truck, and roared up to the side of the house, the hood of the pickup almost touching the front right corner. He left it parked on the grass, left the door open and half ran to the front door.

It was a tall door, with a half-moon inset of stained glass at the top. An old-fashioned knocker hung in the center of the lower part of the door, rusted metal now, probably never used. At the side of the frame was the button of a doorbell.

In the instant Roger started to ring the bell, he heard the sound within the house.

It was faint and far away, an animal cry. Perhaps it came from the deep woodland behind the house. A scream of pain. Roger felt it more than he heard it.

The direction was impossible to judge.

But he leaped off the narrow porch at the front of the house and ran around the side to the new wing, up onto the porch to a door of regular size and thickness, with glass on the top half. He tried the knob and found the door locked.

The cry reached him again, a tortured, terrified scream, and this time Roger could tell it came from within the house. It was not in the new wing, that he knew. It was deadened by many walls and ceilings, and into Roger's mind came a sharp, clear vision of that awful third floor and the narrow landing between lengths of hallways, where the bannister was gone.

He glanced around the porch, looking for something he could use to break the glass, and reached for the closest lawn chair. The glass shattered, changing from a star pattern to what seemed a million pieces as it fell to the floor.

Roger dropped the chair and reached in, raking his wrist across shards of glass that rose like needles from the bottom of the window. The lock clicked as he turned the knob. He kicked the door inward and ran.

Andy turned, twisting, gripping the flashlight in his left hand, striking out with it at the doll. Its face was above him, smiling sweetly, blue glass eyes focused somewhere on the floor beyond him. But the hammer in its hand made a whishing sound as it passed his head. He jerked aside again, but blood was running into his eyes, stinging, hurting so much he could hardly see.

He struck out again with the flashlight, and felt it strike something hard, but he couldn't see what it was.

For a moment the doll's oddly heavy weight fell off him, and Andy rolled onto his stomach and began crawling toward the stairs.

The pain struck the back of his head again, and he heard it inside, a strange, dull sound.

He realized the flashlight was gone. It had dropped out of his fingers without his knowing, and now he had nothing. Nothing but his own hands.

The doll was there again, heavy upon him. With both his hands he caught it by one arm and wrenched hard, and felt the arm tear loose.

They were rolling together, the doll and the boy, and then Andy was aware of falling. He felt the hard jolt of striking something, heard the splintering of wood . . . or was it another of the hammershots in his head? . . . and then he was falling again, but he was holding tightly onto something.

The doll's arm.

He could feel the texture of lace beneath his fingers, the hard curve of the molded shape of an arm.

In the long, slow fall that feeling became important. Lace, old lace, beneath his fingers, rough and fine, covering the hard, cold composition, the bisque—whatever it was—the arm of the doll.

Wherever he was falling, the doll was falling too.

He was on a floor. He had stopped falling, and was still now, was being lifted. He was floating, on a soft, warm cloud that cradled him.

Through the blood in his eyes he gradually saw a face. A kind, warm face, and recognition filtered through the blood and the pain and the feeling that he was part of everything, the wood, the clouds, the sky. The doll.

Roger.

Roger had come to help him.

"Daddy," Andy said. "You're here." He smiled and closed his eyes.

* * *

"Andy!" Roger screamed, holding the boy in his arms. He saw the eyes stare upward, past him, dimming. The boy's body grew horribly still and limp, his arms hanging down.

The doll dropped from his hand.

With an enraged cry Roger kicked the doll, hard, and it spun across the foyer floor and stopped against the wall. One arm, the one Andy had been holding, was pulled out of the socket and hung loose in the lace sleeve of the dress.

Roger turned with Andy in his arms and ran through the house, out the door he had broken in, and to his truck. As he ran he talked to Andy breathlessly, his voice a hoarse plea.

"Andy, you can't die. God, boy, hang on. Just hang on, okay?"

He laid him on the seat of the pickup, bloodied head cradled on his lap, and then he drove, faster than he had ever driven in his life. When a slow car blocked his way he put one hand on the horn and held it down.

The way to the hospital was long and slow, and long before Roger reached the emergency doors, tears of hopelessness made seeing more difficult than it had ever been before.

Laura knew only vaguely when Jill and Fawn came. Moments of darkness interspersed with moments of awareness. Strange images from other times, from a boat trip with her husband, from their wedding day, from the birth of their first child, became blended with the darkness and the beeping of the monitors.

She came more awake when she heard a small voice say tearfully, "Mama?"

She longed to reach out and hug Kara to her. Kara,

thank God, Kara was safe. She wasn't dreaming. She wasn't hallucinating. Kara was here, with her, calling out to her.

I'm coming, baby, I'll be right there. . . .

She was trying to reach the baby who was crying, but she couldn't find her way through the darkness. Then all the sounds were gone, and she found herself in The Mansion again.

As if she were in a nightmare she was wandering halls dead and silent. Where was the light? All windows seemed to have been covered, or boarded. There was no light, only a gray, thick atmosphere swirling with fog and drifting webs.

She realized she had moved in time again, that no one lived there anymore.

She walked the long hall of the third floor, and saw the open door of the playroom. The light was better now, and she knew she had a mission. Her child had been calling her.

She raised her voice, and for the first time heard it as it echoed back at her from distant rooms and other floors.

"Erin. Erin! Jill! Kara!"

Erin. Erin. Erin.

Jill, Jill, Kara, Kara . . .

She stood listening.

Time had moved again, and she saw the broken bannister, and below, on the first floor, she saw the blood on the floor.

Erin . . . Erin . . .

She went running down the stairs, hearing the clatter of her steps, no longer paralyzed, no longer tied to her hospital bed by tubes and helplessness. She ran through the open gate and past the landing to the second-floor bedrooms.

She ran on down, calling, her voice muffled in the

empty house. Where was everyone? Where was Martha? Fawn?

And then she was standing one step away from the blood on the floor and she knew this was not the day Erin had died. Someone else . . .

Something moved against the shadowed wall by the closed front door.

The doll. *Millicent.*

Like a slowly uncoiling wire it moved, a slight struggle that drew Laura's eyes and held them.

It lay against the wall, one arm sagging loosely into the sleeve of its dress. Its legs were twisted, the joints bulging.

Its head turned slowly until the blue glass eyes were staring into Laura's.

The smile was sweet and unblemished, the tiny white teeth gleaming.

Laura started toward it, hatred overriding the fear and terror in her heart. The doll's glistening eyes watched her approach, the head turning almost imperceptibly.

Laura reached down. Someone had tried to destroy the doll. One arm had been pulled out of its socket. Its legs were twisted, its dress torn. Part of the hair on one side of its head was gone. But it was still . . . *alive.*

Laura was going to finish the destruction. Now. Forever.

Beep, beep, beep.

Laura screamed in silence, in helplessness and terror. She was in her bed, unable to move, unable to make herself heard. The sweet voice was still calling her.

"Mama? Can't you hear me?"

A strange female voice said softly, "Would you like to

come with me, dear, and get something to eat? Maybe we can find a nice chocolate chip cookie somewhere."

Footsteps came hurrying down the corridor outside Laura's room, and a man's voice said, "Fawn? Is there someone here named Fawn?"

Jill's voice answered. "She stepped out for just a moment—"

And Kara offered, "Restroom. She took Susan to the restroom."

Jill said quickly, "Shhh, Kara. Why don't you go with the nurse and get a cookie?" Then, "I'm Fawn's niece, can I help you?"

"She's needed down in the emergency room," he said, the breathlessness of his voice unable to cover the urgency.

There was a moment of silence, when it seemed that everyone in the room was holding her breath.

"What happened?" Jill asked.

"The little boy. Andy. He's been hurt. A man named Roger Hamilton has brought him in."

"Oh, my God."

There were sounds of steps, hurrying out of the room in which Laura lay. She heard Jill's voice ask, "Is he . . . alive?"

"Yeah . . . barely."

Andy. Dear God.

Now she knew whose blood she had seen on the foyer floor, and she knew who had tried to destroy the doll *Millicent.*

Chapter Twenty-eight

Jill entered the old mansion alone. It seemed bigger than ever before. And more . . . empty, somehow, as if nothing living existed there. Even though Kara and Susan were in the new wing, Jill felt the emptiness. Even with the double doors that closed off the hall of the old part of the house standing wide open, she felt as if she were alone.

Roger had already taken Fawn out to the cabin at the Village. Jill had brought the two little girls with her. They were here only to get a few things, and when Jill left them they were gathering up books and crayons and things they deemed important.

In her mind Jill could still hear Fawn's cries. *"I can't go back there. I can't go back to that house. Never. Oh, God. Why did I leave him alone?"*

Her cries would live in Jill's mind forever.

How could it have happened? Andy upstairs in the hospital, just two rooms away from her own mother. A team of doctors and nurses had worked over him, and he was going to live.

But like Erin, he had fallen. Why had he gone upstairs? And why had he, too, fallen?

They had almost lost him. First Erin and then Martha, although Martha had been murdered. She hadn't died from a fall.

Jill turned on lights as she entered the darkening hallways. She didn't want to see where Andy had landed, but there it was, in almost the same place Erin had lain. The rug there was wrinkled, accordion folds drawing it away from the darkened place where Erin's blood could never be cleaned from the old wood. And now fresh blood brightened the old.

Jill turned her face away. She was here to get Fawn's and Susan's clothes. That was all.

She ran up the stairs and down the hall to Fawn's room. In the closet she found a cheap suitcase, and in the closet hardly enough clothing to fill it. Was this all Fawn owned? She thought of her own closet at home, in the cottage at the Village. It was packed with clothes. But she didn't think Fawn would be able to wear them. She was probably a size ten, compared to her own size five.

From the dresser drawers Jill took all the underclothes, the two nightgowns. She found house slippers under the bed. Hurriedly she pushed it all down into the suitcase, and then left the bag in the hall while she went into Susan's room.

Blue jeans, mostly, with a stack of knit shirts, underwear, socks. She found it all in a dresser drawer, and put it into the suitcase. From the closet she took three dresses. One of Kara's nicer dresses was there too, and she took it down.

With the two suitcases latched and ready to go, she passed by Andy's room. She didn't want to look in. She didn't want to stop. But she slowly lowered the suitcases to the floor and crossed the threshold. Tears filled her eyes.

What was happening to her family? Andy was a sweet kid, and she didn't want to lose him.

She noticed that one corner of his bed was mussed.

The spread had been pulled back, the pillow overturned. She knew he kept his flashlight under one of his pillows.

She went to the bed and reached beneath the other pillow. The flashlight was gone.

Her gaze drifted upward to the ceiling. "Mama," she could hear him say again, "this place is haunted."

"Why do you say that?" Fawn had asked, smiling. Erin, her nose in a book as usual, had been interested enough to look up, to listen.

"Because I keep hearing things overhead."

"What do you hear?"

"Little kids walking around."

"Andy! No one is on the third floor."

Now Jill remembered the look on Erin's face and how intently she had stared at Andy.

Why hadn't she thought of it until now? Why hadn't she asked Andy about that? It would be a long time before he could tell anybody what happened.

They must have heard something, both Erin and Andy. And gone upstairs to see what it was.

Long, hard chills of terrible fear went over Jill's body. She wasn't going up. She was too scared to want to know. Whatever it was could stay there.

She picked up both suitcases and hurried down the hall. On the landing, just before going down, she looked up inadvertently. She saw the gaping bannister that would never be fixed now, and the deep shadows that always enshrouded that third floor.

Andy's movements now seemed clear to her. He had taken his flashlight and climbed those stairs. And what had he found there? The gate was standing open, she saw. Martha had the key. No one but Martha ever had the key. She must have unlocked it last night.

Jill turned her back to the gate and the rising stairs, and went down as quickly as she could.

When she reached the foyer she glanced, against her will, toward the wrinkled occasional rug and the small round spot of fresh blood beside it. The police would be in later. She had already turned the key over to an officer back at the hospital.

They would search the whole house now. But what would they find? Ghostly footsteps running along the upper halls, sounding like children's?

She started toward the new wing, the suitcases heavy in her hands, when suddenly her eye caught a movement.

Jill stopped, putting the suitcases down, frowning toward the shadows beside the armoire near the front door.

Millicent.

The doll.

For crying out loud, what was that doll doing there?

It looked as if it had been thrown. It looked as if it had been torn apart.

She went back to it, and looked at the perfect face. But the perfect face was now the only thing about it that seemed undamaged. She went down on her knees beside it.

"My God," she whispered aloud. "What happened to you?"

She picked it up and gave it a quick examination. Good Lord, if Mama saw this, she'd have a fit. She'd have to fix it before Mama woke up. Millicent was not a doll to be played with by kids, not anymore. It was far too valuable, and Jill felt sure that Laura had intended it to take its place beside Victoria at the dollhouse in the Village.

Its arm was pulled out of the socket, but the mechanism was still there. Jill could feel it through the lace of the dress sleeve. And the legs weren't as damaged as they had looked at first. Some hair had been lost on the left side of its head. . . .

Jill looked back over her shoulder toward the place where Andy had fallen. There, beneath the folds of the rug, was one bright wad of hair.

Had Andy been carrying the doll when he fell?

Frowning, not understanding, but knowing she had to repair the doll for her mother, Jill cradled it in her arms and took it back through the double doors to the living room.

Subdued, the two little girls were working quietly, putting things into a plastic bag she had given them. Both of them paused, looking up as she entered the room. Susan's eyes fell on the doll instantly. She got to her feet, her lips parted.

"What happened?" she cried.

"I don't know. But would you like to hold her while I go back after the suitcases?"

Susan extended both arms, and Jill placed the doll carefully in the cradle made by Susan's arms.

"You can go on out to the car," Jill said. "Kara, can you take the plastic bag? And open the door for Susan. Be very careful, Susan. Try not to drop her. I'll have to repair her when we get home."

Going back into the shadowy front hall from the bright living room was one of the hardest things Jill had ever done. She started to turn out the lights then remembered the police who would be coming later and left them on. She picked up the suitcases and quickly left.

She had just put the luggage into the trunk of her car when the police car drove in and parked behind her.

"Just a minute," she told the girls, "I might have to show them."

"Show them where Andy fell?" Kara asked.

Jill gave Kara a hard look, but Susan seemed not to have heard. She was crooning softly to the doll, brushing its hair with her fingers, gently, retying the faded ribbon in the doll's hair.

Jill felt glad she had given the doll to Susan instead of Kara, or instead of just putting it on the front seat where it would lie safely untouched. She was glad that Susan was finding comfort in the doll. The poor kid had looked leached of blood ever since she had learned of Andy's accident.

Jill left the car and went back to the porch where the two officers waited, and then she took them into the house, leading the way again through the new wing into the old mansion.

Jill stopped at the foot of the stairs, and felt such weakness in her legs that she reached out for the newel post for support. The small spot of blood was darker now.

One officer stood there, looking up. He was the original investigating officer who had come to the house after Erin's death, a husky man who looked as if he worked out with weights during his spare time. The other man, older, thinner, was walking about in the foyer, looking at the floor.

"Do you have any idea what happened?" the shorter man, who had said his name was Hastings, asked Jill.

She shook her head. "I went down to emergency with my aunt, Andy's mother. A friend, Roger Hamilton, had brought Andy in. The injury was mostly to his head as far as we know. One doctor said he also had a broken back, and that he must have fallen."

"Hamilton didn't say?"

The other officer said, "Hamilton didn't seem capable of saying much. He was almost as out of it as the mother."

Hastings stood with his hands on his hips eyeing the broken bannister on the third floor. "Obviously another fall. Seems kind of strange that two children, within the span of a few days . . ."

Jill said nothing. She clung to the newel post and wished she could leave. She opened her mouth to tell them she had to go, they knew where to find her if they needed her. But her eyes touched the second officer, whose name she couldn't remember, and stopped.

He was bending down, picking up an object from against the wall.

"What's this?" he asked, his voice filled with a quality that drew Jill and Officer Hastings toward him.

In his hand was a small hammer, with a ball-peen at one end. Blood was still wet on the rounded end. The officer held the hammer gingerly by the tip of the handle. With a long, significant gaze at his partner, he pulled a clean white handkerchief from his pocket and knelt.

"I think, Hastings, we've found the weapon used to kill the lady, and maybe . . . Who knows?" He spread the handkerchief on the floor and laid the hammer on it.

"I'll be damned," Hastings muttered.

"Better get on the radio and call forensics."

Jill said, almost in a whisper, "The weapon?"

"Yes, miss. Your housekeeper, as you know, was killed by a series of blows to the head with a small, blunt instrument. I'd bet my life this is it. And the two kids had severe head injuries."

"But . . . Andy fell. Erin fell."

They said nothing. She stared at the hammer's peen, the crusted age of the old hammer, the fresh blood that oozed even now out of the cracks in the metal onto the white handkerchief. And with sudden horror she remembered a murder that happened long ago. Millicent. Killed, Old Charlie had said, by a hammer. Held in the hand of a four-year-old boy.

Old Charlie had never said what happened to the

hammer.

Jill knew. This was it.

She backed away.

"I have to go," she said in a strangled voice. "My little sisters, my sister and my cousin, are waiting in the car. I'm taking them home. To my home, at the Village."

Officer Hastings put his hand on her elbow and guided her down the hall. On the way to the car he said something, but she didn't know what it was. Something, she thought, meant to convey sympathy, to assure her they would find out what happened. Who had hurt Andy and murdered Martha.

And Erin, she thought. And Erin? Had Erin's death not been caused by the fall? Injury to the head, the autopsy said. Such as she would have received if she had struck her head on the bannister or stairs as she fell.

Jill's brain was on overload. She couldn't think. She was hardly able to drive the car.

But in the back seat were Kara and Susan, and she had to concentrate on getting safely onto the street, then onto the lake road, and home to the Village.

The Village gate was unlocked and standing open, so all she had to do was drive in. The two German shepherds came running to the car and then raced alongside it as it moved through the curving and narrow driveway around the edge of the Village park and on past the caretakers' cabins.

Jill pulled her small car up onto the lawn at the side of the driveway. Roger's truck was still parked in the driveway, right outside the garage doors.

Kara got out of the car and started running toward the house, but Jill called her back.

"Remember," she said. "Aunt Fawn isn't feeling well. Keep quiet."

Jill opened the door beside Susan and reached in for the doll. Its arm hung loose in the dress, almost falling away. Jill adjusted it against the body, where she could get a closer hold on it. She saw that Susan was watching her with wide, anxious eyes.

Susan asked, "Are you going to throw her away?"

Jill tried to smile. "No, no. I'm going to repair her. I've repaired dolls before, and I know how it's done. I promise you, when I get her all ready, and get her dress sewn up, you can help me put her right next to Victoria in the House of Dolls, okay?"

Susan nodded.

Leaving the car doors open and the suitcases to be carried in later, Jill took the doll into the house.

She felt a sad relief at being home. In a house that was built on one floor, with windows that overlooked the sparkling waters of the lake and a green lawn that sloped down to the narrow gravel beach.

She went through the bright kitchen and into the hallway. Her bedroom was in the rear corner. Its windows looked out onto the parklike scenery of trees and grass.

She gently laid the doll on her bed. Its head was twisted to one side, the jointed neck looking for one horrible moment as if something had cut into it, nearly severing the head. But when Jill straightened it and adjusted the collar, the face of the doll smiled up at her, its perfection unmarred.

Roger sat holding Fawn's hand between both of his. For a long time she had clung to him. Back at the emergency room one of the doctors had come to see about Fawn, the mother of the unconscious boy, and had handed Roger a small vial of medication to give her. It would do no good for her to try to stay at Andy's bedside, he'd said. They'd take care of the boy.

"Take her home," the doctor told Roger, "And put her

to bed, and give her one of these. If it doesn't help, give her another. Let her sleep. You might as well just give her two to start with. They won't hurt her, they'll just give her a few hours of rest from this stress."

So that was what Roger had done. Jill gave him a key to the cottage, and called ahead and told one of the caretakers to open the big gates. The dobermans, so Roger understood, were kept in a special pen until the gates were closed and locked at night, and the two German shepherds wouldn't bother him, though he was a stranger.

Fawn had been in the guest-room bed for over an hour now. For the first thirty minutes she had clung to him, weeping, saying over and over, "Why did I leave him there? Oh, Roger, why did I leave him there?"

He had no answers for her, only his love. His own hurt ground into his stomach like glass, and every time he thought of that goddamned devil's doll, he felt like vomiting. He wished he had kicked it back to hell, or wherever it came from. Yet he couldn't say anything to Fawn about it, not now, maybe not ever.

And if he told the police, what good would it do? The boy was holding the doll when he fell? So what, they'd probably say. Later, sometime later when he could think of an excuse to get back into the old mansion, he would destroy that awful, horrible doll.

He heard a footstep behind him and turned.

Jill stood just within the room. Her face looked white and thin, her chin narrower than he had ever noticed, her lips pinched and pale.

"She's asleep?" she asked softly.

"Yes."

He got up, aware at last of how stiff and sore he felt from his stooped vigil over the bed.

"Did you give her something?"

"Yes. A doctor at the hospital gave me something for

her, I don't know what. He said it would make her sleep. I guess I'd better go now, unless you need me?"

Jill shook her head. "No, go rest, Roger. We're home now."

Roger nodded. She had said it, *we're home now,* as if to say, it's all over, all the death, the dying, the bad things. They're all over now. We're home.

Roger took a card from his pocket and gave it to her. It had the phone numbers of both his shop and his house.

"If she wakes in the night," he said, "if you need me, call. Please. I'll come back tomorrow morning, if it's all right with you?"

"Sure." She nodded. "Of course."

He left the cottage, got into his truck, and backed out of the short driveway. The dogs accompanied him along the road through the trees, but stopped at the open gate.

Roger stopped and left the truck idling. He sat for a moment, wondering if he should go back and close the gates. But then he shrugged. The caretaker who had opened them would probably shut them soon. The sun was going down, and the woods were filled with growing darkness. Through his open window he could hear the call of whippoorwills, far back in the trees, their shrill, loud voices carrying for miles.

He wanted to go back and sleep on the floor at the side of Fawn's bed, but he put the truck in gear instead and eased it on, toward the highway and the street down to his own lake house.

Jill sat working on the doll in the silence of her room, close to the open window where she could hear the whippoorwills in the woods and the frogs in the still, backwater parts of the lake. Sounds here were so different, she was thinking, from those at her great-granddad's old mansion.

She couldn't think of the mansion now without a terrible sadness, a feeling of doom, of something there that nobody understood or would ever understand.

She thought about it all, fragments of things coming to her mind as she worked over the doll. She thought of old Charlie and of what he had told her. And she thought of the hammer in the foyer with the blood on it. Who had wielded that hammer? To her mind it was like the sounds Andy had heard on the third floor of the house, a ghostly thing that had no explanation.

She thought of the whole day, and the horror of being called to the emergency room where Andy lay on a table. She had only glimpsed him. He had looked as if he were asleep, except for the blood in his hair. The nurses and doctors must have already washed his face.

Fawn and Roger . . . What would Fawn have done without Roger?

And Roger himself. They would never have known him if he hadn't been involved in the wreck with Mama.

The back of Jill's neck ached from the long hours of working on the doll. She had taken off its torn dress and laid it aside, then stripped off the body suit, down to the knees, in order to put the arm back in the socket.

She thought of the evening that had passed so quietly. None of them, the girls or herself, had wanted to eat. So, even though she knew it was bad nutrition, she had made brownies and baked them in the microwave, and that was all they'd had. Brownies and milk. They had spent a quiet hour eating, and then Jill had put them both to bed.

Thank God little children could sleep.

It had taken a long time, but the doll's arm was back in the socket and working well. She twisted it. She had used special tools intended for reaching into the interior of dolls to pull the spring out far enough to hook the end of the arm back onto it. Fortunately neither hook nor spring was broken.

In looking into the arm socket of the doll, she was amazed to see how good the mechanisms still seemed. Not rusted much at all. Being in the trunk all those years, with no humidity, had been the best thing in the world for the doll.

Victoria was in much worse shape, even though the building she was in was as airtight as it could be and, during the wetter months, dehumidifiers hummed day and night.

Jill straightened and put one hand on the back of her neck to ease the ache. The doll, lying across her lap, legs hanging down on one side and the head tilted back on the other, rolled and almost fell off.

Jill grabbed it and pulled it safely back again. She drew a long sigh.

It was past two o'clock, and the night outside her window was very dark and quieter now. Most creatures, even the night ones, seemed to sleep, or at least grow quiet, when the hour passed two or three.

She should probably go to bed, she told herself. But she still wasn't sleepy, and she wasn't quite finished with the doll.

She pulled up its body stocking, covering ugly joints. Then she quickly and loosely stitched up the torn places in the lace dress. What did it matter that her sewing was less than perfect? No one would be examining the doll. At least not right away.

Tomorrow she would take Susan, as she had promised, and they would place the doll in the dollhouse, stand her beside Victoria where she belonged.

Jill stood the doll on the floor, then noticed the bald patch in the wig.

With the doll standing between her knees, Jill worked gently, combing its hair to cover the place where some had been torn out. It was only a small spot, and it would require close examination to be seen.

Jill twisted and reached behind her to get a ribbon from her vanity drawer. Would a new ribbon in the doll's hair hurt anything? She could snap on one of the ribbon clips that—

She felt sharp stabs on her leg, sudden and very painful, as if she had received an animal bite. She cried out instinctively and jerked around.

The doll's hand had clamped down onto her leg, its fingers digging into the flesh of her thigh.

Moaning, half crying, Jill pried loose the tight fingers. It was as if the hand had convulsed, something within it tightening, causing hand and fingers to curl and cut into her.

Jill straightened the fingers one by one, and then a strange unease came over her. She looked into the doll's face—and eyes.

The blue glass was beautiful, and caught the light in a way that made the eyes sparkle like sapphires. Like . . . living eyes.

But there was a coldness, a glassiness, an emptiness, and as Jill looked into the eyes a long, hard chill went over her and she began to tremble.

She slowly pushed the doll away, intending to set it down on the floor at the foot of her bed.

The doll stepped backward, refusing to bend, to sit.

It stepped backward again, and once again. Now it was standing on its own several feet away from Jill.

Jill sat, staring at it, the cold wash of disbelief holding her stone-still.

The doll had moved, walking backward, and it now stood staring at her, its perfect face smiling, its blue eyes glistening in the overhead light, the little bow clamped jauntily on one side of its hair.

It had moved.

That was impossible. There was nothing within the doll, no mechanism, that would cause the movement. Certainly there was no computer. It was an old doll. Circa 1899, maybe earlier.

She didn't believe what she had seen. It was all the other things that were driving her crazy, Jill thought. The deaths, her mother perhaps dying.

Jill sat still, unable to move, and told herself she wasn't seeing the doll move again as it took a step sideways. She watched. The eyes of the doll didn't leave her face as it slowly and carefully walked sideways, one step, pause, another step, to the corner of the room where a dresser stood.

Then, incredulous, and to her growing horror, Jill saw the doll reach behind itself and coil its fingers around a closed umbrella that leaned in the corner.

Quickly now the doll lifted it, the sharp end of the umbrella pointing toward Jill.

When the doll started coming toward her, Jill's disbelief was swept away by pure terror.

Chapter Twenty-nine

Jill tried to stand, but fell backward off the vanity bench. Above her the doll leaped, and the point of the umbrella made a soft whispering sound as it shot past her head just as Jill rolled aside.

Unable to cry out or call for help, she struggled to her feet, ran to the bedroom door, and fumbled with the knob. Minute bits of thoughts flashed through her mind. Help? There was no one in the house but Aunt Fawn, sedated, sleeping. And the little girls. Sleeping. Helpless.

If this horrible thing in the guise of a beautiful doll killed her, it would then turn to them.

Jill had to get it out of the house.

That was their only chance.

The doll was within three feet of her when she finally got the door open. The umbrella was held in its hand much as the hammer must have been when . . .

. . . when it killed Millicent, long ago . . .

. . . when it killed Erin . . .

. . . Martha . . .

. . . when it almost killed Andy. . . .

God, help us.

Roger . . . but what could Roger do? What could anyone do?

If she led it into the lake, would it drown? No. No. She had to get it out of the house.

She had to find a weapon of her own, something with which to batter to death this *thing* with the sharp umbrella clutched in the claws of its right hand.

Walking backward, shaking so hard she had almost no control over her movements, Jill went out into the darkened hall and then the kitchen. Rays from the yardlight streamed through the dinette window, passing over the doll as it followed Jill, glinting on the sharp, metal end of the umbrella that was raised over the doll's head.

Jill didn't dare turn and try to run. She had to keep the doll in her sight, had to lead it . . . somewhere . . . somewhere away from the house.

She found the doorknob and the lock clicked open. The doll followed, across the threshold and into the carport and out onto the driveway.

From the corner of her eye Jill saw the sleek, swift movements of the dogs, and hope filled her. The dobermans were out now, and Jill tried to whistle to them, that low, between-her-teeth whistle that meant attack. But her lips were numb with fear.

To her horror she saw the dogs standing still, their sleek, black coats touched in spots by the yardlights shining through the trees. Watching. Watching.

Not moving.

Not attacking.

Jill heard the crunch of gravel as she kept walking backward, carefully, trying not to lose her footing. She didn't dare think what might happen if . . .

She had to find a weapon. If she could get through the winding walks to the other side of the Village, where the early farming equipment was . . . *if* . . .

Suddenly the dogs were moving, but instead of coming toward her they were going farther away, farther back toward the park.

Then, in the stillness of the night, she heard their howls rise.

Roger listened. He had been sitting on his screened porch, watching the starlight on the water for hours. He hadn't even eaten when he'd gotten home, or changed for bed. He had come out onto the porch to wait for the break of dawn, when he could decently go back to Fawn.

The feel of the little boy in his arms was still there, a weight he never wanted to lose. And he kept hearing in his heart and mind those last words of Andy's. "Daddy. You're here."

As if he could help.

At first the sad and lonely howls seemed to come from Roger's own heart, to be a part of the loneliness of the woods, of the creatures in the woods, of his own despair.

And then he realized the sound was separate from himself.

He stood up and went to the screen door and opened it, as if the screen muffled the sounds.

Wolves?

No. Wolves had a singing quality to their howls, beautiful and wild.

These were dogs. There was sadness in a dog's howl.

The howls rose, quivered, and fell, one repeating the other. Two dogs, howling, and then a third, and a fourth.

The mournful sounds came from around the bends of the hills reaching down into the lake, no more than a half mile away.

The Village dogs.

A terrible urgency filled Roger. He had to get over

there, take his chances with attack dogs who had been turned loose for the night. He had to see what was wrong.

He started running for his pickup, then remembered the roads curved and curled, and it would take him only half as long to go by boat.

He ran down to the boat dock, and felt in his pocket for the key. It was back at the house. He left the boat rocking in the water and ran back for the key.

Jill felt the wooden step behind her. Three steps up, she told herself. Three steps. With her hand out and touching the handrail that kept visitors away from the plate glass at the front of each building, she guided herself along. Her eyes held to the doll, advancing in front of her, the umbrella still raised.

Bright light surrounded them now, light from the long corridors between the display buildings. Jill wasn't sure which little street she was on, or what buildings she was passing. She only wanted a shortcut over to the farm machinery on the other side.

She walked backward, hearing her steps on the boardwalk, a hollow sound. In the distance, beyond the buildings, the dogs kept howling.

The caretaker who looked after the dogs would go out and quiet them, Jill knew, when they woke him. But would he think to look for her? No. He wouldn't.

He would wonder what was causing the dogs to howl, but he would never imagine that it was a kind of primitive terror, some ancient knowledge dogs have, a realization that they were in the presence of the unknown and they were helpless. As helpless as Jill.

Their howls reached toward the heavens, crying for help from some god of their own.

Jill glimpsed on her left, beneath the bright lights,

the glistening of glassware, and knew where she was.

Without planning it, she had come to the corridor of the House of Dolls. On her right, on rising tiers, were hundreds of dolls, among which stood Victoria.

Jill's hand gripped the wood rail as she moved slowly backward, afraid to take her eyes off the doll that stalked her, prepared to kill.

Laura felt the swirling darkness all around her. She knew . . . She knew Roger had taken Fawn out to the cottage . . . Andy had almost died . . . Jill was going to take the little girls out to the cottage . . . *She knew.*

And she knew Jill had taken the doll, too.

Jill had taken the very thing that was destroying them all.

Laura knew without knowing how she knew. The darkness around her, within her, seemed filled with warnings, with voices, with meanings. The voices talked, thinking she couldn't hear.

She had to follow them to the cottage.

Her head felt as if it were bursting with her effort to lift herself from her helplessness, to free herself from the bed and the tubes and monitors, to free herself from the voices of people she couldn't see or make contact with.

She strained mentally to lift herself, and felt the sudden and swift departure from her body.

Not the mansion. Please God, not the mansion. It was dark and empty now, a shell where tragedies had been lived out and where they would live forever in the ears and minds of its wooden walls and ceilings and floors. Not the mansion, but the Village. Please, God, help us. *Take me to the Village.*

She entered through the ceiling, and found herself in the playroom at the mansion. Within the deep darkness, she saw the outline of the toy box.

Despair made her feel heavy and hopeless. She was moving through the mansion again, through dark rooms where no one lived, where no one would ever live again.

She felt her cry of sadness, of helplessness. Her family was being destroyed by something over which they had no control, and she was unable to save them.

No, no, no!

She felt herself moving swiftly through the darkness, spinning, and she wondered, once again, if at last she had entered the tunnel of death.

Jill's hand trembled on the handrail. A splinter jabbed it, causing a small, sharp pain. In front of her the doll lurched forward, closer now. Jill stepped hurriedly backward, and the heel of her house slipper caught on a board that was a fraction of an inch higher than the others. She fell.

She heard the crack as her head struck the board walk between the House of Dolls and the House of Glass, and then the doll was upon her.

Laura was suddenly blinded by brightness. The light . . . the tunnel light? No, it was one of the corridors at the Village, and the bright light came from the bulbs that burned night and day. She could see now, sharply, clearly. She heard the howling of the dogs and the distant shout of a man trying to calm them. She heard the cry of someone . . .

Jill!

Jill was on the floor of the walkway between the House of Dolls and the House of Glass, and she was struggling to get away from the doll.

Millicent.

Laura could hear the sound the umbrella made as it swished through the air toward Jill's head, the movements on the wood floor as Jill twisted away and tried to get to her feet. She was on her hands and knees now, and scrambling forward, slapping and kicking backward, fighting, trying to run. The doll dragged her down again, and with the umbrella struck at Jill's head.

Laura was within reach of her daughter, but her touch was like the soft air that moved through the corridor between the two buildings.

She couldn't help. In despair, she realized that though she had managed to reach the Village and Jill, she could not stop Millicent.

Victoria.

The lovely doll, the duplicate of Millicent, stood on her velvet perch above all the other dolls, beneath the lights of the House of Dolls.

Laura moved through the glass, as if thought propelled her. Within inches of the tall doll, Victoria, she hovered in a state of utter helplessness.

Victoria. Laura's plea was soundless and without form. Her voice part of the wavelength that connected the impossible to the unknown. *Victoria, help us. You were there. You saw the hand of your twin doll used to kill your little friend. You saw the transference of evil . . . you saw . . . you . . .*

The effort to communicate to the motionless, smiling doll became overwhelming. Laura could not reach her. She felt herself drifting away, the light dimming. Her firstborn was fighting an enemy she would never be able to defeat. . . .

Jill kept trying to crawl away, her arms above her head for protection, and then the sharp tip of the umbrella came down. Again. And again. And Jill's cries turned to one long scream, blending with the howls of the dogs. She fell, rolled closer to the wall, her back to the corridor and the doll, pushing her face against the wall for protection. Blood gushed from the wound in her head . . . her cheek, her neck. . . . Laura didn't know the source, only that it was her child's life.

Victoria, Laura screamed in her silence. *Victoria!*

The tall, beautiful doll on the velvet pedestal took an awkward step forward. Her arms reached out as if for support as she stepped again, and fell, rolling from tier to tier, against other dolls, down, down, to the bottom of the dollhouse.

The large doll lay still there, between the lowest tier and the wall, her arms lifted. Her blue glass eyes looked dulled beneath the overhead light, saddened and old.

Victoria! Rise, Victoria! You can do it.

The girl who had taught Millicent to kill had surely taught Victoria to walk.

Victoria, help Jill, the child. Revenge . . . Victoria . . . the death of Victoria.

The doll lifted itself and went to the door. But it was locked, and the knob turned uselessly in its hands.

Then, as Laura watched, as the scenes played out before her as if they were on a screen, as Jill lay unmoving beneath the repeated striking of the umbrella, the doll Victoria turned.

As if it were going back to its place at the top of the tiers, to the pedestal where it was the queen of the antique figures, the doll climbed two tiers.

Laura's child was being killed, and there was nothing she could do.

The howling of the dogs seemed to be coming nearer, interspersed with silence, as if they were running. The shouting of the man to silence them had stopped. No one was coming to help.

Then Victoria reached down, bending, and lifted

one of the wooden pedestals that had been holding a doll that had fallen.

Turning, the pedestal in its right hand, the large doll came back down the tiers. As Laura watched in her helpless silence, Victoria lifted the pedestal and struck it against the plate glass. The glass shattered. Weblike veins moved across it, like distant lightning in the sky. But the glass held.

Victoria struck the glass again and again, and the glass fell, inside and out, and there was an opening.

As if the doll Millicent at last was aware, it lifted itself from the limp and bloody body on the walkway and stood back, the umbrella held high in its hand.

Victoria went through the opening in the glass. Sharp shards ripped through the material of the doll's dress and tore strands of hair from its head. With its mirror image standing on the walkway, the sweet smile never altering, Victoria advanced, holding the pedestal before it in a pair of tiny hands.

Dogs were barking now, running and barking, coming nearer. Shadows slipped beneath the trees, swift and low.

Millicent dropped the umbrella and the evil doll's hands reached out as if to hug its twin. But its hands curled, the fingers made into claws.

Victoria paused, just an instant, and then leaped.

Roger left his boat running and jumped ashore. He saw the dogs above him, slipping swift and silent through the mixture of dark and light that filled the Village. But they weren't coming toward him.

Someone was shouting. A man? Two men? But they were far away, their voices coming from his left, somewhere uphill.

Running up the slope from the lake, Roger followed

the dogs.

The corridor between the buildings was brightly lighted. When Roger ran up the steps, a few feet away from dogs that ordinarily would have attacked him, he stopped, staring, numb with what he saw.

Twin dolls, exactly like each other, were fighting. They rolled together, along the corridor, past the inert and bloody body of someone who had fallen against the wall, face down. Roger watched, stunned and as silent now as the dogs behind him.

The two dolls moved out of sight and into the darkness beyond the building, in an unreal, deadly tangle.

Left behind them lay a small black, high-buttoned shoe and a white shoe, different only in color. Left, too, were bits of clothing and hair, and at the other end of the walkway, at the top of the steps leading down, was the arm of one doll.

Roger ran to Jill and lifted her.

She leaned against him, weeping hysterically, her arms around his neck.

Behind them, men and dogs came running.

"It's okay," Roger told Jill as he carried her. "It's all right now."

Chapter Thirty

As the sun rose over the lake, Roger went out again to the House of Dolls and walked the corridor. The two German shepherds went with him, following at his heels.

Lights were burning along the corridor between the House of Dolls and the House of Glass. He saw the broken glass of the dollhouse, scattered in sharp needles, catching the light and reflecting it like the glassware behind the unbroken pane in the building on his right.

Among the shards of glass he saw something of a different color. Gold. He picked it up.

It was a small, thin identification bracelet. *Millicent.* He murmured the name aloud. "Millicent." It had come from one of the dolls, he knew. It came to him suddenly, a memory undisturbed until now, seeing that bracelet on the arm of the doll James Ruther carried from the wrecked car.

At the bottom of the steps he found the doll's arm, and farther on, as macabre as if it were real, half-hidden beneath the wheels of a rusted old combine, he saw the doll's head.

He stared at it a long while before picking it up. It looked so odd, the face still lovely, though scratched and gouged, one eye pushed back into the head, the smile still perfect. Tiny teeth showing between pink lips. A tip of a red little tongue . . .

Half the hair on the head was gone, the network of the wig dark against the hard, round skull.

He carried the head and arm to the nearest trash can and dropped them in.

Then he noticed one of the dogs digging at the edge of another trash can, and he went over to find one of the doll's legs. It was bare, the stocking gone, the shoe gone.

The caretakers had picked up a bunch of doll parts, they had told him when they'd let him back in through the gate a while ago, after he had taken Jill to the hospital.

"Whoever the hell attacked Jill, sure tore up some of the best dolls in the House of Dolls," the man said. "I put a bunch of stuff in the trash. Doll dresses, shoes. Impossible to repair, I know. What the hell do you suppose they were after? Victoria? I reckon she was worth a lot of money. Jill, we figured, heard them break the glass and came to see what was going on. We can't understand what the hell happened to the dogs. They've never let a stranger in. Makes us wonder if it was someone they knew. The way they carried on was weird, real weird, like it was the devil himself. Did Jill see who it was?"

"I don't think so," Roger said carefully. Jill was still in the hospital for observation, and he hadn't talked to her about what he had seen. Andy was much better, but still groggy from medication, and sleeping. Roger wondered if Andy would ever want to talk about it, or even if he should.

Fawn was sleeping too, the wife of one of the caretakers staying with her and the two little girls. He had kissed her on the lips and told her he loved her.

Roger walked on, slowly, half following the dogs now. When they headed for the timber he continued to follow.

One of the dogs stopped and sniffed carefully at something on the ground, half buried in the leaves. Roger looked, and found another tiny gold identification bracelet. This one was scratched, the chain broken.

Victoria.

So the dolls had worn identical bracelets, except for the names.

He didn't know the story behind the dolls yet, and he wondered if he ever would. A story like that would be kept hushed up. People wouldn't want to know that anything of that nature could happen.

The two dogs stood staring deep into the forest, and one of them whined. But when Roger started walking back toward the Village, they followed him.

Laura opened her eyes.

She saw the face of a woman wearing a white cap with dark blue trim, and she blinked. She heard the beep, beep of the monitors.

"Laura! Laura?" the woman cried. Then she was pushing an emergency button. Other nurses came running in.

"She's awake! She's out of her coma. Hey, Laura, can you hear me? Can you see me?"

"Yes," Laura said, but she was tired, so tired, as if she hadn't rested in the days and nights she had been there. "I can hear you," she said slowly, her voice sounding wobbly and faint. "I can see you."

She saw delighted faces, above her, around her.

"Hey, Laura," a nurse said, smiling, tears in her eyes. "You've made it, kid."

Laura returned the smile.

"Jill," she whispered. "Is Jill all right?"

"Jill is fine. She'll be up to see you later, I'm sure. She's fine. Can you move? See if you can move your fingers."

Laura lifted her hand.

"Hey, great, great. Now the feet. Try wiggling the toes."

Laura moved her leg. The paralysis was over, she was free from that terrible experience of being trapped in a body that wouldn't respond.

"I'm tired," she said. She wanted only to sleep. To sleep and then to go home to the cottage on the lake. "I'm so tired."

"Sure you are, baby." The soft lotion-scented hand patted her arm. "But you're going to be all right."

Laura nodded.

She slept. She thought she slept. She thought she was dreaming about being back at the Village, but then she realized the images were too clear, too sharp and brilliant.

Too real.

She was having another out-of-body experience, and the realization hit her hard. She turned, running through the trees, searching for a way back to her body, to the life that had been given back to her.

The trees were tall, the underbrush sparse, and Laura stopped, staring ahead.

Something was moving there. Something, she felt suddenly, that she was meant to see.

She was still, no longer running, no longer moving at all. She waited.

It came closer, the leaves rustling beneath its hesitant steps. It sounded as if it were half crawling, like a wounded animal.

Laura waited, fear rising within her.

She didn't want to see. But she had no choice.

The doll.

A doll incomplete, hideous, half torn apart. There was no head at all, no clothing. Not even the body stocking. One arm was intact. The right arm. And both legs were functioning, but the left foot was turned aside, so that it walked on the inside of that one. It came toward her through the trees.

Victoria?

Millicent?

The scene began fading, swirls of darkness like fog filling Laura's eyes. In the moment before she left the woods she saw the doll stoop and pick up from the ground a heavy stick. Its fingers curled around it, and lifted it above its headless body.

It was going home.